2007

DARLING JIM

Christian Moerk

><

DARLING JIM

A NOVEL

HENRY HOLT AND COMPANY

NEW YORK

Henry Holt and Company, LLC
Publishers since 1866
175 Fifth Avenue
New York, New York 10010
www.henryholt.com

Henry Holt® and 🏠® are registered trademarks
of Henry Holt and Company, LLC.

Originally published by Politikens Forlag, Denmark in 2007
Published by arrangement with Nordin Agency

Distributed in Canada by H. B. Fenn and Company Ltd.

Library of Congress Cataloging-in-Publication Data

Moerk, Christian.
    Darling Jim : a novel / Christian Moerk.—1st ed.
        p.   cm.
    ISBN-13: 978-0-8050-8947-9
    ISBN-10: 0-8050-8947-0
  1. Postal service—Employees—Fiction.   2. Diaries—Fiction.
3. Storytellers—Fiction.   4. Young women—Crimes against—Fiction.
5. Ireland—Fiction.   6. Psychological fiction.   I. Title.
    PS3613.O34 2009
    813'.6—dc22   2008033074

Henry Holt books are available for special promotions
and premiums. For details contact: Director, Special Markets.

First U.S. Edition 2009

Designed by Victoria Hartman

Printed in the United States of America
    1   3   5   7   9   10   8   6   4   2

Christian Moerk

＞＜

DARLING JIM

A NOVEL

HENRY HOLT AND COMPANY

NEW YORK

Henry Holt and Company, LLC
Publishers since 1866
175 Fifth Avenue
New York, New York 10010
www.henryholt.com

Henry Holt® and 🏛 ® are registered trademarks
of Henry Holt and Company, LLC.

Originally published by Politikens Forlag, Denmark in 2007
Published by arrangement with Nordin Agency

Distributed in Canada by H. B. Fenn and Company Ltd.

Library of Congress Cataloging-in-Publication Data

Moerk, Christian.
    Darling Jim : a novel / Christian Moerk.—1st ed.
        p.   cm.
    ISBN-13: 978-0-8050-8947-9
    ISBN-10: 0-8050-8947-0
    1. Postal service—Employees—Fiction.   2. Diaries—Fiction.
3. Storytellers—Fiction.   4. Young women—Crimes against—Fiction.
5. Ireland—Fiction.   6. Psychological fiction.   I. Title.
    PS3613.O34 2009
    813'.6—dc22   2008033074

Henry Holt books are available for special promotions
and premiums. For details contact: Director, Special Markets.

First U.S. Edition 2009

Designed by Victoria Hartman

Printed in the United States of America
1   3   5   7   9   10   8   6   4   2

For Aoife, wherever you are

In Ireland, in Cromwell's time, wolves were particularly troublesome, and said to be increasing in numbers, so that special measures were taken for their destruction. . . . The date of their final disappearance cannot now be ascertained.

—*Encyclopædia Britannica*, 1911 edition

In Ireland, in Cromwell's time, wolves were particularly troublesome, and said to be increasing in numbers, so that special measures were taken for their destruction. . . . The date of their final disappearance cannot now be ascertained.

—*Encyclopædia Britannica*, 1911 edition

DARLING JIM

✤

WHAT DESMOND SAW

· 1 ·

Malahide, just north of Dublin. Not so long ago.

Long after the house had been disinfected for new occupants and the bodies rested safely in the ground, people still didn't come near it. "Cursed," whispered the neighborhood gossips and nodded meaningfully. "Deadly, a haunted house!" cried the children, but they only ever mustered up the courage to take a step or two into the front yard before losing heart.

Because what Desmond the mailman had been the first to see inside had been unnatural strange.

Everybody liked Desmond, even if he might have been a little too nosy for his own good. He was also a slave to ritual, always noticing if anybody's grass needed tending or whether the paint on a flagpole had begun to chip. Taken together with his guilt of having seen details without understanding their true meaning, these otherwise sociable qualities cost him his sanity.

On the last day of his life that gave him any joy, this most demanding connoisseur of his customers' coffee delivered the day's mail in the

quiet neighborhood just down the street from the train station in Malahide as slowly as he decently could without being called a Peeping Tom.
He started where the bars of New Street met the faux-Bavarian ugliness
of the concrete marina and took a left, continuing out to Bissets Strand.
As usual, old Des peered in the windows to see if anyone he knew might
be waiting inside with a fresh cup, and he wasn't disappointed; he'd
drunk two before reaching the end of the first block. Most residents had
come to accept his lonely need for attention. Just "happening by" for a
spot of the morning java made him feel, it was understood, as if he were
part of someone else's life, just for a bit. He always said, "The bean
smells lovely." He never outstayed his welcome. And he smiled when he
saw you—that's what made everyone surrender to this strange little
creature—flashed a grin as wide as you please.

Before he found the corpses, Desmond was universally viewed as
harmless.

His life off the clock, such as it was, was spent at the safe remove of
Gibney's, where he stole glances at the local wives when their husbands
weren't looking and lost his meager paychecks at the bookmaker's next
door each time there was a hurdles horse race on TV, which was often.
He had trudged his black mailbag up and down the old beach town's
cracked pavements for more than eighteen years, staring at the same
ash-gray houses where the nearby sea had eaten away at the paint, and
found the monotony comforting. Going in to the city, just half an hour
away by train, would have required a desire for surprise and a worldli-
ness he couldn't have imagined pursuing. Besides, it would have upset
his carefully planned route, which netted at least four good cups before
lunch.

When he walked past on the footpath, people inside their kitchens
could hear him hum. Nonsense tunes, really. He had lousy pitch but
bobbed his head to the beat, which counted for more than talent. He
was happy the way only children under the age of twelve usually are.

Later, people took bets on whether that humming should have
warned them.

It was on either the 24th or the 25th of April, just after ten in the morning, as far as anybody could recall, that the town's tolerant opinion of Desmond changed forever. The sun didn't shine. God averted his eyes from number 1 Strand Street and, instead, sent rolling clouds draped in suicide gray in from the sea to obscure something imminent not meant for public consumption. A prophetic color choice, as it should turn out. And so Desmond Kean, waving in blissful ignorance to old Mrs. Dingle on the second floor of Howard's Corner and tipping his cap to that nice Mrs. Moriarty just opening up her hair salon, proceeded toward the end of his daily route.

When he had handed out mail to the drab granny houses out on Bissets Strand, turned back, and again reached number 1, on the corner of Old Street and Gas Yard Lane, he hesitated all the same. The bag was nearly empty, and he only had to deliver two adverts from the local supermarket to Mrs. Hegarty inside. In the days to come, Desmond would go back and forth in his fevered mind, trying to remember how far back he should have noticed that something was wrong with how that house made him feel. It looked ordinary enough, its façade a faded cream with fake Swiss wood latticework above the doorway. But from the very beginning, something just out of reach whispered a warning about the house's occupant that he had been too polite to hear.

Mrs. Hegarty, who let Desmond call her "Moira" only after a year of sporadic—and persistent—visits, had come to town nearly three years ago from nowhere she cared to talk much about. People said it was a small town way out in West Cork. She was still a handsome woman at forty-five, and her face had the lucky kind of defined bone structure that would wear well into old age. On the rare occasions when Desmond's clumsy jokes managed to coax a smile, she was beautiful. But she had also acquired a hardness to her that blossomed into open hostility whenever people tried to get too friendly. Invitations to tea from neighbors were first met with polite refusals. And when some tried bringing her cakes to drive the point home, she left them untouched on her front porch, where wild cats finally ate them.

Among the many curious neighbors, only Desmond was ever invited into the house for coffee, probably because of his innocence or willful blindness to people's hidden side. Then, sometime last January, Mrs. Hegarty had abruptly stopped answering the door when he rang the bell. His subsequent attempts to reconnect with her whenever they happened on each other in the street were also rebuffed. Mrs. Hegarty, rarely seen outside her four walls as it was, would simply trail past him without a word in that old greatcoat, a scarf wrapped around her head like a mummy. She never again asked him inside. Desmond and everyone else simply assumed she'd had a tragedy befall her, didn't pry, and gave her the space she obviously craved.

And yet.

Now that Desmond stood outside Mrs. Hegarty's front door with the colorful adverts in his hand, he hesitated because of that *feeling* he'd had these last few weeks whenever he walked past. Recently, there had been sounds from inside that Desmond had written off as coming from a TV set, or maybe the radio. They had sounded like whimpers, even the cries of a young voice. Once there had been a loud thumping noise, and the drapes on the second floor had been yanked open briefly before being shut once again. But since Desmond was only curious, not investigative or even brave, he explained it away as the eccentricity of the lonely, a tribe to which he himself belonged.

The closer he came to the mail slot, the more the little hairs on his hand stood to attention like a blond forest. He thought he smelled something. Like spoilt stew. He wasn't sure where it was coming from; could have been seaweed rotting on the beach nearby. Or someone's fridge where the power had gone out. But he knew it wasn't.

Desmond finally ignored his imprecise feeling of foreboding, bent down, and pushed open the slot. He jammed one of the Tesco adverts inside. He noticed a pile of unopened mail on the floor.

And then he stopped.

Far inside, near where he knew Mrs. Hegarty's sitting room was, he saw what was probably a hand.

It was blue-black, ballooned thick like a surgical glove, and stuck out from somewhere in the adjoining room. The arm connected to it was fat and sausagelike, too, as if filled with water. A watch lay next to it, its band snapped clean off the wrist from the swelling. Desmond craned his neck and could just glimpse some more of Mrs. Hegarty's remains, dark stains all over her Sunday best. He could have sworn that, despite all that, she was smiling. Des just avoided getting sick all over his shoes and ran down to tell the gardaí.

And for the first and last time in his life, he left a piece of mail undelivered.

AFTER THE REGULAR guards from up the street forced the lock open, they stepped aside and made room for the astronaut-looking forensics team from Garda headquarters in Phoenix Park. Two men silently entered, backed up by a canine unit. The dogs howled and whimpered as the crusted blood called out to them, and their handlers had to hold them back. One astronaut wearing a white full-body HazMat suit knelt by Moira's prostrate body and examined her skull. There were several depressions in it just above one eye, as if someone had struck her over and over with a blunt object, but not hard enough to kill instantly. Cause of death was later determined at the inquest to have been caused by a massive subdural hematoma. In other words, Moira Hegarty had suffered a stroke after being beaten and died only minutes afterward. The body had been lying there for at least three days. One detective superintendent initially thought it was a robbery-homicide. Once he learned the full story, however, he was later heard to remark under his breath that "that fucking bitch deserved every blow she got." Because her death, as far as the cops were interested, was the least of it.

There were scuff marks on most of the walls, too, as if more than one person had tumbled around the ground floor, trying to gain control of the other. Shoe polish and brown leather skid marks had been smeared on the floor panels, and paintings of the Holy Land were askew. Those signs of struggle were replicated in every room downstairs, and it made the rookies nervous. One local garda opened the press under the sink and found rat poison in large quantities. Another discovered a necklace on Moira that was forged in iron and welded shut at the nape. A smaller ring with more than ten different keys was connected to it. Any one of them would have been impossible to pry off. "Must have jangled when she took a shower," another remarked, in a poor attempt at dispelling the unease they all felt. Once removed with bolt cutters, the keys were found to fit every lock in the house—from the outside. They found no other keys. And most of the doors were locked shut.

Forensic analysis indicated that Mrs. Hegarty suffered the injuries upstairs, then managed to make it almost down to her couch, collapsing just inches away. A fine blood trail from upstairs pointed the way.

The cops stopped laughing when they walked up to the second floor to verify this theory. It took two of Malahide's finest to shove the door open. One caught the nervous look of his partner when they put their shoulders into it. Because the smell from inside was stronger than it had been near Mrs. Hegarty. They weren't ashamed to have an armed officer accompany them as they revealed the truth of what Desmond saw and yet had missed so completely.

The girl lay bunched up against the door, her hands folded around a rusty shovel as if in prayer.

"Jesus!" exclaimed the youngest garda, and steadied himself on the doorjamb. Downstairs, the dogs howled, and their claws clicked around on the wooden floor.

Her red hair had been turned nearly black by sweat and filth. The fingers, slender and elegant, had only two nails left on them, and her ribs showed through the thin film of what once had to have been a yellow summer dress. Poor thing had died hard, the Garda established, but they couldn't immediately determine whether it was the knife wounds in her abdomen or something internal that killed her first. The shovel had her fingerprints on it, however, and its head matched the marks on Mrs. Hegarty's forehead. It was concluded that she had followed the older woman halfway down the stairs before something had broken off that chase. A knife was recovered from behind a chair, and Mrs. Hegarty's prints made it clear that she had stabbed the young woman not twice but at least nineteen times.

"Poor child bled out quick," a veteran cop remarked, blowing his nose.

Forensics quickly reconstructed the scene. A desperate battle had taken place on the second floor, where Mrs. Hegarty had tried to beat back the weakened girl's surprise attack and ultimately succeeded. But the young woman hadn't surrendered without a fight. Almost as an afterthought, forensics realized that not only did Mrs. Hegarty's keys fit in all the locks, but no room in the house had a keyhole on the inside. Remains of raw potatoes and moldy bread were found under the bed, where the girl had clearly been forced to save her rationed, meager food. It was determined that she'd lived inside the house for at least three months. Leg irons and handcuffs were gaping open on the bed railing, and both looked well used. The smallest of the self-established prison warden's keys fit snugly in them. Poor divil had cuff burns where the metal had eaten into her skin. Two bent hairpins, caked brown by the girl's own blood on the floorboards, were determined to be her home-made handcuff keys.

She had been a prisoner. For a long time. There was no other conclusion.

And the warden, the kindly woman doling out coffee to Desmond, had never been found out until it was too late.

"We had no idea," said the out-of-breath gentleman from Social Services, blinking in the camera lights right behind the cops, when confronted with the queasy notion that Mrs. Hegarty, the shut-in from somewhere out west, had evidently kept a live-in slave right under the noses of her neighbors. "We shall immediately make further enquiries." But as the man avoided the stares of angry onlookers and exited the house by the front steps, everyone knew that was so much bullshit. The woman who had lived quietly at the end of the street was an unmitigated monster. And nobody had cared enough to notice, least of all the government.

Through all this, while the astronauts, the flatfoot cops from around the corner, and the dogs all dissected their part of the unfolding mystery, Desmond knew that to be true more than anybody else. From the time the first ambulance came to carry that poor girl away, he stood right across the street, clutching a railing for balance, staring at number 1's chocolate-colored front door. And when darkness came, he still hadn't moved. An unhappy, ghostly smile had replaced the genial one he usually wore. And slowly, the same people who had tolerated Desmond's fussy demeanor now began looking askance at the prematurely balding man trying to catch a glimpse of the young girl's battered corpse being loaded into the ambulance. Those furtive glances into their kitchens took on a completely new and unsettling meaning. And it felt so good, besides, to smear one's collective guilt onto the only available patsy.

"Pervert!" a mother was heard to remark, cracked lipstick forming the words. "Sick bastard," added another. Both had served him coffee with a smile days earlier.

But even if his untoward glances could have been taken for untimely curiosity, or even sexual titillation, they were wrong. Had they been able to look into Desmond's heart, they would have discovered nothing but the blackest, stickiest guilt and shame. Those thumping noises now made sense to him. The yelps coming from the top floor could have—no, definitely had—been cries for help mere days before a violent death. Desmond nodded meekly at the neighborhood women, who didn't meet his eyes but kept theirs fixed on the front door of number 1, as if staring at it long enough would make them better neighbors.

NIGHT HAD FALLEN. The astronauts had finally folded their tents and carted the results back down to HQ. The throng of onlookers had thinned, but barely, when Desmond heard a sound from inside the house that fell somewhere between a shout and a yell. Someone had been surprised, and not by anything pleasant. Within seconds, the same young garda who had found the girl appeared in the doorway, his already ashen face pulled in directions that were all wrong. Whatever he'd just seen exceeded his tolerance for human ugliness.

"Sarge," he said, swallowing hard. "Something we missed before."

One of the dogs had refused to move, but instead hugged the carpet and began to weep when it passed a bookcase on the second floor. Not to howl, like before, but to mourn whatever it sensed nearby.

When the gardaí finally moved the bookcase and opened the blinded door hidden behind it, they found the second girl.

"LOOKS YOUNGER THAN the first," said the coroner later in the week, after performing proper autopsies on all three women, and he snapped his rubber gloves off with a practiced gesture that gave him no joy at all.

This last one had been tucked away inside a tiny crawl space that was really part of the outer wall. Reached only through a door tiny enough to have suited a dollhouse, a narrow air duct led from the first girl's room to her damp corner. Absent any ID, she was determined to have been in her early twenties, with black wiry hair that would have been beautiful when it was still clean enough to be brushed. Her skin, except for sores brought about by poor hygiene and lack of protein, was un-blemished by blows. In contrast to the first girl, she had died of massive organ failure, brought about by gradual poisoning and malnourish-ment. Her arms were so thin no muscle tone remained. When they found her, she lay in a dirty blanket like a whipped dog. Like the first girl, she bore marks of having been routinely shackled. In fact, one of the officers gently unlocked a set of leg cuffs that had caused her ankles to bleed. What nobody had a satisfactory answer for was why both palms were ink-stained. A leaky ballpoint pen was eventually found, but no paper. If she had been writing to somebody in the darkness of her prison cell, what had she done with the message?

A few days went by while the guards inventoried every stick of furni-ture found inside the house.

Then, when one of Moira Hegarty's many keys was found to unlock a dresser drawer, the story grew worse. And even the foulest gossip in Malahide was momentarily silenced at the sheer calculated ugliness of what the law dogs found.

The drawer first yielded two driver's licenses. One was made out to a red-haired, well-nourished Fiona Walsh, twenty-four, of Castletownbere,

County Cork; clearly the first girl found on the top floor. The other belonged to twenty-two-year-old Róisín Walsh, whose black locks and pale skin in the photograph bore little resemblance to the skeletal creature now lying on the metal slab next to her sister. It was unclear how and when the girls had arrived at Moira Hegarty's house, but that's not what moved newspapers off racks that week. No, the salient detail that gave the *Evening Herald* and the *Irish Daily Star* golden days for far longer than the initial shock value of the news was something most had already guessed.

Fiona and Róisín weren't just two sisters who had suffered a grim death.

Moira—their jailer and killer—was their aunt.

SLAVE SISTERS SLAIN BY KILLER AUNT, barked one headline. BEAUTIES AND THE BEAST blared another. And despite their lack of tact, both were right. The girls were found to have ingested small, steady amounts of the anticoagulant rat poison coumatetratyl over a period of at least seven weeks, probably mixed in with their water and what passed for food. "Put simply," the coroner said, "the girls' organs gradually fell apart, and any cuts they sustained wouldn't have healed. The youngest died of internal bleeding. And each would appear to have been chained to her bed at night. Their aunt really planned this one out." The newspapers, as well as Desmond's neighbors and former friends, just called it diabolical, which was true enough, too.

But the dresser drawer still didn't offer up any clues as to *why* any of this had happened.

Among the inventoried effects were several sealed plastic bags with clumps of black dirt inside. Upon further analysis, the bags were also found to contain a button, one damask napkin, a crumpled pack of Marlboro Lights, and a used 12-gauge shotgun shell. None of these items seemed connected, but for the fact that the dirt on them had the same pH value. Some stationery was found, too, of which exactly one envelope and a sheet of expensive writing paper had been used. But forensics couldn't determine for what purpose. Perhaps Róisín had used it but, if so, the questions went, for what?

After a few days, the neighborhood grew restless and less enamored of the cops' authority. Kids dared one another to cross the white-and-blue Garda tape and grab a trophy from the wall, a stunt never repeated once the house had been shuttered and silenced and officially become inhabited by ghosts. One boy made off with a plastic Jesus figurine with a 40-watt bulb inside it to illuminate the halo. Another managed to get as far as the corner before a garda nabbed him and made him give back a gilt-edged portrait of the once-so-revered *Taoiseach* Eamon de Valera, the prime minister's long face seeming to disapprove of the dead woman who had hung him above her mantelpiece.

The police were rapidly running out of clues and got ready to close the case.

Then the house offered up one more secret all by itself.

It came in the form of a previously overlooked scuff mark by the back door, which looked like someone had nearly ripped it off the hinges trying to get out. A fingerprint was found on the handle that didn't match any of the three dead women's, and theirs were the only ones otherwise discovered in the house. But a third soiled bed was found in the basement, and more of the same unknown prints were found on a sewage pipe. Whoever it was had managed to saw through the pipe with a primitive cutting tool and had very likely fled the house with handcuffs still attached to at least one wrist.

The two girls hadn't been suffering alone. Someone else had been there with them, until very recently, a someone who was still out there, alive. And undiscovered.

When the last floorboard had been unpeeled and every spoon in the kitchen itemized without turning up anything new, number 1 Strand Street was finally cleaned out, boarded up, and offered for sale by the city. And as tantalizing as the unknown fourth person in that house might have been, with no apparent clues or even a single living relative to suggest any compelling explanation for the carnage, the gardaí quietly shuttered the case after a few months. Even the press eventually moved on to fresher kills.

Around the town's bars, the case was still being tried, however.

"Moira was off her head," went one popular theory. "She had it in for the girls. Murdering their beauty for jealousy's sake." Another version had the girls plotting to murder their aunt for her money in an extortion scheme that had backfired on themselves, but no cash was found anywhere in the house. "What a waste," the neighbors said, and they were right, whatever the truth. "The mystery guest was Moira's lover, who killed them all and left before getting what was coming to him," went one particularly fanciful notion. But none of these theories lasted any longer than the time it took to utter them.

"What happened here began somewhere else," a regular down at Gibney's finally ventured one night after a half pint of stout and a lot of listening to crap gossip from people with more alcohol in them than common sense. "This kind of bloodletting takes years of hatred to ripen properly."

If the boys in blue down on the Mall could have heard him just then and put down their breakfast rolls, they might well have cracked the case. But they still wouldn't have understood the half of it. Because the story the women inside Moira's house nearly took to their graves *did* begin somewhere else, in a small town in West Cork where everyone was driven by something far stronger and more combustible than hate.

It was love that put Moira and her two nieces into the quiet section of the tiny graveyard behind St. Andrew's Church.

The kind of love that burns hotter than a blast furnace.

AT THE SAD little funeral carried out and paid for by Social Services the following week, no relatives or friends came by to pay their last respects to the Walsh sisters and their murderous aunt. Fiona and Róisín were placed a few feet apart from Moira, which the funeral director insisted upon, "because I'll be damned if that awful woman should be able to reach out and touch those poor children." As if to mock the two young girls, God had turned the coke-colored weather cape inside out and now shone bright sunlight through a misty rain, creating a banal rainbow beautiful enough to make the only guest in attendance weep so loudly it bothered mourners at another funeral two graves over.

Desmond appeared to have aged ten years inside of a month.

From the day the two Walsh sisters and their aunt had been carted out to the meat wagon, he hadn't been seen in public. That's because the first thing he did when he came home to his freezing little flat was to take off his uniform and burn it. As days turned to weeks, the usual sounds of rare Jelly Roll Morton tunes seeping like golden pearls underneath the door from his old stereo went silent. Neighbors thought they heard quiet weeping. Children stuck their noses near his windowpane to catch a glimpse of the weirdo, and a few saw a flash of messy hair atop a pallid face. "Freak!" they whispered to one another, threw rocks at his front door, then ran home laughing. Parents knew, of course, but allowed that bit of exorcism. Better someone other than they take the blame for what had happened. What's more, it appeared to have worked. A nice unsuspecting Polish family would eventually move into number 1, which once again looked like just another house on the block.

Desmond wore a shiny black suit with worn elbows and knees, like a waiter at a ferry cafeteria. He trembled as Father Donnelly said the requisite prayer. And he had to cover his mouth with both hands when the priest got to "Blessed art Thou amongst women." Below the church hill, the soot-colored rooftops were slick with rain. Desmond remained standing long after the graves had been properly padded and marked. He still stood there as it really began to pour.

When he started back for his flat and nodded at a group of kids in the street, that's the last anyone ever saw of him.

If it hadn't been for another postman, named Niall, whose curiosity likewise picked him out of his humdrum existence and catapulted the poor lad headlong into the biggest adventure of his short life, the whole story might have ended there.

But the secret of the Walsh sisters was only just beginning to unfold.

Anybody walking near the cemetery that night might have had

enough imagination to see the girls' spirits rise from their cheap state-sponsored coffins and hover in the air near the service window of the post office, tapping on the glass. For they had unfinished business inside.

Desmond, poor soul, had been closer than he thought.

And neither Fiona nor Róisín, even in death, would be denied.

Interlude

⸻

✦

DEAD LETTER

N iall heard no faint, spooky noises outside his window of the post office sorting section. Not because he didn't enjoy a good ghost story as much as the next man and was likewise attuned to the faintest noise after nightfall.

No, it was because his wolf had turned into complete shite once again and he knew it, even before giving up on coloring its amber eyes.

"Arh, bollocks," he muttered, and looked at the fifth drawing of the night. How was this possible? He used to draw felines pretty well back in art school; even old Professor Vassilchikov had to admit as much. Leopards and pumas leaped effortlessly across his pages in living color and burst out of their flat world into the third dimension every comic book fanboy lived for. But his canines never came off right. Niall would finish the head, work his way toward the strong hind legs, and add silver fur, hoping to preserve the animal's feeling of pure lethal menace. But with astounding regularity, the creature always looked like an overfed dog or an arthritic fox by the time he got to the tail.

If he kept at it, he might one day become a decent clean-up artist for one of the comic book creators he admired, like the godlike American penciler Todd Sayles, whose seminal 1980s sci-fi series *Space Colonies* he'd read as a boy. It had featured a heavily armed intergalactic bounty hunter named Stash Brown and his talking monkey, Pickles, as they battled scores of murderous mutated aliens all across the Alpha Centauri star system and points west. But who was he kidding? Realistically, Niall had to admit, he could merely hope to shine the shoes of Mr. Sayles—or of his new prodigy, the artist Jeff Alexander, who had just inked *and* colored the four-part Wild West adventure *Six-guns to Yuma* for DarkWorld Comics and dazzled the bright eyes of boys all over Ireland and the world with classic gunslinger "Ain't-enough-room-for-the-both-of-us-in-this-here-town-pilgrim fantasies."

Niall looked at his pathetic, un-dangerous wolf one more time and realized he'd never get as far as either of those men's front offices. He had been trying to create a cover for some kind of medieval fantasy comic book and had drawn castle keeps all night after clocking out from work, complete with falling-down walls and towers, tree stumps sprouting infestations of verdant moss, and creatures of all kinds roaming the lost world of a distant Ireland that had never even existed. The ravens to the far left, just above the fearsome gibbet, had come off well. Their mouths were red and expectant, and it was possible to believe they were about to swoop down and gnaw off a piece of the condemned man still swinging from the noose below. Knights farther back on the page, returning from the hunt with falcons tethered to thick gloves, were nearly majestic. Even the fair maiden Niall had drawn cowering in the forest clearing was a partial success; her black hair half shielded her milky face as she fled ever deeper into the protective darkness of the branches.

This, of course, is where he'd messed everything up.

Because he'd intended a wolf to appear suddenly in her path, head lowered and eyes ablaze, poised for the attack. It would have set the entire piece apart and guided every snot-nosed preteen lad into a wider world of adventure, where ravenous beasts feasted on defenseless young girls to the tune of at least ten euros per issue. But now, all the maiden would have to do to get past was feed the fat dog a Snickers bar from her handbag. It was pitiful.

Niall crumpled the paper and lobbed the ball where he'd disposed of the previous four—into the massive metal-caged bin where the mail sorters tossed all the dead letters, cases where senders had forgotten postage or a complete address. Each week, unless they came by to pay the penalty or reclaim the posted item, the bin was emptied into the trash.

The crumpled-up wolf didn't go gently. The paper ball glanced off a few envelopes, rattled downward on the white avalanche, and bumped up against a bulky package, which loosed itself from the rest and shifted a few inches until it bounced into one of the steel bars with a loud *thump!* and settled there. Whatever was still inside that last envelope, it wasn't mittens for granny but something with a harder edge and some weight on its bones.

For the first time that night, Niall forgot his self-pity and turned his head at the sound.

The dead-letter bin, which tonight looked to Niall's once-so-excitable, still-adolescent inner eye as a half-lit guard tower in front of the maiden's castle, stood less than three feet from the battered wooden desk his superintendent had recently sandwiched between a boiler and two out-of-order stamp-vending machines. Mr. Raichoudhury had pointed to the chipped piece of furniture with a grave mien as if the gesture would make invisible all its coffee and cigarette stains.

Niall hesitated, then got up. In the two years since quitting art school in silent agony and reluctantly donning the funereal uniform of an entry-level An Post junior postperson so he could pay rent, he had grown to hate opening the latch every Thursday and climbing inside the metal cage to empty its never-sated paper guts. But something about tonight was different. A mean winter draft coughed loose sheets of paper across the floor. Stash Brown would have cocked the hammer on his laser shotgun and expected alien vermin to come crashing out of the bin, Niall thought. Pickles would have bared his teeth and shrieked like the killer monkey he was.

Niall walked over to the bin, opened the latch, and climbed inside.

A fat envelope, dark brown and stained, lay at the bottom of an improvised paper sled run. Niall picked it up and was about to toss it back among the others when he flipped it over and glanced at the sender's name and address. It looked as if it had been scribbled in a hurry. The letters were crooked and smudged, but could still be read:

From: Fiona Walsh
1 Strand Street, Malahide

The name of the murdered girl, who had died in a vain attempt to protect her little sister Róisín? Impossible. A hoax, surely, now. Niall stopped breathing for just a moment. His brain didn't quite know how to proceed after that. Toss it aside as a joke? Freeze in terror at the ghastly implication? After realizing he was involuntarily hugging the bulky package, he went for option number three, one that usually plays more tricks on enlightened minds than the previous two. Niall pretended to suspend judgment, thereby rendering himself secretly more afraid of what might lurk inside. He quickly stepped out of the bin, which to him had begun to resemble the forest from his own pathetic cover drawing, and made for his desk.

Open it right away, yes, of course. That would have been the only natural thing to do. But as the light from the battered desk lamp (which he had recently "liberated" from Mr. Raichoudhury's secret supply by the overseas bins) shone onto the paper, more was revealed that rendered his fingers quite still. No postage had been affixed, which is what had got it sent to the reject bin to begin with. It had been simply addressed to:

Anyone at all
Post Office
Townyard Lane, Malahide

Niall turned the envelope over once more and squinted like an old diamond cutter. Now he could clearly see that a second, more harried message had been added to the brown paper before dispatch. It had once been covered in rain droplets, but was still readable. It was a prayer, a last wish told to an unknown soul from one about to be extinguished. The words, askew and jumbled, read:

We are already gone. Read this tale only to remember us.

At this, Niall couldn't stop the light trembling of his hands, even if he'd wanted to. Of course he'd read the newspapers and knew about what was already being called "the battle on the second floor," where Fiona had fought off the beast who had pretended to be a kindly woman. How could he not follow her written incantation? He began to loosen the flap and could see a shadow of something black inside when he heard a booming voice and a set of heels clacking together behind him as if on the parade ground.

"Please tell me what is the meaning of this, Mr. Cleary, if you'd be so kind?"

Niall turned and saw the regal fearful bearing of Very Senior Post-person Raichoudhury, whose dark tunic was buttoned all the way up past his Adam's apple in a way that made everyone think of an overzealous parking attendant rather than the officer he secretly wished he could have been. The tall ascetic figure cut across the small room and pointed a neatly manicured finger at the floor, where several sheets of paper still lay spread about. He acted as if he had legions under his thumb rather than two people, and Mrs. Cody was out sick.

"I am really quite concerned about your attitude, Mr. Cleary, I don't mind telling you. What on earth are you doing here so late anyway, may I ask?"

"Just drawing, sir."

"Again?"

"'Fraid so, sir."

He now stood so close Niall could see the belt buckle the older man had inherited from his great-great-grandfather, who had "taken Ayub Khan's guns" during a glorious battle against a warlord sometime during the Second Afghan War in the mid-1800s. The gangly supervisor had once taken a sun-stained photograph out of his wallet and showed it around the office. On it, a man very like Mr. Raichoudhury himself sat astride a magnificent horse, wearing a striped turban and carrying a serious-looking lance while daring the photographer to do anything but tremble at the sight. "He was an officer with the Twenty-third Bengal Cavalry," he had once explained to the largely unenthusiastic Mrs. Cody. He always shined the buckle, Niall remembered, on which a complex coat of arms signaled death before dishonor or something.

At present, however, the Bengal Lancer's descendant didn't have death in mind so much as office discipline. He looked at the sorry desk as if he now regretted having given it to this young man, who clearly couldn't be trusted not to mess about after closing time. Then his eye fell on the bin's open latch, and he looked as if he missed his ancestor's weaponry after all.

"What the devil is . . ." He walked over and gently swung the gate shut. Then he turned and fixed Niall with a withering glare every bit as deadly as Ayub Khan's guns. "Go home, please. And come see me tomorrow, first thing. I think there are several things about your . . . deportment which we have to talk about at length."

"Yes, sir," answered Niall. He slipped Fiona Walsh's fat envelope into his bag by using a back issue of Jeff Alexander's most recent comic book, *The Road to Boot Hill*, as a shield. On the cover, three nearly naked female gunfighters aimed their pistols at the reader, which in this case was an increasingly exasperated Mr. Raichoudhury.

"*Now*, please," said the imagined officer, as if ordering about a dim-witted redcoat recruit on the bloody battlefield near Kandahar. He followed Niall all the way through the shoe repair shop (behind which the entire post office was ignobly sandwiched) and pushed him out the front door, which he locked from the inside. He could be heard to mutter something about "no respect" as the sound of his leather heels faded into the bowels of the smallest post office in creation.

ONCE OUTSIDE, NIALL lit up a smoke and through the shuttered keymaker's station could see his boss once more stepping into the dead-letter bin as if to ascertain whether young Niall had somehow be-smirched his holy office. Niall took a deep drag and remembered what he was carrying. He walked over to the main intersection in front of a lit-up newsagent's window, fished the envelope from his bag, and opened it.

A black book lay inside, like a headstone from the graveyard nearby.

Its cover, made from coarse cotton, was rough to the touch. A deep gouge ran across the bottom half, almost as if it had been used for de-fense. He held it up to the light. No, more like it had been wedged some-where for safekeeping, maybe jammed down behind a radiator, which had singed its dark fibers. Niall already imagined how Fiona had man-aged to hide it from her aunt. But what was inside it? Lurid tales? Hid-den accounts? A treasure map, perhaps?

"Shut up, you eejit," he said to himself, dampening expectations. "This isn't *Space Colonies.*"

He was about to turn the first page when he noticed someone staring at him from inside the shop.

"You all right out there?" asked the cashier, a fat man in a white apron whose cheeks had turned the color of ripe plums. Something about his tone made Niall hide the book.

"Why wouldn't I be?"

"Fine, then," said the man, and took a bite out of what from a dis-tance looked like an extremely ambitious-sized tea cake while follow-ing a rugby game on TV.

Niall nodded and continued over to his bicycle, which still waited patiently by the tobacconist's, even if he'd forgot to lock it again. He strapped the bag across his chest and swung his long leg across the iron bar, where the paint was peeling like autumn leaves. As he pedaled up Dublin Road, he could see the faint white glimmer of a jetliner's anti-collision lights as it navigated a landing approach to town right above the professionally cute storefronts. It was nearly midnight.

Niall didn't feel any impatient spirits gliding past on the road next to him as he biked the long trip home, nor did he even sense the faintest whisper of anger from two girls who refused to be forgotten.

But if Stash Brown himself had been the accidental carrier of Fiona Walsh's black book, he would have brought along his very biggest laser gun and never taken his eyes off the handlebars. Because two impatient ghosts were sitting backward right in front of Niall's face on the chromed steel, itching for him to open the damn thing and begin to read.

OSCAR HAD EATEN through everything when Niall stepped into the tiny one-room flat they shared in Ballymun.

When Niall had come to town from way out in the arse end of nowhere, nobody who lived there ever called it anything but "the Mun," which, to him, sounded a bit like war-weary Vietnam veterans describing "the 'Nam." He quickly came to realize that the cluster of concrete towers intended for social regeneration had worked inversely, turning the Mun into something like an urban ghetto straight out of the charming old East German Republic.

Seven buildings—each named after a martyr of the Easter Rising in 1916, when a small band of Irish fighters trying to birth a nation had held out against the British Army—had blighted North Dublin for decades with Stalin chic. A local initiative was finally under way to restore civic pride in the place by leveling the eyesores, one after another, but Niall's own solitary black Lego piece, called Plunkett Tower, still yawned at him each night when he neared home. The Mun always beat a happy mood, hands down, even with new and airy plans for parks and the like. Who were they kidding? he thought. This wasn't cappuccino-land and never would be. It was a place populated by knackers, real ghetto tinkers like the ones they still had out in Tallaght, with sharpened coins and worthless lotto tickets in their pockets. To them and everyone else around, these places would forever be the Knackeraguas and Tallagh-fornias of their past, and fuck their regeneration.

But Oscar didn't care either way, as long as there was enough food. The orange tabby blinked disinterestedly when he heard the door and climbed up on a chair to allow Niall an unobstructed view of the damage he'd been proud to cause: one mangled telephone cord, two eviscer-

ated Mars bars, and at least ten tea bags swiped from the kitchen and scattered to hell and gone like the mummified mice he dreamed of when he looked the most peaceful.

"Love you too, you orange fucker," Niall said, and began cleaning up. But he quickly settled at his work desk, which Oscar never came near because he hated the smell of ink and of the lacquer coating the pens. The cat purred and turned his head toward the first light, still not visible out across the cement ocean, even from the forever grimy windows on the twelfth floor.

Niall dug the black book out of his bag and placed it underneath his brightest architect lamp. Now he could see that someone had carved the initials F. W. into the felt by running a ballpoint pen over the same spot over and over. Fiona Walsh? This could be the genuine article. But he'd have to wait and see. He waited for Oscar to give him a sign to continue, but the sugar-sated cat merely glanced at him with that classic heartlessness peculiar to its kind that seemed to say, Whether it kills you or not, I won't go hungry to bed. So go ahead, stupid fucker, and see if I care.

Should he ring the gardaí? he wondered for a moment, hefting the book in his hands. It could be evidence. It might be important and help solve the murder case. His ears burned. NIALL CLEARY IS TOWN HERO! screamed the headline inside his head. His hand was on the telephone. Then it snaked left, as if by itself, and touched the rough black canvas again.

He finally turned the first page and forgot all about the cops.

Though he couldn't know it then, his life—or at least the repetitive existence he'd so far known—would never again be the same.

Niall's heart quickened as he read the first few words of the tightly lettered scrawl that filled page after page. There were spots of dried blood and tears on the thin onionskin paper. Or was it sweat? He compared the penmanship to the words on the envelope, and they matched. Same ragged downstroke, similar tight loops on the vowels. Written in a hurry. Not cozy like, with tea or a bowl of crisps nearby. Nails had dug into the paper everywhere, desperate half-moons leaving their dirty imprint.

Just then, daylight came up in the shape of a pale streak of sunlight attempting to carry the entire horizon of gray clouds on its lonesome shoulders, but it was quickly overwhelmed, as if concrete made it wither and die on contact. Darkness fell on the tiny flat that was as solid as the blackest night. Niall turned on all the lamps he had and drew his puffa jacket tighter against the cold, because the heating had conked out again. He ran his fingers across the first sentences of Fiona Walsh's story and began to read. Niall was firmly in her grasp already, and knew he wouldn't move until he'd reached the last page.

At the top of the page, she had written:

Dear unknown good friend. Please listen to me. I'm right here, and my time is short. To you I bequeath my story and all my to-morrows, for we will be dead soon. We'll die in this house because we loved a man named Jim without knowing his true nature. Listen carefully as I tell you what happened.

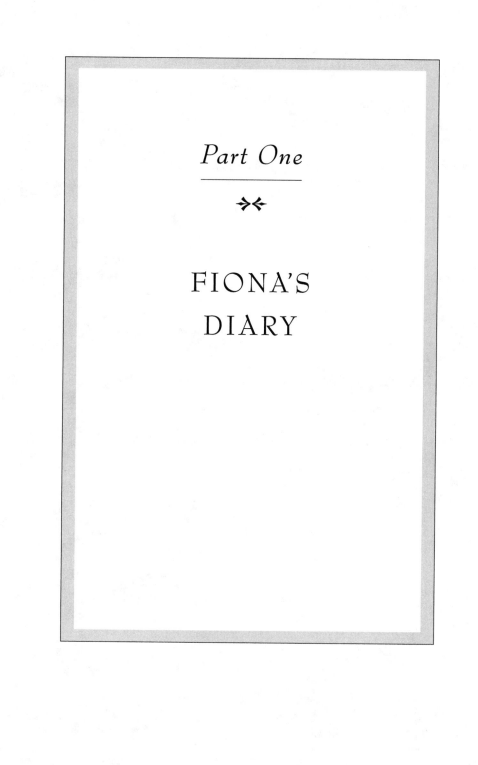

Part One

✦

FIONA'S DIARY

· 3 ·

_____

S he's finally being quiet downstairs.

    I haven't heard my darling aunt ranting and raving for at least an hour. That means I have a little while to write myself warm. So before she starts back up again with her banging on the door and her accusations of murder, I thought I'd better introduce myself to you.

I'm Fiona, Fiona Nora Ann Walsh, and I've been inside this bloody house for nearly three months. I'm manky. Smell like a monkey's arse. The dress I have on is Thai silk, or at least it used to be. People at home told me I was pretty, but usually only after they'd told my sisters first and meant it. Forget your guilty conscience, okay? If you have found this diary, you can't save me. But even so, at least remember me. Promise me you won't forget who I was and how I came to be here. Because being carted out in one of those rubber bags without a soul knowing the true full story is more than I can bear to imagine.

Just so we don't get off on the wrong foot, let's get something straight: Don't start feeling sorry for me. I can take care of myself, even now. A month ago, just before evening room inspection, I found some hairpins and a screwdriver in a drawer she had forgotten to padlock, and I hid them inside my mattress. For the last couple of nights, after I've checked on Róisín, I sharpen the screwdriver on the raspy edge of the brick wall near the window. It's already pointed enough to puncture three demon aunties. And I only need to jam it into one. But I have to wait, to listen. Because when the time comes, I will have just one chance. I sometimes hear scraping from her room downstairs, as if she's dragging something across the floorboards. I bet she's found something heavy to beat my skull in with: a pickax, perhaps, or a shovel. But can she even lift it? I'm not so sure. Last I saw of her about two days ago, through my upstairs window, she looked as shriveled as poor Rosie.

I'm dizzy all the time now, day and night. And that's not just from eating potatoes and bread. It's a feeling somewhere bubbling up inside me that's like my guts being shoved sideways. Or drying up by themselves, leaving a big hole of nothing. I'm not sure I can describe it right, but I know she had a hand in it, whatever it is. I've been bleeding when I pee. Róisín, too. At night, my Rosie whimpers like a barn animal and cries for our mother.

We've heard nothing from the basement for a while, just a clattering sound that could have come from anyplace, really. I'm afraid it's just the two of us up here now on the second floor. I wouldn't put it past that bitch to have flooded the downstairs hole with her garden hose, just to make sure nobody who might be able to help us made it out alive. But we would have heard that, I suppose. So would the neighbors. And from the sound of it, Aunt Moira's strength is ebbing, too. It's become a question of will now, I think, not faith. Endurance. I ran more half marathons than that whore. She may worship her plastic Jesus, but I have my hatred for Moira and my love for little Rosie. And that's stronger than a hundred self-serving rosaries from that wretched woman, now, isn't it?

Help has often been so close I could smell it. But it's never come to visit.

Recently, I've seen a few people right outside on the footpath stopping and staring at my upstairs window, including that funny little postman with the lopsided smile. He always looks like he's thinking about something, making up his mind. His grin always just hangs on his face, even after Auntie Moira stopped inviting him inside.

Because he knows.

I know he does. He just doesn't want to admit it to himself. But what would I have been willing to believe myself before this entire thing began? That one murder can lead to imprisonment and preparing to kill your own family? I doubt that I would. And the postman is putting it out of his mind, too, I'm sure. Because you never believe what your eyes tell you. You trust what you feel in your gut and compare with your own experience. That's the reason old ladies who lived next to serial killers for years always tell the papers what a "wonderful normal boy" he was. You refuse to believe in the presence of evil and go searching for the good "at the bottom of the soul." Me and Rosie, we know better now. If there's black tar in that well, you won't find fresh flowers when you drain it.

Two weeks ago, when I was sure Auntie Moira was listening for the postman downstairs by the front door, I pulled the curtains aside and waved as he started up the front steps. He blinked and stopped for a second. I could see him through the curtains, praying he'd turn around, run down the street, and ring the fucking guards. But he trusted only his eyes, I'm sure. And his eyes had seen a fluttering piece of lace that the wind had moved, not me. The mail was delivered, and we weren't. Lately, when I see him coming, it's as if he averts his glance from my window as he hurries for the mail slot. He wants to make sure he can live with his guilty conscience. And fair play to him, I suppose. You have to be able to tolerate yourself, right?

That means it's up to me to save us. Me and my prison-shank screwdriver. Unless I can find something better before it's time. Something to beat her brains in with.

Wait.

Hold your breath with me. Don't make a sound.

Because I can hear her downstairs. She's rummaging through those drawers of hers, and there's the rattling sound of metal on metal. Scissors, maybe. Or knives. Can you hear it? Clanking together like a dragon gnashing its teeth. She shouldn't be up this late, it's past half two in the morning. Something isn't right. Usually, the yelling and the screaming only begin after what we've got used to calling breakfast around here.

There—now it's quiet again. But she's preparing for something, I know she is. Perhaps she'll make her final assault tonight or tomorrow. So I don't know how long our time together may be. When I stole this book from underneath her Bible last month, I thought we might make it another three weeks. To be honest with you, now it feels more like three days.

But I promise you this: I will write until I can't move my hands any longer. She'll have to pry this pen right out of my fingers, and get past my screwdriver doing it, won't she? So take notes, if you like, because I might remember things out of order, even if I want to tell you everything just the way it happened. We'll never meet, you and I, but it's important for me to know that you can trust me. Just have a little bit of patience. I'll get to all of it.

You need to know something right away, just so you don't go thinking we're innocent lambs, for only children who haven't told their first lie are innocent.

Auntie Moira is right about one thing.

We *are* murderers, as sure as my hand is shaking on this damn paper. And while it's a sin, and I don't look forward one bit to accounting for it on the other side, I'll never regret it. There are good and bad deaths, just as there are innocents and people who need to be killed. We *had* a choice in the matter, I'll tell you that. Only cowards and wankers who whinge when they're caught make up stories about how God or destiny "forced their hand." We used good solid steel to do it and wiped our hands in the grass afterward. And we didn't lose one night's sleep. I'm getting ahead of myself again, sorry. Read on, and perhaps you'll understand how such contradictions can exist inside someone whose biggest concern until recently was trying to remember our lives the way they used to be. Before Jim.

As we've now been introduced, I suppose it's only fair for me to admit something else to you, something that's much harder than labeling us as killers:

It's my fault. All of it.

If I hadn't noticed the handsome young man on his sexy motorcycle to begin with, we would all still be snug in our beds back home in West Cork. But once I'd met his eyes and swum into their black pools, I couldn't forget how it made me feel. It was like something I've only read about in books. Opium, they say, has something of that magic, but this was stronger. When he looked at me, I felt both terrified and relieved. I guess the reason I can't describe it any better, even now, should tell you something of his power.

Because Jim was a force of nature there's no name for yet, unless that word is *ruin*, *fury*, and *seduction* rolled into one. And he did seduce me; he seduced all of us.

It all began with a faulty fuel line, you see. Why didn't I just keep riding past? You be the judge. Pull up a chair and help me figure it out. Because as God is my witness, I still don't understand all of it.

It was barely three years ago, at home in Castletownbere. Sometime in May, I think. The sky was swept of clouds when I noticed a figure bent over his broke-down 1950 Vincent Comet dream machine and cursing under his breath. I slowed on my bicycle, not thinking he'd notice. But he turned to face me on the narrow street.

And with one look, he cracked me open like a safe and stole everything inside.

THE FIRST THING I ever heard him say to anybody was, "Do you think that car is big enough?"

He didn't say it to me, of course, but to the arse of the massive, yacht-sized yellow BMW that nearly clipped him as it roared up the narrow main street near the square. The tourist, whose plates said he and his bejeweled girlfriend came from some country where people drive on the right-hand side, stopped and leaned out the window. The driver had more chins on him than a roomful of butchers. The muscles on his bulging wheel arm might have made reasonable men hesitate. A diver's watch that would have sunk the *Bismarck* glinted in the sun.

"What did you say to me, *din skitstövel?*"

The motorcyclist in the ratty leather jacket raised his head, and I saw the weak sunlight catch his irises. There was no fear in them. He was glorious. Before he answered, he took the time to nod at me as I leaned on my bike to see the show. Even today, I can't tell you what I saw in his eyes. Perhaps it was only aggression. It could have been pure fuck-you-ness, but there was something else hiding there that the motorist didn't immediately catch as he opened the door and took a half step onto the roadway.

"I believe I asked you a question."

"Kalle, get back in the car. Now!" A blond shape in the passenger seat leaned left and grabbed for the heavyset man's suede shirt. But he kept at it, placing both feet on the deck, ready to move down the road under his own power.

Right up until he saw the look in the younger man's eyes.

"Before you get too upset," he asked the Swede, "can I tell you a secret?"

The motorcyclist kept both arms at his sides and smiled as he walked right up to the driver and put his gorgeous lips to the man's meaty ear. I noticed that he didn't just have a great arse, but carried more than muscle inside the tight black jeans and T-shirt. He moved like he had all the time in the world as he bent down to whisper something. The driver was about to protest, and his hands clenched. He could have put one of them around the young fella's tousled black Keanu Reeves hair and squeezed. And for a second, it looked as if the pompous wanker had a mind to. His condescending smile had been widening for several seconds.

And then his jaw went slack, along with his shovel hands.

I couldn't hear what the handsome fella was mumbling, but it didn't sound angry from across the street where I was standing. He even put out a hand and playfully pulled at the other man's earlobe, as if making a point. Then he turned around and, smiling at me, walked back down toward his fire-engine-red motorcycle. The driver just stood there, gob-smacked, letting the wind blow into his open mouth for a bit, while he digested what he'd heard. Whatever it was, it must have come as such a shock that it had robbed him of the power to move, for only the girl-friend tugging hard on his shirttail finally brought him back to the here and now. He got back into his seat faster than my own students after the last bell and gunned the engine so hard he left two fat skid marks on the asphalt. He was past the church steps and gone in seconds, and we never saw them in town since.

Now, I know what you're going to say.

I should have just got back on my bike, continued on my way, and minded my own business, right? Don't think I didn't consider it. But wouldn't you have waited just a few moments more to see if you could find out what had made the driver's anger evaporate so quickly? Of course you would. So I leaned my bike against the window of the realty office and gathered my courage to walk over and talk to the fella, who was once again kneeling next to his mud-splattered machine, which had more loose wires and plastic tubes hanging out of it than a trauma victim. I thought I heard him humming a lullaby. As if he were singing the dirty street racer to sleep right there, next to the gift shop.

He knew I was walking across the street even before my own feet did. I know he did; I could tell by the way he stopped for a second before tightening another screw.

"Howya?" he asked, without turning around, sounding a bit like Dublin, a smidgen of Cork, and a busload of something else not from around here. His voice was as smooth as a cat's.

"All right, I suppose," I answered, feeling stupid for just standing there like an eejit. I was wearing my schoolteacher clothes, regulation skirt length and sensible shoes. Exactly the least sexy outfit to be wearing when talking to any man, and I cursed my rotten luck.

Then he turned to look at me.

I can't say that the ground shifted underneath my feet or any such bullshit. What I will swear to on a stack of Bibles, however, is that look-ing at him filled me with a kind of hope you only get very early in life and can never quite recapture later. It felt to me as if whatever thoughts I had brewing inside me mattered more at that moment than anything else. Because he didn't flirt this time, or wink, or smile. He just peered into my eyes, past the retina, the brain and guts, and all the rest of it, and shone a secret flashlight all around my insides before crawling back out, apparently satisfied with what he'd seen. I can only compare the feeling to being in the grip of a large animal you aren't afraid of; you know it might hurt everyone else, but not you.

But despite his caressing the tourist's ear and fashionably unshaven cheek, it wasn't love that drove that gesture, it was a promise. The promise went something like, "Don't listen to my words, just heed my willingness to tear your ugly head from your body and drop-kick it down the street." I knew it as sure as Easter Sunday, and I still didn't walk away from him.

What made me stay? It wasn't just curiosity or the cheap fantasy of a quick ride somewhere in a quiet alley.

The best I can tell you is that I began to tune in to his voice. Like a lonesome dial waiting to hook on to a good radio station, I stood in my cheap patent-leather Dubarry pumps and let his frequency wash over me.

"What's yer name?" he wanted to know.

"It's not for sale."

He tightened another screw and wiped the fuel line with the bottom part of his shirt, allowing me a full view of a stomach that hadn't seen many chips or pints of stout in its life. I knew later that he did it on purpose. "And now you want to know what I told the Swedish meatball to make him forget about buying his own little slice of Ireland and to drive off into the sunset instead with Miss Bleach 1983, dontcha?"

I toughened up my voice a bit, because the fella was too sure of himself, even if he'd read me dead right. "Maybe I do, and maybe I just wanted to see someone not from around here fiddle around with his fancy toy. What kind of bike is that, anyway?"

He put down the wrench and cocked his head to the side, as if to say, Well, damn, this one's going to take some effort. "Only the most beautiful motorcycle ever made, and that's the truth," he said, stroking the gold leaf lettering on the side of the large fuel tank.

A tattoo-style banner had been carefully inlaid, with the word VIN-CENT offset in white inside. The fella finally smiled. His teeth were perfect, of course, and he spoke with a reverence I'd only heard before in church.

"My Vinnie is a genuine racing machine, the only one left in Ireland, maybe even in the world, and rare as a unicorn. A 1950 Vincent Comet, nine hundred and ninety-eight cubic centimeters, with Albion gears and a wet multiple clutch." He saw my befuddled expression and added, "All that means is she's fast as piss, a bitch to please, and breaks down all the time. But I love her. Want a ride?"

"Quite taken with yourself, aren't you?"

"Just being friendly."

I wanted him to ask me again, but then I looked at my watch. It was nearly nine and, right up the road, twenty-three eleven-year-olds were already piling into their seats for another riveting lesson on the Nile River delta and the construction of the temple at Abu Simbel. He saw me do it and looked a little sad. Before I knew it he had taken my hand and squeezed it, just a tidge, like a gentleman would. He didn't stroke it or anything.

Then he said, "I'm Jim."

"I'm sure you are." I took back my hand, walked back across the road, and stopped. He knew I'd do that, too, because he laughed as I turned around. The wind was making his jacket billow on his lean frame like a leather sail. "Okay," I said. "I'll bite. What *did* you tell that Swedish fella? That you'd take his nice car and make him eat it for breakfast?"

My first real warning came rolling along right there, and I ignored it. I was already past my own good judgment and itching to share a secret.

Jim shook his head and started the engine. It roared louder than a fleet of tugboats at dawn. This made me come closer to him, of course, and he smiled again, gunning every inch of that thing. Thinking about it now still fills me not with dread but with desire. He stuck his head out toward me and with his free hand beckoned me to bend closer to hear. As my hair whipped around in the wind and merged with his, I could at last make out what he was saying.

"All I did was tell him a story."

"Must have been a pretty scary one, then?" I tried, wanting to know more. The Vincent screamed with all its 998 cubic voices, and now my cheek was next to Jim's. He smelled of motor oil and several days of hard road. I think I may have closed my eyes for a second.

"No. Just one that fit what was already inside his head." Whatever that meant. Then he gently patted my cheek, swung back the kickstand, and gave me another one of those small nods. He tightened his grip on the throttle and took a left up the hill to the town of Eyeries, where kids walking to my own class stood and gawped after him. I remained standing in the street so long after the sound of the engine had died down that I was nearly run over by another fancy car. I moved out of the roadway and stood by my bike, listening to the church bell strike nine. I'd be late for class, but so would at least ten students, because the sight of a red Vincent, driven by a gorgeous fucker who knew what lay dormant inside the heads of others, was not regular fare in the town where I grew up.

As I pedaled furiously up the hill to work, I tried to recall the look in the Swede's eyes.

He hadn't just been scared by what he'd heard.

He'd been afraid for his life.

ALL THAT MORNING, I tried my level best to give two shites about the Great Pyramids, the egomaniac who had them built, and how to spell the words *Pharaoh Khufu* on the blackboard without looking too much like the first-year teacher I really was. Except it didn't really play out that way in my sixth classroom. While telling Clarke Riordan three times to put his shagging Game Boy away, I couldn't help wondering what Jim had whispered into the aggressive driver's left ear to leave him so paralyzed.

But most of all, to be honest with you, I just thought about him. I even tuned out the sounds inside the room and listened for distant engine noise that could, perhaps, be emanating from a Vincent Comet.

"Miss, but you didn't answer my *question*," said Mary Catherine Cremin, and she was bang on target. I hadn't listened to a thing she said.

I heard a ripple of nervous laughter around me and snapped out of it. Before me stood the teacher's pet, uniform starched and pressed and every number-two pencil in her drawer sharpened like a lethal weapon. She clutched the piece of chalk as if, by pressing it harder, she could speed up the lesson. Mary Catherine had been halfway through delivering her homework report on the Valley of the Kings and was pissed that I had crawled up my own arse and disappeared before she got to the good parts.

"Oh, erm—sorry, Mary Catherine. What was your question again?"

The future inquisitor crossed both arms and sighed. Her shoelaces were so tight I was surprised the child could even breathe. "David says the sphinx lost its nose because a bunch of French soldiers climbed up and hacked it off, and I say that's just not true. Is it?"

"No, I said they fired a cannon at it." David was a husky boy with a braying voice and eternal bad breath.

"Shut up, ugly," hissed Mary Catherine, adjusting a barrette in her hair.

"Make me."

"Quiet, please," I tried, motioning for Mary Catherine to sit back down, which she did without much speed or enthusiasm. David looked like he had a mind to pelt her with one of the apples from the tree right outside, and I can't say I blamed him. "Nobody knows, really," I said, choosing diplomacy. "Many historians believe local vandals destroyed the nose in the fourteenth century, so it probably wasn't Napoleon's army. But there's no definitive answer."

Both Mary Catherine and David were unimpressed with that Solomonic judgment and dug in their heels. "But *Miss*," started little Miss

Please-give-us-more-homework in a piping voice, "I looked it up, and it says it definitely wasn't the French. It was some loser who—"

"Did *too;* they blasted it off with a cannonball," cried David, thumping his tabletop. "*Boom!* No more nose."

A shouting match erupted across the length of the room, with each side pretending the fight really wasn't about settling a long-brewing power struggle in the class that I'd been unable to quell: Miss Perfect vs. Mr. Know-it-all. Soon, books went flying right after insults, and raising my voice merely seemed to agitate them even more, the little beasts. I glanced at my watch. It was a long time to second bell.

Then I heard this dull roar.

It crept into my ear through the din, growing stronger from somewhere far away, until one by one, the shrieks had been extinguished and the kids were listening, too. I recognized it straightaway. It was the wet sputtering growl of an old motorcycle engine that broke down more than once a day and needed expert tending. I looked out the window but saw only my battered Raleigh next to the even shittier Ford Fiestas in the teachers' car park by the hedgerow. I couldn't see the road but still craned my neck, hoping to catch a glimpse of red zipping past.

Then the sound died down and blended with the drumming of rain on the roof.

One boy, Liam, whose body weight was so low I could have folded him in two and put him into my backpack, smiled. And this was rare. Liam was the kind of lad the others would shove into the water of the bay so often his gray uniform had turned a kind of mottled brown when it dried out. He rarely spoke up in class, and when he did he always looked at boys like David to see what kind of punishment would be meted out later as a consequence. But today, something had happened. He sparkled like a lighthouse.

"You saw it too, Miss," he said, eyes bright and mouth open. "The motorcycle. Didn't you?"

Other expectant faces turned in my direction, and I recognized a handful that had likewise observed the crimson rock 'n' roll machine cutting right through town that morning and wondered where it came from. I considered saying no. Not because I wouldn't let Liam have his hard-earned victory, but because I was afraid that the way I answered would reveal just how affected I was already by my brief encounter with a man who called himself Jim and smelled like pure sex, no chaser. I listened for the sound one more time, but there was only normal traffic from outside, produced by mere mortals driving delivery vans and buses.

I finally looked at Liam and nodded.

"Yes," I told him, keeping my voice as neutral as the sphinx's smile. "Yes, I did."

FINBAR, OF COURSE, had most of his tea in punitive silence.

I loved him, I did. Not because of his spit-shined Mercedes S500L that he always made sure to park somewhere he could keep an eye on it while we ate. And it wasn't because he was the best-looking piece of arse in old Castletownbere, making more than a million a year flogging "authentic Irish dream homes" to people needing fellas like him to interpret their dreams for them in the first place.

No, I'd stayed with Finbar upwards of a year at that time because he always listened. It was as simple as that. Even then, I could tell the difference between feigned interest just to get laid and real inquisitiveness. He cared about what I said, never missing nuances or contradictions. At times, it was a bit like dating a lie detector, though, because nothing passed him by. He would nod and wrinkle his handsome brow, and his blue eyes would narrow while he waited for me to finish telling him about my day.

That's how he interpreted love, I think: to wait—hold himself back—until it was safe to come out and play. I was happy. Or, perhaps, I wasn't unhappy. Back then, they amounted to pretty much the same thing. Our sex life, if you must know, was pretty intense for the first two months. There used to be lots of pushing me up against the wall, because he wanted to live up to driving a piece of Nazi steel that big. But those encounters had become rare by the time he and I sat down for our daily ritual of tea before I was to join my sisters for dinner.

It was precisely because he listened so well that he heard what I *didn't* say.

The sky had got ready for bed and colored the old IRA monument outside the café salmon pink. The shadow of the Celtic stone cross stretched across the street and covered one half of Finbar's face as he prepared to say something unpleasant. I could tell. I squinted and pretended he was really two people: one was my boyfriend, the other a person who existed to point out my faults. I'll leave it up to you to guess which of them took up more space that afternoon. He kept opening and closing the flip-lock bracelet on his Rolex, and I wanted to rip it off his arm and toss it into the harbor and have him spit it out.

"I saw you kissing that . . . tinker this morning," he finally said, not looking at me.

"Get outta here with that."

He smiled without mirth; he was dead serious. At first, I couldn't believe it. "You even leaned your bike up against my window first," he continued, flicking open his watch one more time. "My place of *business*. And then you strode across the street, bent down, and kissed him. The guy in the leather jacket. I saw you." He wasn't waiting for an explanation. Finbar was like that. He preferred his own eyes and ears to a good excuse any time.

I rummaged around in my bag for one of Róisín's ciggies and found none. Now the shadow from the cross had shifted so that only Finbar's left eye was still lit up by the sunset. A Cyclops, I thought, fabulous. My boyfriend is prehistoric and mythological, not to mention so fucking irritating—precisely because he's pointing out something I'm just beginning to feel myself.

"He was telling me—"

I stopped. For what had Jim really been telling me? Nothing I didn't know already. What he had done was reel me in until I didn't know why I had gone near him.

"Telling you what?" asked Finbar, whose pearl-blue Ermenegildo Zegna tie had flopped into his tea like a thirsty eel while he wasn't looking.

I decided to lie. Not to be mean, but because nothing else would have made sense. I hope you agree. Because, honestly, would you have believed that Jim was telling me how he had made a bollixy bodybuilder type fold his tent and fuck off just by whispering a *story*? Exactly.

"That he was totally lost, dead broke, and needed money," I said. "I had to bend down to hear him for the engine noise. Give me one of your smokes, willya?"

"No. You quit." His face scrutinized mine the way it did when he wasn't sure what to believe, his ears or his sixth sense. He hadn't made up his mind.

"Don't be a pain, Finbar, give us a cigarette. He asked, and I answered."

"So what'd ya say back to him?"

I grabbed for his Marlboros and snagged one before he could stop me. I lit it first, blew smoke into the still air, and answered. "I told him to go play with his little red machine somewhere else. Okay?"

"Really?"

"Will you ever listen? What interest would I have in kissing some Dublin homeless person on a red motorcycle fucked out by Father Christmas the last time his reindeer went on strike? Are you off your head?" I took another drag and glanced at him to see how well my act was going over. Because underneath my loyal girlfriend bit, I knew I deserved Finbar's jealousy, you see. I had earned it because I could feel Jim nagging me like a stone in my shoe. Even right then, under the glare of suspicion, I had to wonder where that 1950 Vincent had gone off to.

"Grand, so," he said, reaching for his coat. Apparently, that was the end of it. He even smiled and grabbed his car keys. He'd believed me. For a while, I'd believed it myself, but as I rose to follow him out the door, I was angry that I was lying for a man I didn't even know. Before it was all over, of course, I'd do far worse. But we'll get to that.

"See you tomorrow?" I asked, as I stepped out into the narrow street and listened to the well-fed seagulls dive-bombing a filled trawler crawling into its berth.

"You don't want me to drive you?" asked the lie detector in the nice suit.

"I need to pick up a few things for Auntie Moira," I said, happy at least to be back among truths once more. "She's cooking. I won't survive unless I minimize the damage with some purchases of my own. Like food bought *before* its expiration date, for one."

"God bless Our Lady of Perpetual Suffering." Finbar crossed himself and gave me a genuine smile.

"You blasphemer, you," I said, kissing him good night. "Dinner tomorrow?"

"Only if you come alone and don't bring your Hell's Angel, or whatever he was."

"You're not getting any, you keep that up, Finbar Christopher Minihane," I said, but I laughed because the tension was broken. He trusted me again. I've often thought what would have happened if my lie hadn't worked that day. Perhaps I'd be standing behind you right now in your nicely heated home, alive and well, peering over your shoulder as you read some other poor wench's diary. But here we are, the two of us. And we have to make do.

As I saw Finbar walking back toward his silvery car, I wanted to tell him the truth. How dizzy I had really felt when I saw my feet moving across the street that morning, eager for a story that made no sense yet. That Jim really frightened me as much as I was drawn by his offhand charm and the hidden promise of violence. But I did nothing. More than anything, I was afraid of feeling stupid if I told anybody.

I caught a glimpse of my own reflection in a shopwindow as I stopped by SuperValu to pick up fresh vegetables.

The woman staring back already had someone else's eyes.

They'd seen something I knew she'd never try to explain to anybody.

DAYLIGHT STILL HUNG on by its fingernails when I came back outside and put my bags in the bicycle basket. Out across the water, Bear Island lay resting like a dark blue whale sated from a long day of feeding.

Spring was about to sprout into the kind of summer that ballooned my town from eight-hundred-odd souls to over a thousand more outsiders come June. I rode past the new gourmet restaurant that only ever had two people in it, zigzagged between some of my own students playing football, and stopped near the top of the hill.

I hadn't meant to go this way, because I'd nearly forgotten how it always made me feel to see the old house. Like I was lower than whale shite, to tell you the truth.

But there it was, in all its former glory. An off-license had been crammed into what used to be my father's news agency, and never mind the ghosts. It had been a humble two-story gray pebble-dash house where I grew up with my sisters in relative comfort. Father would rise early to cut the red nylon cord on the newspaper bundles; we all loved helping him do that. The place really was the center of town there, for a while. We got the lotto players, the drunks, the moneyed Eurotrash, and all the rest. Dad worked and kept his own counsel, most days. Mother taught us about the world. She had bought me a map of ancient Egypt, with a watery blue line running right through it from south to north. I drew temples next to it myself, and hung it on the wall over my bed. I never dreamed about Amenhotep and Rameses, even when I tried to, but that's probably because I couldn't spell their names back then.

Then Dad forgot to secure the propane bottles downstairs one night. A simple mistake to forget unhooking them from the spigot, I've always felt.

We girls were upstairs, asleep. Our parents had been downstairs cleaning up the shop for tomorrow. After it was all over, and the neighbors had pulled us out in time, the gardaí and the fire brigade said it was probably an electrical fire that started over by the back of the cooler—which happened to be where the propane had been put to bed. But whatever it was, the explosion was powerful enough to blow out all the windows downstairs and singe the insides so that only the freezer we used for ice cream was spared. We buried what was left of our parents when I was thirteen and moved up the hill to Aunt Moira's house.

It was all right, I suppose. In time, living there became normal, until each of us grew up and found our own place.

I still hated taking this route to anybody's house, if I could help it. My old room on the second floor had become a storage unit for empty crates; I could see them through the salt-caked window. From the street, I couldn't tell if my Egypt map still hung up there. I was sure it didn't. Black smudges on the brick façade still tracked the flames' path. I haven't tasted ice cream since. Sticks in my throat.

I turned back around, took one long look at the majestic trawlers coming in, each with a bellyful of herring, glanced down at the quaint town square, and hated every inch of the sight.

I'm sorry, but I didn't have much of that hometown nostalgia you read about in tourist guides. Still don't. You know, the Irish Spring bullshit with red-haired Colleens on horseback, leaning down to receive a long wet one from rugged George Clooney–looking fellas in tweed caps and vests, while some invisible orchestra in the background plays fiddle-de-dee music until you want to throttle somebody. But that fantasy was the reason Finbar is probably still selling waterfront properties the rest of us wouldn't be caught dead in. From Portugal and Holland they've come, changing a quiet boring town into a slightly louder and richer boring town. I may have red hair, fine, but you try feeding that kind of romantic image on a teacher's starting salary and see how well you do.

I was aching to leave. To see the pyramids for real, not just in my mind's eye. But older sisters don't get to leave, really; they stand their ground and wipe everyone else's arse.

And speaking of that, I was biking over to Tallon Road to pick up my baby sister Róisín for dinner at Aunt Moira's house. I could have met her there, I suppose, but in those days Rosie had a close personal relationship with rapidly changing glasses of stout, to be consumed in the darkest corners with the worst possible men who would never get to see her with her knickers off, no matter how hard they tried. I felt my legs boiling with dutiful fatigue as I pumped the iron horse the last few feet to her flat.

Inside, it smelled like a camel had crawled underneath her bed and promptly died. That meant Rosie was home. Her black locks moved somewhere in the mess of down comforters, a raspy voice snarling and groaning and clearly just waking up for the day at half seven in the evening.

"Mneed a ciggie," she mumbled, and I tossed her an extra one I'd swiped from Finbar. I swept through my sister's layers of black goth clothes and uncovered the coffeemaker. Then I noticed that her most cherished possession, her closest friend in the universe, was still up from last night and hadn't been properly tucked into bed.

The voices still chattered. Like the saints in heaven comparing their favorite sinners below and not caring a whit if we could all hear.

A brand-spanking-new ICOM IC-910H shortwave transceiver ham radio glowed green on a cluttered desk next to the ironing board. It was black and boxy and top-of-the-line. The sound was still on, and low garbled transmissions competed for space on the crowded UHF band. To me, it always sounded like one of those TV programs about moon rockets, where men with buzz cuts and earpieces smiled when they heard the fellas in the tin can up there somewhere saying, "We read you loud and clear, Houston." But to Rosie, it was heaven on a slice of buttered toast. I walked over gently to turn off the knob, and the green light dimmed.

I could bore you with my sister's obsession with faraway voices she'd never even meet, but suffice it to say she and I both dreamt of distant shores, each in our own way. Where I was content to hang a map or a picture, however, she needed to connect. My parents bought her first transistor radio when she was seven. She listened to it so often the plastic backing melted right off within a year. Soon, she spent her money on two things: mascara that made her look like a punk raccoon and ham radios. She detested e-mail, which she called "a playpen for children who can't be bothered to speak," and I suppose she was right, at that. Her voice was always prettier than anybody's.

This particular monster had been given to her by an admirer, and I mean that seriously. She had them by the dozen. Men would hang on her like tree sap in summer, and not just because she treated them like absolute shite, which you can never do often enough, if you want them to stay. No, they were drawn by the rumor, which happened to be absolutely true, that she'd never slept with a man. The fact that she could debate all of them under the table, even when dead drunk, just added to the mystique. And she was gorgeous, as well. I kicked one of her feet.

Another grunt. "Ow! Come to torture me, you schoolmarm dominatrix, you."

"Giddup. If you think I'm having boiled meat and shite potatoes by myself, you're dreaming."

Slowly, two legs swung out and Rosie sat up carefully. She looked like a Japanese porcelain doll who'd got herself mugged by a gang of makeup artists. Her eyes were pink and swollen, and she had little drunk flowers on her cheeks, where some of the mascara had ground itself in with the foundation. Her lips curled up in that guilty smile that every boy, man, and grandfather from here to Skibbereen told their friends about, even if she'd never dignify their grins with so much as a look. It was the kind of smile that could lay waste to empires, if only Róisín had any clue what that meant.

For the time being, she was content to remain on the dole and be the last customer at McSorley's Bar most nights, outdrinking the gobshites who paid for her pints without breaking a sweat. Easily the smartest by a mile in our entire family, Róisín had been accepted to University College Cork the previous year and had been well on her way to an honors degree in physics without straining her active social life.

That is, right until a teacher's aide in her Thermal and Statistical Physics class grabbed her in the girls' bathroom one fine day and tried to force her to suck on his little pecker. It took three grown men to drag Rosie off him. She'd broken his clavicle and the bone around an eye socket and destroyed one testicle in less than a minute, all using only the cleaning woman's mop. They didn't want to expel her, but they also didn't fire that sad little man who'd tried to doink her, so Rosie just told them goodbye and thanks very much all the same, took the bus back

home, and returned to her unseen voices on the airwaves. It had been that way for over six months.

"Didja forget my breakfast?" the creature in the tiny tiger-striped panties wanted to know. I tossed her two pieces of bread with honey that I'd just made on the cluttered windowsill and watched her devour them, legs dangling over the edge of the bed like the girl she still was. While she finally rose and rummaged through a press to find some clean clothes that weren't black, I held all thoughts of that motorcycle charmer at bay. Almost. Rosie finally screwed herself into the tiniest jeans in creation, topping off the ensemble with spiky red heels and a full-length white patent-leather coat. Demon-dark eyeliner made her look like Dracula's favorite relative, and she was already tugging impatiently at the door while I was lost in thought about someone I was trying hard to forget.

"Oi! Whatcha thinking about—Martians?" Rosie wanted to know, as she cracked that deadly smile for me again and stuck a fresh ciggie in it the same way a longshoreman grabs his gaffing hook.

"No," I said, and wanted to mean it.

I ALMOST DIDN'T notice the tiny article about the unexplained death.

We were just about to leave, but Rosie hadn't used her bicycle for so long the tires were flat. So while she emptied her mudroom looking for a pump, I tried to make sense of the mess of overcoats she'd strewn all over the floor. I hung fake leopard coats and paint-stained black leather jackets back up on hooks, and found four days' worth of newspapers underneath. Of course. My sister stubbornly refused to acknowledge the free subscription I'd got her to the *Southern Star* through one of Finbar's clients. She preferred the company of disembodied voices to the ongoing facts of regular life.

"Will you ever put something into your head but that fucking short-wave," I asked, leafing through the most recent issue, "and rejoin the rest of us out here in physical reality?" Because it wasn't her baby sister protest that galled me, but my dead certainty that all her superior brain power would be turning to digital mush before long. My little genius didn't answer but dragged her bike outside and started pedaling away. Typical. I folded the newspaper and was about to throw it into the mud-room before locking up.

And that's when I saw it.

It was a hundred words, if that, and similar to other tragic stories I'd often read before. Because when the tourist stream increases each summer, so do the highway deaths. Simple as that. But what held my attention now was the way this one seemed—well, wrong somehow. I had to read it twice to realize what it was. There was something hidden, something unsaid, that spoke more clearly than what was on the page.

LOCAL WOMAN FOUND DEAD
BY DEIRDRE HOULIHAN

BANTRY, 19 May—Julie Ann Holland, 34, of Drimoleague, was found yesterday by neighbors in her bed, where she had apparently been dead "for some time," according to gardaí. Mrs. Holland, a widow, had not been seen since attending a céilí near Clonakilty last Saturday night. Nobody was noticed entering her house, and there are no signs of a struggle. Even so, whoever may have seen Mrs. Holland that night in anybody's company should contact Macroom Garda District Head Quarters at 026-20590 and ask for Sergeant David Callaghan. Neighbors describe observing a motorcycle parked near her house the last time she was seen alive.

Mrs. Holland leaves behind a young son, Daniel, 6, who was away with his gran on the night in question.

"Are you *comin'* or what?" My brain princess was getting impatient with me, and had stopped halfway down the street. I folded the paper into my bag and locked the door. While I joined my sister and half listened to her needling me for being so absentminded, I wondered how Mrs. Holland had died. She hadn't died in her sleep, because the article would have been worded differently, wouldn't it? *Anybody's company* didn't sound peaceful at all. Why would readers be encouraged to ring the guards if they didn't already suspect out-and-out murder? Then there was the motorcycle. It could have been any color, I suppose. But in my heart, there was only candy-apple red, wasn't there? I shivered, pretending to laugh at my sister's jokes as we rounded the bend and saw Aunt Moira's pink bed-and-breakfast.

Like I told you before, the clichés about happy maidens dancing with leprechauns and fairies on the green meadows of our peaceful emerald island are a load of shite.

Because that summer, there were worse things than Swedish speed demons stalking the hedgerows.

OUR SAVIOR HAD been cleaned up for Friday dinner.

I hadn't seen his haloed face in ages. But as Rosie and I walked through the front door of Moira's two-story on the road facing the bay, he was back and all shiny, as if he'd recently been dunked in Woolite and lovingly hand-dried. Last time I'd seen him in one piece was the final evening our parents were still with us. A customer had given him to our mother and father as a kind of joke, and it stuck. He was made of blue and yellow plastic and posed with both arms out to the sides. The beard had been dyed brown once, but had flaked off, providing a full view into his power and glory, in this case a 40-watt lightbulb. Plastic Jesus had been blown into the street that night, and Auntie Moira had saved him from the trash heap. She'd dusted him off and told us girls it was "a blessing from the Almighty." She had put him in a box by her bed and taken him out once in a while to remember her only sister by. Even the few religious nuts left in town backed up at that point and left the stage to her.

Róisín and I looked at each other without a word as we glanced around the house. Moira had got worse lately. A portrait of old Eamon de Valera, that sexy beast, hung in blazing black and white by the coat rack. All grannies and aunties loved him, don't ask me why. She might have picked Bill Clinton; at least he knew how to party. A rosary hung over Dev's face like a necklace. He would have liked that.

"Howya, Aunt Moira?" Rosie asked, and smiled dutifully, like a girl who'd never had to be driven over to the hospital by me in the dead of night only three days earlier and have her stomach pumped.

"You're late, my darlings," Moira said, but smiled and took our coats. There was the unmistakable smell of overcooked whatever-it-was all over the entire house. The place we sisters grew up had begun to show signs of Moira's failing self-interest and complete surrender to kookiness. The wallpaper we'd hung when we were little now sagged near the bottom of the walls, as if the house were trying to shed some weight. The fireplace in the kitchen was blocked by a chair, because our aunt recently had begun to fear accidental fires. "I'll go up in flames, same as your mother, and that's the truth," she'd said when we'd been there last, and I'd hurried home without commenting. Where she'd once made sure the bed-and-breakfast guests felt welcome, she now rarely spoke to them, except to accept payment and hand out maps of the area. So customers had become scarce lately, and I couldn't say I blamed them.

It wasn't her fault, really. It was Harold's.

Betrayal takes many shapes, but preying on a forty-two-year-old woman with a few good years of lying about her age left in her, that was downright cruel. Sometimes, I could still smell his cheap Brut after-shave in the far corners of the upstairs hallway. Harold hadn't been gone six months, but my aunt's decline had been precipitous. She never even bothered to wash except every other day now and still waited by a silent telephone for a bell that would never come. A steady diet of Mars bars she thought she was keeping a secret added to a waistline that had once been so slim even older men had been afraid to squeeze her too hard, lest they break her in two.

Less than three years earlier, Moira had been the kind of stately creature that other women her age envy and men of every age fantasize about, the same way they sneak peeks at the coolly beautiful librarian. Harold, a tourist who said he came from a place called Rensselaer—somewhere north of New York, I think it was—had been a guest in room number five. He'd paid in advance and said he planned to do some fishing. A high forehead, those massive American horse teeth, and a braying laugh signaled his arrival anywhere, but people soon grew to think he might not be half bad for a Yank. He winked at me once, but not in a creepy way. More like a big brother who knew he wasn't cool but didn't care. I liked him. All he had to do was walk into a room to make even the dogs inside it feel better.

One day, it was time for him to leave. Me and my sisters came home from school and found his bags downstairs, but he was nowhere to be found. It was only when Rosie snuck up the stairs and put her already trained ear to the freshly painted door of room number five that she heard more than giggling. She ran downstairs to tell us that Harold was probably staying after all. And I can still remember a sting of jealousy that he hadn't picked me.

Moira did more than blossom. With Harold staying around, the light behind her eyes, which had long been absent, flared brighter than when the sun reflected over the waves. She kissed him too hard and too often, and in public, but didn't care who saw it. And whenever she had her peculiar ideas crawl onto her shoulder and whisper in her ear, Harold could always be counted on to talk her out of her tree. She rested her head on his chest when they sat together on the couch. I felt perfectly at ease letting Harold take over the responsibility we had shouldered since we were little. He told me that, at last, he'd "found the woman I never want to leave." And so we began to make ourselves scarce to let them have their privacy.

I know; don't even say it. If *you'd* heard a line like that, you'd run for cover. And I should have, too.

Because the Dutch girl made him break his promise in five seconds flat.

Aunt Moira had come home from the market early that day, wanting to surprise Harold with dinner. She hadn't even put the bags down when she heard the moaning from number five. She opened the door and found Harold on top of a little backpacker named Kaatje. Moira had just stood there, mouth moving in silence, wearing the new floral dress she'd bought to be pretty for him. She was still clutching one shopping bag as she realized he wasn't going to stop, even if he'd been caught. Kaatje's technique and her firm Coppertoned skin apparently outweighed the shock of being caught by a quarter mile.

"Could you ask your maid to close the door, Harold?" the nymph had even asked, reaching around and squeezing his bony arse to bring him closer to her shaved crotch without even so much as looking at Moira. Harold had finally turned to the figure in the doorway and stared dumbly as if to say, *Will you* look *at this young girl? Can you blame a guy?* Only then had Aunt Moira taken a step back and closed the door. She cried when she got downstairs but did it so discreetly that nobody but the saints could hear.

Harold left with Kaatje before nightfall. He only took his passport and whatever cash and traveler's checks he found in the register, while Moira hid in her bedroom for the rest of the day, beating her head with her fists. He didn't leave a note.

And now, with nobody to talk some sense into her darkest moments, Moira's eccentric ideas sprouted once again like hungry snakes busting out of a broken jar. Only this time they began to make us uneasy. Plastic Jesus was one thing, but other notions had taken hold. As Rosie and I made our way through the hallway to the dining room, we saw all the landscape paintings were gone. No more scenic lakes and tumbledown castles with deer all around. Instead, our aunt had bought statues of the saints, cast in white plaster, and lined them up like mute security guards every few feet. It looked like God's Army was expected to charge at any moment. There was a new brittle energy to her walk, I noticed, but said nothing. I knew she'd soon have another one of her "episodes" unless I could prevent it. Except Rosie wasn't helping.

"Did the nuns have an early Christmas sale?" Róisín asked her aunt, saying what I had only been thinking, her voice innocent but spoiling for a fight.

"Go on, girls, sit down and eat," replied Moira, refusing to take the bait, and nearly smiling the way she did when we were kids. She ushered us into a room we remembered as a place where damask napkins and clean glasses had blocked our view of each other as children across the spit-shined mahogany top. Now the table was chipped, and our

aunt had folded blue paper napkins with the name of Finbar's realty company into glasses that would never see better days, from the look of them. The source of the smell stood right on the threadbare linen table-cloth, in which pale gray chunks of meat gasped for breath like beached seals under a hot sun. Every vegetable in sight was dead on arrival. The potatoes were, as always, overcooked to the point of being pure muck, and—as usual—Moira had accepted my fresh produce and stashed it far away. Friday dinner was always *her* show, since it was the only time we all came over anymore.

Me and Rosie sat down, and I kept an eye fixed on her, just in case she felt like tempting fate or me some more. An impish smile was get-ting ready to crack my little sister's black makeup when she noticed the sofa bunched up against the second fireplace, like an early season stop-gap against intruding Santas. Only a look from me averted another smart-arse comment cooking in her goth brain.

There was one empty chair. Aoife was late. Again.

And the reason I've not introduced her until now is because she was stronger than the rest of us. Róisín's twin sister looked like her in every respect, but there could never have been any mistaking the two, even in their birthday suits. Because where Rosie emanated a calculated ag-gression that required buckets of eyeliner, Aoife had a kind of story-book purity about her. Remember that Irish Spring commercial look from earlier? That's the one, but with a twist. Instead of whiny uilleann pipes and shamrocks as the soundtrack to her life, she usually blared death metal with some German fella who set fire to himself onstage. She'd sew her own dresses, choosing large floral prints, which she'd wear with anything from slingbacks to bare feet. Well, bare feet most of the time, if she could get away with it. She'd inherited my mother's sunny "You'll see, it'll all be better tomorrow" disposition, and it rubbed off just as surely as Rosie's sexy sullenness drew in the men with more rings in their noses than on their fingers. The trick of it was, where my demon child never had delved into carnal mystery with the opposite sex, her twin didn't exactly sit in the back of the bus in that department, if you get my meaning.

When the insurance company paid us each our share from the fire upon our reaching maturity (and I'd use that term advisedly for Rosie), Aoife had bought an old green Mercedes with those figure-eight headlights and started her own taxi service. It barely kept her in hippie dresses, but she didn't care. Whenever people said it was too dangerous for a single girl to be driving the roads all by herself, Aoife smiled and peeled back the carpet underneath her seat. She'd hid our father's old shotgun there, and even sawed the barrel and stock off. It was ugly-looking, and the fire had turned the gray metal a bright shade of copper. "See how they'll like *that*, they try anything in my cab," she'd reply, smiling widely at nothing in particular.

Finbar had got her a deal the year before on a ramshackle stone cottage way the hell out of town in the middle of a field, over near Eyeries, where you had to watch the rams grazing by the side of the road and irises made the whole world turn yellow after it rained. The roof leaked, but she loved it. Sometimes, when I came to visit unannounced, I'd see her standing among the trees, wearing her wellies and a pair of shorts, as if she were listening to the branches and the birds, lost to the grandeur of it all. I often didn't disturb her for several minutes, because it looked so natural. Peaceful. Something I could never feel for myself.

"I could eat a farmer's arse, I'm so starving!"

We turned and saw herself tumbling inside, grinning and placing a cake of some kind smack on the table before sitting down. She walked over and kissed our aunt on both cheeks with such ferocity Moira momentarily forgot that she was still supposed to be grieving her lost love. Then she sat down and winked at me and Rosie. Aoife's presence inside a room usually made it impossible for our aunt's built-in victimhood to gain full speed. Her green polka-dotted dress was brighter than the neon-lit icon of Our Lady above the door.

"Aoife, will you say grace?" asked Aunt Moira, and Aoife was a good sport and bent her head.

"Our Father," she started as she looked at the image, on autopilot already from years ago, "bless this food and all the people in this house, that we may enjoy what You have provided for us through Your grace."

A swift kick from me made Rosie fold her coal-black fingernails into an acceptable posture of reverence before it was over.

"Amen," concluded Moira, and started serving the sad protein-drained remains.

"When did Our Lady get herself some Las Vegas lights?" asked Rosie, before I could stop her. Aunt Moira looked hurt and mumbled something about getting more bread before rising and going into the kitchen.

"Shut up!" I hissed. "D'you hear me, child of the night? Leave her the fuck alone!" Rosie's cheeks reddened a bit underneath the white pancake makeup, and she shrugged as Moira came back with a basket of stale rolls at least two days old.

Aoife chewed the food as if she liked it and even told Moira how good it tasted. In gratitude, our aunt walked over and planted a kiss on her niece's newly shaved head, where a few centimeters of blond hair made her look like some anemic boy soldier.

"Sorry I'm late," Aoife said, as she pinched Rosie's knee and piled more deceased meat on her own plate. "But a fucking motorcycle nearly ran into me a moment ago. Had to swerve like fuck."

"Language," said Moira, but she was still smiling. Aoife was her favorite by a mile.

"Oh, right, sorry."

"What did you say about a motorcycle?" I asked, as casually as I knew how. But out of the corner of my eye I could see Róisín cocking her head and staring at me.

"He came shootin' past Saint Finian's Cemetery like his hair was on fire." She chewed and shifted her pink combat boots on the floor. "Handsome fella, too."

I didn't have to ask to know the color of the machine.

"Which way was he going, d'ya think?" I asked.

"The next pub over, I'd imagine, judging from the direction. Why?"

"Just wondering if it's the season for those Belgian bankers who think they're Marlon Brando." Each year, you see, leather-faced old men with young wives would carom all over, losing loads of cash and often their legs, besides. The gardaí always had a hell of a time cleaning that up. I figured even Rosie would buy that excuse for my growing interest.

"Too early yet," said Rosie laconically, chewing a lonely stem of near-white broccoli. "That's in July."

"Oh, no, this one wasn't an old fart," continued Aoife, with that predatory gleam in her eye. Just the other day, she'd had to drive some retired football player to the airport up in Shannon. He never made it that far. Instead, he had spent the night at her cottage and, for all I knew, was still providing her with loads of locker-room charm. "This one was thirty, tops."

"Ah, so many men, and only one cab." Rosie sighed.

"Don't you start," said Aoife, and there was a tiny crack in her nature-child act.

"How about some dessert?" asked Aunt Moira.

IT WAS NEARLY ten when Moira reluctantly let us go, making us swear to visit next week. The sky was still promising summer around the corner and appeared nearly green out across the bay. The boats were berthed and the sails taken in. At that moment, I remember, I nearly fell in love with my hometown, just for a bit. Then the feeling was gone.

"Fancy a pint?" asked Róisín. "Too early to think about torturing the men yet."

"I agree," said Aoife, and took off her camouflage jacket, on which she'd painted little men chasing butterflies with nets. A warm breeze rolled up from the bay. "How does the aged member of our fair sorority feel about that?"

"I'll drink the both of yis into next Tuesday," I said, grinning. God, how I loved them, and Christ, they were a lot of work.

The twins looked at each other like co-conspirators and asked, simultaneously, "So would you like to lose to us down at O'Hanlon's or McSorley's?"

"McSorley's," I said, grabbing the handles of my bicycle like I was a proper Hell's Angel. "And yis can suck on my tailpipe."

FRIDAY NIGHT MEANT we'd have to fight for a breath of air.

Fishermen stood by the bar in their sweaters and boots, forking over fistfuls of cash for fruity drinks they didn't know the names of. Two Spanish lads in matching aluminum sunglasses were yelling that someone had stolen their backpacks until Clare, the waitress, told them to calm down and look behind the bar, where she'd put them for safekeeping. The whole place was always a bit too "genuinely Irish" for my money, but it was slap bang in the middle of town and poured the best pints. Sepia-toned prints of Castletownbere's glorious past graced the nicotine-stained walls. There were rumrunners in black oilskin ponchos and IRA volunteers in felt hats with their stolen British rifles hoisted aloft, as well as newer pictures of my own students getting a prize from the mayor for not drowning in that year's regatta. A wooden replica harp hung on the wall, along with a jumbo TV screen that normally showed rugby.

My sisters had forged ahead and charmed a bunch of intimidated Norwegian fellas into giving us the end of their table, inside the only private nook the place had. I was balancing three pints of the dark stuff through the throng when I saw a face I thought I recognized. Then it was gone. I was about to remember where I'd seen it when Rosie howled from her seat like a fire alarm.

"Baby needs her medicine, granny!" she shouted. "She wants her Murphy's sometime in this century, please!"

"Yes, have pity," supplied Aoife, and bent forward, to the delight of the Norwegian boys trying to look down her plunging neckline.

I laughed and put the glasses on our table. Rosie finished hers before her sister could even take a sip. I had just sat down when I heard a voice I now knew I wasn't just pretending to recognize. It came from nowhere and from everywhere, and quickly silenced the surly drunks, the happy visitors, and the iPod-driven jukebox playing a song about the futility of love. When I located the source, I knew who it was.

Jim was already drinking in his audience like a slow pint of Guinness.

"Gentle ladies, brave gentlemen, and honored guests to this fair establishment," said the handsome fella sitting on a high chair back near the toilets. He was wearing the same leather jacket and had his hair slicked back to reveal the face I hadn't been able to forget since that same morning. "My name is Jim Quick, even though I've been called worse and sometimes better. Tonight I have been bid, in the ageless storytelling tradition of the *seanchaí*, to favor you all with a tale of love, of danger, and of sorrow."

The last we'd seen of that kind in town had been at least sixty, fat, and wore a manky old beard for a costume. The audience had consisted of two drunks. This was better.

Cheers went up from the already lubricated crowd. "Tell it, boy!" cried a trawler captain still wearing his smock. "Woo-hoo!" yelled some English girl, pulled her T-shirt up about halfway, and got a better response for it than the fisherman.

And me? I just gawked at Jim. I couldn't help it.

"We *seanchaí* are an old fraternity of tellers, but there are only a handful of us left now. So we subsist on the kindness of strangers," he continued, blinking those amber eyes at men and women alike and getting no glum stares back. Without raising his voice, he had everyone listening. "It's a long tale, and I can only offer you the first chapter tonight. I will be continuing in other towns. But if, when I'm done, you feel you warmed to what you heard, don't hesitate to see my man over there for a consideration." Jim pointed past the bar, where an Asian-looking guy with a hangman's face stood nursing a glass of soda water while covering his face ever so slightly with the collar of an upturned cowboy jacket.

"Are you all right?" asked Aoife, because my face had gone slack.

"She's fine," said Róisín, and patted my hand with too much sisterly deliberation. "She just got what she came for, I think."

I was too wrapped up in Jim to reach around and smack her one. And I wasn't alone. Bronagh the eager rookie had red spots on her cheeks.

Each time we saw her in that spanking-new Garda uniform of hers, it was hard to imagine we'd played with her since before we knew the words for "Ah, shut up, Bronagh, yer full of it." She had always policed us around the playground, so I suppose a desk at the cop shop down the street shouldn't have surprised me. She bit her fingernails as she watched Jim enjoying the spotlight. Little Mary Catherine Cremin's mother, all two hundred pounds of her, had even stopped eating chips with melted cheese on them to stare at the figure up there in the lone spotlight. The only noise was the humming from the fish tank by the door.

In whatever time I may have left, I'll always recall the hush that preceded Jim's story that night. For, in a sense, it was the last moment of peace the three of us would know.

Jim rose from his stool, took off his jacket, and stared into the smoke-filled crowd. His hands weaved back and forth like a magician's, and he leaned into the light.

"Close your eyes and imagine a family brought down by evil," he began. "A castle once stood five towers high and more, not far from this very spot where we're all joined today," Jim intoned, in a level voice reaching even the back of the room.

"Nobody knows when it was built, because when it finally tumbled, no stone remained to tell the tale. It could have loomed right on the other side of the parking lot, or across the fields to the east of here. The old ones who entrusted me with its secrets said only that for hundreds of years it had never been conquered, whether by foreign invaders or traitors inside its moss-covered granite walls. Its gate was sturdy oak, painted black as if the wall itself had a perpetually open mouth, ready to swallow wayward travelers. Whenever it opened, trumpet blasts signaled for man and beast alike to make way, and smartly. Because it meant that men of the Ua Eitirsceoil clan were about to ride past, weapons clanking against their horses' flanks."

"Did the castle have a name?" asked Bronagh, forgetting her newly poured pint entirely. Her cleft chin rested on her uniform, as if she were shy. But her eyes blazed with anything but self-doubt. He could have read the fucking phone book to her, and she would have listened.

Jim allowed Bronagh to break the spell, but only for a moment. A few of the patrons glared at her, and she covered by playing with the zipper on her jacket. Jim reached for his own beer, took a deliberately long sip, and nodded. A forelock of black hair fell across his brow. I noticed Aoife blinking in acknowledgment, getting the scent of a man who was unlike most others. Again, I felt a stab of jealousy. And the story had barely begun.

 Its name was for many years referred to by locals in hushed tones as Dún an Bhaintrigh, the Fort of the Widower. The ruler, King Stiofán, had been mourning the death of his wife, which is why the gate was as black as the shroud they buried her in when she was only nineteen, her body broken from bearing twin sons. The king still ruled the fortress, the fields, and the forests beyond, though he was nearing three score and ten years of age. But even the wolves who sometimes felt brave enough to probe the outer defenses knew to steer clear when the wizened king walked the parapets, his beard reaching nearly to the ground and a tattered shred of black cloth held before him like a relic. His howling outdid the predators of the impenetrable forest in pain and ferocity. Because it was just his wisdom that had been dulled by age. His sorrow and love had been preserved inside his heart as if left underneath everlasting snow. He had no mortal cares of his own any longer. Even his most loyal warriors grumbled that the castle might soon fall, now that there was nothing to rally behind but shadows of glory past.

His sons, Euan and Ned, eventually grew into manhood, in the nick of time to defend their home and their ailing father. For the war that had consumed the rest of Ireland now stood on the borders of Munster and, with it, West Cork.

The year was 1177, and the victorious Norman and English armies had been sweeping through much of Ulster, Leinster, and Connacht for seven years already. Leinster's king, Dermot Mac-Murrough, had lit the fuse around 1168, when he was thrown out of his castle and forced to go begging for help across the Irish Sea. The Welsh-Norman Lord Richard de Clare, the second Earl of Pembroke, whom everybody called Strongbow, was more than willing to lend a hand and helped reconquer vast parts of the lost territories.

The Norman invasion had begun.

It didn't end there, of course. Because power is as stable as a forest fire.

Local feuds soon erupted, and the newly empowered Irish warlords became a real danger to the English masters who had backed them. For the next two hundred years, battles raged, both between Irish kings and Normans and among the Irish themselves. Maps were redrawn. Allegiances shifted faster than the tide. And only the fiercest and the smartest still raised their flags around the high councils each evening after battle.

Through it all, no invading force ever penetrated the walls of Dún an Bhaintrigh.

"I want a suit of armor and a sword, Father," demanded Ned upon his seventeenth birthday, when the forces of the Norman Lord Miles de Cogan rolled across the landscape in eastern Cork, exacting tribute and brooking no opposition. Soon, they would be at the black gates, preparing to rend them asunder. De Cogan had archers from Wales and cavalry from France. His troops were well fed and armed, and his hair perfectly groomed. He had no fear whatever, except that he was too late to be granted an earldom somewhere beautiful after victory was won.

Ned, always more headstrong than his more timid brother, Euan, got his wish, mostly because his father only answered unseen ghosts rather than him. So at dawn, Ned rode out to meet the invader, all five feet six inches of him. But lest you get the wrong idea, Ned didn't burn with a desire for glory. He merely wanted to preserve the castle, and knew the forest better than the Normans, as they should soon learn. His red mane and already fearsome physique looked magnificent upon his father's black steed, and a trail of the Ua Eitirsceoil clan's best horsemen behind him made the rain-soaked earth shudder and shake as they rode into the forest.

But someone stayed behind inside the castle walls.

Twin brotherhood doesn't mean twin courage. Euan had hid inside his bedroom when the head yeoman came around calling all able-bodied men to arms. He sat there still, fists clenched, watching his brother's flag whipping in the wind, unable to move, hating his own fear more than his brother's ability to shake off similar feelings of dread. When he finally emerged on the ramparts upon the afternoon, even the washerwomen turned their backs on him when he pretended that he had slept through the call to arms. His own father, momentarily awakened from the blurry images of the past, stared at him without a word. Then he bowed his head in shame and walked past, not reacting to Euan's excuses as he tried to follow.

As evening fell, the clanging of broadswords could be heard beyond the oak trees in the far distance. Whatever Ned had found wasn't yielding.

Euan finally grabbed one of the last horses left in the pen and rode through the gates, furiously slashing at thin air with a sword at least two sizes too big for him. When his brother had trained with at least three of his father's biggest soldiers each day, Euan had preferred to spend his time putting on disguises and visiting pubs in the local towns. He'd bring his lute and strum it any time he saw a pretty dress. Townsfolk knew who he was, of course, and looked the other way, even if he hadn't bothered pretending to be something common, like a minstrel. But sometimes, girls came back down from Dún an Bhaintrigh late the next day with tales only their eyes revealed. Euan had forced them to do things they'd never find absolution for in church.

The sky had lowered itself almost to the point of touching the tree crowns, Euan felt, and blue-black clouds were sending bolts of lightning down so close to his horse's mane that he could smell the singed hairs. He whipped the scared animal on.

As Euan entered the forest, the sounds of battle changed. Screams and cries for mercy faded. A more primeval, and patient, chorus began to rise.

Now he heard what sounded like whispers and creaking noises, as if the trees themselves turned to stare at him as he followed the hoofprints, barely visible even when carrying a torch. Amber points of light floated in pairs just beyond the trees, making him dizzy. He knew the wolves in his father's parish had multiplied since the wars, now that all swords were pointed at

Norman throats, not theirs. Sometimes it felt to Euan as if the beasts knew the humans had left them alone and therefore had less fear of their weapons. A low steady growl followed him all the way to a clearing he knew by heart; he and his brother had often played there, dueling with wooden swords until one cried out in pain—usually Euan himself.

It was there that Euan now saw a sight that made his previous anger pale in comparison to what he felt clawing at his smooth throat.

Ned had lured the enemy cavalry into a trap.

He had sent out a small probe of horsemen, hoping to draw the largest part of the invader's force into a place from which they could not escape. Unaware of the land's many dark places, the Normans had taken the bait and soon found their horses surrounded on all sides by trees and stuck to their bellies in fresh Irish mud. Welsh archers, disoriented underneath the low black canopy, began firing at their own officers by mistake. Ned's foot soldiers made short work of them all, sticking the horses in the belly where they stood and leaving no quarter for their riders as soon as their handmade Parisian cuirasses hit the ground. The forest groaned louder now, and blood was sucked into the bog faster than rainwater.

Euan waited. If he showed himself now, his earlier hesitation would mark him forever as a coward. He dismounted, crept low to the grass, and watched his brother swivel around on his father's great horse, taking down a lanky Welsh colonel of infantry before he had a chance to draw his weapon. The man shielded his pale gray eyes even as Ned gored him. Ned wiped his blade, wheeled around, and looked for more prey.

Then, God smiled on cowardice.

"Prince Ned!" A cry went up from an Irish vassal. "They're trying to flank us!"

A small group of Welsh archers had broken through the forest on the far left side, their tunics ripped to ribbons by the thorns but their voices undaunted. They screamed like banshees as they cut a bloody swath through the victorious Irish horsemen.

And exactly then is when Euan rose and seized his one and only chance.

Because with their backs turned, nobody was watching his corner of the battlefield. Besides, most of the torches were flickering
and dying faster than the soldiers. Euan snuck up on his brother's
horse and hacked at its hind legs. In the chaos and tumult, nobody
heard the keening when the animal fell, crushing the rider underneath.

Ned lay with both legs and most of his body trapped. His eyes
rolled around in his head as he tried to comprehend what had
happened. Euan approached cautiously, scanning the battlefield.
Ned's men were massing for a counterattack, torches illuminating them like hundreds of giants against the leaves, but they were
still disoriented by the ferocity of the Welsh surprise.

"Br-brother?" Ned mumbled, gasping for air, recognizing the
figure bent over him.

"Yes," said Euan, and mounted his own horse. He tightened
the straps on his armor and put his good kidskin gloves back on.
Then he reached down and took his brother's shield. A painted
ship with three furled sails shone on its steel.

"You will be damned for all time," Ned said, his eyes burning
gold in the light.

"Only God and fortune know," answered Euan, and rode his
horse over his one and only twin brother until its hooves had
stopped Ned's breathing. Then he turned his attention to the Ua
Eitirsceoil cavalry and galloped, full-bore, out into their van-
guard. The sight of his red hair whipping around, and of his
brother's shield held aloft, roused the troops, and they quickly
surged to fill the gap the Welsh had opened. The Irish yeomanry
used their short swords to check the enemy advance, showing
even less mercy than before. It was over in minutes.

Moments later, even the trees were quiet.

The Irish celebrated their victory, most praising Prince Euan's
timely arrival, now that their beloved leader had suffered such a
dishonorable death, probably brought about by a callow Frenchman. The enemy retreated and sought other lands to conquer.
Dún an Bhaintrigh still stood against any foe.

Now began Euan's reign.

He made sure, upon his triumphant return, to have his father
bestow upon Ned a hero's funeral. Euan even delivered a fitting

eulogy that touched upon "the warrior spirit that cost Ned his life." When his father, racked with yet another loved one to mourn, followed Ned to the grave less than a month later, the eulogy was markedly shorter and less heartfelt. Euan had turned his father's quarters into a bordello within a day, making his soldiers round up a sampling of young women from the surrounding countryside to celebrate his victory and rapid ascendancy to the throne. Servants looked the other way. And the stories of his peculiar tastes spread even wider each time a young woman came walking back down the hill with her eyes cast down.

Sometimes, it was whispered, they never came home at all.

More than anything, though, King Euan soon found a passion far greater than preying on women.

He had begun to venture ever deeper into the forest in search of wolves.

Within a year, he had more than a hundred grayback heads on pikes in the Great Hall where his father had once overseen the annual flower festival. Now, hunters his family would never have deigned to look at in public drank the castle's mead barrels dry. Clad in black leather skins, they bragged about the day's hunt and compared kills. In thanks, one of them even fashioned a hollowed-out wolf's head for Euan as a present. He accepted it with genuine tears in his eyes and pulled it down over his head. It fit almost too well, making the twin sets of eyes reflect the low candlelight. He wore it all night, even to bed with three girls barely old enough to know why they had been brought to his chambers. And in the morning, he baptized his family's home to fit his newest passion.

Dún an Bhaintrigh was no longer a fitting name, he decided, now that the widower had died. Henceforth, the castle with the black gate would forever come to be known as Dún an Fhaoil. For what had a better ring to it than Fort of the Wolf? He struck his family's age-old nautical crest from the castle's banners and shields and replaced it with a fearsome wolf leaping through a forest clearing, a sign of his own good fortune and ferocious human appetites.

King Euan lived almost three more years this way.

Until God finally decided to frown on cowardice and treachery.

Euan was riding on the outskirts of his land with just a small escort. He felt glorious. His servants, trailing a mile or two behind him because they picked up his kills, already had three magnificent graybacks and two of their young in leather nets. He spurred his horse on, picking a trail leading into a part of the forest he didn't recognize. Fear welled up in him for the first time in years, but he fought to quell it. It was only three upon the afternoon, but the shade beneath the trees seemed to have solid form. The groaning, twisting sound he had heard years earlier, right before he found his brother's war party, now writhed out of every branch.

"Superstition," he cried aloud to the trees, which didn't answer. "Old fairy tales!" His guard shouted his name far behind. And he held his tongue. If he couldn't conquer this childish fear of the dark, how could he hope to rule all of Cork? Or, perhaps, to retake all of Munster one day and drive the Normans back into the waves? He rode on alone, and the nervous voices behind him were soon swallowed up by the leaves. He turned around a bend and saw he wasn't alone.

A wolf sat on the path before him.

It seemed to wait patiently, as a human might have. Euan's horse became spooked, and threw him to the ground before it whinnied and galloped off in a panic. Euan quickly drew his sword and scrambled to his feet. His wolf helmet had fallen off his head and tumbled limply toward its living namesake, still sitting perfectly immobile, as if waiting for a sign.

"Are you real?" Euan finally dared to ask, panting for breath.

The wolf blinked slowly, then began to walk toward him. Euan slashed before him with the blade, warding off the vision. But without making a sound upon the autumn leaves, the creature continued until it stood so near him he could see the black splinters in its honey-colored irises.

"As real as you," it said, without moving its mouth. The voice ricocheted only inside Euan's own head. "Answer me this: Did the life you stole make you happy?"

"Get *back*!" Euan screamed, and hacked at the wolf, who sidestepped his amateur thrusts with ease before returning like a lost dog.

"Do the murders of young women and of all my fellow creatures make you feel less afraid?" Its head was lowered now, and the bristles stood out from its body as if it had been struck by lighting. Fangs the size of human fingers appeared as it curled its lips.

"I beg forgiveness," said Euan, though he didn't mean it in his heart, "for all my sins."

"You will pay for every life you took," said the wolf, as it charged Euan and pushed him onto his back. The second before he felt its teeth closing around his throat, Euan heard the voice inside his head saying, "I promise you that you will know fear. You will learn what it is like to roam the countryside and be despised, hunted, and murdered for sport. But just remember this: The only way to get your old life back is to make someone love you despite their hatred of you, and sacrifice yourself for them. But also consider this: What if you no longer remember what it was like before?" It glared right through Euan's outer defenses and glanced straight into his darkest desires. "You may see me again," said the wolf. "You may not. It is up to you."

"What does that mean?"

If wolves have the capacity to smile, this one nearly did. It turned its head coyly. "You'll see. In time."

"How long . . . will that take?" gasped Euan, unable to breathe.

The animal's eyes bored through him like the torch he'd carried the night he murdered his brother.

"Only God and fortune know," it said, and bit harder.

Euan passed out as the pain in his throat overwhelmed him.

When he woke up, he thought he was in heaven.

Skylarks twittered, and the sun made his face burn hot. A terrible dream still lingered in his head, in which a wolf had ripped out his throat, but it quickly faded. Very carefully, he opened his eyes and saw that he was still in the forest, where night had turned to day. Leaves rustled somehow louder in the breeze. The smell of freshly harvested grain burned in his nostrils more than it had before, and before he could reflect on why, another scent almost made him faint. It was the smell of a freshly killed deer somewhere nearby, its salty juices both sweet and pungent in the gathering heat. He felt that peculiar blood song in his ears that he'd only experienced once before, when stomping his brother, that sweet quickening just before the kill.

"There he is!" someone shouted nearby. "Over here!"

"Thank God," Euan said, because he recognized his most merciless hunter by the sound of his voice. "I've prayed that—"

He stopped, because his own mouth didn't make the sounds it should have. All he heard was a nonsensical kind of gargling. Then he remembered the bite on his neck; knew his vocal cords were probably damaged. He rose. Before he could wave to his own hunting party, an arrow spiked the tree right next to him, and he flinched.

"Padraic, it's me, don't!" he tried to shout in anger, but he couldn't get the words out as a rider in black leather skins charged straight at him, brandishing a mallet. Euan ran as he'd never run in his short life. God, his heart beat in his chest as if it had grown to three times its regular size. He sprinted past crags of rock and over hedges with an ease he could only have dreamed of as a boy, feeling his muscles quiver with a spasm that sent him nearly flying. And when he finally allowed himself to rest, he discovered that he'd come to a brook where not a breath of wind stirred. Euan bent down to get a drink of water.

And he heard his own broken throat growling in horror at the sight.

A wolf stared back at him from the still surface.

He looked down at himself and saw thick fur and paws where his hands should have been. Euan closed his eyes and shook his head. He had to still be dreaming. He opened his eyes again, leaned all the way down to the water this time, and felt his black snout touch the cold stream. He could smell the salmon and frogs that had died in it, and instantly sensed that it was fresher just a few feet upstream. There was dead Welsh blood in it, too, its stink blending with rotting branches. He withdrew his whiskered face and sat there, panting, looking at his skin, which had become gray fur. His body was large and muscular now, and only a little of his own wound had encrusted itself where the wolf from the forest had bit him earlier. Against his own better judgment, he had to admire himself. No longer was he the scrawny twin people laughed at behind his back, despite his father's crown. What power! Such strength! He could only have dreamed—

"This way!" cheered another of his most ardent wolf killers a few hedgerows behind him, and he heard the horses' hooves like an explosion.

Euan ran again and didn't stop until the heavens had grown black and its diamond carpet had been unfurled, blinding him with its brilliance. Was that Ursa Minor up there? What was the beaded string of twinkly lights next to it? He wondered if his brother was looking down on him from the stars or if he could even recognize him now. But the images in his mind of Ned teaching him long ago about "God's shiny eyes" were wiped clean by his hungry new blood. It didn't matter to a wolf what the constellations signified; the absence of a moon now only meant the hunters wouldn't find him so easily. He turned his head and listened. Something moving in the grass. Easy prey.

That same night, he feasted on a rabbit he'd caught, eating it in three bites while it still squirmed in his grip. As the flesh went down, he felt a new, hungry rhythm briefly silencing all other sounds around him. He finally curled up underneath a tree, wet and tired of running. Euan's paws were swollen and hurt. His last memories of a life in silks, between women's legs, and in the Great Hall, where hundreds of stuffed wolf heads stared balefully down at him drifted slowly away and were replaced by a desire to survive, no matter how.

The wolf in him rejoiced at having been turned into this exquisite predator.

Whatever remained in him that was still human felt nothing but childish fear.

He lay for a while by the brook, listening to the trees' creaking voices and sensing the heartbeat of every doe, rat, and owl as far into the woods as his new eyes could see. The transformation was complete. The wolf's curse hung all about him, like incense, its warning still echoing inside his head. He felt the pressure building between his ears and opened his jaws.

Without having to think about it, he threw back his head and howled.

I can still see Jim sitting there on his stool, lapping up the applause, the bastard.

"So endeth the first part of my tale," he said, like a practiced *seanchaí,* calmly as you please, while everyone from hard-bitten trawlermen and Paris Hilton–wannabe girlies still in their training bras put their hands together for him. He nodded and was about to walk down into the crowd when a voice piped up.

"So what happens to Euan? Will he be a wolf forever?"

I turned and looked. It wasn't hard to locate the source of that flirty little query. Sarah McDonnell had walked right up to him, wearing her best come-hither outfit, the one where being able to see the color of one's knickers is practically standard when picking out a pair of low-slung jeans and a black shirt that ends just at the lowest edge of your tits. She wore shoes with fake diamond sparkles on them. She looked out from under her blue-tinted eyelids and smiled at him. I'd seen her practicing that look in front of a pocket mirror down at the bank, when she thought no customers noticed. She was no more than twenty then, pretty as a spring morning and dumb as a bag of hair. Her earrings looked like she'd stolen them from the wall decoration in an Indian restaurant.

All right, perhaps she wasn't that bad, and it's petty of me to speak ill of the dead. Our Lady, forgive me. But if a girl can't be allowed to feel a pinch of jealousy, even as she's rushing to tell you this while probably not long for this world herself, then when, I ask you?

Anyway, Jim didn't care for her pushiness and answered both her and the rest of the crowd at once. He turned the charm down like a dimmer switch on a lamp and left Sarah in the dark while illuminating the rest of us. "All true and honest tales have a beginning, a middle, and an end, so have patience," he said, which made the girlie in the acid-washed jeans wrinkle her brow. It had been a simple enough question. She'd probably never had a man tell her no, either, especially not when flashing her skin at him dressed up like an eejit.

"You may find me in one of the towns nearby over the next few days," he continued, motioning his hand in the direction of the Asian gentleman by the bar. "Tomo over there is my . . . I suppose you might call him a road manager, isn't that right? The trusty compass needle around which my humble life revolves, eh, Tomo?"

Tomo half turned and smiled without much conviction. What I thought was a denim jacket earlier was now clearly an oilskin coat, the kind with millions of pockets for fishing tackle and such. All the pockets were weighted down with something. The garment was the color of a winter bog. His eyes were telling Jim to put a sock in it and get the hell out, for whatever reason. I remember noticing him glaring at me, too. But I didn't think about it then. When he realized how many local eyes were on his fourth-world-looking face, he performed an exaggerated bow and threw out his arm like a drunken ballet dancer.

"True enough, ladies, gentlemen, and any boy or girl brave enough to hear the next part of the tale," Tomo said, in a voice so nearly child-like in its softness that it startled me. There wasn't any no-tickee-no-shirtee Chinaman humbug with this fella. He could have come from slap bang in the middle of Castletownbere by the sound of him, even if his showman delivery was a discount version of Jim's. Tomo was probably no more than twenty-five, but he looked ancient, as if strong drink and cigarettes had pulled fluid from his sallow cheeks since he was ten. "There is no telling exactly where we shall be, but rumor has it that the good town of Adrigole might repay a visit two nights from today. At the Auld Swords Inn. So come one, come all. And tell a friend who likes a good scare."

Tomo put his hand over an old gray felt hat and scooped it onto his head. I could hear change hitting his head inside. Children laughed. Then he sent Jim another penetrating look and bowed.

"Well said, old friend Tomo," crowed Jim, downing his lukewarm pint. "Thank you. And with that ringing endorsement, fair ladies and honest gentlemen, we bid you adieu."

I felt myself rising from my chair before I quite knew what I had done.

Jim had been following his manager out the door when he turned and looked at me. You could have burnt your fingers on Sarah McDonnell's head just then, she was so hopping mad. Jim whispered something into Tomo's ear, and the Japanese Irishman looked like he'd just been slapped across the mouth. He hissed something back at Jim, who stopped him with just one hand gesture. Moments later, as Jim came strolling over to me, Tomo walked slowly out the door with a face like a trout someone pulled ashore and left to rot.

"Are there two of you, or are you just everywhere in town?" he asked me, sitting down right next to us without being asked. Róisín rolled her eyes before I could kick her leg, but Aoife carelessly drank in whatever sex-and-leather combination his face radiated out into the room so thickly even dogs outside stirred. She started fussing with her nails, which I'd never seen her do that obviously before, with a man present.

"Could be more of me waiting outside, you just never can tell," I shot back, right proud of myself. "Are you here for the guzzle, like, or is your day job still to deport Swedes?"

He just grinned.

Róisín said, "The hell you talking about, anyway?"

"A private joke, miss," said Jim, not looking at anyone but me in that way he'd done earlier. Before I had even touched his hand, I knew I'd be cheating on Finbar more than once that same night and felt nearly awful. My sisters started to get up and grab their bags, as if I'd sent them a get-lost telegram. Aoife winked. Rosie drank both our pints in two shotgun swallows and tousled my hair before leaving.

Those syrup-colored eyes now rested only on me.

"So, how Quick are ya?" I asked, but that was just to watch his pupils move. I knew well enough.

And come the morning bell, the sphinx would have to handle my little sixth-class monsters all by himself.

NEED I TELL you more about that night?

Well, I suppose I do, if you can't guess for yer own self. So let's get it out of the way. But if you imagine that he had me arse over teacups and begging for it before I'd even got my knickers off, you're wrong, and get yer mind out of the gutter, besides. Because this was different: What Jim did better than anybody was listen to what you needed and then hold out until finally giving it seemed almost predestined.

We were in my kitchen, and I was making two strong mugs of Bewley's with milk before I even asked him if he wanted tea. And while I prattled on about Rosie's radio obsession, and how Aoife probably thought she was Robert fucking De Niro himself in *Taxi Driver*, he didn't say much at first. He looked around for something, like he was expecting company. So as I stole glances at myself in the windowpane's reflection to check my hair, I told him about our Aunt Moira, and her newfound love for early Catholic home decoration. I may even have made a joke about it, I don't remember.

What I do recall is that he first touched me on the neck.

It was a light brush, nothing more, before he moved past me to get comfortable in my place. Had it happened now, I would probably recognize the signs of someone marking his territory before pouncing. Back then, I just thought he was cool for not immediately throwing me up against a wall and fumbling with his zipper, like Finbar had done the first time we'd gone out to dinner together. Jim stopped by my figurines and smiled. I blushed. There were a lot of them, you see. Totems of places I wanted to visit some day when I got the hell out of town, but knew I never would.

The Statue of Liberty with fake green patina, the Colosseum, and even the shagging Eiffel Tower stood on the windowsill next to a brass hurling trophy my father had won as a boy. It featured him wielding a hurley above his head, like an old Celtic warrior might have. At least, that's what he had always said. Nearby, postcards of Mallorca hung on my fridge, and photo snaps of me and my sisters wearing lobsterlike first-degree burns, with dodgy cocktails and cigarettes somewhere in the vicinity. I'm afraid to admit there were pictures of old Tutankhamun about as well, just for good measure. When Jim smiled, I noticed how white his teeth were. He still hadn't kissed me, and I was beginning to get second thoughts. Finbar had already texted me three times without getting an answer.

"So where are the Hanging Gardens of Babylon?" Jim wanted to know. "You're missing those."

I snapped my fingers. "Ah, I forgot. Think they don't water them anymore, besides."

He sat back down next to me at the kitchen table. He smelled like motor oil and the stout still on his breath. "What's your name?"

I heard myself saying "Fiona" right before he kissed me.

I've told you before how I felt both naked and safe when he really looked at me in the street earlier that day. Multiply that by infinity. He took his time getting my clothes off and wouldn't let me do it myself. His teeth grinned above and next to me as he unzipped my skirt, removed my blouse and T-shirt, and unlaced each of my admittedly very unsexy shoes, while gently slapping my hands away when I tried to help. Through it all, I just lay there and wondered how many times he'd done that, because there was a practiced fluidity to his movements, a ritual, almost. I wouldn't have minded even if I knew the answer, and that's the truth.

Because he shagged me good and proper and in every possible corner of my tiny flat. What surprised me is that he let me lead him, rather than acting like the hard-core sex desperado I had imagined him to be. And where Finbar had needed a map to get anywhere near my most tender places without losing his way, Jim could read my desires with his eyes closed, tracing my breathing and the way I'd flinch when he touched me inside, and didn't stop even when he knew he had reached a way station we both liked. It felt like I danced some furious Cuban number with him, standing, sitting, and lying down, while I ventured into new areas he knew intimately but wanted me to discover without being led by the nose.

Even as I was being shagged out of all proportion, this wasn't just physical; I knew that much.

He was seducing every bit of me I could name, and then some. And I gave up all of it willingly. Of course I'd had boyfriends before Finbar. And naturally some of them had been sweet and kind, or even experienced enough with their hands and tongues to make me blush. But Jim wasn't just interested in proving his manhood and coming in record time, and in the loudest way possible, the way most every man I'd ever known had been. He was unpredictable, which both irritated me and turned me on. This one's passion lay deeper, buried underneath all that skill and refinement, just barely out of reach. It was that elusiveness, I think, that had me aching for it again each time we'd finished. He had all of me, and I still only tasted a smidgen of what he kept inside. Now that I think about it, it was probably just as well, since that sliver made me higher than a kite. The full dose might have killed me.

It must have been five hours later or so that I could even think straight again.

I was lying on the floor with my cheek resting on Jim's perfectly smooth, hairless chest and dreaming of a cigarette I didn't have. He read my mind again and reached over to his jacket, digging around for two ciggies. We didn't move for a while, but watched the smoke rings disintegrate as the seagulls' cawing outside informed us it would be dawn soon.

"What's his name?" asked Jim, curling the other arm around me again.

"Who d'you mean?" I said, knowing exactly who he meant. Because my mobile phone had been buzzing louder and more often than Courtney Love's vibrator. There'd be hell to pay this time. And no amount of careful lying would get me out of it.

"You don't have to tell him about this." A half smile to make it all better.

"Everyone from here to Bantry already knows. People saw us leave together. Are you joking or wha'?"

He grinned and touched the inside of my thigh. "Then don't tell him everything."

"I never do," I said, not stopping his hand as it continued higher.

HE WAS PUTTING his jeans on when the sun told me I was already late for class.

I sat on a kitchen chair, pretending to leaf through assignments. But I was thinking of the fairy tale Jim hadn't finished yet. "So what happens to the werewolf?" I asked, just noticing his tattoo before the T-shirt covered up the inside of his left arm. It had looked like a symbol, with lettering underneath. I had been too busy admiring other parts of him to pay attention to it before. Something told me it wasn't just MOM FOREVER in his case.

"Euan is not a werewolf," Jim said, suddenly serious. "He doesn't change back to human every time the full moon vanishes. That's comic books you're talking about. Silver bullets and the bullshit mythology. No, this one's a wolf like all the other animals. Roaming the earth as fugitive prey and predator at the same time. For as long as it takes for him to find someone to love."

"Will he do that ever?" I wanted desperately for the wolf to be changed back, I can't tell you why. Perhaps because of the loneliness of the forest, the way Jim had described it.

"How should I know?"

I felt a twinge of disappointment. He had acted last night as if the whole story was planned out, like a saga or something. I found his ciggie pack, which was empty. "So you just make it up as you go, like?"

He smiled in a way I couldn't interpret. "The other way around, love," he said. "The story's in charge, not me. I just say the words as they happen in my head. And like my trusty old Tomo said, when we get to Adrigole tomorrow night, we'll all know a little bit more. Until then, even I couldn't tell ya." He was lacing his boots, which looked like he had walked in them to the ends of the world and beyond. They had steel-toed caps.

"Where'd you find the Chinaman, anyway? Yer man looked unimpressed with you last night."

"He's Japanese, actually, not that he cares. He managed a rock band I was in years ago. The rest of the lads got a fat record contract and threw the two of us out first. Been together like peaches and cream ever since. His name means *companion* in his language, I think."

"So if you're the sheriff and he's yer trusty Injun friend, where's *his* iron horse?"

"He gets seasick on motorcycles. Never could figure it. He drives a van with mikes and such."

"He was pissed off at you, but?"

He looked at me without trying to flirt. "No, just jealous when he saw me with you."

I twirled the buttons on my sleeve without looking at him. "That happens a lot, I imagine." I hadn't phrased it like a question, because I knew I wouldn't care for the answer.

"Less than you think."

I looked out the window and saw the sun-drenched red bike in all its glory. Jim's Vincent Comet had traffic slowing down to gawk just as it had yesterday. He got up, put on his leather jacket, and opened his arms to hug me. I moved toward him, angry that I didn't have the guts to ask him if we'd see each other again.

"Don't be breaking yer neck on that thing, now," I said, trying for brave.

"Never have," he answered, touching the small of my back just once below the panty elastic, the fucker. "Take care until we meet again."

And with that he was out the door, giving me a two-finger wave that I wanted to hate but couldn't. I closed the door instead of lingering like the lovelorn girlfriend. Moments later, my windows rattled as he gunned the chromed animal and started up the street. I stood by the door, listening for the sound until it was gone.

Then I heard my mobile buzzing again.

Finbar, I thought, dreading that conversation. I already had a wobbly excuse on deck when I saw it was my demon sister calling.

"Will you ever kick yer poet out of bed and answer the shagging phone?" she bellowed, when I picked it up. "Have you heard what happened to Sarah McDonnell?"

"What, did she finally bribe one of yer Norwegians to bone her?"

Róisín sighed at my ignorance. "She's dead as Aunt Moira's saints. Heard it on the radio. Bronagh is already up by the Glebe Graveyard with all the other mice in blue."

BRONAGH'S FACE WAS beet red as she draped Garda tape around a small mess of trees inside the low stone wall, which was invisible from the main road. She'd been crying and was clearly sick of answering questions, even if nobody had begun asking them yet.

"Can't talk about it," she said flatly, when she saw me puffing up the hill on my bike. "Shagging press is already on its way, from as far away as Cork."

"Sure, Bronagh," I said, patting her shoulder.

Her face cracked, and she clenched her teeth to make it stop. A senior garda who was pushing two photographers away sent her a stare that said, Keep it together or leave. "Never seen anything like it, you know?" she said, in a hushed whisper.

Sarah hadn't been covered completely by the temporary plastic cloth. She lay halfway down the twisty path where the cemetery is too overgrown for new customers. The wind took hold of a corner and exposed her legs. One of her shoes was missing, but the remaining one twinkled gold as the sun hit it. Another rattle of the cheap shroud and Bronagh ran to refasten it as best she could.

But not before I saw that one of Sarah's earrings was missing.

Her face? I can't talk about that. Any description I could give you would be a cliché. But use your imagination and try to picture a face that's no longer there.

I pulled Bronagh aside as two new patrol cars arrived in the dirt road, distracting her superior. "What happened?"

"Sergeant Murphy says a drug crazy did it, because her face is so done in." She chewed a nail and stole another glance at Castletownbere's former reigning sex queen.

"But you don't think so?" I asked.

"Garda, a moment?" Another stern look from Bronagh's top cop from Main Street, and she turned on her spit-shined boots and ran over to him without another word. As she bowed her head to receive what I'm guessing was a dressing-down, I had my answer.

And for the life of me, I couldn't help thinking of that lone widow over in Drimoleague, who they said died from no foul play at all.

RÓISÍN'S FARAWAY VOICES were already whispering about all kinds of colorful death long before me and Aoife came by for dinner.

She sat hunched over her blinking contraption and didn't even hear us coming through the front door. It had always been like that. Only tonight, Rosie's facial expression had taken on more color than usual, enough to bore right through that powdery punk makeup.

". . . a rumor that *another* girl was found as far over as Kenmare five days ago," said an excited female voice on the massive loudspeakers Rosie had hung from hooks in the black ceiling. "Cops aren't talking, of course. Because that one had the same things done to her, and you know what I'm talking about, Nightwing; over."

Nightwing. That would be my darling sister's shortwave handle. Not a stretch, exactly.

"Tell me anyway, Master Blaster, come on back; over," said Róisín, finally noticing and waving us inside with a smile.

"Panties down to her ankles, same as with Sarah," continued the voice. "And her head beat in like a lorry hit her. Trophies were taken. My source says she had at least four earrings, including one from her fiancé. They're gone. Over."

"Same as with Mrs. Holland, over," repeated Róisín, making furious scribbles on her notepad, which she always kept handy, as if issues of world importance were about to break any moment. But that last comment made me stop and listen hard. Because Master Blaster was talking about someone who had suffered exactly like the dead woman from Drimoleague.

"Arh, give it a rest, will ya," said Aoife, and put down the shopping bags on the kitchen table. She always got cranky if she didn't eat, and had most of the uncooked food on the counter before I shushed her. I can't explain, even today, what made me feel adamant that what was happening around our area wasn't accidental. You see, this wasn't anything like the previous year, when a Romanian gang had been knocking over banks and killing the tellers for good measure. This was closer to home. There was a demonstrative rattling of pots and pans as Rosie and I leaned over the shortwave.

"That's affirmative, Nightwing, only *her* face was intact. Otherwise, same idea, right down to the missing earrings. No fingerprints, says my Garda spy; over."

There was a wash of static, and Master Blaster was drowned out by a laconic male voice that sounded like its owner was still in elementary school.

"I'm hearing the woman over in Drimoleague wasn't alone that night; over," he said, satisfied at having trumped the scandal-seeking adults listening in on the airwaves.

"Medium or well done, my media darlings?" yelled Aoife, as the smell of steaks filled the tiny apartment, where filled ashtrays competed for space with Róisín's bad paintings of Oscar Wilde wearing nothing but leather pants in postures not sanctioned by the Kerry Archdiocese. We both waved her off, and she shook her head.

"Who was she with then, young man; over?" asked a very terse Master Blaster.

"That's Overlord, to you, madam, and I have it on good authority that Mrs. Holland was seen wi—"

Zzzzt!

A spike of electricity buzzed out the rest of the message. Rosie turned the knobs on her machine this way and that, but the kid never came back.

"I'll take that to mean just a bit pink in the center, then," called Aoife, setting the table and fixing us with a determined look only our sainted mother could have replicated.

"Until next time, Master Blaster, Nightwing out," Rosie said with resignation, and keyed her hand mike twice.

"Same to you, watch yer back, girlie, and out," wished the voice, and there was another double click. Then the band went dead.

"Madame and madame are served," intoned Aoife. "And I won't hear another word about that shagging murder until *after* we eat." That was fine with me. I hadn't much of a mind to talk about it at all.

We hadn't even taken the first bite when Rosie looked me up and down and grinned. "You have the glow of the recently shagged all over ya. Do tell."

"Not a word," I answered, unable to be really mad at her.

"On a scale from one to ten?" said Aoife, piling on as only the twins could.

Rosie wrinkled her nose. "Wait, that all depends. Do you mean the hot-guy scale or the Finbar scale?"

"Get out with that," I said, sawing a piece of meat off with what was supposed to be anger. Truth is, I was flattered. Finbar had never given me such good press in my own family. "All right, he was all that, okay?"

"How many times?" Róisín wanted to know.

"Only God and fortune know," I said, in a fake-serious voice, twirling my plate.

"Leave Him out of it," said Aoife.

I put down my knife and fork and looked out the window. It was still light enough to see the trees against the sky. I wondered who Jim was serenading tonight.

"I need your Mercer tomorrow night, will that be all right?" I asked, smiling at Aoife. "It's Sunday, besides. I'll pay you the two lousy fares you would have got."

"No worries," said Aoife, running her green-lacquered nails through her commando hair.

"*That* good?" asked Rosie, and tried to catch my eye.

"You don't know the half of it," I said, trying to get the sudden vision of Sarah McDonnell's missing face out of my mind and prevent the steak from coming back up all by itself.

THERE WAS ALREADY a queue outside the Auld Swords in Adrigole when I pulled up in my sister's battered Idi Amin staff car.

Word had clearly spread from two nights before, because I saw more makeup than stubble on the eager faces sorting through their change. Bronagh was there, too, in civvies and trying not to be noticed, and I recognized at least three others from home. The muttering ahead of me as I stood in the back and waited for my turn became clearer by the minute and rose in excitement as it got closer to the appointed hour, despite an Old Testament downpour. I heard snippets of "sexy" and "just deadly," and knew they weren't whispering about the barmaids inside.

All heads turned as a throaty growl rose up the street.

Jim was even Quicker than Friday night. He zoomed right up to the line, winked at nobody and everybody at the same time, and parked that glorious machine as women who had to have been grandmothers several times over just stood there and swooned.

"How are you going, ladies?"

"Come for that second chapter, sonny," said a red-cheeked stocky mother of two, whose barely teenage daughters fixed the *seanchaí* with a glare that was more adult than the cheap blue glitter on their eyelids.

"We'll be taking care of that in a moment now," he said, ducking inside to set up. He'd picked a new T-shirt for the occasion, which fit even tighter around his waist than the black one I'd already got used to touching.

I hid behind the shoulder of a tall woman in a rain slicker as I saw Tomo follow him through the doorway. The truculent assistant did his best to charm the ladies, but none of the main event's appeal rubbed off on his surly face, and the halfhearted smile soon became a scowl as they both vanished from sight. When they let in the guests a few minutes later, there was a sound like someone uncorking a bottle filled with shaken-up soda.

I can't tell you exactly why, but I had picked a spot far in the back of the room, next to a busted cigarette machine and three girlies with eyes wider than if they'd ingested uncut cocaine. The low tin ceiling did nothing to dampen anyone's spirits as I heard Tomo doing a microphone check that made the sound system whine and squeal. I could only see women's shoulders and necks and done-up hair from my bar stool, and I couldn't understand why I didn't just get up, elbow my way past all the others, and let Jim see me. It was silly, of course, so I finally stood and made my way forward.

Which is when I saw my Aunt Moira.

She sat at a table quite near the stage, wearing the teardrop-shaped earrings she had inherited from Mother, and she clearly still remembered how to apply lipstick, for she looked like a horny Madame Butterfly in her short-hemmed summer dress and heels. I retreated to the back wall and ducked my head. There was something about her pose that had me frightened. I just wanted to see Jim, without dragging my family into it. I'd seen her dolled up before, when she was trying to impress Harold, but tonight there was something rigid about her face that went beyond determination.

Right before Jim tapped on the mike as a way of confirming his ritual power over the room, Aunt Moira half rose and turned her head. I hadn't been fast enough. Those eyes that sometimes still reminded me of Mother's trained themselves on mine. She didn't smile, but assessed me like a prizefighter might do before the big bout. You or me? No quarter asked, and none given.

I swear to Christ but the woman stared like she wanted me dead and buried.

"How is everybody doing tonight?" crooned a voice I knew well enough to make my stomach do jumps I still didn't understand.

"Grand!" a chorus yelled back.

I couldn't see Jim, but it didn't matter. Aunt Moira broke the stare and returned her attention to the figure onstage, who was probably sending the ladies all the way over by the door his most winning smile. I heard the sound of a bar stool scraping the stage. Jim coughed once, and the silence that ensued was both instant and deafening.

"Did you ever wonder why you can never trust a wolf?" he asked.

 The animal who was once Prince Euan had just tasted human blood for the first time.

He hadn't meant to, because the last two winter equinoxes had told him how quickly the creatures that walked on two legs could defend themselves. Just one new moon ago, as the wolf was tearing asunder its kill of a small deer, that throat sound the humans made startled him. He had turned and seen three figures wearing leather jerkins and carrying sharp steel in their hands. There was a crunching of feet on the dry autumn leaves. He could hear the beating of each man's heart and considered, for a moment, to charge them, but saw the net that a fourth man, just ahead of him, was holding. The largest human made a louder throat noise, and Euan the wolf feinted left, then right, before fleeing right between his legs.

As he fled past a small coastal village in the middle of nowhere that the human in him would have called Allihies if he still remembered having ever walked upright, he had seen more evidence of what the humans could do. Men in black leather skins had assembled in front of a gibbet by the side of a road. The landscape was so desolate near the edge of the cliffs that only yellow moss grew on giant rocks poking through the earth's surface like giants' thumbs. Each hunter had with him a still-writhing gray wolf in each hand, and they took their time hanging them from their hind legs and slowly beating them to death. Euan's fellow creatures had cried like the cat he had killed himself for sport the other day. No. Worse. They had shrieked like human babies.

He had stayed hidden, unable to stand the sound but with no place to run.

And he felt an even deeper sense of terror than the old wolf from the forest had promised.

He stayed low to the rocks and hid behind the sparse tufts of grass as the men mounted their horses and rode back up into the pass from whence they'd come. Anger stung in his eyes, and his legs shook, the closer he dared to creep. Finally, he stood quite near the hanging wolves, whose maws were open wide, their lives dripping out of them. The sharp-edged faces were swollen and the eyes he knew had to be there were hidden behind black welts. He took one last look and ran so fast his heart drowned out the thoughts of revenge in his head.

The human blood called to him just a few days later, and by accident.

It had been midday when a doe stepped into the forest clearing near the old castle with the black gate. Euan didn't know why, but it always made him even more afraid to come near its towers even as they'd begun to crumble. There were fewer riders now than before, but they all had nets. Still, he was drawn to the crisp trumpet sounds inside, and even to the strange moans that could sometimes be heard from the small windows near the base of the west wall. Something about these particular throat sounds filled him with a feeling very close to pleasure, if he could still recall what that meant. In brief flashes that would stab his brain like a dagger, he saw pictures of naked women underneath him, before the visions were gone forever, like storm clouds.

That's why, when he heard a softer throat noise nearby as he chased the doe into the woods, he dared draw closer.

He forgot all about the doe.

His autumn-colored eyes could hardly believe what they saw.

A man was rolling on the ground, trying to unfasten his metal breastplate, like a turtle in heat. Next to him was a woman, giggling, always a little too quick, herself taking off her dress as he stumbled after. Finally, after much good-natured slapping and grinning, they both grew quiet and Euan could see two human skins, rubbing against each other's hairiest parts, getting cut from the brambles but caring not at all. The woman's eyes were as blue as the cornflowers near the brook where he had once seen soldiers' bodies come to rest, like logs at low tide.

He circled them now, his heart a thunderbolt, a raging sea. Their bodies called to him in a familiar way that was even stronger than what he had felt when taking down a stag ten times his size last snowfall. The woman was kissing the man's stomach, which was smooth and pale, and neither heard a twig snap as Euan chose the highest angle of attack, while waiting for his breath to match the rhythm of the blood in his ears. Not even when he started to creep up on them did they sit up and take notice, for the woman had taken the man's member in her mouth by then, moving her head up and down while his throat made sounds Euan finally recognized as the same he'd heard from inside the stone wall with the windows in it. Grunts of desire. Another image almost tapped its way through to his mind from behind his eyes but stayed in the past.

The man turned the woman over and prepared to mount her.

When he lifted his head, it was too late.

Euan's jaws clamped on the man's neck before he could cry out. He moved his strong head from side to side, not resting until he heard the first snap. His mouth was instantly filled with blood, sticky and warm and wonderful; he couldn't decide which he liked better, the man's death spasms or the woman's throat shrieks.

He had chewed through half the neck and started on a soft cheek when he realized the woman wasn't there anymore. He felt confusion, mixed in with the sated bloodlust, because he should feel content and safe. Instead, those strange sensations he'd sometimes have when he saw washerwomen bending over to smash white linen against the rocks wouldn't let him go. It was like a low, constant pressure somewhere inside him that he couldn't name. But he knew the woman with the blue eyes could help him find out. He couldn't quite put it together in his head, because her throat noises hadn't sounded truly frightened, but more as if she had decided to act that way.

Euan put his bloody snout into the dirt and sniffed.

Instantly, he saw in his mind's eye exactly which way the naked creature had fled. He turned briefly, tore off another piece of blue and red threads sticking out of the man's neck, and gave chase.

The rains came down, blurring his vision and muddying the trail, and soon Euan had trouble tracking the scent. The trees twisted and creaked their eternal warnings of danger ahead, but even as a wolf he didn't pay them any heed. His snout sensed the naked woman somewhere ahead of a sunken cemetery, which was overgrown with vines to resemble hibernating moles, ready to pop through the surface at any moment. He caught a flash of skin on the trail ahead, and his hind legs kicked harder, propelling him forward.

He didn't even see the net.

But now there were loud throat sounds all around, and the smell of strong drink. Euan writhed helplessly several inches from the ground, but merely managed to get himself caught up even farther in the trap that suspended him from a tree. He twisted his head and saw a young man with wide eyes and thin black hair, baring his teeth and laughing. Another instant memory played across Euan's eyes. In it, this young man lifted a cup next to Euan and presented him with a gift. It looked like a wolf's head. He remembered! The castle, his brother, everything! This man was his friend, he was sure of it.

The image evaporated with the first kick he felt from someone's boot.

"Padraic!" screamed Euan, while he could still remember the vision. "It's me, Euan! We know each other!"

But the hunting party only heard a melodic growl that sounded like the wolf was trying to tell them something. "This one talks more than the others," said Padraic. He grabbed Euan around the throat before he could bite and shook him hard. "Let's see if he can sing when we hang him from his paws with the others."

Euan understood none of that, but he knew from the tone of Padraic's throat noise that he would soon end up like the wolves he'd seen in the gibbet by the bay.

And with that, the men slung Euan across a horse's flank and rode as quickly as they could back through the forest, where the trees looked down in silent sorrow that nobody ever listened to a thing they said. He gnawed at the leather net, but it was spun too tightly to give. Before long, the castle rose out of the clearing, and the black gates opened with a long yawning sound. When Euan heard the clattering of horses' hooves on the cobblestone, he closed his eyes and remembered more. The shame of his father's eyes on him the day Ned had rounded up men to meet the enemy. His own triumphant return. Ned's funeral. And the scores of nameless women he had savaged, and often choked for his own pleasure, right behind the same castle walls. There was a smell of freshly dried blood on the square, as if killing there was now a habit. He opened his eyes and saw a set of gallows, in which several wolves already hung by the hind legs, twisting and howling as they waited for the pain. He kicked and screamed, but the hunters just laughed harder, and the washerwomen brayed even louder than the men.

"Sing us a song, playful one," said Padraic, and dragged Euan out of the net by the tail. Euan dug in his claws, but they skidded on the slick stone, and the women kicked and belted him with sticks.

"Skin him alive!" a little boy's voice called out.

For the first time in his life, Euan regretted the part of him that enjoyed killing. He remembered his past life as a prince who delighted in watching young girls' eyes go wide, as he put his thumbs on their throats and squeezed until the light in them dimmed and vanished. He howled for forgiveness to a God he couldn't even name anymore, as the other wolves were being clubbed to death, one after the next. He was dragged up the steps and felt the leather straps tighten around his paws.

"Give him to me."

It was a woman's throat noise, and Euan could understand the words now. It was delicate, but carried with it more authority than Padraic's brute force, and the chorus of bloodthirsty voices subsided. Warriors, hunters, and maids parted as all heads turned to see a young woman making her way through the crowd. She wore a green ankle-length dress with a golden belt, and her hair was tied at the neck with a brooch in the shape of a wolf's head.

Her eyes were blue, and she had a recent scrape on her chin where brambles had cut her.

It was the woman from the forest.

"These men are merely paying tribute to Your Highness's family's honor, and—"

"And they will continue to render that service, Master Huntsman. But this particular wolf will not be touched, is that clear?"

She smiled, leaving no one in doubt of what strength hid under-neath that sweet expression if she was now refused.

Padraic took a step back and bowed deeply. "Your Highness may do your pleasure."

"I'm delighted you agree, Padraic. Please continue."

Strong hands undid Euan's bonds and lifted him back into a net, which was carried up several flights of granite stairs. All the while, he could see the woman's shape floating before him, al-ways a few steps ahead, the curve of her back and hips making even his mortal fears subside. Behind them, the sounds of hard objects striking flesh and bone echoed across the courtyard. Ani-mal shrieks and howls were drowned out by the appreciative roar of the crowd, relieved at not having been deprived of an after-noon's entertainment.

Soon, a door opened and Euan was carried into a room he recognized with something like dread.

It was his old bedchamber. The last woman he'd seen in here had been tied up to the bedposts for four days and put through her paces before she begged him to kill her.

"Chain him up over there," said the woman, and sat on the bed, looking at him.

"As you wish, Your Highness," said the guard, and put Euan's neck into the dog chain by the wall that Euan had installed him-self. He could now recall having used it many times on the maids from town.

"Leave us," she said, and never took her eyes off Euan. The guard closed the door and the footsteps faded.

Where Euan had first been relieved at being delivered from death, a wellspring of conflicting emotions made his jaws hurt. Why did she just sit there, scrutinizing him? Had he been brought up here so she could torture him in private? He was unsure if he should try to escape or jump onto that bed and mate with her. The blood in his finely tuned ears, which had never steered him wrong in the forest when he searched for prey or dodged pursu-ers, now sang out of key. He felt a desire he couldn't name; it was a longing for the woman, but also a need to see her blood spilled by nightfall. It made no sense to him, because the twin Euans inside the gray pelt were trying to decide whether the wolf or the residual human was in charge. He leaped up toward the bed as far as the chain would go. Then he whimpered and lay down at her feet.

She undid the clasp behind her head, and strawberry-blond locks fell past her shoulders. Something stirred in Euan's groin that felt familiar yet terrifying. The woman bent down and put a hand onto the wolf's forehead, quite unafraid she might lose some fingers.

"I know you, cousin," she said, in that honeyed voice. "I know you so well."

"Who are you?" Euan heard his own throat say, and jumped back at the surprise.

"When you vanished in the forest, the castle fell into disrepair. The head yeoman sent for help from my father, but he was chasing the Normans all the way back to Leinster. So I gathered up what remained, a few archers and a handful of horsemen, and took your castle." She bent even farther down, and Euan could see her cleavage and the white globes inside the dress. "I'm Aisling, your cousin. Our fathers weren't much as warriors, I have to admit, but it would appear both of us did our level best to even that score, wouldn't you say?"

Euan's head swam. The pain in his jaw had now spread to his entire skull. It felt as if his body were trying to turn itself inside out, shedding the fur and showing only the fair pink skin it was once born with. Sinew by sinew, it waited to see if it would soon be changed once more.

"It hurts, doesn't it?" she said, patting his head. "I could make you human again. Get you what you so richly deserve."

He recognized the glint in her eye as his own former delight in observing pain that wasn't his own. He felt fear gushing through him again, stronger than before. "What will you do with me?" he asked.

"I looked in your eyes today and knew you were family," she said, taking off her belt. "Padraic told me often enough how you seemed to have melted into the grass, and I never believed him. He's sweet, but dumb. I've heard the legends and paid soothsayers a small fortune to find out what happened to you. I even had one of them read the entrails of an old wolf we captured shortly after your disappearance. All signs pointed the same way: You were close by, yet not in human form. And ever since, I've held these ridiculous hunts that amuse the public, but which only serve one purpose: to find you. And when I saw you back in the forest, I knew my search was at an end."

"You wish to avenge Ned," said Euan, sure he wouldn't leave her chambers alive.

At this, Princess Aisling merely laughed so delightfully it would appear she was watching a basketful of kittens squinting against the light. "The true soldier, who lived to serve his father? No. My interest has always been you. Your strength, your cunning. You won a victory by biding your time and ruled a kingdom while you still had only fuzz on your chin." Another little smile. "Do you really think I would have dragged that poor soldier out into the woods today for a bit of fun if I didn't believe you could still tell the difference between family and bait?"

Euan was too speechless to reply. His old life in furs and royal robes lay just ahead. And if that wasn't enough, they had gutted the old wolf who put the curse on him to begin with. So much for God and fortune, he thought, and felt a surge of triumph.

Aisling finally rose and knelt down to undo his metal collar. She smelled of honeydew and freshly washed hair, and put a hand on his beating heart. Her eyes appeared to change color for just a moment, the heavenly blue yielding to his own golden brown before turning back to normal.

"I have ruled this castle alone for over three years," she said. "During that time, poor Padraic has kept forgetting his station and believes he might someday wear the crown next to me on the throne. I occasionally take a servant or two to my chambers for amusement's sake. But I have waited only for you." She reached behind her and unfastened the dress, which fell to the ground with a soft *whussh*. "My soothsayers told me there is only one way to end the curse. Approach, then, and prove them right."

She stood naked before him, unafraid, and didn't even attempt to cover up her sparse tuft of hair as Euan crawled slowly toward the bed.

For guidance, he listened to the blood coursing through his ears but kept getting different messages.

"Slay her!" said one voice, which had never steered him wrong out in the wild.

"No, love her," called another, unfamiliar accent, which resonated in parts of him he was just now beginning to remember.

"Come to me, cousin," said Aisling.

Euan lowered his head and sniffed the ground at her feet before looking up. Her breasts were small and pink and her fingers as delicate as a rabbit's foot. Those blue eyes made it impossible not to rise and crawl slowly toward his prize.

His lips curled away from the gums, and the dueling impulses inside his animal body fused and became one. His snout touched her shin. He licked it and tasted soap. The sound of blood in his ears was like a hundred men shouting havoc all at once.

A growl that began far inside his predator's heart began to work its way into the strong throat, gathering strength as it went.

The wolf had made up its mind.

The applause never came. I looked at the backs of everyone's heads as they bent forward to hear the punch line, but Jim had stopped talking.

"So?" asked an impatient older woman's voice. "What did the wolf decide to do?"

The shoulders of the Single Women's Legion parted, and I caught a glimpse of Jim leaning back on his stool and lighting up, and smoking ban be damned. No one protested. He crossed his legs and grimaced, enjoying the tension. He smiled, wider than when he'd been unzipping my trousers just two nights ago, and brushed away a forelock of hair.

"Well, what d'you think, yourselves?" he said. "Will he kill her or love her?"

Without hesitation, most voices in the room voted for love, while only a few broken hearts found Princess Aisling a touch too forward for a cousin and suggested Euan should make a meal of her right away.

"Love her!" a voice I recognized had shouted, just a half second before everyone else.

Aunt Moira's cheeks were flaming red, and her eyes shone like a true believer's.

"Well, now, ladies, that'll just have to keep for about a week, I'm afraid," said Jim, taking a deep magician's bow, his fingertips sweeping the floor. "My assistant and I need to rest up from all the traveling we've done. But never fear, Euan and Aisling's adventures will continue next Sunday at O'Shea's Pub over in lovely Eyeries, where even the colors of the buildings are as cheerful as the people inside them." He leaned forward and actually winked. "And don't tell anybody, but my money's always on love."

Torrential applause finally broke out, even as a few ladies cried "Aww" in disappointment that the handsome Elvis impersonator was going to hold out on them yet again. One of them even reached out and touched his lapel as he passed, as if he'd been Saint Bono himself.

While the dour Tomo had given up pretending to be genial and now just passed the hat like a busker, Jim leaped off his stool, threw on his motorcycle jacket, and strode over toward me. A few girls made way as I whipped a pocket mirror out to check my lipstick, which looked crap. When I'd put it away, I glanced up again and couldn't see him anywhere.

I turned because the soft murmur of his voice was rising right behind me.

"Kelly? Lovely name, Kelly. Rolls right off the tongue, doesn't it?"

And there he was, lightly touching the forearm of the prettiest girl in the room. Mind you, she had a fella with her but suddenly didn't seem to mind. I know that Jim didn't either, and rather than have the pitying stares of scores of women on him, the cuckolded boyfriend soon left, alone and disgraced.

I wanted to walk over there, I did. But not while Aunt Moira was still in the room, eyeing her chance to talk to Jim herself. I stole a pack of smokes from the girl next to me while she had her back turned and lit one up while I waited. My darling aunt blinked first, realizing she had no chance against Kelly's ample chest, expensive dress, and miles of endless lips. She ducked out with the same downcast look in her eyes I'd seen the night Harold had left her with nothing but shame and a bank debt.

I was eating out my guts, too, as Jim escorted Kelly home half an hour later. She jumped on the back of the Vincent while I followed behind as casually as I could. Yes, you heard me right. What the hell else would you have had me do? Go home and cry about it? At this point, he was under my skin, and I couldn't help it. I looked for the white van as I pulled out in the green Mercer, but saw only Jim's adoring crowd headed for home on the footpath, talking eagerly among themselves like trained penguins at the fair.

The red motorcycle rode down the coastal road toward Glengarriff, then took a left up into the hay-colored Caha Mountains, where houses are a bit thin on the ground, so I had to hang back as much as I could. The car bucked and yawed as I took the hairpin turns worse than the racer, dodging blue-gray cliffs as large as Volkswagens. Irises ripped from the ground by the strong wind tumbled across my bonnet in a yellow spray. The summer evenings were almost upon us, and on any other night than this I would have called it beautiful.

Jim pulled into a stone gate, behind which I could see a small cottage in better shape than most. Two stories of limestone, with new windows and doors and a spanking new Audi out front. She must have left the spare in town, I figured. New money, no doubt. They kissed before the engine had gone silent. I looked around for a suitable rock to plant in his head but stayed my hand. I waited until they'd gone inside before I parked the car down a blind dirt road and approached the house like a thief.

I should have worn better shoes than these heels, I thought, as I stole behind the house and stepped in mud up to my ankles. I heard sounds from upstairs I'd rather not tell you about, but I'm sure you can guess. Didn't take him five minutes to get in her knickers, did it? I was again thinking about doing something drastic, when I heard the soft whine of an engine coming nearer. I looked up the hill and saw a white van pulling behind a boulder and stopping. Tomo walked quietly but quickly down to the front door and put his ear to the pine. Apparently satisfied, his gloved hand touched the handle and turned it. He let himself inside without a sound, leaving the door wide open.

The thrusting sounds from upstairs grew louder as I saw my own feet following Tomo inside and trying to keep my heartbeat from getting noticed.

"My darling . . . darling Jim," she moaned, the cow, while I kept an eye out for Tomo. If Jim's Chinaman had been mostly immobile before, he wasted no time here. I hid behind the kitchen counter and watched him sweep silver candelabras, iPods, jewelry, gobs of cash, and what looked like a real Cartier watch into a leather satchel without making a sound. The ceiling was creaking as Jim apparently really put his back into it; Tomo could have set off hand grenades and she wouldn't have noticed. With a graceful last sweep of the right hand, he checked to see if he'd nicked it all before ducking back out.

I waited a full minute before following him. Upstairs, the show was nearing the rousing finale, and I still don't like thinking about it too much, to be honest. I waited until I saw the leather-faced man carrying the heavy satchel up past the rock to the left before leaving the house myself. I can recall my sense of satisfaction that the price Kelly had just paid for a piece of Jim's charms was everything in the house that wasn't nailed down. And be honest, now, you would have felt that way, too.

I had the car key in the door when I felt the knife at my throat.

"Why can't you people ever be satisfied with just the one time?" Tomo hissed in my ear, smelling of wet wool. "I keep telling him it's too dangerous to keep doing it this way, but will he listen? Take a guess."

"I don't . . . know who you are, so you don't have to—"

He grabbed my hair with the other hand, twisting my head backward like a pig in the abattoir. "Sure you do. I'm the last mad gook you'll ever see this side of the Resurrection, and old Jim in there can't have girlies like you crying to some sketch artist down at the Garda station, now, isn't that right?"

I made a fist around my keys and tried to breathe. I haven't a clue where I found the courage, but Jim had put enough anger in me to say it. "Is that what you told that poor creature over in Drimoleague?" I yelled back. "Or little Sarah McDonnell? What had she done to you, anyway, you oogly fooker, steal yer rice bowl? I'll buy ya a new one!"

He hesitated long enough after that insult for me to reach back and jam the key into what I suppose was his eye, for he howled and yelled like the damned as I unlocked the car and drove out of there without looking back.

It's either the cops or my sisters next, I thought, and I wasn't in doubt about where to go.

"YOU'RE MAD, YOU know that?" said Aoife, as she cast a weary glance at her mud-splattered car. She wore one of our father's tweed racing caps, back to front, which made her look like a newsboy from one of those Hollywood gangster films. I could tell she was angry, because she smiled too much for the occasion, and her voice was covered in something sharper than cut glass.

"But I saw that Tomo fella clean her out, and—"

"Grand so; now you can tell Bronagh and her fellow uniforms that you've solved a burglary. I'm sure they will get right on it—soon as they've finished their lunch."

"You're not listening," I said, exasperated, while a nasty feeling was prickling inside me. It wasn't like my youngest sister to be this skeptical in the face of bald evidence. "He had a blade to my throat, right? He's the one who killed Sarah, and that woman over in . . . wherever it was. You know I'm right. And Jim is in on it. It's how they operate. Tomo practically told me so his own self."

Aoife took her time fixing the garden hose to the outside faucet and turning it on. While she demonstratively sprayed the Mercedes, I could see she had already made up her mind.

"Did he, now? So you're *assuming*"—God, how she loved to drag that word out to the ends of the earth—"that yer man Jim and his proper criminal friend finish each show with a festive murder? How does that make any sense at all?" Some of the muddy water hit me on the cheek. By accident, I'm sure. "Besides, Jim's hot buns was in your sack the night Sarah was killed, wasn't he? You saw to that. And how do you even know he performed the night of the first murder? Give it a rest. I think you're seeing things."

I was about to protest when I saw the look in her baby sister eyes as she brought the hose around the rear bumper.

It was the same look of undiluted jealousy I'd seen in our aunt Moira's face the night before, accompanied by a tight little smile that said, "Don't look to me for pity, now that Jim has gone and found himself someone better. You made your own bed." She put the hose away and went in her house without asking me inside for tea.

So much for sisterly love.

"Give you a bell later," I said, and got a self-pitying mumble in return. I stood there awhile, dumbstruck, happy about only one thing.

Our father's sawed-off shotgun now rested snugly inside *my* bag. And I'd sleep with it in my arms that same night, praying for that ugly bastard to come try his luck again.

I'M NOT A coward, no matter what you might think of me by now.

That's why I got up before dawn, when I couldn't sleep a wink anyway, and went over to see Finbar. The flood of his text messages had abated, but the ones still trickling in were shorter and more plaintive. WHERE R U? and PLS CALL had a better ring to them than I'M HEARING THINGS I DON'T LIKE BUT STILL LUV U and, a second later, WHAT THE FUCK DO U THINK YER DOING, F?!

By now, they could have emptied all of Bantry Bay and poured my guilty conscience into it instead, and there still wouldn't have been enough room. Truth of it is, I cheated on him the moment I laid eyes on Jim, not when Jim finally put his hands on me.

I walked across town to Finbar's front door with the chip in it, from the time Rosie threw a six-inch-heel shoe at last New Year's party, and waited a moment. Tallon Road led up a hill where a cluster of houses had the best seaside view, of course, and my boyfriend had the one with double-paned glass and the kind of burglar alarm I've only ever seen in films. You know, the one where some American white fella's actor-voice tells you the "system is armed," as if that was supposed to make burglars compliment him on his nice language or something.

The streetlights shone on Finbar's car, which was spotless next to two others that looked like they just had fresh mud poured over them. I could see him through the kitchen window, drying the dishes and toweling them off, even though he had spent a fortune on a German dishwasher that cost more than me and my sisters' Mallorca vacation way back when. From the way he cocked his head, I could tell he was doing it because he was angry enough to come down the hill and kick in my door, and this kind of meditation made him rethink his plan. His hands moved efficiently, without any real joy or irritation, the way he did everything. Like he had lukewarm water for blood. I felt like hauling off and throwing a rock through his window to get a different reaction.

Instead, I wiped my feet, listened to the sound of my own breath, and rang the bell.

"Fiona," he just said, as if I'd forgotten the name myself. He had shaved his face so often and so close over the last handful of days I counted three nicks that had barely healed. I could smell the lemon soap, which hung about the place like hospital disinfectant and made my eyes water.

"Can I come in?" I said, smiling wanly like I sometimes do at Father Malloy in the street. Lots of teeth and no real eye contact. Because I knew what Finbar's eyes looked like without having to see. They'd be filled with questions instead of recrimination, and I'd have taken the anger any day. Because the last thing I felt like giving him were answers to where the old Fiona had gone off to.

"I was just doing the dishes," he said, in a voice I didn't recognize as his. It was too thick, as if he'd just eaten honey and forgotten to swallow.

I sat down on one of the white IKEA couches he'd spent a load of cash to have delivered all the way from London two months earlier, making me sit on the floor and assemble it with him for two days straight. I'd learned to hate Scandinavian L-shaped tools and cute pictograms that only make you feel like a total eejit. Finbar wiped his hands on the angel-white apron and sat down on the matching couch on the opposite side. A crystal rendition of a mermaid caressing some kind of horny fish was the silent referee, as she stood on the slick marble coffee table between us, looking unhappy at the task. The fish looked as if he couldn't have cared much either way.

"I have no excuse, Finbar, and I'm really sorry," I began lamely, trying to breathe at the same time. Now that I was actually here, it was as if some of the mystical opium Jim had squirted into me was fading, and I was again beginning to feel the familiar thumping signs above my heart that meant raw shame lay right beneath and was trying to claw itself out by force.

Finbar said nothing, at first, and kept wiping his already bone-dry fingers on the fabric. It was then I noticed he was drunk. I'd only ever seen him give up control twice in my time with him. Once was when he'd become the top salesman in the whole county, and envious colleagues had dragged the both of us to a fancy restaurant in Cork City with an Italian name. He had drunk two bottles of champagne by himself, and when I drove us home the only thing he did all night was inspect his suit for dirt that wasn't there. The other was when we'd had sex for the first time, and he told me he loved me right before finishing. I understood why he wanted the place to smell of fake lemons and not single malt. His eyes were pink, but that could be from either tears or another five fingers of whisky.

"You have to come to the dinner with me," is all he said at first.

I waited for the rest, but Finbar put both hands on his kneecaps, having spoken his piece.

"What are you talking about?"

"Next Saturday. At Rabenga's *ristorante* over in Glengarriff. The company dinner. Everyone expects to see both of us there." He belted the words out as if longer sentences would cause him physical pain. He still hadn't tried to smile, which actually is the only thing about that night that made me happy.

"Maybe . . . it's not such a good idea, okay? I mean, the way things are now and all."

Finbar covered his mouth before answering. "And how are things? Can you tell me exactly, Fiona, what *things* you think I'm talking about?" He was lisping, like his lips had begun acting on their own, telling tales the rest of the mouth knew nothing about. He looked at the crystal mermaid, not at me, and from the looks of it she was in for a hell of a beating.

"I didn't plan it," I said. "And I'm sorry I lied to you about seeing him. But I did, and I can't take it back now." I looked at Finbar's hands and wondered how it was that he could massage my breasts like he was kneading dough, and it took me a while to feel anything at all, when all Jim had to do was look in my direction to make me drenched.

"Does that mean you're not coming to the dinner?" he said.

I rose, went over behind him, and put my hand on his neck. I considered staying and sleeping with him for pity's sake, but that would only completely mess with the poor fella's head. So I let my fingers linger there a moment, feeling his pulse and the love we'd never really shared, until he reached up and brushed them away.

"See ya later, Finbar," I said, opening the door, and knew I probably wouldn't.

I KNEW THE headmistress didn't believe a word I said when I rang her that morning.

"Well, then, feel better, won't you, Fiona," said Mrs. Gately, who had just heard me hand out some weepy excuse about pneumonia for leaving my evil sixth class to the tender mercies of a substitute teacher they'd no doubt tear to little bits before second bell.

"Thank you, Missus," I said, being careful not to cough and oversell the story. "I am sure I'll be much better next week." Truth is, I had begun to feel a bit haggard since meeting Jim and losing him again. I traipsed out in front of the bathroom mirror and saw dark shades under my eyes, with a kind of gray pastiness in my cheeks.

"Nice work, Fiona," I said to the reflection, before putting on my jacket and heading out the door. As you've figured out by now, I wasn't just shirking the sixth-class monsters for the hell of it. The sensation of Tomo's knife at my throat had kept me awake every bit as much as pictures playing in my head of poor Kelly, who had probably lain in her bed out in that cottage all night by herself, blood already hardened to a paste.

That's why I decided to go see Bronagh, brave defender of truth and justice.

"Yer looking well for a person with galloping pneumonia," she said tartly, eyeballing me from behind her cramped desk. It was round breakfast, and all the other gardaí were stuffing their heads with eggs and toast at the café down the street, leaving the rampant criminality to the youngest garda on the squad.

"Us Walshes, we mend quick, ya know," I said, sitting down and handing her a cup of coffee with lots of sugar and milk, which is how she drank everything. If anybody had made a beer that tasted like java, she would have clapped her hands, poured in the cream, and drunk down two pints at once.

She accepted the peace offering without much enthusiasm, looking me over with the same kind of frank distaste my own sister had displayed the night before. I felt like saying how bitter Finbar had been but decided that wouldn't buy me any mercy.

"Whatcha doing here?" Bronagh said, slurping the coffee while keeping an eye out for Sergeant Murphy, who had called her blubbering to attention at the old graveyard. A picture of a still-living and flirting Sarah McDonnell hung on the bulletin board, under a heading that said ENQUIRIES SOUGHT. There was no mug shot yet of the dead girl I'd read about in the paper. But I was sure Jim and his Chinaman were just itching to participate in clearing up that little mess.

"I saw something," I said, working up the nerve to risk sounding stupid. "Last night. Out in the mountains toward Glengarriff." I remembered Kelly's voice from her upstairs bedroom, and it made me angrier—even then—than recalling Tomo's breathy promises of death in my ear.

"Didja, now? What was it, d'ya think? That Armenian pickpocket who escaped from my esteemed colleagues over there? Was he wearing that busker's black suit with white stripes on it?"

"Get outta here with that, Bronagh, I'm really serious."

She leaned forward, forgetting all about the steaming peace offering. Her face turned bright pink. She pointed at a pile of papers next to her. "And what d'ya think *I* am? Fucking desperate, like you? We're only open four hours a day to handle this workload, Mum *always* brings Ava home half-filthy and filled to the eyeballs with sweets, and Gary is getting ready to make his move on that brunette over at the SuperValu and leave me for good. I can't listen to yer half-baked visions, Fiona Walsh, I really can't. Not today." Her cleft chin burrowed into her regulation tie as if she were on parade—or trying not to cry.

"Remember that Japanese fella?" I persisted. "The one who passes the hat around for Jim? I think he may have killed someone last night."

Bronagh didn't move a muscle but just stared at me in a way that made me remember why she'd wanted to join the guards to begin with. Her eyes bored through me, through the wall, past Castletownbere, and to the farthest edge of Ireland until it came to rest on the unknown crime she hadn't solved yet. "Last night?" she asked, hiding a nugget of something secret behind her vocal cords. Her eyes grew confident again.

I nodded, eager to be heard. "Yeah. A few miles past Adrigole, going east. I followed Jim up the road, and this guy Tomo, he was there, too. This woman, I don't know her full name, but she goes by Kelly, she lives in a stone cottage by herself. Jim went upstairs with her, while Tomo robbed her blind. When he saw me, he tried to cut my throat, but I got away in time. Bronagh, you have to send someone up there right away."

It took a full five seconds. Then Bronagh's face lit up in one of those kinds of smiles people feeling suddenly superior can't help showering you with. I think guards practice them every day before breakfast. She rose and beckoned me down the stairs with her.

"Did you hear a thing I said?" I asked, nodding at two returning gardaí with crumbs still on their duty blues. One of them mumbled something about "pneumonia" and made a disapproving face at me as he passed.

"Clear as a bell," said my little cop in a self-satisfied voice, descending ever deeper into the dusty stairwell, until we both came to a steel door that was pitted with rust. She opened it with a smart turn of the wrist.

"You're *quite* sure it was last night that all this happened?" she asked.

"Don't be such a witch, Bronagh. I told you. And if you sweep that farmhouse properly, you'll probably see that this woman, Kelly something-or-other, was murdered in the same way that Chinaman did both Sarah and that Holland woman over in Drimoleague."

"Sounds like a proper crime wave, is what it does," continued Bronagh, unlocking a metal cabinet and sliding the tray out with a flourish.

There was a loud *clang!* and she whipped a rubber sheet aside.

Right under my nose, on a slab, lay my Chinaman, dead as Plastic Jesus.

His slim equine face had swelled to twice its normal size, and it looked like something massive had pummeled his cheekbones until they gave under the weight. God Himself had sat on him, I thought. Either that, or Jim had taken a baseball bat to his tobacco leaf skin. No amount of hit-and-run drunk driving could have produced this kind of rag doll, unless someone had put it in reverse to do the job right.

"You want to tell me how he could try killing ya looking like *this*?" Bronagh asked.

"Jaysus!" I said, reeling backward and banging my head against the cooler where they kept the rest of the departed.

"Exactly. That's what *I* said when old Mrs. Monaghan called early this morning because her grandchild had found something nasty in the water," said Bronagh, enjoying my gobsmacked expression. "Haven't done a proper forensic analysis yet, but it looks to me like someone really put the boots to him before he got wet."

"He was still alive last night. Because I was there." I turned my head so Bronagh could see the red line where his blade had nicked me. "See that?"

"You should take more care when shaving," she said, and shrugged, shoving Tomo back to his everlasting reward and ushering me out the door onto the footpath. We walked out on the main street, where Bronagh pulled me aside and put a hand on my shoulder, as if she'd seen it in a movie first. A couple of fishermen in the middle of yapping about some girl pretended not to look but lowered their voices, just enough to hear every word.

"Now, you listen," she said. "It's one thing to break poor Finbar's heart by whoring around with that tramp. But it's quite another to mess about with our enquiries. So in future, stick to yer pyramids and mummies and leave the dead to us, all right?"

"I know what I saw," I said, trying to keep my voice down. That ever-nosy Sergeant Murphy had opened the window upstairs to take a look at us, and Bronagh used her big-girl voice in order not to disappoint him.

"Go home," she said. "And nurse that . . . pneumonia, was it? Maybe one of yer new boyfriend's fairy stories can make it all better." And with that, she turned and walked back into the station house, hoping for the kind of collegial respect that would never come her way, no matter how many tin badges she shined.

My own blood had spurned me, and my old best friend thought I was a crack.

For the first time since I could remember, I felt completely alone.

THE WIND HAD taken hold of the bunchgrass up in the Caha Mountains and started to tug hard.

I had biked with the wind in my face for two hours to get back up to the sloping meadow below the rocks. Now I lay arse up and nose to the ground, trying to figure if anybody was still alive in the cottage below. Fine, laugh if you must, but *you* try playing Hercule fucking Poirot with skylarks chirping away right over your head, the tattletales, and wayward sheep coming over to nibble at grass not two feet from your secret hiding place. I was roasting in my too-warm overcoat, and the tails flapped loudly in the wind like the ragged banners from some long-forgotten and buried army.

The house seemed quiet. The Audi I'd seen before hadn't been moved, and there was also a crusty old Land Rover that looked like it had come straight out of a hunting catalog, dirt, scratches, and all. I wanted to go down there, I did, but something held me back. It was probably fear, even if I would have called it prudence at the time.

When I blocked out the birdsong and the whispering grass, I could hear a faint thumping noise. It sounded like someone smacking their palm against a tabletop, holding their breath to see if anybody noticed, and then trying it again.

I inched closer in the grass, smearing green skid marks onto the yellow floral dress that I'd nicked from Aoife, until I saw what it was.

The front door yawned as open as it had been the night before, banging against the lock as only the wind guided it. I dared to rise and felt like someone had dumped a load of cold water straight into my veins. If Kelly lay upstairs with flies crawling in and out of her, I didn't want to see it. But if the brave sheriff in town thought I was a shirker and a nutcase, what choice did I have?

"Hello?" I said, but the wind snatched the word away before it reached the door. I was close to where I'd been before and could see my old hardened footprints in the mud. *Thump!* went the door one more time, making me jump an inch off the ground. I put my nose to the window and peered through the glass but saw nothing new, no milk carton or coffee cup to ward off the fear of fresh corpses in the bedroom, courtesy of one darling Jim Quick. I cursed my own curiosity, but more so my desire to see him again. Because this much was the truth: I wanted to solve what I remained sure was a murder spree that traced back to him, but mostly as a means once more to stare into those amber eyes and try to divine their secrets. Judge me if you must, but there it is. That solidarity with my fellow girlies went only so far. Despite what I knew, Jim still owned the rest.

So I took a deep breath, turned the corner, and went inside.

The living room was still, but for the soft creaking the wind made against the glass door leading down to the bay. Sails filled the bay like white napkins on Neptune's blue dinner table. I stood there a second, dreading what I had to do, and then started for the stairs.

"Hello?" I tried one more time, but heard only the insistent *thump!* in reply. I was halfway to the top when it dawned on me I hadn't brought as much as a kitchen knife for protection. And Father's dreaded shotgun was still fast asleep in my bed. I looked down and rummaged through my bag for at least a set of keys to use for brass knuckles, when I heard the dead speak for the first time.

"And what exactly might you be doing here?" asked a woman's voice.

I raised my head and looked into the eyes of a barely toweled-off Kelly, who held a giant robe about her waist with one hand and a heavy wooden bowl in the other.

I was dumbstruck and relieved not to have to see another dead body and was surprised to feel myself actually smiling. "I—erm, the door was open, so—"

"That's 'cause I opened it to get some fresh air. See how that works?" Her voice was as sharp as her lantern jaw, but she'd begun to tremble at the left knee as she took a step down toward me. "And you're not invited. So answer the question, or I'll plant this in your skull."

I backed down the way I'd come, trying to keep my voice from breaking into a million pieces myself as I answered. "My name's Fiona Walsh, and I'm a schoolteacher from over in Castletownbere." There was no reaction in Kelly's face, and she took another two steps down the stairs. My brief rush of joy at not having to see encrusted blood gave way to the kind of fear I hadn't felt since I dragged my sisters out the back door while the fire below burned the soles of our feet. "You know, Sacred Heart? Right behind the church?"

"And yer pay is so crap you have to come stealing from honest people, is that it?" She took a swing at me, and I tumbled ass over teacups down the last few feet as I ducked, smacking my head into her nicely polished cherrywood floor.

"No," I croaked. "This is a misunderstanding."

"*You're* the misunderstanding, whatever your real name is." Her blood was up, and I could feel her circling me to have another go while I was down. "Do you manky illegal immigrants really think you can just use law-abiding folk as your own personal cash machine, is that it? So what's yer real name, anyway? Sveta? Valeriya? Or, no, don't tell me, you're a *tinker* from some caravan up north. I thought you people had become extinct with the introduction of mobile phones."

"I just came to see if you were all right," I said, half sitting and rubbing my head. "God's honest truth. Call the Castletownbere Garda station if you don't believe me. Ask for Bronagh."

Kelly blinked and cinched a terry-cloth belt around her slim waist to make what was probably her steady—and cuckolded—boyfriend's bathrobe fit. She was cute. Jim had good taste, I had to give him that. Once again, my jealousy jumped into the driver's seat and threw caution and righteousness onto the roadway. For the first time that day, I felt like choking her bony arse to death my own self.

"If *I* was all right?" she asked.

"Yeah. After what happened last night. I saw someone go upstairs with you. And I just thought—" I remembered how she'd screamed when Jim really gave it to her and felt my face redden. Now I felt both ashamed and stupid. I knew I should have listened to Bronagh.

She wrinkled her brow and put the bowl in her lap as she sat down. A brief moment passed, as both of us listened to the other's willingness to take this all the way. Then her eyebrows shot up, and she reached for her weapon again with something like joy. "It was *you!*" she shouted, rushing me like a hurler. "I knew I'd seen your face somewhere. Yeah. You were at the pub, weren't you? And you followed me and Jim up here, you perv?" Her face had gone foam-white. "The ring my mother left me, my passport, cash, car keys to the Audi, and every single phone number I own! And you have the bloody cheek to come back and see if I had *more*? C'mere, you!"

Swisshh! went the wooden missile, and I bolted out the door to avoid it, losing a shoe as I ran. "Come back here, you tinker bitch!" Kelly raved.

"Remember the Asian fella who was there, too?" I screamed, running as fast and as far as I could.

"Liar!" she yelled, gaining on me like a mad dog. "What fella?" Up on the road, a car had pulled over to watch the show, and someone rolled down the window.

"Jim's assistant; he followed you here, too," I gasped. "I came by last night because I was jealous that Jim had found someone else, I admit it. But this guy, I saw him take everything. It's how they work it. One man to open the door, one to keep it open." She fumbled for my hair, pulling out a few strands before I found a few ounces of adrenaline, and escaped again.

"Try again," she said, wheezing. "Jim is a gentleman."

"Yes," I said, "until his little helpers say the wrong thing. Then he kills them. That Chinaman is deader than shite."

I looked back at her, and she'd stopped running. Both hands hung by her sides as if suddenly heavy.

"What'd you say?" she said.

"That's right." I pressed on, slumping to the grass. "Saw him not one hour ago, head beaten in." Kelly sat down, too, mouth chewing on an invisible blade of grass, so I decided to plunge the last knife of knowledge I had straight into her little yuppie heart. "And tell me this much," I asked, trying not to smile as I said it. "Did he tell you all about how the *story* is in charge, not him? I'll just bet he did. And didja get a look at that tattoo of his? What's on it—I forget—Porky Pig or the heroic Cúchulainn? Sometimes they dress alike."

"Shut up," she said, looking down, but I could tell I'd scored a bull's-eye. Everybody wants the prize, don't they? But nobody likes to share.

"Jim charms and tells tales, and his little servant cleans up the rest," I said, this time without anger, because it really was simply brilliant and you had to admire it.

"Jim had nothing to do with this," Kelly said, not quite trusting what her own voice was saying. She rose and brushed the grass off her bathrobe with a pinched expression as if someone were holding her nose shut against her will. "That man's death was an accident, I'm sure. And now I would like for you to leave. Because I told you, Jim is a real gentleman."

I looked up at the ridge and saw Bronagh slowly walking down toward us between the rocks, the smile of the triumphant beaming on her face like a lighthouse.

"Isn't he just," I said.

MY DEMON SISTER took pity on me. Who else would do that for the girl who had cried wolf? As it was, the whole town had heard of my ridiculous murder-spree theory by nightfall. Bronagh saw to that. Snickers followed me on the footpath from the Garda station all the way back to my house.

After Bronagh delivered another lecture on the way home on how easily she could have done me for burglary since my footprints were outside *and* inside Kelly's place, the last thing I felt like that evening was more judgment.

Instead, what I got was a healthy dose of Evgeniya when I knocked on Rosie's door and saw a blond girl with freckles open up.

Evgeniya was my sister's girlfriend, even if none of us called her that but still let Aunt Moira refer to her as "that old flatmate of yours." I suppose we could all have fought it, but *you* try coming out in a part of the world where anyone other than a boy whose hand you want to hold had better be your sister or else.

She was from Russia somewhere, and I could never pronounce her name, even with a head full of Guinness and the patience of saints, but that didn't matter. I just called her Evvie. She was grand, and the only outside influence who did anything to raise Rosie's spirits. Elfinlike and gracious where Róisín was spawned from the darker corners of God's imagination, Evvie moved with a fluid grace I would have expected to see in swimmers, except she did it on dry land. They had shared a flat at UCC, where Evvie still lived, and she came out to visit whenever she felt like it. The hand that shook mine was small and applied just enough pressure to let me know she was happy I'd come by. She had the brown fleece sweater zipped all the way up to her fine seahorse-shaped ears, because the wisdom behind my sister's casual unwillingness to pay bills on time had been lost on the power company, which had promptly shut her off. Again.

"Hey, how are ya?" Evvie said, in that peculiar choppy accent of hers, and walked back out into the kitchen, which hadn't seen actual cooking since she'd last been there.

"Not too bad," I lied. "Whatcha making?"

"Steamed salmon with vegetables," she said, attacking each syllable with deliberation. Even Rosie, who had kissed her narrow lips for over a year and still hadn't a clue how to say her name properly, only ever called her Ivana the Terrible.

"Grand. Where's the lovely one?"

Evvie jerked a thumb toward the bedroom, where the familiar chatter of electronic voices told me where to find the only member of my family with a reputation more nefarious than mine. The muttering rose and fell, like a chorus of angels locked inside a radio for all eternity and still searching for the exit.

"Oi, genius," I said, feeling relief at seeing the crouched-over figure in the pink POG MA HON T-shirt manning the controls and trying to suck the life out of a ciggie at the same time. I knew Evvie hadn't given her an item of clothing inviting the general public to kiss her arse. She'd probably made it herself.

"About time ya showed yer face," she said, giving me a fierce hug. "The Russian princess is staying for a coupla days, which means you and I will do better than rashers and old bread for breakfast." Her face grew unnaturally serious, and she looked like someone whom you could hurt just by looking at her sideways. "I hear our little Columbo sold you out to get in good with the boys in blue. Fuck her." Her chewed black nails dug into my wrist. She would have killed for me then. As it would turn out, we'd both soon kill for someone else.

"Thanks, Rosie," I said, and had to look away a moment in order not to cry from pure happiness. "Hear anything from Taxi Driver today?"

"Ah, don't worry too much about Aoife," said Róisín, dialing an inch to the left, seeking a voice farther out on the band, where only the true hard-core devotees hung about. "She wanted to give your *seanchaí* a tumble herself and called me to say she had told you some things she already regretted. Typical. She's back with that football player of hers, the shades are drawn, and she's not taking any trips tonight." She smiled at Evvie, who was setting the table. "What is it with all these beautiful people, I wonder? Taking advantage of nice, proper girlies like us?" The skull ring on her index finger shone as she adjusted the knob around a man's voice, barely audible through the carpet of static, still eluding easy capture.

"I feel like an eejit, Rosie," I said, taking the newspaper article about the "accidentally" dead Mrs. Holland out of my pocket and handing it to her. "I was so sure that—"

"Yer my big sister, and I'd drink donkey piss for ya," she said, grabbing hold of my hand. "But you have got to give it a rest, now. Yer man there isn't all shiny and fabulous; I think everyone knows that. Maybe he even stole more than hearts. But if you see murderers everyplace, you'll come apart at the seams." Her mouth curled upward in a smile so wide the tip of the cigarette nearly burned her cheek. "And who would take care of me then?"

I squeezed her hand but didn't answer. I was thinking about how much time it had taken for Tomo to stop feeling whatever it was that had punched him to death. I made a mental note to look at Jim's knuckles if I ever laid eyes on him again.

"I mean it," Rosie said, seeing that I only nodded and didn't pay attention to a thing she said.

"Five minutes, guys," said Evvie, and shot Rosie a look like she meant it.

"Yes, ma'am, general, sir," said Rosie, and saluted with her ciggie hand, but she gave the wheel another spin to the left with the other and was finally rewarded.

". . . from my castle on the hill deep in the forest. Can anybody hear me, I wonder?" came someone's fragmented message from the great beyond. The voice was male and soothing and reminded me of something familiar, but I couldn't put my finger on what.

"This is Nightwing, deep in the arse end of Cork, reading you five by five; over," Rosie barked, into her old-fashioned CB radio mike, which was black and as large as a hand grenade.

"And a pleasure to meet such a charming lady, I'm sure," continued the voice, while Rosie tuned a few other knobs to get rid of the distortion. "Why might you be sitting by yourself by the mike on a summer night like this?"

"Come and get it," said Evvie, setting the filled plates, "or the vegetables will get cold." I signaled that we'd be there just as soon as I understood why we still listened to this man, rather than flip the switch and be done with him. My opium receptor, the place Jim had touched with his eyes before anything else, that hidden part of me I didn't want to acknowledge was still driving me to search for him, was throbbing now. It felt as if liquid hope surged into my heart, pumping an unknown kind of wonderful lethal drug back out through my fingertips.

"Why? Because that's where the action is, fella," said Rosie, and I could hear from her sneer that she was annoyed the voice didn't observe ham radio protocol and end each transmission with an *"over."* "What might a fine young man such as yerself be called when yer at home in yer castle, then? *Over.*"

There was a long silence. For a moment, I thought we'd lost him.

"Lads," Evvie persisted, already seated and demonstratively clanking her fork.

"Never thought about that," the man said, and nearly chuckled at the idea. "I suppose you could call me . . . Gatekeeper. Yes. I like the sound of that."

I listened harder for the edges around the voice; they kept moving like wet marble. I wanted desperately for Rosie to shut off her infernal machine. And yet I didn't, the more the voice grabbed hold of me. Because my blood ran faster at the sound.

"Grand, so," said Rosie. "So you're out in the forest, are ya? Have to rush off, but the girlfriend's waiting with dinner. She'll ship my arse off to some Siberian labor camp if it gets cold; *over.*"

"It *is* cold," said Evvie, and couldn't help laughing. My demon sister had that effect on everybody.

"That's good to hear," said the voice calling itself Gatekeeper. "Because sometimes the things coming out of the woods should have stayed th—" There was a long melodic whine as some pop station from Kerry drowned out the rest; then it stopped. ". . . reful when you talk to handsome men telling tales."

I grabbed the handset away from Rosie and clicked the key. "What did you say? About men telling tales? What is it they do?" I had a feeling my life depended on making the voice answer me.

Another measured pause, but the signal was lost amid the whistles of stations trying to get our attention.

"Are you there?" I almost shouted, keying the mike again. "Gatekeeper?"

"You're not the same young woman as before," said the man, and from farther away this time, as if transmitting from deep down inside a digital well. "But I like the sound of your voice. You seem sincere in your question. The storytellers, you understand, make you look at anything but what's inside themselves. They gain your confidence and make you feel every story is invented for you and you alone. Don't believe them."

"I met one," I admitted, and hadn't a clue why I'd said it the second the words had left my mouth. I swear to Christ, but it felt like I was in confession. Except this time I wanted to reach into the radio and touch the man at the other end, and Father Malloy had nothing I wanted to touch, except maybe while wearing rubber gloves. "I'm beginning to suspect that he's . . ." I paused, sensing Gatekeeper holding his breath and listening. "I think he's hurt women—not just their feelings, I mean, but much worse."

"I see," said the voice, giving me no idea what he thought of that. It had got so quiet in the low-ceilinged room I could hear Rosie's wristwatch ticking, and the clicking noise of the frying pan cooling off in the sink. "He's kissed you already, hasn't he? It's what he does. If he's been really crafty, you've already let him stay the night." The voice had grown insistent but not judgmental. "You should forget all about him, whoever you both are, and get on with your lives. Nothing good comes from him, in the end."

Rosie and I looked at each other the way kids imagining they've just seen a ghost might do.

"G'wan outta here with that," said the least spiritual goth child I've ever met in my life, and snatched the mike back. "That's the biggest load of shite I've ever had shoveled, Gatekeeper. Sure ya haven't stared at yer Ouija board after smoking a big doobie? Over."

"Suit yourselves," said the man, as the electronic gates slowly swung shut on our little séance. "Perhaps these are mere nonsense ravings."

There was one last sharp burst of signal, and Gatekeeper's voice came out of the speakers as clearly as if he had sat on the couch in the flesh, staring at me.

"But if he speaks to you about love," he said, "run for your life."

LOOKING BACK, EVEN now, most of what had happened until that night was almost bearable, as crazy as it might seem to you. But by the time Friday dinner at Aunt Moira's came around again, our lives had changed forever.

I stayed for a while and ate Evvie's food, laughing at my sister's jokes and pretending to be entirely over my obsession with traveling story-tellers who might also in my mind have been serial murderers. But between mouthfuls of corn and salmon, it was all I could do not to get up out of my chair and put both hands on the shortwave radio one last time, hoping to coax back the hypnotic voice from the forest. "A lonely perv from some council flat with too much time on his hands," quipped Róisín, pulling a face. "Ooh, *spooky*, almost as if he *knows* Jim, and gives himself a name that makes you think of the black castle gate from Jim's dream world, isn't it? Please. Cheap storytelling gimmick. Probably an accountant or a clerk. Castle? All fairy tales have one of them. More peas?"

But I knew better.

So did Evvie, but she wisely kept silent, squeezing Rosie's hand gently when she waved a lit cigarette around like a loaded weapon, ranting on about how gullible her big sister was, despite her schoolmarm smarts. Both Evvie and I had heard something between the spoken words of warning, a message from somewhere beyond the forest I was sorry I'd ever been able to imagine.

In the days that followed, I reaped the full harvest of shame I'd sown when I chased after Jim and Tomo, pretending all the while to be sicker than a hatful of priests at a boy scouts' convention. People on the footpath smiled too widely as I passed. Father Malloy tripped on his own tongue as he said good morning.

But that was nothing compared to the scorn I received from my sixth class.

"Mrs. Harrington didn't know *nearly* enough about the Egyptian Second Dynasty," exclaimed little Mary Catherine Cremin when I finally made it back to school, shooting me a look that could have wilted flowers. "So I've made a list of all the things we're behind on in the last three days since you've been . . . away. Substitute teachers are just not the same." She placed a neatly printed note on the desk in front of me and smiled so sweetly I could have belted her one. I knew then how the sub had suffered. After that, no amount of stern finger-wagging or even threats to report David to the headmistress each time he swiped the girls' iPods had any effect at all. That little bitch ran the class like the she-wolf Ilse from the SS.

I had been forever tagged as "the hoor who shagged that tinker on the hot bike."

Finbar had ceased his text messages and now had taken to passing me in the street with a condescending nod, such as you'd do to lepers. He received lots of sympathy from the blue-haired ladies down at the Lobster Bar.

I kept scouring the papers for news of Jim, of course, and to see if anyone else had met an untimely end in some other two-horse town. But there was not a peep about young girls raped and strangled, just more stories in the *Southern Star* about cake-faced lotto winners from Clonakilty and about what a nice summer we were having. I didn't dare ask Bronagh any more questions, and it seemed that, whatever may have gone on, everything was back to the way it had been before that red 1950 Vincent Comet thrummed its arrival in my town.

That is, unless you'd taken a closer look at my aunt.

For one thing, she had lost weight and started to wear high heels

again. Aoife had seen her down at the hairdresser's asking for high-
lights. When one of the girls at the market asked Aunt Moira if she'd
got a piece of good news, she just smiled and kept mum. And she made
sure to call each of us to make sure we'd make it to dinner on Friday.

"Hello, my lovelies," she crooned, as she opened the door and let
us in. Aoife and me had just made up in the way we always did, by
making fun of Finbar, who now refused to say hello to any of us. But
as we went inside our aunt's house with Rosie in tow, an unfamiliar
scent greeted our nostrils, which were attuned to smelling only burnt
meat and soupy vegetables. God help me, but it smelled wonderful.
Like chicken and steak and some kind of exotic spice all rolled together in a sauce too complex to describe. All things being equal, I'd
have run past the statues and into the dining room ahead of my sisters. But things weren't.

"Whatcha cooking, Aunt Moira?" asked Róisín sweetly.

"Didja bring yer appetites?" is the only answer she got. That, and a
smile more secretive than the Sphinx's.

There was an extra chair at the dinner table. New crystal glasses
graced a starched white tablecloth, and Moira had hoovered the place
cleaner than a hospital's operating theater. As we all sat, Aoife shot me a
look of complete puzzlement, as if none of this made any sense. Rosie
just gawped after our aunt, who whisked out of the room again with a
toothy grin, no doubt getting ready for the big entrance.

"What's she on about?" hissed my demon child, unsettled by Aunt
Moira's newfound confidence. Her instinct was dead on. It was downright scary to watch Moira's energy. Something feverish and other-
wordly about it.

"Haven't a clue," said Aoife, touching a lacy napkin so new the price
tag was still on it. "But I don't think I have to pretend to like her cooking any longer."

There were footsteps in the hallway, accompanied by the sizzling of
food in a skillet. My sisters and me leaned forward in our chairs in anticipation. I swear it was like a magic show before the elephant vanishes
behind the curtain, only to reappear with a drumroll.

Jim emerged, holding two frying pans filled with the most delicious food I'd ever seen. His knuckles were scratched and swollen, and he didn't try to hide them.

"Well, there you are again, ladies," he said with that grin, but it was me he looked straight in the eye.

JIM WAS ALWAYS a step ahead.

Without anyone noticing, he had called up Aunt Moira earlier that week and asked for a room. In one of the biggest acts of irony I could remember, she'd given him the keys to number five, where Harold had once ruined her life on that creaky old bed.

"He's *such* an easy guest to have," tittered our star-struck aunt. She smiled at me between forkfuls of Jim's chicken cordon bleu and gave his forearm a possessive squeeze. He didn't seem to mind, but entrapped her in that snakelike gaze that already made women from Mizen Head to Kenmare forget what their husbands' faces looked like.

"Got tired of small bed-and-breakfasts," explained Jim, allowing himself to stroke Aunt Moira's hand in return, as my sisters worked very hard not to look at me for a reaction. "And your aunt here has let me move in, just as long as I help out around the house. A fair trade, wouldn't you say?"

Oh, yes, I thought, and I know in just what way you're planning to help.

I know that you know, his eyes seemed to signal back to me across the wineglasses. And we also both know that nobody believes you.

NOW BEGAN SEVERAL weeks of agony for me.

I don't want your pity and I'm no whinger. I told you that before. But I have to tell you how surreal it was to watch my frumpy aunt shed the Mars bar complexion and once again reveal the confidence she used to have before the Harolds of the world stole off with it. Jim still cranked up that gorgeous Vincent to race off in search of audiences who would pay for his stories, but he came back home to our aunt every night.

Room number five was soon properly christened, with Jim shimmying off our aunt's new dress and underwear. After that, his backpack and sleeping bag were moved into the master bedroom for good.

I have to admit to you that I once stood outside their bedroom window, listening for the kinds of noises he'd once coaxed out of me but all I heard was muttering. I didn't understand it, at first, but when I moved so close to the wall I was nearly touching it, I understood. They weren't having mad monkey sex, at least not right then. Jim was doing something far more seductive.

He was telling her a story.

From having been a weekly exercise in stark boredom, Friday dinners now became a showpiece, in which Moira would appear in ever more revealing costumes with plunging necklines, tarted up with our mother's good jewelry. She was now as skinny-arsed as those models whose hips she used to envy, and Jim beamed like a proud proper boyfriend. Whenever he carved a steak or deboned his wonderful steamed trout *amandine,* I looked at his hands around the knife handle, thinking of Tomo, Mrs. Holland, and little Sarah McDonnell. But as the months passed and no new grisly murders were reported, whatever suspicion he might have aroused back then was washed away like a bad dream in most people's minds. Except for mine.

"Ya got to get over it," said Aoife one night, as we sat in her kitchen drinking tea. "I mean, *I* did. At least you got to enjoy it for a moment." She tried to act her old brave self, but I could see a twinge of envy still lodging itself somewhere near her heart. The gorgeous footballer had finally left town a few weeks earlier and reunited with his anorexic trophy wife back home in lovely Dalkey.

"I suppose," I said, noticing how she patted her missing hair when she was irritated. "There's just something . . . off . . . about how he moved in exactly at the time when the murders stopped."

"Oh, willya give the Perry Mason bit a rest?" Her face, which was always a harder version of Rosie's pixie complexion, grew a touch bitter. "Yer Chinaman was hit by a car, most likely, Sarah was done by one of those roving Armenian or Ukrainian gangsters we had last year, and Mrs. Holland died in her sleep, all right?"

"All right," I said, and we both knew I didn't mean it.

I'm not proud of it, but I soon took to spying around my aunt's house every Friday night.

I'd use any excuse to get upstairs and rummage through Jim's belongings, and it wasn't easy, since he knew what was stewing in my brain. It meant creative bathroom breaks whenever he was busy in the kitchen, or each time my aunt pulled him down the street to show off his pearly whites to the adoring neighbors. I soon acquired the silent skill I'd once ascribed to Tomo, opening cabinets and lifting sweaters, unzipping pockets and closing them again without a trace. It was almost a game, but not quite. Because I had a very good idea what might happen if he caught me doing it.

Besides, I found very little, at first.

There were restaurant receipts, phone cards, and chewing gum wrappers bundled up with girls' phone numbers and ballpoint pens. Nothing to suggest anything other than what I already knew him to be, a traveling charmer.

But I was patient. For nearly a month, I kept my head down, suffered the daily toil with the little monsters at school, and dutifully ate Jim's expertly prepared food every Friday night, all without sending him any more suspicious glares. I convinced myself he felt less threatened by me, because his stares had become friendly again, almost like a brother's. That meant I sometimes had a full two minutes to steal glances in all corners of the upstairs rooms, turning over mattresses and rugs, searching for anything at all to convince myself, once and for all, that I could prove what I knew in my heart to be true.

My first clue to what lay beneath Jim's considerate-boyfriend act came one night when he passed by in the upstairs hallway without noticing me inside one of the rooms. There was a large gilt-edged mirror there, flanked by candles. He stopped in front of the glass, leaning in to meet his own reflection. Then he bared his teeth, pulling the lips as far back as they would go, so that just the incisors and several centimeters of red gums showed. He didn't blink, but just stood there, eyes narrowed to black pencil strokes, admiring his choppers.

I didn't breathe as I peered at him from behind a crack in the door to room number seven, but in my brain all I could remember was a thing he'd once asked the audience down at the pub over in Adrigole.

Will he kill her or love her?

I knew his money was on anything but love.

A few more weeks went by without anything but tourists littering our streets with burger wrappers, beer bottles, and themselves.

Then, one Friday night when Jim and our aunt stood outside kissing, I found it.

I had already been through rooms number five, seven, and nine that night and discovered nothing but a used condom. The master bedroom had only his leather jacket, hanging from a chair like it was waiting for James fucking Dean to come back from the dead. I was just about to walk back out when I slid my hand inside the hidden motorcycle pocket I knew was sewn into the lining on the back. It's where he'd kept his ciggies the night he was at my place. I listened for footfalls on the stairs but heard nothing but Aunt Moira's girlish giggles from downstairs and knew I had at least thirty more seconds.

I unzipped the pocket and stuck two fingers inside.

What I felt was cold metal. I pulled out something golden and jangly that I'd seen a dead woman wear on the last night she drew a breath:

Sarah McDonnell's missing earring.

I held it in my hands long enough to know for sure that my aunt's new boyfriend, and the object of my fantasies, was a stone-cold killer. For the briefest moment, I considered slipping the gold hoop into my own pocket, but I knew Jim would notice it was gone. So as quietly as I could, I put it back, went back downstairs, and selected a smile appropriate for the occasion. Only Róisín read my blank expression and knew something ugly hid underneath.

Later, when my sisters helped serve the coffee, I was finally alone with Jim.

I stood with my back turned, putting spoons on saucers and trying to act normally, when I felt his breath on my neck. And I have to be honest with you. It was a toss-up between terror and thrill. Because, despite everything I knew, I couldn't get that night on the floor out of my head.

"You're ungrateful, you know that?" he said, never raising his voice or even bothering to sound threatening. "We had a good business, me and old Tomo. And then you go and follow us up the shagging mountain and see what we do. Can you blame him for wanting to carve you up like a flank steak? I mean, honestly?"

"Tomo killed Sarah McDonnell," I said. "Killed her sure as rain. But you kept the trophy."

He leaned over my shoulder with those wolf's teeth and didn't listen to anything but the black music in his own head. "And I killed Tomo for your bright eyes, d'you know that? He was going to do you and your two sisters and leave you in a ditch somewhere. Wouldn't be persuaded otherwise. I took a hammer to his face, don't ask me why. Maybe I'm becoming a soft touch. Or you were a hair better than most with yer skirt off."

The smile widened and became warmer as the voice dripped nothing but honeydew.

"But I make you this promise. I like hiding behind your Aunt Moira's skirts, confounding the gardaí. Fuck up that snug arrangement, like talking to yer good friend Bronagh one more time, and one of you three won't see the light of day." He gave my neck an almost friendly, reassuring brush. "So relax. We can all have a lot of fun."

I was about to ask him how much fun Mrs. Holland had when he squeezed the life out of her, but Aunt Moira came in the kitchen just then, with empty plates and a short come-hither dress.

"What are you two plotting?" she asked in jest, but still searched me with those radar eyes that remembered where Jim's pecker had been shortly before it chose her.

"Nothing but mayhem, darling," he said, turning slowly and kissing her on the neck. I could feel her delighted shuddering from where I stood. "And how to keep other men away from you."

It was so blatant, so obviously fake, I was sure Aunt Moira must have seen what lay beneath the smooth voice and easy smile. Instead, she let herself be wrapped in his arms as I carried out the tray and served dessert. She was a true believer, even with evidence staring her in the face.

I DIDN'T CARE about Jim's threats. God forgive me, I didn't, and I called down the wrath of all the most sinister demons on one of the two people I'll soon die for. For two days, I thought of how to tell Bronagh about Jim in a way that wouldn't make her lock me up right then and there, and also not arouse Jim's suspicions.

But he wasn't done shoring up his defenses, oh, no. I told you he was always a step ahead. So when me and my sisters each got a phone call from our aunt to meet her for tea on a regular Sunday afternoon, we knew it wasn't to discuss the menu for next week.

Aunt Moira had dressed in her new come-hither best—a black dress with a leather sash—and wore heels that would have caused a nun to make the sign of the cross.

On her finger, a diamond sparkled brighter than her eyes.

"We wanted you three to be the first to know," she said, lowering her voice to convey the idea that we were privy to a great announcement. "He's asked me to marry him. Two weeks from today, down at Sacred Heart." Moira looked at me and pursed her lips. "He especially asked that you be there, Fiona."

You bastard, I thought, not knowing what to answer, *of course you did.*

"I'd be honored," I managed to croak, and took a deep swig of red wine. Our aunt smiled, thanked us, and left a generous tip before sashaying out the door. My sisters and I repaired to McSorley's Bar afterward, trying to make sense of it all over several dirty pints of stout. I felt like Jim had fashioned a noose, made from equal parts charm, jealousy, and pure calculation, and was now strangling me in my own desires. And I still didn't know how to walk just down the street to Bronagh and tell her about the earring. I had half a mind to pump two shells into that ugly shotgun of Aoife's and finish the job myself.

ONE MORNING, JUST as I was in the middle of basic Irish history, Finbar moved things along all by himself.

"Where is she?" I could hear him yelling out in the school hallway, and even Mary Catherine looked startled. "Get your hands off! I want to talk to her. Fiona! You can't hide from me!"

The door banged open and I saw a version of my ex-boyfriend I'd never imagined.

His shirt looked like he'd slept in it, and the tie was frayed as he wobbled into my classroom smelling of expensive whisky. While only Mary Catherine held her ground at the desk right in front of me, a spot she'd won through ruthless infighting, everybody else shrank to the back wall.

"How could you do this to me?" he asked.

"Finbar, I have no idea what you're trying to—"

"You let him move in with your aunt like that? Your tinker whore? And you still sit down and have dinner with him, calmly as you please? Have you any clue what people are whispering about me?" His voice stumbled over that last *me* and became a sob.

"This has nothing to do with you," I said. "Now, will you please leave. You're scaring the children."

"*I'm* not scared," said Mary Catherine, both hands grabbing her desk as if Finbar was about to make off with it. Her face was a defiant little dinner roll of anger.

"Shut up, Mary Catherine," I snapped, feeling glorious about finally saying it. I had taken my eyes off Finbar for just a second to do so, when I felt his fist in my eye. The force of the blow socked me clear across the room, where I tumbled in a heap amid upturned desks and screaming children.

When Bronagh came with the other blue mice, I looked a fright. My cheek was swollen, little David was crying, and the entire school was in uproar.

"You want to file a complaint?" asked Bronagh, feeling sorry for me for the first time since I could remember. I could see her grumpy sergeant holding Finbar by the arm and whispering something unpleasant in his ear. Finbar was sobbing and kept nodding his head, big drops of teary snot dripping onto his Italian shoes.

"No, let it go," I said, feeling guilty as hell.

Bronagh seemed to like that decision, for she put her notebook away and again gave me that American-cop-show pat on the shoulder that meant I was all right. Mrs. Gately, into whose good graces I had recently hoped I could return, let me go home for the rest of the day. Her tight smile meant I had to start all over from the bottom, now that I had brought destruction to her tranquil school, loose woman that I was.

I slept like the dead all afternoon. Aoife and Róisín were both supposed to be over for dinner, but only my goth sibling made it on time, carrying a bottle of cheap red wine like a baby she'd kidnapped from an evil orphanage. We drank it and puffed half a pack of ciggies while we cooked. But Aoife still hadn't shown up by nine and didn't answer her mobile.

"I saw her car earlier," said Rosie. "It's been sitting up by her house all day long. She's not out with a fare."

"She'll be here," I said, trying to taste the sauce but feeling dread well up in me like an underground volcano. "She's probably just found herself a new boy."

"Probably," said Rosie, and looked sad. "I miss Evvie," she added, pouting, "but she's coming out next week."

When it was past midnight, even Rosie got worried. She'd texted Aoife all night and heard nothing, which had never happened before, even if our Taxi Driver had got lucky with someone. So up we went on our bikes, as skylarks twittered above us in the summer sky, pedaling faster than we ever had before, because both of us had a sense of foreboding we didn't dare tell each other about. In the pit of my stomach, I had saved Jim's warning like a black diamond that grew in size and frightening carat the more I thought about it.

Thump-thump!

I recognized the sound long before I saw the open door flapping in the wind.

"Aoife?" I called out, but got no answer. I looked at Rosie, who seemed unsure of what to do for the first time in years. The house was dark, and the hallway with all the dried hippie flowers on the wall was empty. A handful of leaves danced by themselves on the tiled floor, whipped around by the wind. Me and Rosie entered slowly, hearing nothing but the sound of our own thoughts.

"Aoif, are you here?" whispered Rosie, scaring herself, I could tell.

When we reached the living room, my fingers fumbled for the light switch and finally found it.

And now it became clear what had happened.

Both her comfy couches had been cut up like cattle, with woolen tufts hanging out of ragged gashes. Glass shards lay everywhere, along with Aoife's favorite books, which had been torn to bits. White wine still pooled in eddies near the door, which meant this had happened recently.

We were so stunned we didn't notice right away that we weren't alone.

A figure sat in the corner, huddled in a blanket and cradling herself. She looked ancient, her eyes glazed over and staring inward at something horrible. Not a sound escaped her throat.

"Aoife!" screamed Rosie, leaping over and taking her twin in her arms. Very gently, we removed the blanket and saw the beating she'd got. Red welts covered her arms and chest, and the polka-dotted dress had been torn to rags. She didn't react to the sound of her name. For hours, we just sat there, huddled together like red Indians at camp, trying to forget the gruesome raid visited upon us by white cavalry and listening to the sound of our sister's beating heart.

When dawn came up, Aoife turned her head to me and said, "He told me it was your fault." Her voice had been run through a filter that removed all emotion.

It was Jim. Of course it was.

While I made tea and tried to get Aoife to at least sip some of it, she told us how he'd come by under the guise of having to tell her a secret.

As soon as the door had closed behind him, however, he had wiped the floor with her, torn her clothing, and raped her for hours.

"He said the only reason he didn't kill me this time is that Aunt Moira was expecting him home for dinner," said Aoife, in that graveyard voice. "But he promised he'd be back."

I've told you before that the three of us became murderers, and that early morning is when we took our vows. While Aoife finally slept in my arms, I noticed Róisín picking out the sharpest knife in the kitchen and putting it in her bag.

"Time to shut that fucker down," she said, in the tone of voice that left no doubt she meant it.

BUT WAIT.

I hear my darling aunt downstairs again. Remember how I told you, when you first picked up this book, that I wasn't sure how much time we'd have together? Well, we just ran out. So if you've read this far, say a prayer for us and hope that me and Rosie's diaries find their way out of here somehow. Mine may make its way to the post office, and hers will be sent to where old Father Malloy, that old devil, can throw flowers on it. Perhaps I can hold off Moira long enough to keep her from hurting Rosie, but I'm not so sure. Maybe she'll nail us both before I can get my licks in. All I'm begging for is one good chance to run her through. I won't be seeing the pyramids now, so if you get the chance, take a picture of them for me.

Here she comes. Easy, Rosie, easy. Don't cry. Wait for it. I'll protect you for as long as I can.

And you, dear unknown reader, remember what I told you. Despite our faults, think kindly on my sisters and me. God bless you for turning the pages. Everything you've read is the truth, the good and the bad.

Remember me.

Remember us.

And should you ever pass by our sainted aunt's grave, feel free to spit on it.

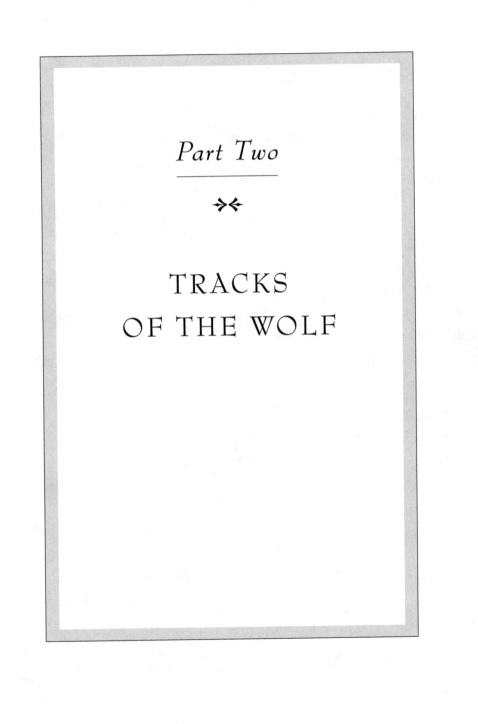

Part Two

TRACKS
OF THE WOLF

· 4 ·

Niall rested his fingertips on the word *grave* for a long time and felt like he was drunk on a black exotic wine he would never be able to stop drinking.

He could feel the blood thrumming in his ears and didn't know which image from Fiona's tale to hold up to the light for further inspection. Her first meeting with Jim? No, that was believable enough. The brief affair that changed her life, then? Should he reexamine the violent death she and her sister suffered along with their aunt, not a quarter mile from where Niall had sorted mail day after day? Impossible to choose. Disjointed, angry pictures raced through his head, both real and imagined, in which wolves and men in black skins pursued women up craggy hillsides and impenetrable forests. He touched that last page and felt as if he could see Jim, could almost reach out past the onionskin paper and touch his scruffy cheeks, to make sure he wasn't just a creative figment of Fiona's imagination. It impressed him that up until the final printed words, her handwriting hadn't wavered or broken from fear. It was steady as a killer's pistol eye right down to the last period. A fat line had been drawn underneath, like a final curtain. But what did it mean that Father Malloy "can throw flowers on it"?

More than anything, he wanted to sit down with Fiona and just talk to her. He'd never met a girl like that, who dared to admit her faults and vulnerabilities while also making clear that her spine was made from some kind of rare, still undiscovered chromium steel. Would they have been friends? he wondered. Most likely she wouldn't even have noticed he was there, like most girls he'd wanted to sit close enough to touch. He'd been past what people called "the murder house" on Strand Street a while ago and knew exactly where Fiona had swung that shovel, which didn't quite cut off Moira's head but secured her a headstone, all the same. Niall wasn't going to go to Fiona's grave and make some senti-mental promise to see the pyramids, because he knew she would have rolled her eyes and called him an eejit for wasting his time with the dead.

What to do, then?

He turned the diary over in his hands, but differently this time, as if it were filled with liquid thoughts that could leak out if handled roughly. The guards, was it? Would he sit in a front office while some sergeant listened to how Niall had lifted the diary from the post office illegally and taken it home? Suppose as he tried to smile and extricate himself like a good Samaritan, that same fat-faced mucksavage put his sausage fingers to the keyboard and found out that one Niall Francis Cleary, only child to Martin and Sarah, had once barely escaped an assault charge?

So what if it had happened when he was fifteen and had stood, back to the stone wall at school, while crazy Larry and his eager helper Char-lie the rat had pelted him with rocks and called his mother a fucking cripple because she used a cane? So what if Charlie's and Larry's parents had withdrawn the charge only because Niall's father had provided them with free plumbing and supplies and silent apologies for years afterward? They had never spoken of it at home. But whenever his mother made him dinner and asked him how it tasted, he could hear the gratitude in her voice.

Sure. The cops would listen to *him*, wouldn't they? Would they fuck.

But the rest of what happened to Róisín and Aoife lay somewhere at the Sacred Heart Church in Castletownbere, if old Father Malloy was still there. He closed his eyes and tried to imagine who had managed to escape from the basement in Moira's murder house. Was it Aoife and, if so, why hadn't she been found? Could it have been the stalwart Evvie, coming to the party late and leaving early? Or maybe poor Finbar had finally stopped crying and tried for a rescue but failed? It couldn't possibly have been the town skeptic and brownnoser Bronagh, unless she'd begun doing actual police work instead of kissing up to her senior colleagues. Niall chose a fat elastic band from his desk and wrapped it around Fiona's diary before stuffing it into his backpack. He was going to keep this accidental book of the dead to point him in the right direction whenever he needed some extra courage.

This was one mystery he had to solve by himself.

Brringg!

Niall knew from the impatient intake of breath who it was before even hearing Mr. Raichoudhury's overbearing voice.

"It is half ten, Mr. Cleary," said the most senior postperson in all of Ireland, whom Niall had forgotten about since opening the book and reading the first page. "Is one therefore to presume that you either have a terminal illness or that dastardly bandits stole into your abode last night and made off with all the clocks in the house? Because I expected you here at eight. Please, Mr. Cleary, be so kind as to enlighten me."

Jesus! Niall glanced out the salt-caked windows and saw the sun already hanging high above the construction cranes transforming the Mun into yuppie nirvana. Oscar glared at him and sprinted out into the kitchen rather than witness the impending humiliation. His orangeade-colored tail gave Niall a swat on its way out, just in case he'd forgotten who was boss.

"I really apologize, Mr. Raichoudh—"

"Am I to understand, then, that you aren't missing a lung or some other vital organ? And that no intruders are holding you hostage to your duties, even now?"

"I was reading a book, sir," said Niall, running his fingertips over the black fibers again. He pretended he was speaking to Fiona on some divine two-way shortwave and tried tuning out the words of the little Napoleon.

"While that is no doubt a vast improvement on your predilection for drawing childish pictures, Mr. Cleary, as the senior representative for An Post in Malahide, I see no other choice but to let you go. I trust you don't find this in any way unreasonable or harsh?" Mr. Raichoudhury sounded wounded at having to finally lower the boom after three warnings. It would have been trite to call him a mentor. But the older man had the born officer's concern for his men—even those who kept letting him down.

Niall could hear his aristocratic nose exhaling two years of disappointment. "No worries at all, Mr. Raichoudhury. You've every right. I haven't been at my best."

"I will make sure you receive your last check in no more than five working days," said the voice, sounding almost fatherly. "Good luck to you, Mr. Cleary, and don't hesitate to ask for a recommendation." There was a slight pause, before the martinet added, "Would you permit me to make a personal observation? You may say no, of course."

"I'd be curious, sir," said Niall, watching Oscar mangle a bag of lemon crèmes he'd bought for himself. The green eyes swung his way and told him to mind his own business.

"I once had a teacher who was mesmerized by pictures and images of every kind," Mr. Raichoudhury began. The keeper of the Bengal Lancer's flame sounded many centuries away as he went to the faraway place he liked best. "His wife and children had begun to disinterest him. One day, in the market square, he saw a painting of Vishnu, in the image of the deity resting on the eternal sea, with many worlds pouring through his skin, shaping the universe. But he couldn't afford to buy it. So he bought paper and colored ink instead, and sat in front of it, day and night, attempting to copy its magnificence in detail. Rains came, and withering droughts. My teacher started to cough, but still he painted. His wife and daughters pleaded with him to come home, but he wouldn't listen." Mr. Raichoudhury coughed once, signaling that the punch line was right around the corner. "You see, Mr. Cleary, my teacher died in the street one night, overcome with pneumonia and exhaustion. His family was left destitute, and only by the grace of God did the children avoid being thrown into the street. Now do you see what I'm trying to tell you?"

Niall felt a pinprick of anger punching through his guilt at having slacked off at work but tried to hold his tongue. "To be straight with you, sir, no, I don't, really."

The imaginary officer sighed, as if he'd just thrown pearls before the dumbest swine in the yard. "Don't live for dead pictures, Mr. Cleary," he said, clucking his tongue like a disappointed mother. "They will suck you in and bury you alive."

Mr. Raichoudhury rang off, and Niall knew that the senior postperson had been all too right. He already had in his mind an image of three women circling a gray-backed wolf, knives low to the ground as they waited for the right moment to attack. At some point, he knew, he'd have to draw that scene. Otherwise, he'd get a headache from the backlog of pictures in his mind.

Niall quickly stuffed some T-shirts into his backpack, scooped up Oscar in his arms, and asked the two biology students across the hall to take care of him for a while. As Jennifer and Alex smiled and closed the door, Niall caught one last glimpse of those judgmental feline eyes. They seemed to say, *Wherever you go now, I hope you break your neck doing it.*

THE WOLF CAME more alive the farther west the train went.

Niall had boarded the early InterCity at Heuston Station and plunked himself down by the window. The car was nearly empty, and he had no one but someone's lost suitcase and a sleeping teenage girl wearing headphones for company. He took a few bites of a sandwich and stared out the windows, wondering how long his meager reserves of less than a hundred euros would last.

As the concrete suburban row houses gave way to tumbledown stone walls and rain-soaked fields, Niall took out his sketch pad and, almost without conscious thought, brought to life a monstrous eye, watchful and unblinking. While the girl and the rocking motion of the train disappeared, he was sucked into the blank paper, just as Mr. Raichoudhury had predicted. The eye soon was ringed with stiff fur, a narrow, hungry face, and teeth only barely covered by the black color of the snout.

Niall didn't hear the announcer welcoming travelers on board the green-and-white train and informing them that the next station was Thurles, with terminus in Cork City. For around his wolf a forest slowly grew, dense and lush, with trees you could almost hear whisper warnings of ominous creatures, if you leaned down and put your ear right next to the paper. He was in the middle of drawing a castle, with a coal-black gate in the middle of an imposing wall, when he looked at the wolf again. The legs were pretty good but still not right. There was something innate in the creature's physique, in its very nature, he was unable to capture. Perhaps, he realized, the secret to rendering true danger lay not in copying its physical shape but in trying to sense a predator's pulse, his built-in reflexes and atavistic fear of capture. Niall leaned back, sighed, and put down the pencil. The wolf still looked like a dog, albeit a slightly more dangerous one. The girl awoke and fixed him with a disinterested glare before turning her shoulder to him and going back to sleep. As the tea cart came past, Niall folded the drawing and put it back into his portfolio. He had to admit how little he knew about danger, or evil, or any of the myriad of strange events Fiona had described. If he were going to get through the journey he had embarked upon, he would have to heed the senior postmaster's warning, at least for a bit.

The announcer's voice came back on the loudspeakers, soothing and authoritative.

"Good morning, and thank you for traveling with Iarnród Éireann. The next station is Limerick Junction. Connections for Limerick, Ennis, and Tralee. This train is for Cork."

Niall ate the rest of his sandwich and stared out the window again. Before him, beyond the scratched glass, lay an open field, sloping up toward a range of blue-black trees. Beyond them, he couldn't see.

But for the first time since picking up Fiona's diary and becoming the impulsive guardian of her story, he felt afraid.

IT WAS NEAR dark by the time Niall succeeded in getting himself a ride anywhere near where he needed to go. No buses ran from Cork all the way to Castletownbere until six in the evening anyway, so he had stood in the freezing rain for hours by the train station, wondering if it was worth it. Cork City, lying below the iron railing anchoring Kent Station to the rest of town, appeared to him as a vast gray carpet of uniform cement blocks that could have been anywhere in the world at all.

Cabdrivers, shuttering themselves against the downpour, had walked back and forth across the road to the pub, glaring at him as the itinerant hard-class traveler running out of cash he so obviously was. Niall waved at them halfheartedly and wondered whether Jim had experienced the same feelings of inadequacy when he had roamed the same landscape. Probably he hadn't. Jim would have already talked his way into someone's dry and warm bed, now, wouldn't he?

A kid on a motorcycle pulled over, double-tapped his brake lights, and turned his head.

"Where ya goin'?"

"As close to Castletownbere as possible," answered Niall, picking up a strange music somewhere in his ears that told him he might want to remain where he was. But his trainers were coming apart at the seams, and nobody had stopped for him in the last five hours.

There was a flash of teeth behind the smoke-colored visor, and the fella behind the handlebars nodded and said, "Hop on, then, unless ya want to grow roots."

Niall soon regretted clambering on behind the rider and grabbing hold of his waist, because the black bike bucked and roared off the hill with a scream that rattled the panes in the well-behaved pink and green row houses. His stomach soon pressed against his spine from the inside.

With the rain whipping into his eyes, Niall peered around the leather-jacketed shoulder of what he assumed was a younger man than himself, judging by the slim build, but saw only a blurred onrush of trees they barely missed. He felt his fingers slowly losing their grip from the amount of torque, and yelled at the guy to slow the fuck down. But whether on purpose or because he just couldn't hear, the man whose waist felt bony to the touch merely squeezed the throttle even further.

"What are ya doing way the hell out on Beara?" the man asked, leaning hard left onto the soft shoulder to avoid a delivery lorry coming straight for them in the middle of the road. "Nothing much to do besides drink and chase Euro-babes around, anyway. What are ya, then, some sort of writer? Or a damn nature walker?"

"Postal clerk," Niall yelled back, teeth chattering like castanets.

"Fair play to ya!" The rider laughed and straightened out the bike as the road plunged down a steep incline, revealing the frothing sea just beyond the coastal road. "Ya never see a State employee actually caring about delivering mail anymore in weather like this. It's admirable, is what it is." The rain abated and was transformed into fog, which blew across the narrow blacktop like clouds that had taken a wrong turn at the last roundabout. The engine drowned out something else the cheerful speed freak tried to say, and he managed to coax another jerky acceleration out of the whining engine as Niall was carried deeper into a territory where not even the patient boulders cared if he lived or died.

It was almost an hour before they finally stopped. Niall had considered throwing himself off the seat and into a muddy ditch several times but decided he'd kill himself trying. When the road had begun to wind and unwind like a fist the closer west they came, he nearly threw up on the rider's back. As a weather-beaten road sign proclaimed they were near BANTRY—BEANNTRAÍ, Niall tapped the guy on the back, hoping he'd finally stop squeezing that gas handle. To his amazement, the deafening noise abated and he felt the bike coming to an abrupt stop on the gravel near a fork in the road. Niall staggered off, trying to smile as he stuck out his hand in thanks. Wet pine branches swished against one another like brooms in the hard wind.

The rider flipped open the visor and winked.

Now Niall could see that the racer who had nearly got them both killed several times over was a girl, not much more than eighteen years old.

"Thanks a million," Niall said, "but I think I'll walk the rest of the way from here."

"You're welcome," the girl said, giving Niall a wry smile that seemed to judge his weak stomach. "You lasted longer than most. Remember: On this road, don't wait until you see headlights coming, but jump off as soon as you hear the engine, my advice. Otherwise, you'll feel the thump before ya know it. And then it's curtains, right?"

"Thanks."

The girl cocked her head and examined the sorry figure before her, whose long matted hair and frayed jeans didn't seem at all like regulation postal dress. "What's yer business out on Beara anyway, did you say?"

"I didn't say," answered Niall, feeling very alone at this bend in the road, wondering how many people had decided to jump off that bike before him and take their chances. "I'm looking for someone."

"Then find them quickly." The rider slammed the visor back down and squeezed the gas. There was another warning, but it came out muffled from behind the plastic, and was lost as she made a U-turn, roaring up the hill into a fresh low-lying cloud.

Niall stood on the shoulder for a while, listening to the sound of the engine fading away, leaving only the slapping noise of rain hitting the road sign. He still had more than thirty miles to go. One tennis shoe had opened far enough for his black sock to peer out like a curious salamander. There was one more echo far beyond the rocks, as the unknown rider forced the engine into higher gear. Then it was gone.

"I don't believe in omens," Niall said to the trees, in an effort to convince both them and himself and not believing a word of it.

· 5 ·

The only thing staring at Niall when he finally sloshed into Castletownbere was the lone IRA monument he remembered from Fiona's diary. Recognizing it immediately, he knew he was in the center of town.

Niall looked around the empty square, where early dawn did nothing to make the place feel more welcoming. It made his ill-conceived quest to discover the truth behind the Walsh sisters' deaths seem more hopeless as the weak sunlight brushed against the top of every structure. The unsmiling figure in the center of the stone cross, wearing a bandolier across its natty overcoat, face turned sternly to the left, was depicted cradling a captured British Lee-Enfield rifle and waiting for orders to use it. The man's granite eye looked into Niall's and didn't whisper any kind of greeting.

The Lobster Bar and the Spinnaker Café on the far side were both shuttered. A sorry-looking crêpe stand made from flimsy white plasterboard had been torn loose from its mooring by the wind and now banged into parked cars like a blind dog. O'Hanlon's and McSorley's pubs had their shades drawn, but voices carried ever so faintly out past the thick walls, daring him to enter and find out. Niall looked down at himself and decided, What the hell. I need a pint, I'm only starved, and I have to get dry somewhere. I need to think about what I've set out to do.

Nearly eleven hours of dodging lorries on the side of the road within an inch of his life had made him jumpy, and his nerves jangled as the brass bell above the doorway heralded his arrival.

The front of the bar tricked Niall's eye for a moment.

Dry goods were piled high on shelves to the left; there were Bewley's tea bags, soda crackers, and sweets, and he felt as if Fiona had been wrong about having first heard Jim begin to tell the story of the cursed Prince Euan in there. But the farther into the hushed room he went, the more he realized how much smaller the place was than he had originally imagined. A narrow bar section was separated from the grocery by an open doorway, and there was no real stage at all. Jim would have been able to maintain eye contact with everybody in the place from the back door next to the toilets. That would have been his point, of course: stare them full of that snake charm, then do what you will with any and all of the ones who don't have the sense to look away.

Split-in-half boat models with no masts or rigging hung next to wooden harps. Rapidly yellowing newspaper cutouts lauding the charm of the place were everywhere. God, was he thirsty all of a sudden, having eaten nothing but a packet of crushed crisps at the bottom of his bag that he'd forgotten about until Castletownbere was in sight. But there was no bartender that he could see, and he looked futilely into the darkened kitchen for signs of life.

"Help ya?" The voice was both low and patient and belonged to someone behind him.

Niall spun around and saw nothing at first. Next to where he'd entered, he now discovered there was a small enclosure to the right, the kind of squared-off wooden booth his mother once told him had been used for matchmaking in places where she grew up. Perhaps this one still served its intended purpose. On this evening, however, a head finally came into view from inside it that seemed uninterested in joining together two hearts beating in the same key. It was mean and flat, teeth hiding underneath a fleshy overhang that too many beers had turned from an upper lip into a permanent speech impediment. As Niall approached slowly, he could see the man was not alone in the former love nest; another pair of ruddy knuckles lay folded, for now, in a lap that also cradled a black pint of stout and one recently illicit cigarette, smoked down to the nub.

"Come for a pint," Niall tried, standing his ground. He may have looked like a geek, and he still wore T-shirts with drawings of Pickles the space monkey in its best attack mode, but nobody who had seen him in a fight would approach him lightly. Two years ago, he'd come to his first day of work next to Mr. Raichoudhury's desk sporting a swollen eye. The other guy had looked worse, whispered a girl from down in the emergency ward. A real mess.

The first man rose with the same sound a sofa cushion makes if you squeeze it really hard, and he regarded Niall for some time. Then he lumbered over behind the bar, pulled half a pint, waited for it to settle, and finished the job. Fingers with hardly any nails left on them pushed the glass in front of Niall with a deliberation that was neither friendly nor hostile. But he remained standing in the same spot while his young visitor tasted the first head. Reading him like a door opening very slowly.

"Yer here for the fishing, I take it?" asked the man, and his eyes connected briefly with the fella in the love nest. "Yer too early. Weather's turned, and the boats are coming back half empty, now." His dark brown gaze met Niall's, already reading his answer in there before listening to the lie that was right around the corner.

"Not really," said Niall, stalling for a fitting answer and feeling the silence in the room envelop him like a shroud. He'd grown up in a small town like this one, in a place called Kinnitty, out in County Offaly, where someone's first answer was never forgotten and always checked against what you might carelessly have told others. In places like that, a clumsy lie was discovered immediately, a talented one only slightly later. Niall considered telling the truth, then looked at the bartender's slack smile and low-to-the ground center of gravity and reconsidered. "Just meeting some friends," he said.

"Really?" said the man, who smiled for the first time, revealing a set of beautiful teeth that looked as if they had been lovingly fashioned by hand in some Beverly Hills dentist's office. Niall was certain they were fake. The real ones probably lay scattered in some other bar. The man in the wooden corral shifted his feet impatiently, waiting for the right moment to back up his friend. "I might know them, at that. What would their names be?"

"They're not from around here," said Niall, dodging that clumsy jab, taking a deep swig of his glass, and feeling that old defensive itch returning and spreading like warm jet fuel inside his belly. If everything goes to shite and this fucking skanger wants to make a meal of it, he thought, then I'm yer man, extra helpers or no. "There are three of them, in fact. Friends of mine from way back. Dated one of them. Great girl, ya see."

What was he *doing*? Why had he said that? Too late to take it back now. His fingers tightened as the fella in the love nest rose and walked slowly up to the bar, muddied shoes coming to a stop not two feet away. Before Niall saw the man's face, it was the shoes he couldn't tear his eyes away from. They were obviously expensive, and had once been lovingly made somewhere in Gucci-land, where it never snowed or rained. Now they looked crap, with the little brass horseshoes across the last looking like dull key chains. The tie around his neck, dyed a kind of dusty gray by sweat and sun alike, might once have been royal blue.

"Did you say *three* friends?" asked the rumpled man, who had risen from the enclosure, and the sheer emptiness of his voice finally made Niall look up and examine his face. It had once been handsome, with that high brow found mostly on the fortunate, but wrinkles now made it older than what might have been a good thirty-five years. Deep bags under his eyes were as distended and dark as ripe figs. This was a man, thought Niall, whom life had kicked right in the heart and then made sure to cut it out afterward for good measure. He couldn't get a read of the fella's eyes, because whatever light might once have emanated from them had been turned off from the inside and the cord yanked out permanently.

"Yes, three of them," lied Niall, keeping both hands steady. The man behind the bar had begun to shift his weight to the balls of his feet. This could end badly right now, old son, thought Niall, and felt his own body twitch with fresh rivers of adrenaline, which made him woozy and nearly high with pre-explosive excitement. "But I don't think they've made it here yet. They said for me to meet them here, when this place opened up."

"Lucky for you, then, that we never closed last night," said the bartender, sliding a fresh pint in front of Niall and the man with the hollow eyes.

"What are their names?" asked the man with the faded tie, his voice nearly begging for an answer. His mouth was open in supplication, and it frightened Niall more than it made him wonder which one of them he should try to hit first if that big fella behind the bar came out with a bat or some other foul surprise. "Please," persisted the man. "You see, I had three friends once too, ya know." His voice seemed to run out of air as he looked at the beer and added, "Funny how things work out. Funny . . ."

"Easy, Finbar," said the bartender, with surprising tenderness, including Niall in a stare that was meant to tell him that the figure in the Guccis ignoring the fresh pint in front of him might not be quite right in the head. "You ask everybody that who comes in here. This nice young man was just leaving." Another Hollywood denture smile that seemed considerably less patient with strangers who couldn't even be counted on to arrive with a decent cover story. "Weren't ya?"

"Thanks for the pint," said Niall, hefting his soaked bag and making for the door. The despondent guy with the wretched tie seemed familiar, but not enough to trigger a memory. Niall passed the old engagement booth, feeling both men's eyes on his back like darts, and realized that Fiona and her sisters had once sat exactly where the broken man had just nursed his cigarette moments ago and waited for Jim to spin his tales.

It was only as Niall emerged out in the narrow main street that it struck him who that disheveled creature was.

Fiona hadn't just broken Finbar's heart. The way she'd died had ensured he'd never grow a new one.

Castletownbere was still silent as darkness faded into silver out across the bay. The IRA volunteer's stony face looked as unsmiling as ever, even from a distance. The crêpe cart had finally escaped its noose and was being carried toward the wharf by a stiff offshore breeze that shook bicycles parked in racks. Niall squinted against the low sunlight, which rose just above Bear Island and crawled onto the moss-covered walls of a nearby roof, dyeing it dusty pink. He was going to slump in an alley nearby and try to sleep when he saw a Garda patrol car rolling slowly up the street, driven by a humorless-looking woman with her chin buried in her uniform blues. Niall sighed and began walking back out of town. There had been a sign near the road earlier, he remembered, barely visible by the dull orange streetlight. It had said something in Irish next to the words BED AND BREAKFAST.

He knew he was just being twitchy from the mad motorcycle ride. But the eyes of the town all looked at him as he went. What will I answer the next time someone asks me why I'm really here? Niall wondered, and found he couldn't answer it himself.

THE WOMAN CUTTING up strips of salmon for her guests' breakfast looked outside at the breaking dawn and, almost as if by instinct, put the boning knife down.

A sorry-looking figure came walking up her driveway, carrying something on its back. She was sure she had seen that same young man trudging by on the coastal road a few hours earlier, headed into town. When it was still dark, his chin had hung lower on those skinny shoulders, but the slouching gait was the same. At the time, she had stared out her bedroom window and dismissed him as one of those drugged-out kids come for that damn punker music and throwing up in her rosebushes on their penniless walk home.

Bing-bong went the doorbell, and she turned her head. That damn tramp stood outside the frosted glass, shuffling his feet as only the truly destitute could.

Laura Crimmins had lived her whole life in the modest split-level house by the bay where she was born. She was a mannish woman of indeterminate age, with larger upper arms than most of the fellas. Her shock-white hair was worn short to the head, and she preferred to treat guests at her tiny bed-and-breakfast cottage with a sharp dose of so much motherly friendliness at all times that they never saw how close she was to crying. Clark, her husband of thirty-eight years, had been dead just long enough for her to learn how to smile without anger at the ladies nodding silent pity at her down at the SuperValu. She wiped the knife and put it in her back pocket before going to answer the doorbell. Father Malloy would have called this situation "an opportunity for kindness." Laura agreed. But if she didn't like the look on the stranger's face—and all the neighbors said she read them better than cards in a deck—he wasn't stepping foot inside. After that Jim business, everyone looked twice now before they crossed the street, didn't they?

"Come about a room?" said the poor fella outside, and Laura felt genuine pity. He was practically a boy, with one shoe forever opening its mouth to speak, too.

"Right this way, my dear," said Laura, putting a hand on the young man's shoulder and feeling the water pressing through from the inside. It was happening again, even if she had promised herself to take on no more hard cases. Because despite his eejit T-shirt with that wretched monkey on it, this boy seemed utterly lost. "Yer drenched, poor lad," she said, already the mother she hadn't had occasion to be for many years. "Now, I want you to go into number eight and wash up. I will leave dry clothes for you outside the door. I want no argument."

Niall smiled in thanks and nodded his head. Perhaps, he thought, the myths about Munster folk being a suspicious and curmudgeonly lot were about as true as the legend about fairy unicorns roaming free next to them. "Ah, thanks a million," he said, squishing past. He turned, a look of apprehension on his face. One hand dove into a jeans pocket, fishing for whatever money was left. "What's the tariff?"

Laura took another hard look, past the wet hair and the carefree smile. She saw something beneath the eagerness to please. A defensive barrier, made from something she couldn't figure out yet. It could withstand temptation and flattery, though, she was sure of it. Whatever this young man harbored wouldn't encourage him in the dead of night to open the door to her quarters that had STAFF ONLY printed on it, ready to cut her throat. His hair was too damn long. But this boy was solid. "Say, thirty euro per night, and I'll make ya breakfast, as well?" she said, feeling the still-cold blade next to her butt cheek.

"Brilliant," said Niall, and walked over to his room. Then he stopped and turned.

"Was there something else?" asked the innkeeper. The young man's face looked like someone had just walked over his grave.

"This might sound odd, but . . . have you ever heard of a young girl riding a black motorcycle near these parts? Quite fast, like. And—erm, dangerous?"

Laura shook her head, eyes on the ceiling as she appeared to search her memory. "Och, no. Nobody like that." Then she lit up in a smile. "Is that a friend of yours I should be making up another room for?"

"No, just someone I met," Niall said, waving both hands in apology. "Thanks again. I'll see you tomorrow."

Laura watched him go inside his room and close the door behind him. Then she locked the front door and daubed her index finger in the Virgin Mary pool of holy water that hung by the mini-altar on the wall. Black riders. Never heard of such a thing, not around here. Still, everything was possible. She made the sign of the cross as she looked outside.

Because despite a gut feeling telling her this kid was honest enough, whatever haunted him surely wasn't.

NIALL HAD SAT at the tiny desk for just a few moments when Jim stirred inside him again.

He took out the plastic bag that contained his precious drawing paper and withdrew a single sheet. Fiona's diary already lay opened on the bed next to him, dog-eared in places where there was a scribble he couldn't quite decipher or where he'd found what could be an important clue to how the story might have continued. For instance, she had drawn crosses and check marks in the margin in several places, but it didn't appear to be connected to any one direction that Niall could figure out.

On one separate page, Fiona appeared to have made some kind of crude map of the area, with an X through a few towns, leaving others unmarked: Castletownbere had two crosses, while Drimoleague deserved just one. Niall guessed that meant both Sarah and Tomo had died in the first, while the Holland widow merited only one marker. Adrigole, Eyeries, and Bantry were unblemished. Question marks dotted almost every other town nearby, as if roving death on a motorbike stalked sheep, goats, schoolboys, and fair maidens of the distant past. Despite his own creative imagination, Niall had to frown at that. It was all too perfect. But as much as he wanted to doubt Fiona's ever-decreasing sanity inside her aunt's murder house as she had jotted her version of events down for him to read, there had still been a real wolf out there, hadn't there?

Jim hadn't just bragged about hammering Tomo to death, Niall's good sense told him. He looked again at Fiona's testimony about where he had committed either acts of love or of a darker nature, and her story seemed logical again. Niall felt the *seanchaí*'s presence very closely, as if he were standing outside the windowpane even now, breathing on the glass and writing his name in the hot breath. Niall flipped back to the final page again. "Murderers," Fiona had said they vowed to become, but did she and her sisters ever have the time to fulfill that promise, before Aunt Moira turned out *their* lights?

There was that stirring again, just as he'd felt from the balls of his feet to the top of his head that first night at the post office. It was almost a pain inside his skull, so forceful were the images contained therein, tapping on the bone from inside to be let out and play.

This time, a hand grew, almost without Niall's help, on the middle of the blank page.

It was soon connected to a leather-jacketed arm, which became a whole man, lunging forward for someone, mouth half open. Niall drew the fingers longer than he'd wanted, but they fit with the slender legs, rendered in mid-run, thigh muscles visible through the ripped denim. Jim's eyes, strangely, were the last thing to become animated, but they were too dull and lifeless. He erased them and tried for a genuine set of wolf eyes, but that looked even worse, like a bad Japanese *anime* cartoon. Niall was about to try rendering Jim's prey with the well-chewed charcoal pencil, when the door swung open behind him without warning.

"Can't have ya running around catching pneumonia, now can w—"

Mrs. Crimmins cut herself off in mid-sentence, and Niall threw the diary on top of the half-finished drawing, a second too late for privacy. He read something in his hostess's eyes that the bright smile couldn't quite cover up fast enough. She'd seen a brief flicker of what swam around in his brain. And nobody—except, perhaps, that famous American comic book artist Todd Sayles—was allowed to see that.

"Thanks so much, Mrs. Crimmins," said Niall, seeing the neatly folded clothes in her arms. "That's too kind."

Mrs. Crimmins set down a pair of men's jeans, a sweater, an overcoat, and a pair of barely used boots at the foot of the bed and wiped her perfectly dry palms in the apron, as if to wash herself of the items forever. "Not at all, young man. Not at all." She turned up the warmth dial in her eyes, as if she'd never noticed a thing. "And will you be having breakfast tomorrow?"

"Yes, please. Is half eight all right?"

"Salmon and eggs at half eight, my love," repeated Mrs. Crimmins in her singsong incantation that signified professional distance, exiting the room quickly. She shut the door without a sound.

Niall sat there a moment, feeling like his mother had just surprised him with a porno mag in his free hand. He brushed aside the diary and looked at the unfinished sketch. He'd gone about this all wrong, as usual. It wasn't just the wolf from earlier that he'd failed at. If you can't properly imagine what the predator is *chasing,* how can you ever hope to make his desire lifelike? Niall rose, locked the door, and sat back down. Mrs. Crimmins probably thought he was some pervy artist, but it was too late to change that now. He bent over the paper and tried to imagine how it might have felt to have Jim's hand seizing his own neck right before squeezing the life from it. He remembered Sarah McDonnell's earring and her lifeless feet, Tomo's shattered face. "How are you going, ladies?" the storyteller had asked with a grin, before setting to work. And Mrs. Holland, if Jim had been her murderer, may have got herself no flirting hellos at all.

Something began to happen.

A female form appeared under Niall's pencil, just ahead of Jim's lunging hands.

Her shoulders came first, twisted as she ran, and sprouted a slim back, hips, and legs, kicking against the pursuer's grip. Why am I so drawn to all this? Niall asked himself, but felt the answer coming in the shape of a lovely brow and a set of wide-open blue eyes, rather than intellectual thought. Now the entire composition made more sense, with prey and predator entwined in a dynamic dance of death.

But even if the wolf was human this time, the eyes were still wrong. Niall erased them yet again and tried for a narrow, hungry gleam to go with the murderous pose. He added dark shades to make the rest of the face disappear. Shit! Now Jim looked sleepy, not dangerous. Niall put down the pencil, disgusted with himself. Maybe bringing evil to life meant actually having to touch it in the flesh first?

The only real death Niall had seen had been when little Danny Egan from across the street had come out second in a game of chicken with a bus. They had both been around eleven or so, and Danny had just left Niall's house, where they had tried to tape their hurling sticks the way the pros did it, ten thumbs and all. Niall's mum had called after him not to run across the street, and her voice was cut off by the thudding noise. From the front yard, Niall could clearly see the naked legs beneath the undercarriage, one shoe still untied. They had looked like wax.

That same night, feeling like a ghoul, Niall had taken pencil and paper and stolen underneath his blanket with a flashlight. The adults had talked about "the tragedy" and "a young life snuffed out," but those words didn't kick-start any feelings inside himself, just a thick, aching sense that none of it had seemed real.

So he put pencil to paper and watched something happen he barely understood, even now. A pair of shoes became two *real* legs, fused to a real boy's prone body. He began to feel pangs of fear and loss. Danny, his best friend, was dead! By the time he was finished, bus on top of Danny's unseen torso and a garda added in the drawing for good measure, Niall was sobbing so loudly both his parents came to see what was the matter.

The pen and pencil had become magic. Everything else since then, to Niall, had been an echo of the real world that existed only in two dimensions.

Niall got up and walked over to the window, where the sun now rose high above Bear Island, transforming it back into a peaceful tourist trap. No wolves lurked anywhere, even those wearing jeans. There was no opportunity to meet anything dangerous. Perhaps, he thought, he'd made a mistake coming out here. He lay down on the bed just for a moment, testing the springs. Tomorrow, he'd begin exploring the tracks of the wolf, beginning with that school. Perhaps, he imagined, Fiona had left something behind she didn't even think to include in the diary.

Soon, he was asleep. And in his dreams, the black gate opened, sending an army of mounted cavalry into the world, each horseman armed only with the deadliest smile in creation.

"WHO ARE YOU?"

The voice was brisk as a cold shower and about as pleasant. Niall stood in the empty classroom at Sacred Heart Primary School, hunched over at least the eighteenth teacher's desk in as many minutes that afternoon, and had just put his fingers on an old copy of a book called *Lost Treasures of the Pharaoh* when it dawned on him that he wasn't alone. He raised his head and was greeted by a set of eyes that demanded nothing less than unwavering answers.

"Are you that Mr. Breen?" the little girl wanted to know, heels together like a drum majorette. "That would make you our *third* substitute teacher this month."

Niall regarded the spit-shined patent leather shoes and the fingers
clutching her desk set and didn't need to think twice to know the identity of his inquisitor.

"You must be Mary Catherine," he said, trying not to grin at her like
some kind of weird stranger with candy.

Mary Catherine adjusted her barrette and eyed him warily. "Maybe,"
she said, looking behind her out the half-open door. "I show up early
for class, making sure the blackboard has been cleaned and that there is
enough chalk." She narrowed her eyes and her mouth became a tight
ringlet of distrust. "Where are your books?"

"I . . . thought it best first to see what your class is learning now," he
answered, thinking on his feet, but not quickly enough to make this
child unclutch her weapon. In about a minute, Niall knew, she'd be
howling bloody murder down the hallway, and he'd be done for burglary or worse. "Must be confusing to have had so many teachers since
Miss Walsh. Did you like her?"

Mary Catherine sat down behind her front-row desk, which was still
only inches away from the teacher's. Her hands lay folded across an impressive stack of notebooks that would have made a librarian envious.
That little brow loosed somewhat, and her voice dripped with the kind
of melancholy people use to describe doddering relatives, long passed.
"She wasn't a bad sort," said the child, "except when that Jim person
was around. Then she went nuts. They say their aunt killed her and her
sisters, but my mum tells me it was the other way around." For the first
time, the eyes looked unguarded, even curious. "Did you know Miss
Walsh? I mean, know her outside of work?"

"Only a little. We were old friends from Dublin." Niall eyed the door
without appearing to do so and hoped the kid didn't notice. Less than
two minutes left before the next bell, and he still hadn't found any more
clues. He would go down to find Father Malloy next, and invent some
kind of airtight excuse about wanting to see Róisín's diary, if it still ex-

isted. "Did she keep any kind of notebook here at school anywhere, do you know? Just in case I need to see a record of your studies?"

Any hope Niall might have had of uncovering another of Fiona's hidden treasure troves about the town's most famous scandal faded as the girl searched her book pile without even looking. She pulled out a pristine pink hardback with Hello Kitty stickers neatly affixed by the animal's head size. "I took notes on everything she taught us," said Mary Catherine with a smile wider than a cat's to spilled cream. "And even more on what she missed whenever she was seeing . . . him."

Niall took the notebook and leafed through endless rows of missing lessons, indexed in four different colors of Magic Marker. There was nothing about what he really wanted to know. How did Jim manage to blur the traces he had left all over the surrounding countryside and on any number of people who already knew better? He should have gone straight to Father Malloy for the next chapter of the sisters' story. Jim's opium, even from a distance, had begun to dull Niall's good senses, too.

"This Jim character," said Niall, in too bright a voice for the occasion, pretending to study Mary Catherine's demerit list with real interest. "Did he die suddenly?"

Mary Catherine's proud look expecting of praise evaporated, and her smile turned nastier than a summer storm. "Everybody here knows what happened to *him*," she said, looking Niall's ill-fitting wardrobe up and down for the first time and smelling a rat. "If you were such a close friend of Miss Walsh's, why don't you?"

"We haven't been . . . close for a while," Niall said, stalling, feeling uncomfortably like the worm at the end of the hook in a very large ocean. He wasn't encouraged by Mary Catherine's metal smile, braces and all, as she rose and took back her pink attendance sheet with a hard yank.

Brringg! went the bell. Niall wondered why none of the other children had come barging in, and didn't like how he could hear no voices squealing in the hallway.

"Are you *really* Mr. Breen?" she asked, cocking that efficient little head like it was spring-loaded.

"Never said I was," Niall answered, shooting her an apologetic smile that failed to impress. "I'm sorry, but I'm not your new substitute teacher."

The girl straightened her back like the Queen of Sheba on her throne, just before pronouncing judgment on captured enemies.

Niall followed her gaze out the window, where the garda woman he'd seen earlier that morning was walking up the steps.

"Never believed you were. And now we'll see what *they* have to say about it," Mary Catherine chirped, walking out and leaving Niall alone with Fiona's dead pharaohs.

BRONAGH'S FINGERS TOOK their time turning over the long-haired fella's An Post ID card.

"Now, yer not chasing down stamp thieves out here," she said with a sigh. "So what are ya doing? Frightening children for the fun of it? Or exposing yerself to them, more like." They sat in the squad car she'd inherited after Sergeant Murphy, her eternal shadow of discipline, had finally retired. Outside its windows, Mrs. Gately, the headmistress, stood at a polite distance, sweatered arms crossed, glaring at Niall. Mary Catherine, never too far behind to be noticed, was next to her, no doubt fantasizing about a violent spectacle to top off the arrest.

"I did nothing of the sort!"

Bronagh caught Mary Catherine's eye. "Not what *I* heard. So what are ya doing?"

"I'm looking for someone."

"So you tell everyone who cares to listen. Except yer not telling them much else, are ya? Poor Finbar is only at his wits' end every time he sees a stranger at McSorley's. I know what yer all like. Come for the scoop? To find out 'how it all began'?" She pursed her lips as if getting ready to belt him one. "Your kind have trampled through here since Fiona and Róisín died. Vampires, all of yis!" Bronagh looked through Niall's still-damp backpack with the same distaste as if the contents were raw sewage. "Some ratty old T-shirts, spare trousers, socks. Cadbury milk bar, half eaten." She looked up in surprise. "Didja leave the camera at Laura's? Figure it would give you away? No shame in you. No shame at all."

"I'm no journalist," said Niall, watching some of the parents huddle close enough to the car door to make a rush for it and tear him into little bits. "I—"

I'm what, then? he thought, knowing he'd never imagined ending up in this mess. I'm a thief, a liar, and a slacker squandering the public's trust, is what. And I'm about to join Fiona's Chinaman soon unless I think of something.

Bronagh's mouth hung open, one eyebrow ready to believe him, but not much else. "Yer what? One of those crystal worshippers come to save us from the 'evil that lives in this town'? Believe me, now the news cameras finally left, I'm still cleaning up those crazies every now and again. So let's have it."

"I'm a postal clerk in the town where those girls died," Niall finally admitted, drawing a breath of air to steady his hands, which had begun to shake. "Right after it happened, one of them, Fiona, posted her diary. It ended up in my dead-letter bin. I read it. There are more questions than answers in it. And that's why I'm here."

Outside the window, parents had started to gather. One of the fathers hefted a hurley and looked back at Niall with something like vulpine hunger for blood. Mary Catherine walked over to him with a puppy-dog face and pointed at the car. Daddy, look what the bad man made me do. That little witch! thought Niall. It won't be long now.

But to his surprise, Bronagh started the car and waved at the obviously disappointed lynch mob. Her face was impassive, as people informed of a great loss usually are right before the feelings kick in. As the car sped down the hill, the last thing Niall saw was Mary Catherine's patient face. Can't keep running in a town this small, it seemed to say. You and my father will meet again soon enough.

"This conversation we're about to have," said Bronagh, in a voice much less cocksure than the New York City TV cop she had always pretended to be, "I'll swear on my mother's name never happened. And we're not going to the station to talk."

THE DARK BUTTER-COLORED grass covering the Caha Mountains like hundreds of sparse wigs whipped in the wind, as it always did. Sheep glared with mild disinterest.

Niall sat in the passenger seat of the patrol car, stomach curling into knots of embarrassment as he listened to Bronagh verifying his story over the phone with the only person who could. Even from the next seat over, that voice of well-thought-out disappointment in a raw recruit was more than he could bear.

Bronagh smirked and turned her head to him. "He says he expected better of you, pretending to be a postal clerk when you've really been fired and all."

"I never said I wasn't."

She held out an admonishing finger while listening to the rest, coming through the mobile like the very essence of a Bengal Lancer's honor code. "Now he says something about how you didn't listen to what he tried to warn you against," Bronagh added. "And how he's sure you've been sucked into the pictures again. Have you any idea what he's talking about?"

"Yes," admitted Niall, and locked eyes with a sheep right outside, chewing the grass. He thought of the wolf once more, except this time it had meshed with Jim's image in his mind, creating a kind of half-human figure. "Unfortunately, I do."

"Thanks a million, Mr. Raichoudhury," said Bronagh, ringing off. She exhaled while she shooed the animal away, then looked out at the sea. "I failed her, you know. She was my best friend once, Fiona was, and she came to me needing help. Róisín did, too. And I *didn't* help. Now it's too late."

"Maybe it isn't." Niall reached in the back of his jacket, and Bronagh jumped at him with a can of mace ready to go.

"Wait! I have something to show you!" shouted Niall, less than a second before eating pepper spray. Slowly, he withdrew the now even more battered diary and handed it over. "Here it is. See? I couldn't help reading it, when it was just lying there with a dead woman's name on it, could I? I'm sorry. But I've come too far already to worry about an arrest for stealing public property, Garda." He hesitated, watching Bronagh's eyes brimming with tears as she carefully opened the book, touching the pages as if they would burn if she looked at them for too long. "She was your friend, I know," he continued, a bit more carefully. "But I've come to know her, too. In my own way."

There was only the sound of the wind rocking the car, and of the sheep trying to nibble on the paint job. Out in the bay, two trawlers bucked against a headwind, aerials bending as far back as they would go.

"Thanks for letting me see this, really," said Bronagh, having got some of her composure back. "But you still haven't told me why you've come. And what you were doing inside the school. Parents will be calling me. Soon."

"Then tell 'em I was Fiona's exotic Dublin ghetto boyfriend," said Niall, frustrated with all the gaps in his knowledge. "I wanted to find out more of what took place in that house, and of what happened out here. To Aoife. And to Jim."

Bronagh's eyes grew distant, and that frightened Niall more than her anger.

"We never speak much of that man out here anymore," she said. "And neither should you."

"Oh, really? Then what about Julie Ann Holland over in Drimoleague? I suppose she died from slipping on a banana skin, is that it?"

Bronagh's hand clutched the pepper spray again. "You haven't a fiddler's fuck what yer talking—"

"There's another diary in town somewhere," Niall said, so loudly that a sheep outside flinched and scurried at the sound. "Róisín wrote one as well, if you believe what your friend Fiona says! I haven't a clue how either book made it out of that house, but Róisín's was sent to Father Malloy, unless it never got—"

Bronagh grabbed Niall by the scruff of the neck and pulled. "Police brutality is just a word, Niall. Until I break both yer arms and leave you here." She saw no fear in his eyes and let go after a long breath, even smoothing out his collar.

"I forgot," said Niall, heart racing. "You always wanted to be a TV cop in America."

The husky garda fished around in the console for a cigarette and pushed some angry air out her nostrils when she found none. "Shut up. I've chased away goth girlies, journos, and yer ordinary sick souvenir hunters for weeks. The first place they all go is to Father Malloy's, since a Dublin newspaper article had the grace to mention our church by name." She tapped on the glass to make that same persistent sheep go away. "Trouble with that is, the good Father passed away more than a month ago now, God rest him. If anybody sent him anything, I would have found it. Me and some of Fiona's students cleaned out his office afterward. But people like you still come. Looking for 'the truth.' Right?"

"Only the truth about what Fiona and her sisters did to Jim," said Niall, without hesitating. "And to whether or not he killed more than just his old friend Tomo." He felt his face flushing the same way it had when he thought the bartender was going to stomp his guts. What the hell was she holding out on him for? Hadn't he proved his good intentions? "But you wouldn't know about that, would you? Sarah McDonnell? And one more girl in Kenmare, if you believe Róisín's radio voice. Ring any bells? What happened to Aoife? She go the same way as them? Shall I go look for her in old Glebe Graveyard, or what?"

Bronagh started the engine. Her chin was again resting firmly on the slick uniform jacket. When she spoke, the last trace of friendliness was gone. She handed Niall the diary as if it contained thoughts that could contaminate by touch. "I would have gone to Fiona's and Róisín's funeral, but I only heard after it had already happened. I spent weeks trying to find the postman who discovered them. You have no idea what it's been like for us out here since. Living in the town that spawned 'Moira's murder house.'"

"Desmond," said Niall, remembering a stooped-over figure, transformed by guilt into Malahide's whipping boy. "Nobody ever heard from him after that."

"Think about that the next time you poke around stories people want to forget."

Niall tried to ignore the threat. The wind shifted and blew onshore, dusting the fields with a fine spray of salty rain. "He's dead, isn't he? Jim? Just tell me that much."

Bronagh reached over and opened the passenger door. Her face betrayed a ghastly memory, before it vanished again. "Doesn't matter," she said, and pushed him out. "Memories die harder than people out here."

Darkness crawled up on his ankles in the tall grass. The sheep scattered, as if an inaudible shotgun blast had gone off. Niall dug into his pocket and was reassured he could still catch the train back home and forget this entire story. Not that Oscar the cat would care either way. Niall looked west toward the setting sun, back the way they had come, and knew he couldn't let it go. If he hurried, he might still be able to find a clue about where Róisín's diary could be found, despite what Bronagh had tried to warn him about.

Somewhere Father Malloy could throw flowers on it, isn't that what Fiona had written?

It was time to go treasure hunting in the graveyard.

He picked up his rucksack and began to walk.

· 6 ·

There was something wrong with the lights.

Niall had chosen a new route back to Castletownbere, just in case Bronagh was waiting for him on the way. The rains had finally ceased, so he'd managed to reach town limits by walking across the rolling hills and following the last gleam of the evening sun. He'd twisted an ankle because it was too dark to see the rocks, jutting out of the ground like frozen gray hands.

That's why he was surprised when he reached a back road and saw what looked, at first glance, to be thousands of candles on a giant birthday cake, looming out of the void. It appeared that an entire hillside was on fire, but the lights neither grew nor dimmed. Instead, they flickered on and off steadily, illuminating odd shapes it was impossible to distinguish even as he inched closer. This place was nowhere near anything Fiona had described in her diary but lay north of town, on the winding road toward Eyeries.

When Niall had walked around an endless hedgerow, he finally stood in front of an ancient stone wall, slick with rainwater and eroded by time. The lights, hungry and dark red, lit up the moist air beyond and produced a cloud that seemed to breathe on its own. Niall's fingers found a rusted gate and gave it a tug. It was locked. He fumbled his way past and stopped.

There. Letters. Hammered into the limestone. They had been worn down but were still traceable. A quick fumble for his mobile phone produced enough weak blue light to read that this was the old Saint Finian's Cemetery, whatever that was. He looked both ways in the road and scaled the wall, minding the foot, swollen and tender already.

He stumbled off the wall and fell, feeling something warm and wet spilling over his hand. There was the tinkling of broken glass. Niall brought his fingers up to his face and smelled candle wax. All around, as far as he could see, someone had placed what appeared as thousands of votive candles encased in red glass. Many of the graves he could see were overgrown, while others were as lovingly tended as a war memorial. But this only appeared to be the outer circle from which the strongest source of light emanated. At the lowest point in the terracelike cemetery, the fiercest red gleam lit up even the distant trees, like floating embers.

"Who's there?"

It was a young woman's voice, both assertive and scared. Niall crept closer to a hedgerow, behind which he could see the vague outline of a female form, prostrate on a grave. He didn't answer. The figure rose, impatient swoosh of the long hair, and began combing the grounds.

"Is that you, Séamus, come to steal our holy offerings again? I won't just warn you this time, and that's a promise." How old could she be? wondered Niall, wedging himself down between two sunken headstones, and guessed about sixteen. There was in her voice the clarity and lack of hesitation found only in true believers. He stayed low and didn't get a good look at her before she returned to her original spot, sitting back down this time in the lotus position.

Soon, a humming sound rose up into the fine crimson mist that first sounded like singing. Niall crawled out of his twin grave and edged closer. When he was near enough to smell the singer's patchouli perfume, he could hear the words quite clearly, and they made his flesh crawl.

The girl was chanting the praises of the person on whose grave she sat.

"... the most beautiful, blessed are your eyes. You are the most kind, blessed is your heart. You are the most generous, blessed are your acts. You are the most—"

"—the most homicidal raving lunatic ever to visit hell on West Cork?"

The girl leaped several feet into the air at the sound of Niall's voice and turned to face the long-haired intruder, who had risen right in front of her like Lazarus from his grave. "Who . . . you've no right to be here!"

"As much right as you or anybody else, I reckon."

"You're a tourist? Come to take the name of a good man in vain?" Her mouth was hidden by the half darkness, but the sound of her breathing through clenched teeth was loud and unsettling.

Niall stepped all the way in front of the girl and could now see the headstone.

> HERE LIES JIM QUICK
> BORN OF WOMAN
> SLAIN BY WOMAN
> REST IN PEACE

There was no mention of God or any other benediction. Niall guessed even getting the bastard a half-decent burial had nearly caused a revolution at the parish. A mess of candles, rosaries, Tibetan prayer beads, and what appeared to be a human skull with a heart carved into its forehead covered the earth before the headstone. Rotting fruit, half-drunk bottles of whiskey, and hundreds—no, thousands!—of handwritten notes merely added to the reverence. The girl stroked the cold stone. Even in death, Niall thought, old Jim still knows how to reel them in.

"I don't think some of the women he met on his way would agree," said Niall, trying to keep his eyes on the girl's hands, which she kept low and out of sight. He thought of the image he'd had in his mind on the train, of a wolf beset by furies with knives, and backed away from her.

"I suppose you believe the ones who murdered him to be *heroes*?" spat the girl. "Doing it far away from town, where nobody could see? Bleeding him like a dog?" Her ankle-length dress shivered as anger coursed through her body like fresh poison.

"They managed to do it after all? The Walsh sisters?"

The girl crossed her arms and regarded Niall for a moment, as some of the candles hissed and died. She seemed to squint at him in the darkness with new interest. "You're that fella who broke into Sacred Heart today, aren't ya? Sure." She stepped into a ring of light next to a group of candles on a stone, and now Niall saw she could not have been a day over fourteen. Her eyes, evenly placed in an almost masculine face, now sought only answers where all they had wanted moments ago was Niall's untimely end. "That means you must have the first diary. Can I see it? Is it true? Please."

Niall backed a few feet farther away, to the edge of the uppermost terrace plot. Below him, there was nothing but steep darkness. It was impossible to measure how far he'd fall or how hard he might land. "So then you've seen Róisín's diary?" he said. "It's real?"

The star child held out a hand, as if to touch Niall to make sure he was flesh and blood and not some prophet from her wish-dreams, who might soon again depart into the ether. "I never saw it myself," said the girl, who Niall could now see was wearing a necklace of dried irises around a thin neck. For some reason, this scared him more than anything. "But old Mrs. Kane says Father Malloy did receive it before his death. No one knows where it is now. It's gone." Her eyes flickered, and her voice broke as she repeated, "Gone. All gone."

"Do your—erm, parents know you're out here all alone?" Niall said, and caught a glimpse of something caroming off the treetops in the near distance. It looked like a flicker of headlights. "Seems they'd be worried about you."

The creature didn't answer but gazed behind Niall. She had a look of confusion on her narrow face, as if the cavalry was too early. Or, perhaps, never invited at all.

"*They're* not welcome here either!" she said, setting her small jaw for a fight.

Niall turned and saw several beams of light in the road just beyond the stone wall, pinwheeling around as if held by many hands. The low muttering of men's voices made the blood begin to beat faster in his throat. His way out was blocked. Niall stared into the darkness behind him and knew he had no choice, especially if one of those men was Mary Catherine's father and half the parent-teacher council.

"Take care of yourself, kid," he said, and ran past the waif.

He jumped as far into the black distance as he could, and waited for the pain.

Ba-da-thump! Niall landed, several terraces down, on soft ground. His ankle hurt, but he could move it about. He smelled fresh mud and praised the rainfall. Above him, broad-chested figures had reached the promontory and tried to shine their flashlights on him. They were silhouetted by red candlelight as the celestial embodiments of that poor girl's visions.

"There he is!" one of them shouted. "Over here!"

Niall slipped in the marsh, but fear quickened his step, and he began to run. Despite the pain, he ran faster and farther than he ever had before in his life. His ankle hurt like someone had shoved glass up the ball of his foot all the way to the knee, but he didn't stop. The last thing he heard before disappearing over a hill and losing sight of the red glow was a pleading, hysterical girl's voice. It carried across the fields like a lost shepherd's.

"Come back!" it cried. "I want that diary. Come *baaack!*"

NIALL FELT A prim, insistent whisper in his ear before he awoke. A child's voice cut through the hazy dream he'd had about hippie girls chanting the dead back to life.

"Wake up, mister postman."

He jolted awake and sat up. It was still dark, and all he could see before him were his own wet boots. He didn't even remember dozing off. How long had he slept in his hiding place between an outcropping of moss-overgrown rock? Panic squeezed through him once more, and his eyes whipped around, expecting to see a lynch mob carrying druid lanterns and a hanging rope. But there was nothing, just the scratching sounds of nocturnal animals. It irritated Niall how right Mr. Raichoudhury continued to be, even from a distance. And he wondered how long it had taken that old teacher to die as he sat in the dusty marketplace, trying to copy the majesty of one perfect image.

"Over here!"

Niall nearly jumped out of his skin and scrambled to his feet. It hadn't been a dream! The bloated ankle reminded him of its existence, and dropped him right back on his fugitive arse. That voice nearby sounded like the pursuers, who—

"Relax," said the child again, giggling. "They're looking along the coastal road so far, not here. But they won't be gone for long."

"Who is . . . ?"

A girl stepped out from behind a tree, dressed in a black rain slicker and rubber boots at least two sizes too big, probably her mother's. She had the hood cinched tightly to her round face, but there was no mistaking the identity of the most ambitious sixth-class pupil Fiona Walsh had ever taught.

Mary Catherine Cremin knelt next to Niall and smiled.

"Come to lead the hunters to the prey, have you?" he asked.

"You have something I want. I'll trade you for it. And don't pretend you've no clue what I'm talking about." She produced a large old-fashioned rifled metal flashlight from her pocket, and put her thumb on the power slide. "Because my father and the others react to one of these faster than if I called him on the phone. They're all out looking. For the stranger who was alone with Mr. Cremin's only daughter for a long, long time. Imagine that."

Niall looked around. He could now see a faint cluster of bluish beams down by the main road, uncertain of where to search next. All they needed was one pinprick of light to lead them up the hill.

Mary Catherine took something else out of her schoolbag, neatly affixed across her chest. It was still wrapped in a plain brown envelope and looked like it had lived underwater for years.

"An even swap, right?" she said. The pages on the notebook she slid out of the paper were warped and bent out of shape from humidity. "I have already copied down the entire thing and don't need it anymore. But I need the first part of the story. Miss Walsh's diary. So show me."

She had leaned so close to him that Niall could see her wide blue eyes. There was no pity or hesitation there. He reached back into the lining of his pants, found the plastic sheet covering Fiona's dying thoughts, and held it out in front of him.

"Who was the girl back there? At the cemetery?" he asked.

The kid shrugged. "They keep showing up, and the groundskeeper keeps chasing them away. Some of them smoke so much skunk it reeks for miles." A sly smile. "But my father tells me to be on guard for strange men like you, not hippie girls."

"What does your father think I did inside that classroom?"

"Use your imagination. After Jim, parents have been easy to give a good scare."

"You little witch."

Her free hand made a gesturing motion. "You should be grateful I'm giving you Róisín's diary at all. I could have sold it to them journalists who came around."

"How'd *you* get it?"

Mary Catherine smiled. To Niall's left, the flashlight grouping below him now seemed less confused. It marched, silently, back up the mountain. Toward him. "I helped clean out the rectory after Father Malloy died," she said. "And the envelope was just lying there. His housekeeper, Mrs. Kane, never saw me do it. Some of the pages are destroyed, but. Must have been in some rainy bin somewhere." She looked out into the darkness and the first beam of light strafed her forehead. "Out of time. Do we have a deal?"

Niall handed her Fiona's diary. After a quick second, she handed him hers.

"Don't stay here too long," said Mary Catherine, sounding genuinely concerned for his safety. She pointed north, past the dark hills leading up to Eyeries. "Stay off the roads. Walk for another half hour or so. You'll find an abandoned cottage. I won't send anybody there. Promise."

Niall's ankle was throbbing, but fear gave him one last shot of adrenaline. He ran a thumb across Róisín's diary, and it felt exactly like her sister's, but even more damaged. The entire first half was illegible pulp. "Why are you letting me have this?"

At this, the little girl frowned, as if that was the dumbest question she'd ever heard. "Because Miss Walsh always said to be kind to strangers." Then she was gone into the darkness, and Niall was alone with the rain and his new treasure.

HE HAD WALKED for over an hour across open ground when he walked right into a stone wall.

It was impossible to tell what else might be next to it, for the mountains had been covered by clouds, undulating between the peaks like fat gray snakes. Niall fumbled his way over to what appeared to be a door. A light push, followed by a reluctant creak, and he was inside. His fingers found a light switch, which didn't work. Another light stumble, and he was standing next to something soft. A couch? A chair? He gently eased his way into it, and it appeared to be dry. There was the rhythmic drumming of water dripping through the roof from somewhere upstairs. Niall's ankle was on fire. But his curiosity was greater than that discomfort.

He powered on his mobile phone and pointed the small LED screen down toward the notebook in his lap. Would the pursuers see the faint blue reflection? He moved the phone along the floor and saw rat droppings and strewn paper. Nobody had been here for a long time. Niall hid the mobile and stared out where he imagined the window might be.

There were no lights to be seen anywhere. Had Mary Catherine sent her father up the hill after all? Niall took his pathetic reading lamp back out, and decided to take the chance. The phone's battery had three bars left. And dawn had to be coming soon.

"Tell me a secret, Róisín," he said, and turned the first page.

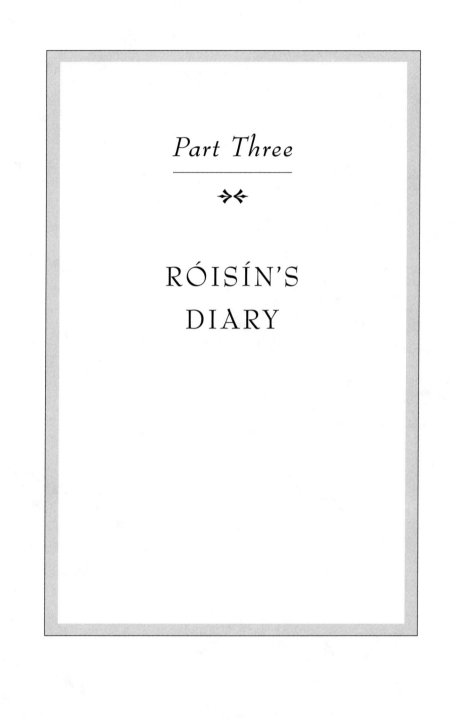

Part Three

❊

RÓISÍN'S DIARY

· 7 ·

I've been hearing voices since I was six years old.

Now, I know what you're thinking. Poor girl, a recluse, shut-in and withdrawn from infancy. No doubt this kind of antisocial behavior is what led to her alcoholism and unquenchable appetite for wireless radios rather than fuzzy human contact. Bound to end up in black jeans and in the arms of some tart. Right? But you can take that politically correct pity and stick the label on somebody else. I've lived a life of dreams, you see. I've surfed on a many-layered cloud of strangers' vocal cords, drifting out at me since the very beginning from cheap handheld transistors, where I could close my eyes and walk in the Kalahari or sail the seven seas. All without leaving the house. The room I shared with my sisters as a girl was tiny, you understand? Aoife and I slept in the same bed until the accident that left us orphaned. And in all those years I spent at Aunt Moira's bed-and-breakfast, those invisible radio waves made every dreary Sunday bearable, each dull everyday sound glorious.

I've been loyal to those voices ever since. Because they never deserted me.

The room where I'm writing these words to you now is so small I can barely even call it a room. It's a hollow section of the wall in my Aunt Moira's house in Dublin, from where Fiona says we may never emerge alive. She could be right, I don't know anymore. I'm usually too tired all the time now to analyze anything but the sinking feeling inside my chest. But Fiona talks a mile a minute, doesn't she? Always did. I love her to pieces, but you sometimes have to subtract half of her ire to get at what she's really trying to say. Not to mention her bleedin' pharaoh fetish.

I know I'm as weakened as she at this point, and I look a fright besides, but this much I'll give her: I feel that same gnawing inside that she moans about in her sleep. Like claw marks in my stomach lining. Something in the food, she says. Yeah, right, try calling it food one more time, willya? I'd brain ya with something hard if only I had the energy to get up anymore and look for the shovel Fiona's just found.

Rescue.

I dream of it, even when I'm awake and trying to blink the blurry strangeness out of my eyes that's there all the time now. I close them and think of endless horizons. Sometimes I dream of mountain climbers, plucked from howling summits by helicopter at the last moment. Other times it's submariners, tapping a code on the steel hull to the divers outside before the oxygen runs out.

Just now, for instance, I see in my mind a lone mariner somewhere on the endless ocean. She's been marooned inside a rescue raft when her ship foundered and sank, trying to signal planes flying past for weeks without noticing her. She's survived this long by catching birds and sucking them clean, sparing only the feathers. It hasn't rained for days, and her tongue is swollen like a bug. Then, disoriented by thirst and hopelessness, she hears the sound of propellers and looks up. There! It's a seaplane, white and large and beautiful. It's tipping its wings and droning so low overhead she can see the dried-up fuel spills on the battered silver fuselage. She leans back and tries to remember the sound of her own name. She hasn't spoken a word for over a month.

Neither have I, come to think of it. Except for *thank you* and *I love you* to my sister, but those don't count.

I have waking dreams like this, even during the day. Visions of freedom, images of escape. Of being outside, smelling grass. I watch over Fiona when she sleeps, or tries to. I listen to our demon aunt, scurrying downstairs like a roach at all hours of the night, or like one of those homeless fellas who used to sort through our rubbish bins at home. For some reason, it makes me homesick.

But mostly, behind my eyelids, I think of Jim.

And I dream of murder.

ONE OF THE last times I saw Jim alive, he was helping two girls across Main Street with their groceries.

Easy as you please, hand gently on one of their elbows, and a polite nod to traffic on the way. He was wearing one of Harold's old Hawaiian shirts, green pineapples flapping on red silk in the sun. I hate to admit it, but it suited him.

I was coming down the hill on my bicycle, on my way to buy supplies for Aoife, who still refused to leave her house. It had been almost a week since that pikey bastard tried to shut us all up. And then I nearly ran him and those two girlies over, only stomping on the pedals at the last moment. Jim danced past my front tire and did a little jig, which made the girls laugh. He placed a steady hand on my handlebars, giving it a playful shake. My sister's blade still lay at the bottom of my bag, inches away. I swear to Christ I could have bled him right then and there.

And then he smiled. Not too wide or too flirtatiously, just a lightning glimpse of whatever lurked beneath the handsome, suntanned skin.

If I'd had doubts before about whether I could go through with turning that skin permanently gray, I no longer had them as Jim continued to the parking lot by the harbor. I wanted him deader than Judas Iscariot. But I did what I've done to every gobshite hard-on in this town whenever I wanted him to feel like a big man, just to make him feel safe: I cocked my head at him like I was charmed or impressed, and flashed him my pearly whites. And as I got off my bike and went into the SuperValu, I could feel his eyes on my arse. It was almost depressing how easy it was with men, even for a cunning specimen like our resident storyteller. And you may wonder yourself, dear reader, why I did it at all. But trust me when I tell you that I was already devising my own plan to somehow plant Aoife's steak knife in his back soon enough. In the meantime, I needed him to fear nothing from this cowed little goth girl.

When I came out of the store with my bags ten minutes later, he was nowhere to be seen. The two girls he'd helped were sitting in an old Renault, smoking cigarettes and laughing at something I couldn't hear. Trawler diesel fumes mixed with stout wafted across the road and made me think of my father. He used to buy us ice cream cones right here with both vanilla and strawberry, nursing a pint he would savor slowly. Today, the crêpe cart was doing brisk business, and boys shoved each other to get the vendor's attention. To anybody else, it was a day for taking a stroll down to the square.

But for me, it might just as well have been the dead of winter. I felt nothing but cold around the heart as I pedaled back up that hill.

AOIFE STILL REFUSED to eat anything but carrots.

I'd tried feeding her salmon, bread, rashers, and all manner of vegetables, but it was no use. She wouldn't even touch the dark chocolate, which she always steals from my fridge. My twin sat in bed for days, chewing nothing but those little peeled carrots with a smiling rabbit on the bag's label. I'd stupidly expected her to be as murderously amped up as me, to check the action on Father's shotgun and aim it out the window every few minutes. But Aoife just shook her head silently whenever Fiona or I told her it was time to tell the gardaí, or at least let a doctor come by. She'd walk outside barefoot and stand, immobile, in the forest clearing near the back of the house, letting the wind blowing through the trees grab hold of her dress and slap it against her thighs. For hours Aoife would remain there, and when she came back, she only nodded at us and went back under the covers, tucking into another bag of that rabbit food.

At night, Fiona and me took turns keeping watch outside.

I'd never spent that much time outside in the fresh air at one time, and my head swam for the first couple of days. I looked down at our town and tried to remember how it had been before everyone became dazzled by the *seanchaí* and unable to think for themselves. Tourist season had begun in earnest, and the sounds of lads drifting down Main Street having drunk the last pint carried up the hill like crows fighting for scraps.

Fiona fetched her books and got comfortable on the couch.

I brought along my shortwave.

On one particularly beautiful night, when the stars crept along the back of the Slieve Miskish Mountains like glass marbles thrown in front of a flashlight, I cranked it up. Fiona was asleep on the couch already, with a coffee-table book about Amenhotep across her chest like a pup tent, and the sounds coming from old Aoife's room told me she was watching one of those shite TV programs about who the most wretched dancer in the nation might be.

My hand steadied the biggest dial, and I began my search for a new voice. Evvie was visiting with her parents in their Russian country house and couldn't come visit for at least a month. I hated the place named Sochi where she'd sometimes text me from, because I had to stay behind. I was lonely and angry. I needed to talk to someone other than my siblings for a change. And on that night, the voices popped up on the band quickly, as if I had hung a net into the air, catching each one.

There were fishermen out in the Irish Sea, trolling for salmon on the way out and easy women coming back in. I saluted them and dialed past, leaving them in the sizzling electronic wake of my very own invisible ship. Next, a political voice, sounding old and disillusioned, belonged to a woman calling herself SocialConscience and advocating that we rescind all public ownership for the good of the land. She vanished aft like those boys on the trawler. The signals dimmed. And just when I thought that night would be another waste of time with teenage shortwave surfers asking me what I was wearing, a voice broke through the din after I'd keyed the mike for the hundreth time and found only people I'd never have nodded to in the street.

"This is Nightwing, flying across your rooftops and trees and hair-pieces," I repeated to the great void, disheartened. "Someone come on back; over?"

There was a crackle, like someone turning on a switch far away. And then I heard it.

"I'm so glad to be speaking with you again," the male voice replied, so softly it felt as if he were stroking the airwaves that had brought him to me. "I have missed you and your friend. Can you tell me how you are?"

My heart beat in my throat and cheeks, because I knew instantly who this was. And still I had to ask to make sure.

"Can you identify yourself before we proceed; over?"

I stared at the green band, and at the needle resting next to 3101.3 MHz, and heard the voice tell me what I already knew. Because proph-ets and madmen use the same door to people's hearts, don't they? They always grab hold of your hope and start turning the handle until it gives, whether you want them to or not.

"Gatekeeper is what I believe your friend christened me the last time," he said, and chuckled pleasantly, the way my father used to. "We were speaking of storytellers. You didn't believe me, as I recall." He took a deep breath and let out more than air as he exhaled. It sounded to me like frustration, or even grief. "Tell me something, dear Nightwing. Think of what has gone on all over West Cork in the last months. Then tell me what you are *now* willing to believe."

I didn't answer right away, and turned my head toward the living room, but Fiona's snoring and those fucking waltzing tunes from be-hind Aoife's door convinced me I'd better not wake them; I'd do this alone.

"How come you know him so well? Our storyteller out here?"

A sound like the burning of paper crackled merrily. Gatekeeper was having a ciggie and taking a long drag of it at that. "Because he sends me things, you see. He has for years."

"What kind of . . . things are you talking about?" I asked, trying to keep my voice low and unaffected and feeling terrified within an inch of my life.

"Souvenirs," said Gatekeeper, lingering on the word, as if it was far too mild for what he had really intended to say. "From his travels. They arrive in envelopes or boxes, depending on what he has decided I should have in the house." He blew some smoke into the microphone and added with a sigh, "Postman came twice this week, dropping them off."

I had to look away from the shortwave and out across the darkened waves as I asked, "What was inside?"

"A gift you'd never want to see," said Gatekeeper, sounding profoundly sad. The fatherly color had drained out of his voice, leaving only regret. "Or think about."

"I don't know if we're talking about the same storyteller, Gatekeeper," I said, feeling the warm breeze from the bay turning frosty and damp. "But ours is a fucking rapist and a murderer, and you can take that to the bank."

"Still riding that red Vincent Comet, is he?" Gatekeeper wanted to know.

How could any of us forget that thing? Jim had at least three kids from Sacred Heart on permanent guard duty at this point, making sure no clumsy tourist or drunk looder from town scratched it up. He paid the lads in cash, which gave the chip shop glory days.

"The only one he loves more than that thing is his own bad self," I said.

"But the murders have stopped, am I correct? Those young women in the towns he visits? No more headlines lately. There's a reason for that."

I knew why. I'd seen Jim parading down the bar at McSorley's, buying pints for anyone with a set of teeth to flash him a smile with. He held poker night each Friday with the lads at the Garda shop. Not to mention the way he'd turned the head of Father Malloy by singing in the choir twice on Sunday. But I wanted to hear Gatekeeper say it.

"Why is that?" I asked.

"You know just as well as I," said the voice, now fatherly and admonishing again. "He's getting comfortable in your town. Like a cuckoo throwing other birds out of the nest and taking it for himself. He'll never leave. I'm guessing he's already made plans for something permanent. Am I right?"

I thought of the diamond he'd bought our aunt Moira and felt like barging into their bedroom and stabbing that bastard through his sorry excuse for a heart right away. Something permanent, all right. "Who are you?" I asked, wanting to tear the metal box apart and pull the jack out of it. "Why don't you come out here and fix it, then, if you and yer crystal ball are so smart?"

"Because I'm afraid of him. And you should be, too."

"What are his weaknesses? How do I stop him?"

Once again, I had the answer. But I guess I needed a friendly voice to tell me I wasn't alone with that understanding.

"You've seen him look at women, haven't you?" said Gatekeeper, stabbing his cigarette into what sounded like a crater-sized ashtray. "There's your weakness, Nightwing. There it is, naked and out there for all to see."

"Did you ever try to stop him yourself?" I asked. But there was nothing but the eternal megahertz ocean, its waves cresting and falling no matter who was listening on the other side.

I heard something stirring behind me and turned.

Aoife emerged in the doorway, pale face framed by the rising sun. She was wearing my motorcycle jacket against the morning cold and those flowery rubber boots. My twin came out and ruffled my hair with both hands. I felt like crying, I was so happy to see her up. Fiona shuffled out on the porch to join us, three of my ciggies in her mouth, all of which she had lit and now passed out like solemn gifts. I regarded my family and felt the kind of pride I can imagine mothers feel for their children when they fall and get back on their feet.

I turned to both of them and smiled. They only looked glorious, my sphinxy sister and my blond double. And I knew what we had to do next.

"I've just had a brilliant idea," I said.

OUR MOTHER'S WEDDING dress shimmered in the sun, a silk ghost from my childhood.

At first, I thought it was a mirage, buried deep inside the dress-maker's shop I was passing on Main Street. I'd been up the road with more groceries for Aoife, who had broadened her diet to apples and bread, thank God. I pulled my banjaxed bicycle over on the footpath and put my nose to the glass. In a sense, I was both right and wrong about the strange vision. It *had* been an old family snapshot come to life, except the face on the figure wearing the dress was no longer my mother's.

Instead, my aunt Moira beamed like a teenage bride, beckoning me to come inside.

"A bit more around the left," she whispered to the seamstress, a quiet girl with freckles none of us could ever quite remember the name of. Aunt Moira waited for her to cinch the long ruffled fabric even tighter to her newly acquired slim supermodel hips. Then she faced me, cheeks aglow and eyes seeing a future I couldn't bear to imagine. What did she hope for? I wondered. A happy, healthy home, with "the romp-ing of sturdy children and the laughter of happy maidens," as Eamon de Valera had once prescribed for us all? I asked myself if old Dev had ever imagined creatures like Jim starting a family.

"You look beautiful, Aunt Moira," I said, feeling like taking a lit match to that dress.

"Thank you, dear," she answered, but there was an alertness in her eyes that showed she caught just how hollow my greeting really was. "Stay awhile. I need to talk to you."

"Sure," I answered, picking a red velvet stool to perch myself on while the girl whose name I forgot made herself scarce out back. The look she sent the bride-to-be might just as well have been from the lowliest commoner to the queen just before her coronation. Aunt Moira was now as close as anyone in Castletownbere could get to true celebrity, and she smiled back at the girl with her head tilted in the fashion of 1940s movie stars.

When she was satisfied we were alone, however, the screen siren vanished.

"Didn't see you and your sisters last Friday for dinner."

"I suppose that's right, so," I replied. What did she expect, after what Jim did, sing-alongs over the roast beef? Rousing card games after dessert?

Moira leaned in, because little miss servant to Her Exalted Majesty was probably eavesdropping. Damn it if my aunt wasn't wearing Mother's good pearl earrings, too, the ones our father gave her for an anniversary gift one summer. I remembered them, because we had gone to the movies that same night, and mum had kept checking her earlobes to make sure Tom Cruise hadn't reached out from the screen and made off with them before intermission.

"I hear the rumors, too," Aunt Moira said, and looked over my shoulder at something in the street. "They say terrible things about my Jim, you know. They always have, he tells me. And I'm not blind, despite what you girls may think." She reached up and touched my forearm. "He's had some wild ways, no doubt about it. Some fooling around and hard drinking, perhaps. But that's over now. He promised me. And what they're whispering he did to Aoife—well, I just can't. . . ." She stopped speaking and still wasn't looking me in the eye.

"I can," I said, and reclaimed my hand without seeming obvious about it.

Something shifted behind those Bette Davis eyes, and the blushing bride was banished to whatever dungeon she lived in when the dirty work had to be done. A more steely Aunt Moira leaned forward and nodded for a long time, as if something had just dawned on her. When she looked at me again, I might as well have told her that Plastic Jesus was the evil one himself. If she'd had a needle, she woulda stuck me with it, no doubt.

"I see," she said, pursing her lips. "So you saw him do it?"

"No," I answered, catching the loyal seamstress sticking her nose out behind the curtain at the sound of raised voices. "I didn't."

Moira shook her head, making the earrings jangle. "Then how can you be sure? How can any of you know enough to accuse him of something that monstrous?" Her face was covered in red spots, and her chest heaved. She had begun to pick at a perfectly manicured nail, and the red flecks fell on the floor like fresh paint.

The monstrous part began long before he touched my sister, I thought, remembering Sarah McDonnell's missing face. I wondered if Aunt Moira would be missing her own in a few weeks.

"I don't know anything, Aunt Moira," I said, in as neutral and obedient a tone as I could muster. "And I'm sorry, but now I really have to go. My sisters are waiting at home."

At this, Moira smiled, because some memories can't be buried in a hazy cloud of whatever love voodoo Jim was practicing. Perhaps she saw us girls when we were children, just one unblemished slide from a time without her *seanchaí*. Or maybe she just wished me six feet under but disguised it well, I'll never know for sure. Then the eyes became narrow again, and she carefully wiped some lipstick from the corner of her mouth.

"The wedding is this Saturday," she said, in a voice drunk on fantasy. "Sacred Heart at two. A cake has been ordered. With violet candies and fresh strawberries." She smiled now, all the way back to the molars, and the anticipation of that moment overwhelmed whatever anger she held toward anyone who might think ill of her darling Jim.

Or so I believed. For about two seconds.

"We are going to be happy together," she said, still smiling like the fairy godmother from folk tales Jim would never tell. "And if any of you girls plan to disrupt the ceremony? Or slag off my Jim around town until then?" She looked at me like a stranger as she smoothed a stray wrinkle in the dress. "Father Malloy and God himself won't protect you from me."

AS I STAGGERED out of the dressmaker's shop, I ran straight into the woman with the shiniest uniform buttons in town. She had also turned my sisters and me into the invisible women. I mean, for over a week, Fiona and me had walked the length of Main Street without getting a single nod. People were caught in a loyalty crisis, we knew that. Believe the town mascot or the crazy Walshes? Even odds they'd pick Jim's amber eyes. But we had expected better from our former best friend.

"How are you going, Bronagh?" I said, picking up my bike and not really wanting to know if she was going anywhere at all.

"Get in the car," she said, chin to her spotless shirt. God, she loved that shitty Ford Mondeo. A dirty bar of soap on wheels.

"It's *Get in the car,* now, is it? First time yeh say so much as a single word to me, and you put on this bollixy Bronx detective act? Am I under arrest for being ignored?"

"Please," said Bronagh, drawing stares from two boys from Sacred Heart with illicit ciggies cupped in their hands.

"I'm busy."

"I know. I've seen you shopping for"—she blinked a moment—"for Aoife."

"Now, look at *that*. You still remember how to pronounce her name."

By now, I was walking on the footpath, pushing my bike along. Bronagh blocked traffic as she crawled next to me, doing two kilometers an hour. Passersby whispered. I could even hear them from the other side of the street. A girl pointed at the white patrol car and covered her mouth. And I knew that, at least for a short while, the brave Sergeant Bronagh Daltry was losing in the public opinion polls.

"Get in the car, Rosie. Jaysus' sake."

"Only if you put my bike on the back. And stop pretending to be on TV."

Bronagh didn't answer but stepped out and grabbed the handlebars while her face grew slowly paler. As I got in and fiddled with her radio, I could hear my old Bessie taking a beating as it was clumsily strapped to the bumper and felt secretly happy for Bronagh's trouble. When she got in and started up the engine, her lips were zipped as tight as a body bag.

"Satisfied?" she asked, smiling tartly at the two boys, who gave us finger waves.

"A little," I answered, getting only routine traffic-stop calls from her radio.

She turned it off, rummaged around for the sweets I knew she always kept in the glove compartment, but found none. "How would you like to talk about a certain man known as Jim?" she said.

"Suppose you arrest him instead of yapping about doing it. How would that be?"

"Oh, that'd be fine," Bronagh said, so angry with me and with herself she could barely keep her voice down. She drove the car out to the end of the pier, where we'd played as kids. Trawlers were coming in, squadrons of gulls hard on their rudders, and men in wool sweaters stood in silence on the stone pier awaiting the catch.

Bronagh held something in her lap. And I'd be damned if I was going to ask her what it was.

"Dontcha think I've tried? I want his brown eyes behind the gates at the Rathmore Road prison before Saturday at two P.M., and that's a fact."

"Glad to hear it," I said, beginning to feel sorry for her despite myself. Somehow, I didn't imagine that wee Sergeant Daltry was invited to the future bridegroom's Friday poker games. "So why are we still sitting here, shiting on about it?"

The edges of Bronagh's mouth moved downward, and she stifled a sigh that could have become a sob if left unattended. I caught in that sound more than sorrow at my sister's violation and her own impotence as town sheriff. I also heard ten months of frustration from the shite she took from old Sergeant Murphy and the cumulative effect of never getting respect even from snot-nosed schoolboys. "Because I wanted to tell you I've turned over every stone to nab yer man. To do him for *anything*. He's too good to be true, I know that. Everybody knows."

"But you're still coming to the wedding?" I asked, finding a crushed ciggie in my pocket and trying to reshape enough of it to light up. "Am I right, Lieutenant Columbo?"

"The invitation came today. I can't see how I couldn't. . . ." She sent me a pleading look. "Did you all get one?"

"I got my own special one a moment ago, from Herself."

Bronagh opened the file in her hands.

"The girl's name was Laura Hilliard, from somewhere near Stoke-on-Trent, in England. That girl murdered over in Kenmare last month?" Bronagh looked out at two men in rubber waders tripping on the slick deck surface and spilling a silver carpet of writhing fish all over the dock. "The murderer left no DNA of his own. Same as with Sarah Mc-Donnell and that Holland woman from Drimoleague way, in case ye're wondering. You understand? No skin samples, no sperm, not even a shagging drop of blood. So either he's wearing rubber gloves or condoms the entire time, or nobody really puts up much of a fight."

I looked at the dying haddock flapping all around the car and thought of the look in those girls' eyes a day earlier, when Jim had helped them across the street. True devotion. You could have set off a cannon next to their ears and they'd have called it distant thunder. "You see anybody in town putting up a fight, do ya?"

She withdrew one sheet of paper.

"Until today. Someone's spittle was found on a cup in the Holland woman's home. Missed it the first time. No match for anyone we know, but it's a man's, all right. Forensics said the victim had her head caved in after protected sex. No sperm, either."

"Sounds like a party."

"Make Aoife sign an official complaint. Then I arrest the bugger and we can at least get a legal DNA sample and compare—"

"You know she won't. I do nothing but ask her to come see you. She goes out and listens to her trees, instead."

"Maybe if we could get some samples of *her*—"

"Afraid that's a few showers ago, Sergeant Daltry."

Bronagh returned the sheet to its folder and stuffed it underneath her seat. We sat there, not saying anything, and listened to the smacking sounds of fish tails against the hot asphalt. I remembered smoking my first ciggie with her not three feet from where we sat. When I looked up, she was crying.

"Hey, easy, Bronagh," I said, feeling like an awful bitch but not knowing what to say to make her stop. "It will be okay."

She wiped her nose with the pristine blue sleeve and sent me a glare that revealed she already knew what I dreamed of more than anything else. "You know it won't."

"CAN I HAVE another Murphy's, please, Jonno?"

The voice was mine. I knew it, because of the vibrations in my throat as I said the words. But almost nothing else was, not even the costume. You see, I was acting the part of Mysterious Town Harlot whose myth most everyone was so fond of repeating to one another under their breaths. Especially the part about how I'd never let any man have his way with me. If I couldn't shake that image, I damn sure was going to make use of it. I'd gone home to my place—after Bronagh finally stopped sniveling—and picked the shortest black skirt I could find, then ripped off another few inches. I'd spritzed something French and expensive on my neck that Evvie had left behind and wondered how far to push the sex-witch look as I baited the hook to land one Jim Quick. Then I'd biked down the hill, taken a deep breath, and opened the pub's front door.

Wednesday, you understand, was the night everyone at McSorley's took leave of their senses, because Jim always favored them with a song or a wee story. And it was my one last chance before the wedding to get what was mine.

Jonno had manned the bar at McSorley's since before I was born, God bless his plastic teeth. He walked across the floor in that unbalanced trawler cowboy way of his and put a glass before me. Sweet

Jonno. He looked at my too-heavily-made-up face and was about to ask me why I was acting this way but thought better of it. Jonno shot me one of those brilliant Hollywood smiles as he returned to his post. To this day, I'll never forget him for that. He could have ruined everything for me that night. Because though wolves aren't used to prey hunting *them*, they still get spooked if they sense something's off.

Instead, I remained inside the booth my sisters and me had practically hung our names on and quaffed my beer slowly. For over an hour, I acted bored as a housewife, when the only set of eyes I wanted on me heralded their arrival by making my skin crawl. I lit up another Marlboro, then broke off the filter to get down to business faster. Not once did I acknowledge the presence of Castletownbere's favorite son until he practically sat in my lap.

"Drinking alone is bad for the humor, my father always said."

"Did he really?" I answered, looking at the yellow wallpaper. "Smart man."

"He also said—"

"Did I hang an invitation on this booth reading *Will manky random-ers and traveling folk please come inside and have a chat*?" I asked, turning my head but careful not to overdo it. Jim would smell a bad actor a mile away, being one himself. I had one ace in my deck. I'd been treating men this way my entire life. And all of them came back for more.

"I don't suppose you did." He grinned and nodded, as if realizing something profound.

"Then we understand each other," I said, turning my head away from his.

The room hummed with chatter and the scraping of boots. But I knew that everyone was hanging on the next words out of the *seanchaí*'s mouth. Not since he came to town had anybody seen me wipe the floor with someone wanting to get a closer look at my underwear. Besides, half of them had been sent packing already and hated my guts, while fantasizing about me when they were in bed with their wives.

"I know why you're angry," he began, in a voice so covered in sugar it was hard, even for me, to hold on to myself and not just break off a piece and lick it.

I pretended to look around the room. "You're here all alone? What, yer mammy lets you go out all by yourself now? I thought she expected you back for dinner."

Even the wooden harp on the wall held its breath. I could hear the tinkling of glasses but nothing else, as I took a vicious drag on my ciggie and blew the smoke down toward my green painted toenails. He was going to have to fight for this one. And it was only round one.

"I'm not the one you should be angry at," he said, in that same Obi-Wan Kenobi voice that apparently was his favorite weapon. "I know what your sister is probably saying, but I had nothing to do with any of—"

"Why are you still talking to me?" I asked, looking him dead between his amber magnets, not having to feign wanting to rip his lungs out of that nice body.

"Aoife and me, we slept together, we did," he said, hands up as if he expected the law to come bursting in. "And I'm not proud of it. It just . . . happened. But when I left her, God strike me dead, she was fine. I swear to you, Róisín, she was waving at me as I rode away."

I thought of Aoife's bruises and dead stare and nearly broke my glass to stick it into his face. But I took another breath and manufactured a surprised, perplexed look.

"I . . . listen, my sister sleeps with several people," I said, "some of them as manky as you, so it's not really my affair, if—"

And then he touched me.

Saints in heaven, he put his long fingers right on my knee and gave it a gentle squeeze, like I was one of his little girlie conquests who just didn't know it yet. Is that how easy it is? I wondered, as I saw him rest his hand there a moment, then pull it away as delicately as it had appeared. Does nobody realize how staged, how completely unreal, he is? Why doesn't anyone but me see the mirror he hides behind, blowing green smoke into your eyes as you look? It dawned on me that no one but Gatekeeper knew what that even meant.

"I have enough trouble with your aunt knowing what I did," he said, looking like a schoolboy caught stealing from the church collection to buy chocolate. "And I'm making amends for that. But the rumors bother me more. Would you please tell your sister I'm so sorry?"

"What are you sorry for," I asked, no longer acting, myself, "if you did nothing wrong?"

"Look, maybe she made up the story because she regretted what happened. And she knew you and Fiona would rush to protect her."

"You got that right." I had my hand in the bag and on the handle of that knife, already seeing his limp body in my mind, slumped over the table.

His eyebrows knotted together, and those gorgeous lips curled in what seemed like real mental agony. "So, I was thinking that maybe . . . you and I could meet up before the wedding, just the two of us," he said. "Maybe you can act as a go-between of sorts between me and Aoife. Now that we're going to be family and everything. I don't want anybody to feel hurt."

I nearly belly-laughed right in his face but held it back at the last moment. Oh, you clever, clever bastard, I thought, as I pretended to frown and think it over like the caring twin sister I was. I also noticed his eyes resting on my chest for just a bit too long before settling again on my face. Just the two of us. Alone. That would mean either my knickers off or a hammer to the skull. Or both, most likely.

I looked up at him and shrugged, making sure to squeeze my breasts by putting both hands between my legs and bringing my shoulders together. Bingo. It was the only place he looked as I appeared to stumble into some kind of gradual understanding of my role as middleman between my sister and her rapist.

"What are you like?" I asked him, because surrendering right away would have made him suspicious. "Why me?" I caught Jonno sending me a look that said, *If he tries anything, you give us a wink.* Even with the town's love for this charlatan, Jonno would have killed him for me, and that's a fact. But I wanted him all to myself.

"I spent some time with Fiona as well, as I'm sure you know," he said, smiling again, acting ashamed to have slept with every Walsh woman in town, bar one. "She still won't speak to me. I'm afraid I left her hanging, a bit. But you and I, we have no bad blood between us. Can we meet? Maybe sometime tomorrow afternoon? I'm sure you can tell me a new place I haven't been yet. I'll bring some wine. Okay?"

To this day, I'm not sure whether to call it bravery, audacity, or the most brilliant conjurer's trick I ever saw. Trying to convince your most recent rape victim's sister of your innocence by asking her out on a date was probably all three, with a cherry on top. And there was only one answer to the question. I even let him have the ghost of a smile as I grabbed my bag and rose to leave.

"You know the beach down by Eyeries?" I asked. I'd heard he'd been there last week with a bunch of the lads from Sacred Heart, holding a fishing competition. Boys had come back with a new hero and their heads filled to the brim with stories. "To the left, there, just before you reach town?"

"I think I can find it, sure." He even looked relieved I'd said yes. God, I had to admire his technique. Every Susie homemaker would have fallen for that one ten times over.

"Half one, by the old stone pier," I said, grabbing my pint and finishing it in one swallow. I hoped he didn't see my hand shaking as I put it down, although he was narcissistic enough to have taken it for anticipation. "And I drink sauvignon blanc. Cold."

I walked out of McSorley's without stopping to hear his exit line, but then I didn't need to. He'd be there, chilled bottle in hand, and a pair of gloves in his back pocket for when the rough stuff began. He'd be there sure as the apple-sized bruise on Aoife's thigh.

And so would I.

It's strange, thinking back on it now, but that's the last time I can recall touching a drop of alcohol. Never tasted right since.

I nearly threw up with adrenaline shock as I rode back up the hill to my sisters, dodging tourists driving on the wrong side of the road. The sound of waves breaking on the cliffs roared in my head as I saw the warm pinpricks of light in the blue darkness up ahead.

"Soon enough," I said to myself, and stomped harder on the pedals.

WHY DO I hesitate to tell you the rest, I wonder? It's not out of shame for what we did, nor is it disgust. No, it feels more like disappointment, to be honest. Because I'd plotted it so well. Stayed up all night before to think it through, back to front. I'd lain there, next to my twin sister, holding her hand, feeling her pulse, and seeing Jim in my mind's eye, smiling for the last time.

But then, things didn't quite go as planned, did they?

I was early that next day, by at least twenty minutes. And the first thing I saw, rounding a tricky last bend on the beach road, was that shiny red machine, parked on the pier. I cursed under my breath as I steered Aoife's Mercer through the wet sand, feeling like an eejit for not anticipating that he would beat me to it. Now it would be impossible to set up a proper ambush.

I couldn't see the bugger anywhere. There was just his lone motor-cycle, buffeted by the wind and surrounded by shrieking U-necked herons. It was as if the *seanchaí* and tormentor of my sister were dead already or, perhaps, had vanished into the forest primeval of his own fairy tales. A cluster of trees overhanging the water's edge rustled in the wind, and if they'd tried to warn me, they weren't speaking loudly enough. I'd wished Jim gone and buried so hard I could almost have believed that God finally smiled on righteousness.

"It's Chablis, I'm afraid. Couldn't find the other kind," said his voice close by.

Jim had chosen one of Harold's white linen jackets for the occasion and an open-necked shirt, as if we were doomed clandestine lovers from a bad aristocratic romance. He sat cross-legged, hidden by a patch of high grass, a Buddha of destruction. I could smell the mango roast chicken before I was even out of the car, and I hated him for being a good cook, too. He'd not only brought along a picnic basket, and spread out a checkered blanket I recognized as my mother's, but also the good crystal glasses Aunt Moira never used because they cracked too easily. His delicate fingers held out a chilled flute of white wine for me to take.

"How hard did you try?" I asked, walking slowly over to him, deciding on a neutral expression with just the whisper of a smirk. The tiniest hint of an opening for future forgiveness. My dress was even shorter than the night before, and the breeze did its job just fine. He didn't look at my face as I sat down.

"Ah, now," he said, shaking his head and sipping the drink himself. "Give the man a chance."

I reached into the wicker basket and pulled out a wing. I stared at the burnt skin, knowing there was no earthly way I could sit there and pretend to enjoy it. "Aoife," I said, nibbling at it. "What's yer grand plan for her? She hasn't left the house for over a week."

"Can I talk to her?"

"Oh, that's brilliant, muppet. Perhaps you can bring *her* some white wine, too, while yer at it." My mouth was dry, but I'd be damned if I was going to drink from the same glass as him. "Maybe I can arrange something with Father Malloy. At the church."

Jim's face lit up as if I'd suggested unzipping his fly and having at it. "D'you really think you could—"

"Calm down, Billy Shakespeare, I said maybe. But if you think I can perform miracles before you walk my beloved aunt up the aisle? Yer only dreaming. That's two days." I looked around and saw nobody watching us but two squirrels. And they didn't care.

He smiled in a way I cared for not one bit. "Don't like her much, do ya—Moira?"

"She's family."

"So were the Mansons. Tell me the truth."

The glass covered everything but his eyes, zooming in on mine all dark and mysterious like. Oh, this tinker was so septic he deserved for me to end it right there. But that wasn't the plan. "Me and my sisters have always taken care of each other. Okay?"

"You know, I always wondered something about you," Jim said, using less of his magician's voice than he had a moment earlier. "Ever since I met you three at McSorley's that first night. And it still rattles around my head like a pebble I can't get out."

"Enough space for it in there, I think." My voice was steady, but just barely. I glanced over at the Mercer, pretending to brush some hair out of my face. Far away, beyond the trees, there was the sound of another car, idling. For some reason, I didn't want it to leave, but it soon did. Even the seabirds were gone as I looked back up at him.

"You're smarter than your sisters," he said, shaking his head. "By a mile. Isn't that right? You never put yourself in any kind of vulnerable situation, even with ten pints inside ya." He finished the wine and smacked his gums. "And yet here you are, the lesbian love of my life, prancing in front of me like a bad porno actress. So here's my question. What made you wait so long? Why not just stick that boning knife you have in yer bag into my chest last night?"

I couldn't move. It was time to act, to pounce, and I just watched my hands immobile in my lap, like some drugged-out granny. "Will he kill her or love her?" I said, but so low the sound of the waves crashed over the words.

"What was that?" he asked, pouring himself another glass like a country gent out with his best girl.

"That's my question for you: kill her or love her? Wasn't that the choice Prince Euan had to make? And the decision *you* make every time you pick a flower you like? What was the matter with Julie Ann Holland, bloom off the rose too quick for ya? Or did she just look at yer real face underneath the makeup and see the wolf?"

Jim put the glass down and applauded. His face was a mask of pure delight.

"You know, we should have met ages ago. You could have taken Tomo's place as emcee, easy, and we could have cleaned out twice as many homes. Girls for me, girls for you, and split the loot down the middle. Ah, well." He rose and brushed some grass off his pants. "So. We best get this done, before my bride thinks I'm having it on with some tart, right?"

"I didn't come alone." I still just sat there as he moved in closer.

Jim turned his head to the green Mercer and yelled, in the merriest voice I'd ever heard, "Oi, Fiona! You can come out of the car now. This will go much faster that way, ya see."

There was no movement inside Aoife's Teutonic taxicab, at first. Then the boot slowly creaked open, and Fiona clambered out, carrying something heavy between her hands. She advanced toward us like those soldiers in tintype drawings, knowing they'll die in the assault, chin up, eyes front. "Move away from her," she said. "Do it!"

"Why does everybody in this town talk like Bronagh the make-believe cop? Put that thing down, or I'll bleed you both slower than I need to."

You see, that was the whole extent of my plan, all of it.

Brilliant, right? I hook the bait, and Fiona sweeps in and beats his brains in while we're at it. Now do you understand why I didn't want to share any of this with you? Christ, it's embarrassing enough to look like one of Jim's groupies. Preparing to die like one was even worse. Jim reached into the wicker basket one more time, and I knew he wasn't offering any more chicken.

What happened next was either a magical sprinkle from Jim's own stories or just the most solid proof I've ever had that love is stronger than fear.

Booom!

The sound made all three of us flinch and turn toward it.

My twin, glorious in that army jacket with the butterfly men painted all over it, pointed our father's shotgun at Jim's head. She quickly removed the spent cartridge and inserted a fresh one as she walked up on him from behind. I'd never seen her eyes look so alive until that moment, and her cheeks were as red as candy apples. It was like she was running on pure oxygen. Her hands didn't shake, even when she stood three feet away from him.

"That's enough picnicking for one day," Aoife said. "Too cold, anyway."

Jim was poleaxed; his shock at seeing the girl he had left a bloody, sobbing mess on the floor shone through his eternal charm. Because this was impossible. Me and Fiona couldn't hide our surprise either. You see, Aoife was never part of my ingenious plan. And here she was, the cavalry rescuing the two Indian squaws who had screwed up and were about to be killed themselves. It was better than one of Jim's stories, is what it was. A last-minute plot twist. The heroes laugh and the villains cry. Except our villain was a long way from crying.

"Yer brilliant, Aoife!" I said, feeling a lump in my throat.

The *seanchaí* soon recovered and poured honey on his next threat. "People heard that blast," said Jim, keeping calmer than a mortician. "And even if they didn't, they'll know who killed me. I've spread enough stories about you three around town to fill two Italian operas."

"Shoot him!" hissed Fiona, crying in embarrassment at having to stand there, doing nothing. Or maybe she hated herself for having loved him a little bit, too, not so long ago.

"Wait, let's see what other goodies he brought along," I said, feeling my hands come alive and duck into Jim's wicker basket. There was a claw hammer inside, wrapped in duct tape. The last thing Tomo saw while he was alive, I thought. Him and several girls I could mention. I waved the thing in the air. "Out of chicken, are ya?" I asked him.

"Home decorating should be done at home," Aoife said, gesturing for Jim to start walking toward the woods. "You should have brought silverware, instead."

"Ever kill anybody?" Jim asked her, nodding at the gun barrel. "It's messy."

"Yer wasting my time; now walk," she answered.

Jim had reached the edge of the woods when he stopped and leaned on a tree. A faun wouldn't have looked half as good in the flecks of green sunlight coming through the leaves, and he knew that, too. "Admit it," he said, "you're just a little bit curious. About why all those women died. And you won't put me in the ground until you hear it from me. Isn't that right?"

"No," said Aoife.

I didn't say anything. By then, second thoughts were crawling into my brain through a hole in my heart that I thought I'd stopped with plenty of hatred beforehand.

"But then Róisín won't get the answer to her question," Jim said, picking a piece of bark off the tree. "Will you, little rose?"

"Shut *up!*" I said, moving toward him with the knife drawn.

"What's he talking about, Rosie?" Aoife had forgotten about the weapon in her own hands. She looked at me with the slightest echo of doubt.

"Nothing," I said, shame burning in my cheeks, waving the blade about. "Pull the trigger and be done with him. Or I'll—"

"Wait," said Fiona, out of breath, even if she had just been standing there, not moving a muscle. Her hand shook as she brought it up to her lips.

And Jim smiled, didn't he? Grinned from there all the way to the coast of Donegal. Oh, but he was a champion at this, turning a dead-certain execution into a session of mental pinball, with himself as the guy causing the machine to tilt right before the bonus round.

"What d'ya mean, *wait?*" asked Aoife, shifting her feet in those shocking pink commando boots. Her healthy color had turned gray. She raised the gun one more time, pointing it at Jim's pretty haircut. "Will *someone* tell me—"

"I just wanted to ask him something first," explained Fiona, looking at us like someone caught at the SuperValu stealing food for her children.

"Except you don't care about Sarah," Jim said to Fiona, sitting down with his back to the tree and getting comfortable. "*Do* ya? Or Laura Hilliard, or Julie Ann Holland, or any other flaxen-haired soul that crossed my path. You really want to know about what happened to them? Say something any time." Fiona looked away, for just a second, and he continued, driving that invisible wedge between us like a hot scalpel. "No, that's not it. You want to know about me and you. Why I left. Why I picked little Kelly and your aunt instead. Right?"

Ker-lick! sang both hammers on our father's trusty old shotgun as Aoife got ready to end the intermission and move on to the main event. "Everyone's talking too much."

"So which is it?" I heard myself asking the man I'd promised to kill with my own bare hands only the night before. "Love her or kill her? Or doesn't it matter?"

Even Aoife stopped, blinking her eyes as her index finger tensed on the trigger. "Oh, this one, he kills," she said. "I guarantee you that."

Jim folded his hands the way a shaman would, cocking his head like he had just heard something wise whispered into his ear. Far behind him, at the edge of the beach, someone walking two German shepherds ambled our way, apparently unaware of the gunshot. One black dog leaped into the waves, retrieving a stick. *Tick-tock*, I thought. Time's a-wastin'.

"Ten minutes," he said, staring down the twin gun barrels. "I know I'll die today. I may even deserve it. But if you let me live for just ten more minutes, right underneath this tree? I'll tell you how the story ends. Prince Euan's and mine, both."

The dogs' barking reached us in snippets. I imagined I could hear the wolf's blood song in my own ears as Aoife appeared to think it over. Fiona nodded at her.

"Five minutes," Aoife said, not lowering her gun. "And then time's up."

"Tough audience," said the *seanchaí,* and pointed in the direction of an empty field sloping down toward us from town. "But fair play to ya. Now, let's pretend the Fort of the Wolf stood on that spot right over there, standards snapping in the wind. It's near evening, and you can look inside its grandest tower." His voice slipped into a hazy monotone that existed in some other time. "Then imagine you see a wolf standing in front of a beautiful woman who does nothing to defend herself. That's Prince Euan, deciding between life as a hunted animal or as a human being who was never quite human. He's been kneeling in front of the princess, but now he rises. And she can see her fate reflected in his eyes."

 "Can you feel it, cousin?" said Aisling, as she watched the man before her stagger to his feet like a beggar.

Yes, his *feet,* because the wolf's body was changing even as he put the weight on his hind legs, feeling them stretch and bend backward. Prince Euan felt such searing pain he'd never imagined possible as he dared to kiss her on the lips for the first time. His gray coat, still thick and matted from foraging during the winter months, was peeling back from the muscles flexing underneath all by itself, and each hair plucked from his body. God had finally punished him for his wickedness, and he knew the final judgment was near. His full memory as a murderous pretender to the throne rushed back into his head, blurring his vision. Brother Ned and his poor father would no doubt be waiting for him on the other side, seeking revenge. He was afraid to live. Terrified of death. And unable to reverse the process he saw transforming his body as he smelled her perfume; his chest muscles convulsed and shrank down to half their size, and the knife-sized teeth he'd grown accustomed to having withdrew up into his gums with a sucking sound.

He crawled on top of his cousin, steadied himself on the headboard, and entered her. It was as if the men he'd slain now howled in his ears, and every killer instinct he'd felt collided in this moment, squeezing the last animal reflex out of him and into forever after.

"It . . . I'm dying," he said, listening to his heart sounding a last rhythmic tattoo.

Princess Aisling just smiled and touched his smooth cheek. "No, only one of you," she said, kissing him on the tip of his once again aristocratic nose. "The beast has to die so that the man may live. That's what my soothsayers have foretold. But you must wait for dawn. Stay with me until the sun rises and your delivery is complete. And we can rule this kingdom as man and wife."

Euan first rode her like a man who hadn't ever been with a woman. It was clumsy and furtive, and he felt like a boy. The wolf memory still contained somewhere deep in his own skin bade him sever her arteries in one quick tear, but it was overcome with the warm sensation of her all around him and inside his head. As the night wore on, he was carried on a purple ocean of calm seas, leading him into safe harbor. It was a sensation he couldn't equate with anything he'd ever felt before in his life.

Human beings would have called it contentment, trust, even feelings of love.

But to Euan, former lord of his father's mighty fort, slayer of wolves become a creature of the forest himself, it seemed a trick of the mind. He closed his eyes and realized he had performed this act before, with many women, without ever attaining this unfamiliar sensation of belonging. It calmed his vexation. Aisling's movements underneath him grew in strength until she gripped his newly slimmed-down forearms and lay quite still.

Euan found his own release just as the far side of the woods outside drank in the first pale ghost of morning. He held her and tried to recapture the image of a wolf, paws nearly silent on the ground, mere inches away from its chosen prey. But the vision fluttered behind his eyelids and faded as the sun grew stronger. He remembered playing with his father as a boy. There had been trumpets. And sweets.

All he recalled of his recent existence as an animal was the eyes of the wolf that had cursed him. "Only God and fortune know," it had promised, threatening him with eternal damnation. And hadn't he shown it how wrong it was, how utterly ludicrous? He had been in purgatory as a savage beast but made it back to safety, thank the Lord. As he fell asleep with sunlight stroking his new face, he kissed Princess Aisling's neck.

Euan slept until the first bell for morning prayers.

Then he awoke, as if snatched from a nightmarish dream. It felt like his body was in the grip of a fever such as he'd seen the insane suffer. The blood in his ears thrummed like the battle drums that had accompanied his entry into manhood on the battlefield. It swished along the deeper, instinctual canal that humans cannot hear or even perceive. And there was no doubt what it needed him to do, despite his smooth pink-flesh costume pretending to clothe a human. It knew what really lay beneath, no matter what that creature be called by man or beast.

Euan looked over at Princess Aisling, curled up around his upper arm for anchorage, a mess of hair bleeding out over the silken pillows. He stared through the open window at the forest, where myriad smells of newly opened roses blended with the raw, musky scent of deer secreted onto trees for mating season. A dove fluttered by. The world expanded. His heart began to thump; yes, he believed it was even attempting to grow large enough to fit a roving animal once again, all by itself.

The young woman stirred, rubbed her nose, and began to open her eyes.

"Good morning, cousin," she said, craning her neck for a kiss.

I made my choice long ago, Euan thought, knowing that the old wolf hadn't told him everything. His real torment was contained in this moment. I was formed before I even murdered my brother and before I felt the red thrill at terrorizing women as I stole their last breath. Even in human form, I will forever remain what I've always been.

A predator.

Driven by the fear of what I'm chasing before me, relishing only in the kill.

"Cousin?" asked Aisling, sensing something shifting inside the body next to hers.

Prince Euan's head felt like it would explode. His skull distended and expanded downward, and the sharp yellow teeth descended from the roof of his mouth until the pain was too much to bear. He opened his jaw and saw gray hair appearing on his forearms faster than a fleeting thought. There was a brief carnal hesitation about ending the young life next to him.

Then he bit down on Aisling's neck and shook it until he heard the soft crack.

The day watch out on the ramparts could have sworn they saw a wolf leap from the tower, land on the ground, and vanish into the trees.

Jim picked at his nails, humming a tune. He watched us stand there and continue to listen for a story that was long over. He grinned and patted his shirt pocket down for smokes. But it was me his eyes returned to more than the others. The knife in my hand was slick with sweat. Out by the sea, the man with the dogs was gone. I could hear my sisters breathing.

"You forgot to tell us how your *own* story ends," said Aoife tone-lessly. The 12-gauge dangled from her gun hand like a gardening tool.

"What, do I have a spare minute left?" the storyteller wanted to know.

Fiona tightened her grip around something ugly and heavy. I no-ticed she'd picked up Jim's own hammer. "You need to clear something up for me," she said, sounding grim. But her eyes flitted around be-tween me and Aoife too much for her to scare anybody.

Jim chuckled. I can still hear the sound. Like an uncle you don't like, whispering a dirty secret in your ear at your parents' party, that kind of laugh. Ya know?

"What'd ya really say to that Swedish fella?" Fiona's voice sounded like someone held her throat in a vise.

Jim shook his head. "Use your imagination. What would make a man twice my size turn into a scared wee lad? No fairy tale, I guarantee you that." He stared up into the sky as if he were going to fly a kite later on. "Told him I'd kill his girlfriend and let him watch. Are you *really* that naïve?"

"But those women," Fiona persisted, breathing too hard not to cry as she asked the question. "Why kill them at all? They were no threat to you. Sarah, she—"

"Just got in the way, is all," said Jim, sounding bored. "Overheard me and Tomo talking about our method. Poor Julie Ann Holland? She heard Tomo robbing her downstairs, so she had to go, while Kelly, whom I know you remember—well, she lived because she didn't notice anything but me. Luck of the draw, really. If you want a mysterious an-swer from my deprived childhood, yer wasting time here."

Fiona appeared to look inward, seeing something I could tell she didn't care to find. When she stared at the *seanchaí* again, her eyes re-vealed more than she cared to about what lay inside. The real question finally escaped her throat. "Why didn't you kill me, then?" she asked, trying not to ask why he hadn't properly loved her, too.

Jim's smile was neither rueful nor guilty. "You didn't need killing," he answered.

"So the wolf was powerless, just like you, is that it?" asked Aoife, fingers gripping the butt of the gun tighter than before. "A slave to biology, yeah? Built for speed and murder, even with 'the love of a good woman' right around the corner? Christ, but you're pathetic. It's not even a good ending to the story. Just another cheap male sex fantasy."

Jim shrugged and crumpled an empty ciggie pack before tossing it away. The sugar coating his voice earlier had hardened and flecked off, leaving only rusty steel.

"I saved the ending for the three of you," he said. "You deserved it. Never had an audience that willing to"—he grinned again—"participate. Come morning, I will still be alive, safe and snug in your aunt's bed. And all three of you will wonder why you lost yer nerve." He pointed at Aoife. "Come *on*! You would have shot me ages ago if you really wanted to, and that goes for your avenging fury sisters as well."

My eyes met Fiona's. Each of us waited for the other to do something. Anything. I'd never been more ashamed in my life. And nothing happened.

"But they catch Euan in the end, don't they?" I asked him, gripping the knife so tightly even the handle drew blood. "The hunters? And then they hang his manky pelt from the nearest tree."

Jim glanced at me in approval. An audience member who makes up her own ending, now, how about that? "Afraid not, my love," he said. "Euan was never found, and all that wandering travelers ever saw of him was a gray shadow, calculating how best to track them down. And with Aisling dead, the Fort of the Wolf soon fell to the invaders, who left not a single stone standing. But they did let the defeated soldiers use the wood from the black gate to make a coffin for the princess."

He looked up at Aoife with the oddest expression. I'm not even sure I can recall it correctly now, but it was something like fatigue or resignation. Like an animal knowing the arrow is coming.

"And as for me?" He took a deep breath and told my twin, "You know why I chose you, right? And neither of these two? It wasn't just because I knew you'd slept with half the town and would suspect nothing. No, it's because I knew it would hurt you so much more than it would the others, especially afterward. Fiona, there, she's tougher than she thinks, and little sis likes the girls herself. But the sound *you* made when I turned you over and stu-*uurgghh!* . . ."

I had jammed the knife into his chest, all the way to the hilt, before I could even think. I wrenched it out and planted it in him again. I got blood in my eye and wiped it away like sticky rain. I felt nothing. I understood nothing. My ears pounded, telling me something a wolf might have understood that I didn't want to hear.

Someone took the knife out of my hand, I think it was Fiona, because I saw her bend over Jim herself and move her arm up and down. She only stopped when Aoife put a hand on her shoulder.

Something red and metallic caught the sun, and I turned toward it. I stumbled and fell before I reached the 1950 Vincent Comet, parked on the edge of the pier. There wasn't as much as a speck of fly shit on the gas tank, and it sloshed as I rocked it back and forth. My hands tingled. The dark blood on them had already begun to coagulate. I looked back at my sisters. Aoife held Fiona, who waved one hand in the air and tried to get some words out between sobs. The heat beat down on us, turning even the sky paper-white, and it made me squint as I remembered how Sarah McDonnell was missing one shoe when they found her.

I broke the key off in the ignition and put the other piece in my bag. For a trophy, perhaps, I couldn't tell ya. I just did it. Then I kicked the motorcycle into the water. When it was gone, you couldn't even see a glint of red underneath the surface. Perhaps, I thought for a fleeting second, Jim Quick had never come our way after all. I could almost imagine it. Some of the pressure on my chest lifted as I walked back to join my sisters.

Jim's eyes were half open. A white butterfly landed on his neck, drawn by the crimson of a fresh neck wound. I kicked him, and he slumped to the side. He felt like a bag of rotten apples already. He didn't move as I put my foot into his back one more time and felt something breaking inside.

There again was the barking of a dog, somewhere close by. Without a word, Aoife slung the shotgun around her shoulder and grabbed each of us by the hand. My body was numb. I became aware of my hands once more when I sat in the passenger seat, wiping them on that stupid dress. They hurt, as if I'd beat him to death. I'll never understand why that is. Do hands that kill also swallow a portion of the anguish they cause? Perhaps. Since then, they've always felt sore.

I looked out the rear window of Aoife's taxi and saw Jim, still sitting underneath that tree, like a lad who just fell asleep. He even made a gorgeous corpse. I can remember wishing we'd hung him up by the heels, instead. Or asked him first if he knew that fella from my radio, who seemed to know all about *him*. Aoife stepped on it, and we were off. The sound of the sand crunching around the tires was louder than anything else I could hear.

Then we stopped so abruptly I nearly hit my head on the dash. Aoife left the Mercer idling and ran out the door, back to the tree. Fiona and I stared after her, silenced by the blood on our faces and this act we now shared equally. That damn dog hadn't stopped barking and sounded closer now. Aoife came back, floored the gas pedal, and we drove with the door still flapping open like in one of those western saloons. God, but she looked like one of Fiona's sphinxes just then. Eyes straight ahead, and no part of her face moving at all. She raced so fast all the way back to the cottage I couldn't even read the road signs.

"Whatcha go . . . back for?" I finally asked her, finding my own breath in a stranger's lungs.

"The knife," she said, sounding centuries away. "You'd left it in his chest."

IF YOU WANT to hear all about how we wallowed in mental anguish for what we did, I'm sorry to disappoint you. There was no frantic scurrying around for a spare rosary in the days that followed what can only be called an execution. None of us, so far as I know, asked forgiveness for our sins. And that old Lady Macbeth was wrong, as it turned out. Jim's blood washed off nicely with ordinary soap and water.

And let me just stop you right there, for I can tell you're thinking we relished what we'd done, right? Whooped and hollered around in

Aoife's living room like mad Indian squaws who had taken our favorite Seventh Cavalry scalp? We were corrupted youth with no sense of how serious it all was, knocking back firewater for days afterward? Did I hear you right? But that's not how it was, not at all.

If you care to hear the truth, it's simply that we knew there would be no more young women found half naked in a ditch somewhere. Yes, I'll admit it was also revenge for Aoife, but there was something else, too. My sisters and I had begun to drift apart even before Jim made it worse. Aoife and Fiona had nearly fought over that bastard, and it pained me to watch. Not to mention our dear aunt's threats of late. So if I say out loud that killing the *seanchaí* made me and my sisters a family again, you have my permission to roll yer eyes. Let's just agree that we three grew closer the second Jim stopped breathing air and leave it at that.

Once we got to Aoife's cottage, we didn't leave that desolate spot of ground for days. I know that may seem stupid to you, us being the logical suspects, and all, but we needed one another more than planning a good defense for the first Garda enquiry. To be honest, the last thing on our minds was any kind of cozy future. For a brief time, we lived inside a bubble of our own making. And when we closed our eyes, it seemed to us all that we had returned to the second floor above the newsagent's, with Father and Mother still downstairs, soon coming up to join us for dinner.

We spent the first night getting our heads together, but it didn't work. In the end, we collapsed in a heap at dawn, our bodies heavy with the work we'd done. All the next day, so far as I can remember any of it, was spent rummaging through the kitchen for something more than chocolate fingers to eat. I found some frozen shepherd's pie, which I divvied up by three. It tasted manky. We watched the night dissolve once more into gray, then black, while our stomachs rumbled.

The following day, we all seemed to wake up a bit. Perhaps, I thought, nothing had really happened that we couldn't wish away by boring ourselves stiff. And still, the guards hadn't come. So I decided to shake up the boredom by removing some evidence. I read about it in a book. It's what you're supposed to do, right?

While Fiona tried to make something edible out of spaghetti and tomato ketchup, I doused our clothes with petrol and burned them. Even Aoife's favorite jacket, the one where yellow butterflies only just evaded the men chasing them with nets, went the same way as my demon-slut skirt. The knife was harder to make disappear. I used pliers to rip the blade from the handle, which I melted into a black glob. Then I took a shovel and trudged far into Aoife's mysterious woods, where I often before had seen her stand in silence, just listening. It gave me the shivers as dew-covered trees seemed to close in on me, but I found the right spot. I heard the tide coming in and realized I had wandered so far away from the house that I was now close to the spot where we'd left Jim's darling bones. I dug a hole three feet deep next to a decapitated oak with just one live branch left, dropped the blade into it, then filled in the dirt and covered everything up with fallen branches. As I turned to walk away, I was struck by something I'd been too caught up to realize earlier.

Jim had *directed* his own death right on the spot, hadn't he? There was no other explanation for the way he'd spat his delight at tormenting Aoife into our faces like that. He drew my blade just as surely as if the fingers around the handle had been his own. I can remember feeling angry at the thought. Cheated, really. I knew why he'd done it. Sooner or later, some lucky garda would have caught him making a mistake and put the cuffs on him, perhaps even as soon as on his wedding day. And prison was out of the question. Perhaps, I wondered, he also knew that legends grow faster if they first suffer a spectacular death. I finally shivered and couldn't get out of there fast enough. That forest scared me more than the sucking sound coming from Jim's chest when I yanked out the knife. Was that the power of a story, I wonder, a lingering effect of Jim's fairy tales? Or just the invisible nature of what killing does to the human mind? You tell me.

As I stoked the fire and watched the last shreds of fabric turn to ashes, I stared out across the field. When you stood at the edge of the gravel driveway and stared back toward town, you could see a few people's kitchen windows lit up like dim stars. Moira's house was over beyond the next ridge, just out of sight. But I imagined her pacing up and down the hallway, flanked by those plaster saints, checking her watch every few seconds. Because Jim still hadn't come home. And I swear to you, I nearly felt sorry for her. I smelled something like burnt tomato from the kitchen and went back inside. My sisters had already ruined dinner, no doubt.

I wondered, as I closed the door behind me, when our aunt would be standing right outside, demanding more than an answer.

LATER THAT SAME night, I dreamed of Evvie. She had been un-furling the sails on a schooner built from used Egyptian sarcophagi, and we both sailed on a velvet sea, under a sky with no moon. I held her hand, noticing that it was changing color from pale snow to obsidian black. When I looked up at her face, afraid of what I'd see, an explosion somewhere beyond the tranquil horizon, in the real world, ripped our hands apart and I sat bolt upright in Aoife's bed, wondering where I was. The windows rattled, and everything on the shelf came crashing to the floor. Outside, the flickering orange signature of a fire waved its many fingers.

Fiona had been curled up around me and she boxed a solid fist into my stomach as she started awake. Both of us knocked our heads to-gether before finding our bathrobes and stumbling outside. Aoife was nowhere in the house as we found our way to the front door and opened it. I can remember thinking it was Aunt Moira, come to firebomb us back to Revelation.

The Mercer was burning. Flames poured out of its broken windows so quickly I could see the roof starting to buckle in the heat, before the tires were even flat yet. The lime green paint curled up in ever-widening craters. Another dull *whoomph!* from inside the wreck made me and Fiona fall down on our arses before we saw my twin sister, illuminated by the glow as she stood quite calmly, smoking a ciggie and toting the shotgun.

"What happened?" I shouted across the din.

Aoife shrugged and gave me a puff. "What happened was, we all saw a group of unidentified men flee over that hedge over there. See them?"

Boo-boom!

Before either of us could react, my twin had leveled the weapon and emptied both barrels into the sky.

"What the—" started Fiona, but Aoife wasn't done yet. She spoke to us as if from a film script she'd just written for the occasion, expecting us to pay attention to how each part ought to be played. She pointed toward town.

"They ran *that* way, ya see, because they had just set fire to my car, hadn't they?" She was asking the dark skies, not us. "And none of yis saw their faces clearly, because you had been asleep, but that's all right. Because all Bronagh needs to know is that people have thought for weeks that we'd kill darling Jim Quick sooner or later. Now, those lads had just heard rumors of the *seanchaí*'s death and wanted revenge. And wouldn't ya know it? They go and torch the *very* car we smeared his blood all over. But there's nothing for it now, I suppose. The gardaí will be lucky if they can even lift the serial number from the engine block after this. Dontcha think?"

I had to admire her. I mean, none of us had thought of hiding the most obvious evidence, like in one of those detective shows Bronagh loved so much. But one look at Aoife would tell anybody that my sister had changed in just a few weeks. The last hippie slice of her, the girl who listened to trees, perished in the oil drum where I'd burnt our clothes. Fiona grabbed my hand, as if the sight of her two baby sisters preparing to deny murder, even for a good reason, frightened her more than she could say. A fat sharp petrol stench wafted around us like some mad demon and gave me a headache.

Aoife smiled in a way I'd never seen before, as she ground the butt into the ground with her naked heel. It wasn't serene or vengeful. There was no hatred in her eyes. I suppose, more than anything, she was relieved that she could do something about how she was feeling inside, rather than just sit there and take it. I never did ask her how she felt about Fiona and me using that knife before she could shoot.

Maybe that's why she had set fire to her car. I know I would have wanted to blow something up, if it were me. Anything at all. As it happened, I'd become a murderer instead of her. And I felt nothing yet, nothing at all. My feelings were still sailing on the purple sea of dreams, holding Evvie's hand and wondering if I'd ever get to see her face.

Bronagh and the other uniforms didn't take long to show up.

"What did you do?" asked our intrepid sergeant, glaring impotently at the flames as they consumed any possible link to the dead man she'd probably just found, judging from her scowl.

"What d'you mean, *I* did?" said Aoife, acting pissed off for the camera, if there had been one. "A herd of mucksavage bollixes set fire to my taxi and ran off. They wore balaclavas, the lot of them, like they was auditioning for a spot in the IRA or worse. What, did ya not see them jumping the hedgerows, coming your way?"

Bronagh held her notebook out before her like the .357 Magnum she no doubt would have wanted instead. The other guards radioed for the fire brigade and got busy doing nothing, but in that most concerned and active-looking way cops learn early.

"Convenient, I'd say," said Bronagh, looking at me and Fiona.

"Convenient for whom?" I heard myself shouting. "Some knuckle draggers decide to burn my sister's livelihood to the ground, and you stand there and tell us she *wanted* it to happen? What are ya like, anyway?"

"You get a look at these . . . men?" Bronagh asked Fiona, who had been staring off into the distance. The other cops had found the garden hose and tried feebly to extinguish the flames, which still had plenty of plastic insulation to eat.

"I was asleep," said Fiona, yawning. "We all were. All I saw was their backsides, and that wasn't an impressive sight, let me tell ya. Aren't ya gonna go and catch them?"

I haven't seen Bronagh in the grip of inchoate rage very often, perhaps only once, when Martin Clarke from class stole her favorite doll and threw it into the bay when we were six. But now she simmered, as she put the notebook back in her pocket and walked up to Aoife, nose to button nose.

"We just found him," she hissed, not knowing whether to cry or threaten, "still sitting underneath his tree, far from prying eyes, like he just rang an ambulance. But you knew that, didn't ya? More holes in him than I could count. Tell me, did you all have a go? Because he bled so dry he's only white like the ghost of Christmas Past. And don't tell me 'Who are you talking about?' because I deserve better than that."

"Jim is dead," said Aoife, in a voice so neutral and devoid of judgment she might as well have told Bronagh the time of day. "Is that it? Well, no shortage of suspects, I imagine. If yer looking for sympathy, you've come to the wrong front door, I don't mind telling ya."

"Let me hear you say how none of you had anything to do with that. Go on."

Aoife obliged. "We had nothing to do with it."

"Tell me anything at all," said Bronagh, in a voice so low I could barely hear the words. "It was revenge for what he did to you. Self-defense, even. Did he attack you with a weapon? Or one of your sisters?" When Aoife just stared at her without blinking, she went on, but mostly to herself. "You probably won't do a day in jail if you tell me everything now. Everyone will understand."

"What about Sarah McDonnell?" I asked. "Will she understand, too?"

Aoife shot me a look that couldn't be interpreted any other way than *Shut the hell up, ya eejit.*

"So, did yis kill him?" Bronagh asked me, her face transformed into a visage of forgiveness. If I'd just say the words. Confess. The fire crackled and hissed as it ran out of food.

"No," I said, pretending to be angry. "But I love this part about everybody understanding us. Tell me something. Did they understand that yer man under the tree there, or wherever it is, raped my twin sister? Oh, I see. They *understood* it so well they decided to shut us out afterward, isn't that it? Like lepers. Even you. Sergeant."

"If I leave here and have to bring back the big boys from Cork City or

Macroom HQ? Deal's off." She searched our eyes in the blazing glare to see if there were any takers. All three of us stared back and said nothing.

"Why don'tcha turn yer horse around, sheriff, and catch those varmints who just burned our stagecoach?" said Fiona, cracking a smile despite herself. "They can't have got far. It's Injun country out there, haven't ya heard? Pure Fort Apache, where even the squaws are desperate." I had to cover my mouth to keep from bursting out laughing. My stomach turned into triangular shapes to keep from howling. And I felt tears on my knuckles. *I murdered someone,* my brain whispered to my stomach for the first time, *so let me see some waterworks to prove ya understand what that means.*

"I always believed you," Bronagh told Aoife, but there was shame in her eyes now.

"Sure you did," said my twin, in a voice as hollow as the wind through a dead tree.

Bronagh looked out across the dark road, which turned increasingly neon blue the closer the fire tender from town climbed toward us. All the fight had drained out of her. She waved her men back in the car and adjusted her cap, so we couldn't see her eyes.

"Just tell me this," she asked Aoife, but made sure we all heard. "Are you ready for this? All of it? Enquiries, maybe interrogations, court app—"

"Thanks for coming, Bronagh," answered Aoife, and snapped the empty shotgun closed with a *clack!*

Bronagh recognized the gun she'd seen since we were little girls, but couldn't resist one last fishing expedition. "Got a license for that thing?"

"You wrote it out yerself," said Aoife, keeping the sarcasm out of her voice. "But if you find any steel shot in those fellas' backsides, feel free to come back and arrest me."

WHERE I'M FROM, funerals are usually a solemn affair where even the corpse is bored. They begin with folded hands at Sacred Heart

Church, where we gawk at who got seated closest to the casket, and there are lots of downcast eyes during the *In Paradisum* hymn. When it's over, everyone's invited to Father Malloy's for sour white wine and a conversation about how "life is changed, not ended." And then, when the father is pickled, a few of the living go for a pint at McSorley's to gossip about the deceased.

But for Jim, those rules were changing before his body was even cold.

We all knew the final journey of the town's slain mascot would be different when the mourners started drifting into town, one starry-eyed face after the other. There were the morbidly curious, of course, and some journos who had heard rumors of the sex-and-violence trail the *seanchai* was rumored to have cut across all of County Cork. It was said he had been slain by three sisters from the area. Hot stuff. The funeral was bound to look great on camera. And the people have a right to know, don't they? I suppose that's why TV vans with satellite dishes soon occupied the square so you couldn't even see the cross in the middle of it. Jonno made a killing serving them all overpriced beer and telling lies about "the butcher of Castletownbere," who paralyzed girls with only the sound of his voice. He even got his name in the paper that way and framed the article over the bar. I'm guessing it's still there.

But the typical pilgrim dragging her worn-out tennies along the Glengarriff Road was usually a young girl, hopelessly devoted to a man she felt was "just misunderstood." Old Mrs. Crimmins was the first to notice this wasn't just a random trickle of crazies. On Wednesday before the service, as she watered her daffodils, she saw clusters of ten, maybe fifteen, women passing by the bed-and-breakfast. Most carried knapsacks and water bottles, and none had enough cash to stay in any of her rooms, even for one night. All of them called him "Darling Jim," long before the press got wind of that nickname and made it the catchphrase the town is still trying to get rid of.

"Something strange about the way they *talk*," she tried to explain to Jonno, who's the one told me about it. "Won't look ya in the eye but are already somewhere else. I wouldn't let a single one of those manky hippies sleep in *my* house."

But the scattered clumps of wanderers on the roadside soon grew to whole caravans. It was as if the lost tribes of Israel had bypassed Egypt and come straight to our town instead. Bronagh arrested two fourteen-year-old girls who had refused to disperse and had chained themselves to the lamppost outside the Garda station because they'd got it in their heads that Jim was on a slab in the morgue. As it happened, he was in an icebox in the harbormaster's shack to throw groupies off the scent until it was time to dress him for the final journey. Three grown women camped out in front of Father Malloy's rectory so they could be the first to see the mourners come. Oh, yes. A proper circus with nothing in it but clowns. If people thought the Walsh sisters were nuts, they hadn't seen anything yet.

ON JIM'S LAST day aboveground, the church was so mobbed Bronagh had to call in help from as far away as Kenmare. Five patrol cars' worth. The stone steps leading from Main Street up to the heavy oak door at Sacred Heart was a panoply of girls with flowers painted on their cheeks, sobbing grannies, and cameramen shoving at one another for a better shot. Mary Catherine Cremin had brought her father's best camera and mounted a telescopic lens big enough to catch the mole on Father Malloy's cheek.

My sisters and I had decided not to attend. With most of our days that week spent apart from one another in front of yet another garda pressuring us to confess, it seemed wrong, somehow. None of us gave an inch, although Fiona cried so much during the interrogations the cops thought *she* was the one Jim had attacked.

But when Saturday came, I couldn't resist.

"We're out of milk," I told my sisters, who stayed home to keep the curious from peering in our windows. "I'll be right back," I lied. And so I picked out a baseball cap one of Aoife's American gentleman callers had once left behind, and biked down toward the noise of a thousand expectant throats. It sounded like the Colosseum around feeding time, and made me shiver more than when I thought of what Jim probably looked like inside his casket. An elderly couple pointed at me and snapped a few photos as I rode past. For a brief moment, I wished Jim were there to whisper into their ears what he'd told that Swedish fella—and immediately hated myself for it. Why wasn't Evvie answering my text messages, anyway? I wondered what the girls looked like down in old Sochi, as the church spire came into view, and I hoped to God they were ugly.

I didn't see Aunt Moira right away.

It was only as I snuck in through the back door near where the nuns are buried that I saw the still-empty altar. A white casket, even more spotless than Jim's Vincent, refracted the light streaming in through the stained-glass windows. Father Malloy was bent down to console a figure kneeling in front of it, hands clasped in prayer.

"Please, I'm begging you," he said. "We must begin. Come this way."

My aunt was wearing a mourner's costume so black the ravens in our backyard would have been jealous. I couldn't see her face, because the veil covering it was so tightly sewn it looked like a fencing mask. Even so, I ducked around the corner when she rose and looked my way.

When Father Malloy let everyone else in, it sounded like stampeding elephants. I didn't dare remain inside for the service. What, I wondered, would happen to me if some of Jim's devoted disciples discovered me there? The *Southern Star* had already run several articles, with headlines blaring GARDA HOT ON MURDERERS' TRAIL, echoed by the *Irish Mirror* all the way in Dublin, which had dubbed us THE STILETTO SISTERS. Of course, there was no proof to convict or even indict us; Aoife had seen to that. And that dog walker near the murder site had seen nothing but the tweety birds that day. Besides, it had rained so much after we left that no footprints or tire tracks remained.

Fiona had described that Kelly woman to me, the one from the cottage out in the mountains, and I think I saw her before sneaking back out to my bike. She was beautiful, in a black silk dress that came to her ankles, and tears streaming down her face, like in a proper opera. Kelly gave Aunt Moira's hand a reassuring squeeze before the father intoned the benediction. If she'd got her hands on me, that would have been the end.

But it was after the service that the true madness showed its face.

Jim, you see, was beginning to divide opinions around Castletown-bere's dinner tables, especially since Bronagh had started to do her job right for a change. That Tomo fella had done time in both Cork and Dublin prisons and had a criminal record longer than most. It was said he'd met Jim at school, some rough corner of the state reform program, but that couldn't be verified. Stories of girls raped or murdered didn't sit well with most anyway, even those who had heard the fairy tales and listened to that mellifluous voice. That meant interment in Glebe Grave-yard was out, and so was anything within town limits. Wouldn't do to seem soft on mass murder, no matter how adorable the chief suspect. A compromise was therefore struck.

Saint Finian's was a strange old burial ground, stuck on the side of the road and with no church on that side of the asphalt to keep it com-pany. It looked ancient when we were children, and time had done nothing to make it less decrepit. Since Jim left behind no relatives who could be found, the city council decided to allow his many fans to erect a headstone there and place him underneath it. There were secret do-nors to pay for the damn thing as well, people said. From all corners of the country. Fucking hell, I thought, how many times did he flog that damn story about the wolf's demolition tour? As hundreds of sobbing women trailed his white casket up the winding road, dodging traffic as they went, the city fathers soon lived to regret that decision.

TV cameras caught the procession, keening as if possessed, as it streamed in the narrow iron gate and beyond. I had snuck out of church before the service finished and ended up in the grass near Aoife's cot-tage, pointing our father's old binoculars at the spectacle. A cloud of dust whirled in the air, obscuring my view, because more than twenty people scrambled to throw dirt on the casket as it was lowered. Their screams carried across the slopes of the mountain like vultures on car-rion. Kill her or love her, Jimmy boy, I thought to myself, shaking my head. These poor souls didn't much care which you chose, did they? The crowd only thinned out as darkness began to crawl across the ridge and cover the road with a fine sprinkle of rain.

But a few faces were still visible, even from that distance. I could see two girls who looked no more than twelve, smoothing the dirt in front of the headstone. I couldn't help thinking of old Fiona's pharaohs and wondered if they had got a send-off this insane. A woman was taking her time placing a candle and lighting it. Her dress whipped around her scrawny body in the wind, but she didn't care. She just kept striking matches until she ran out.

When she left, there was one woman remaining on the grave itself.

She had her back to me and was again on her knees in supplication to a God who had taken everything from her more than once. She lifted the veil and turned her head, as if she could sense my intrusion. I pulled my eyes off the binoculars, as quickly as I could.

But Aunt Moira saw me. I know she did.

And I've been paying for it ever since.

IT'S A FUNNY old thing, time. It doesn't heal all wounds the way they say. But it does make everybody forget details. I suppose it's nature's own discreet mercy.

First, people can't remember around the edges of a thing that happened, even if they were there themselves. Did Jim kill three women or only two? Were his eyes hazel, as most insisted, or did they look green? Questions like that. Given enough time, people will forget the actual event altogether and just settle for the myth. And so it was with the murdering Walshes, because we were acquitted on all charges. After four weeks of trudging down to Main Street to stare at the same wallpaper or being driven to Cork City to meet gardaí with even more gold on their epaulets, the cops let us go.

Bronagh, bless her heart, knew we'd done it, of course. Most of Castletownbere and the surrounding area did, too. It conferred upon us the instant status of living legends, desperate women not to be trifled with. My previous reputation as a sex witch couldn't even compare to this new level of notoriety. None of us could unshackle ourselves from the myth, so we just nodded at people and kept to ourselves.

Eventually, the TV cameras and freelance snoops left our front yard, where they'd trampled it to mud for months. The boys from Sacred Heart whispered when any of us walked past, but not like they did before, when they'd sneak looks at our backsides. Now they didn't dare look us in the eye. Fiona even said people had begun to think we possessed some kind of dark magic. All I wanted was enough of that voodoo to get Evvie to return my calls.

Time had done nothing to blur the most painful parts of Moira's memory.

"Gone wrong in the head" is how I heard Jonno try to describe what had happened to her. She'd been coughing up a lung since catching a bad case of pneumonia from sitting on Jim's grave for over a week. We all dreaded running into her in town, but that never happened. I snuck past the bed-and-breakfast once or twice and saw a FOR SALE sign in the window. A few weeks later, it was gone, and a work crew was busy repairing the chimney, which had been badly in need for some time.

On the days when Fiona taught at school (you didn't honestly think the headmistress would dismiss a genuine *celebrity*, did ya?) and Aoife shuttled tourists around the area in an old Vauxhall she'd bought with the insurance money from the Mercer, I tried to find traces of our aunt. Call me morbid or sick, I've been called worse and lived. But I wanted an answer to why she hadn't shown up on our doorstep, breathing Old Testament threats and waving her Bible about. Having her in one place had kept me calm for years. Knowing she was everywhere and nowhere gave me the willies. I snuck out with the binoculars like some demented border guard, hoping to catch a glimpse.

What worried me more than anything is that she never returned to the cemetery—which was always swarming with women, by the way. The place was forever flower-strewn, and Bronagh had to place a permanent guard to make sure nobody made off with Jim's headstone. In the end, she even had to pour concrete around the casket and be done with it, rather than having to call Macroom HQ one fine day and say someone had stolen the corpse, too. As it was, avid disciples had already salvaged Jim's Vincent Comet and sold most of it for a fortune on eBay. The last relic, half a brake line, was wrapped around the skull on Jim's grave, like a crown of thorns. I ate many dry ham sandwiches staring at it, waiting for the widow to reappear. Only she never did.

One ordinary Tuesday, down by the old beach near Eyeries, I saw a green scarf catching the wind.

It had been a Christmas present to Moira from the three of us not long ago, and our aunt wore it around her face like someone still stuck in the 1950s. She was poking in the dirt by the tree where I'd knifed her precious Jim into next Sunday. At first I had trouble breathing, and then I calmed down. There was nothing to find. Perhaps, I reasoned, she had taken up residence in the forest. Did she spend all her waking hours in the spot where her fiancé died? Not even Aunt Moira was that sentimental. Butter wouldn't have melted in her mouth, even before she became loony. She hopped about like a sparrow, unable to find ground that suited her. She's looking for something, I thought, feeling sick about it. She's searching and won't give up until she finds it. But there was no more proof to dig up, because the cops had been out there with the bloodhounds and all.

I crawled away and biked home as fast as I could. Something about the way she'd moved had unsettled me more than the fear she knew something I didn't. Like a crab, or an unfeeling animal, prodding until whatever it was after broke like an eggshell.

"Have yis heard the news?" asked Aoife a few days later, setting two grocery bags down on the counter. "Jonno says Aunt Moira moved away. He saw her at the bus station this morning, loading suitcases on the bus to Dublin. Sold her place, apparently."

I felt a gray pallor lift from my heart, and I hugged her like a mad-woman. "I could kiss ya," I yelled, leading her around the living room in what was supposed to be a waltz, and we both ended up on the chair. We couldn't afford to buy new furniture yet but had covered the gashes in the sofa with duct tape. Every time I walked past, I thought of Jim.

I can't imagine how Aoife felt. Fiona shook her wise old head and lit up a ciggie for the three of us to share.

It was another week or two before I realized that Aoife's day trips had grown longer than before.

"Ya driving them all the way to New York through some underground tunnel now, or what?" I tried, but my twin just grinned and said something about having to take on more shifts to make ends meet. When she thought I wasn't looking, that muscle right between the eyebrows curled up and looked serious, the way it does on me when I have something to hide. So I decided not to press it.

You'll be relieved to know I finally got hold of Evvie, who all this time had been in the arms of some Abkhazian architect woman who was apparently "sooo smart and sensitive," and we had a fight that kept my sisters up three nights in a row.

The last time I can remember me and Aoife sitting down together was the following week, when all three of us had invited Jonno up for dinner. While Fiona prepared the steaks he'd brought, me and Aoife sat outside, breathing in the last light of the day. I should have noticed that there was something about her, something beyond reach that didn't seem natural, but then none of our compasses had worked perfectly since meeting that bastard, had they? She was wearing my favorite leather jacket, the one with the hand-painted Oscar Wilde portrait on the back. I could hear Jonno's hollow bear laugh at something Fiona said. I didn't want to spoil the mood, but there was something I had to know. Because, like I said, I know a thing or two about the nature of time. And it bothers me when something about it doesn't fit.

"When you went back to Jim that day," I began, not looking at her, "you were gone a long time. Too long to just take the knife back."

The wind rolled in from the sea, drowning out what she answered, so I had to ask again. This time, Aoife tried to smile, as if she were over the entire thing.

"I rolled up his sleeve," she said, keeping the cigarette in both hands as anchorage, "because I wanted to see that tattoo properly. Fiona had told me about it. Everyone had a theory of what it looked like. And when he was on top of me, he shoved it in my face like a boy scout merit badge. But he beat me with the other hand, so I never got a look." She took a breath, and it dawned on me that we'd never really talked about that night, only plotted a murder to avenge it. Her stomach heaved underneath the silk dress she'd filched off Fiona.

"Listen," I said, "you don't have to—"

"Yes, I do. I wanted to make sure he was really dead, do you understand? So I stabbed him myself. Didn't want you two to carry the whole burden, in case old Bronagh grew a new brain or something." She exhaled. "It wasn't a wolf, in case yer wondering. That tattoo. At first I couldn't see what it was supposed to be and brushed some blood away. Then I got it. It was twins. Two boys, holding hands. In a forest. Like in that story of his, I suppose."

I thought of another face from my recent memory, and saw a flash of brown skin and two quick eyes that wanted nobody too close to him. The devil's handler. The man with the felt hat who pretended to be satisfied with spare change from children and their mothers after a good show.

"Tomo," I said. "Jim's setup man."

"What about him?"

"*Tomo* means *companion* in Japanese, right?" I continued. "Jim must have loved that fella enough to ink himself for him. Like they were twins or something."

"Yeah," said Aoife, stubbing out the ciggie before even taking a drag. "Before he beat his face in."

"Dinner, lads!" yelled Fiona, trying to get Jonno's hands off her while she opened the wine.

As I sit here and write all this, I'm kicking myself for not putting two and two together before I went back inside with my twin. All I'd had to do was stop and think about what I already knew. But that kind of self-criticism gets me nowhere, Fiona keeps saying. And maybe she's right.

AOIFE WAS GONE before the first autumn leaves had turned yellow.

It was on a Thursday, it must have been, because those were usually the days I'd go to town to pick up our mail at the post office on Main Street. I found the key, opened our mail slot, and withdrew a few crap adverts and one letter. I was about to put it in my bag when I took a second look. All sounds around me slowed down to murmurs, even the children's screams as they fought over ice creams.

I opened the letter. It started off with a jaunty

Hey, girls.

I biked back up to the cottage so fast my lungs felt like someone had poured battery acid in them. Without saying anything first, I grabbed Fiona by the scruff of the neck and made her look at it, too. I crawled up on the couch and held my ears. I couldn't even look, because I'd seen Aoife's eyes that night and knew what they were trying to say. They had telegraphed a long goodbye.

Fiona read the letter inside the envelope. Then she smoothed it out with her palm and looked at me. I don't know how long it took me to gather my courage, but in the end, I walked over there and began to read, too. Aoife had written:

> *I had to go away. Don't worry, especially you, Rosie, ya moan bag, it's not forever. But I may not come back to town for a good long time. It's nothing to do with either of you, and I'm not losing my mind because of what Jim did to me, either. Someday, I'll explain everything. And when that day comes, I hope you can both forgive me for what I am about to do.*
>
> *Until then, may our parents in their heaven watch over you and keep you safe.*
>
> *I love you both more than you can know.*
>
> *Ever your sister,*
> *Aoife*

I must have read that letter hundreds of times, and it still didn't make sense to me. As days turned to weeks and then to months, her message remained a love letter that sounded more like a permanent farewell each time I reached her final word.

What I couldn't know is that another letter would follow.

And nowhere did it mention love.

YOU KNOW HOW I told you I knew a thing or two about time? Forget that. Turns out I was a complete eejit. Time does whatever it likes, no matter who claims to know its mysteries. And Heraclitus and Einstein can both shut the hell up about trying to figure it out.

Because the three years we spent without Aoife felt like twenty.

Fiona and me shuttered her stone cottage. It seemed like the right thing to do. Photographers still combed the ground, especially during tourist season, when every kid with so much as a mobile phone had to come and bother us. And the leaks in the roof grew worse, forcing us up at all hours of the night, placing buckets everywhere. Finbar, bless his greedy little heart, even offered us a good price for it, but I think Fiona told him to stick it.

So I moved into Fiona's Egyptian temple and had to be careful to mind all the knickknacks every time I cleaned. She made money for the rent the same way she always did, which might strike you as being in poor taste. Morbid, even, to have a sure-as-shite murderer prancing around Sacred Heart after all this lark, corrupting impressionable young minds.

True enough, there were those parents who tried to brand my sister as some kind of desperate killer. Donald Cremin, Mary Catherine's father, was one to have a go, and there were others who did more than merely whisper in Mrs. Gately's half-deaf ear about sexual depravity, witch covens, and all such nonsense.

The only thing they hadn't counted on was their own kids.

Whenever some of Fiona's snot-nosed monsters were pulled from her class under some vague pretext, others were just as eager to learn from Castletownbere's very own female Jesse James. She had them lining up in the hallway. Some even had autograph books. In the end, before events took another sharp turn, she had randomers following her down the street from work.

At home, I'd watch her thumb through countless travel brochures and maps, as if either one of us would really leave town as long as Aoife was still missing. It comforted her, I know, to keep looking at rock piles strewn in the desert sand. But she never said a word about it. She didn't have to. I could hear her thinking from across the room. Between the three of us, she always had the loudest thoughts.

Meanwhile, I grew into a real expert at gabbing on the radio, if I dare say so myself. Not like before, either, where I'd talk to any gobshite just to pass the time. I soon had shortwave spies from Clontarf to Killala on the lookout for a close-cropped blonde driving a dented brown Vauxhall Royale. There were even eager Welsh schoolgirls from Aberystwyth on the lookout, just as I had long broken-up conversations with harbormasters in both Liverpool and Cherbourg, in case she'd gone that way. I quit the ciggies during all this, imagine that? Gained weight like a shut-in, which Fiona said suited me, and I could have belted her one for that. With Evvie gone, who the hell did I have to look sexy for? I gave away most of my raccoon makeup to a couple of reed-thin girlies from Sacred Heart, and they nearly kissed me, they were so ecstatic. I left the house only to buy groceries and then headed home to my dials and my transceiver microphone, where I felt safe.

Except none of it helped. Aoife was gone.

And something else had happened that I didn't notice until months afterward. Someone was missing from my invisible megahertz world.

Gatekeeper, that self-satisfied voice who seemed to know everything about Jim before I did, had closed his doors. I dialed left and right, switched frequencies, and even asked other ham operators to key me a message if they found him on their band. But nobody did. I began to wonder if the smooth talker had been Jim himself, messing with our heads in case face-to-face wasn't enough.

"Heard someone the other day who sounded like him," claimed one of my nerdiest shortwave admirers from across the sea in Brighton. "He just opened the channel and rambled on about the nature of evil for a bit. Quite pissed, he was. Then he began to play the piano. It went on forever. Boring, you ask me. Cole Porter, it sounded like. 'Anything

Goes.' And I suppose it does. But he never said anything after that, so I switched off."

I might have believed a word of that if it had come from a reputable sort, not a mouth breather who wanted a peek at my gicker. Besides, Gatekeeper didn't sound like a music lover. He was too mesmerized by his own voice to bother with other instruments.

Bronagh stayed away for a while but eventually began speaking to us again. The case against Jim and Tomo, such as it was, was still circumstantial, but the sexual assaults and murders had stopped. Even if there was no proof, everybody knew those boys had done it. Each year, Jonno held a fund-raiser down in the town square, to benefit the victims' families. Me and Fiona were reluctant guests of honor, but we did it for him. He always told me there was a pint waiting for me inside, and I declined every time. Mrs. Crimmins, who had taken all the guests Aunt Moira scared away, built a new wing to her place and always treated us with respect. "Never liked that fella either," she'd always say.

With things settled back as far into normal as possible for a town like ours, you would've thought that was the end of it, right? Two kooky sisters scouring the world for their lost sibling and trying to forget about their loving aunt. Turn off the TV and go to bed. What a shitty movie *that* would have been.

Time *is* a funny thing. Bobs and weaves around you in ways it takes too long to explain. Because it was nearly three years to the day from picking up Aoife's letter that there was another one in our mailbox. The envelope was made from thick cotton paper and had been posted from a place called

1 Strand Street, Malahide, County Dublin.

It had been rerouted from Aoife's old cottage, so I knew it wasn't from her. The intended recipients weren't listed, just the postal address. I ripped open the envelope myself this time, ignoring nosy stares from my neighbors. *My dears,* it read:

*I hope this letter finds you well. I will get right to the point, be-
cause I hate writing as it is and have no desire to waste your
time. I have proof positive that all three of you murdered my Jim.
I'm not interested in having you arrested. I've something else in
mind. The cancer's got me, and there's not that much time left,
the doctors say. A month, at most.*

*Here's the arrangement: I want you all to come to Dublin
and care for me until the end. I have nobody anymore. Do me
this last kindness, or the gardaí get all my information. In case
you don't believe me, I've enclosed a sample. And I have more.
You girls didn't clean up properly after yourselves. You'll find the
address on the back of this envelope. Come as soon as you've read
this. If not, I'll be visiting you up in Dochas Prison, won't I, my
dears?*

Big kisses to you all,
Your aunt,
Moira

A sample? Of what? I wasn't even thinking but just did as she said, a
child's reflex. I rattled the envelope, and something fell out into the
palm of my hand. It was something I'd looked at each time I promised
my lungs it would be the last time they'd choke.

My own cigarette lighter, the one with the skull and crossbones that
I'd won in a poker game once. That wretched woman had put it in a
plastic bag. Small clumps of dirt still stuck to it. I couldn't remember
having dropped it anywhere, much less in front of a guy I'd just stabbed.
When did I use it last? I tried to rewind the tape three years and failed.
But I usually kept the lighter in my bag. And I'd brought the bag that
day. What else did Moira have? I wondered, as I pedaled over to see my
sister. I stopped on the way to throw up.

As trees and curious stares blew by, I tried to imagine what would
happen if I just ripped up the letter and didn't tell Fiona. It was all a
bluff, a scam from a woman who had truly lost the last bit of sense her
plastic Jesus ever gave her to begin with. Right? But then I began to

doubt myself. Had we left fingerprints on something else? Jim's shirt buttons, perhaps? But surely the cops would have found those long ago. My head whirled like a hair dryer as I pushed open the door to Fiona's place and barged inside, waving the letter about like a lunatic.

Except my favorite big sister wasn't alone.

The figure sitting on the couch and wearing what looked like a ratty old fireman's coat didn't rise straightaway. I was about to ask Fiona if the local volunteer brigade had come to help us rebuild the stone cottage when I got near enough to see who was inside that getup. I dropped the letter on the floor and took a step forward and felt at the same time a soft caramel love around my heart and such cast-iron rage I could never even begin to describe it to you. Because the visitor raised her head and smiled shyly.

"Now yer gonna tell me I'm in trouble, aren't ya?" said Aoife.

FOR THE LONGEST time, nothing happened. No cries of joy, no screams of anger. I just picked up the letter and sat down as far away from Aoife as I could. Nothing came to me to say. The wind outside made the door creak. Fiona poured me a cup of tea without my asking for it, and I took it without hesitating. It was something to do while my head reoriented itself.

"I have lots to explain, I know I do," said my twin, and nodded into her empty cup.

"Fifty-five cents," I finally said, attempting to sound calm.

"Róisín—" said Fiona, sounding like our mother used to.

"That's all it would have cost ya," I persisted. "A shagging fifty-five-cent stamp on a postcard to let us know you weren't face down in some ditch. Too hard for ya, was it? Too complicated to lick a stamp? Why didn't you wait for damp weather, then, and go outside until it was wet enough to stick on the envelope? That would have been fine."

"Rosie," Aoife tried, only now becoming aware of the letter in my hand. "Can I just—"

"Actually, no, you cannot," I said, holding back the tears, but barely. "We've only had a lovely time, me and Fiona, dragging that stiletto

sisters nonsense about our necks like a dead albatross. Didja go to the
south of France with one of yer football players? Or with that Belgian
fella who kept trying to teach us to whistle?"

"I had to go take care of something" is all Aoife finally said, by way
of explanation, and drew her coat tightly around her body, like a rookie
hiding from the fire chief during inspection. Fiona put a hand on my
shoulder, but I ignored it. I may know nothing about time, but I'm not
so stupid I can't feel what three years of trying to pretend being fine
feels like when the cork finally pops out of the bottle. I folded the piece
of paper in my hand several times, nearly forgetting it wasn't a dinner
invitation, but the devil's origami.

"Well, I can only hope you paid our aunt Moira a visit," I said. "If
that's what you meant in your letter by all that 'forgive me for what I'm
about to do' lark. So? Didja track her down, set fire to her house or
something?"

"That's enough!" said Fiona, actually scandalized, I think, to hear
me wishing such a thing aloud, despite everything. But she'd thought it
herself, which is why her voice was now shrill and shocked like a grandmother's.

"No, I didn't," said Aoife, and reached out for my hand. After a few
moments, I grabbed hold of it, but I still couldn't look her in the face. I
want nobody to see me cry, not even my sisters. Back when Evvie still
came to visit, I always went to the bathroom if she'd upset me, and only
came back out with dry eyes. I make no apologies, because that's just
how it is. But at that moment, I'll admit to you, it felt like nothing on
this earth to touch Aoife's fingers again. Fiona knew better than to open
her mouth and ruin it.

"So what didja do?" I asked.

"Give me a little time, and I'll tell you both everything," Aoife said,
sniffling a bit herself there, around the end. I noticed her hands looked
rough, like a dishwasher's. "Don't know where to begin. But I'll stay for
a while. So we don't have to rush."

I unfolded Aunt Moira's threat as slowly as I could, watching my sisters' faces tighten in anticipation. The paper bird I'd tried to make out of our aunt's letter was unfolding itself into a boat. "Yes, we do," I said, feeling whatever remnants of safety or joy that still swirled around inside me harden and turn to stone. "Because we're going to Malahide."

NONE OF US said much on the train.

The nine-thirty from Cork City was packed to the gills that morning, and everyone's wet clothes made the windows steam up like a Russian bathhouse. My sisters and I found a window seat as far from the dining car as possible. Because if anyone had heard our sparse conversation, they would have pulled the emergency brake straightaway and called for the nearest garda.

Try to understand. We weren't hardened criminals, just three girls who couldn't act any differently than we did. If that's how proper hard men and women excuse themselves in front of the judge, so be it. Put yourself in my shoes, and the arithmetic becomes simpler to grasp. Love him or kill him? Remember that old audience question? Problem is, if you've already killed once, it kinda takes the sting out. And then where does *that* end? See what I mean?

"I didn't bring a weapon," I told the others, keeping my voice down and smiling at two elderly men sharing a bag of crisps on the other side of the aisle.

"Shut up, ya eejit!" whispered Fiona. She had made us sandwiches and tea for the trip, just like she did when our parents went out for the night, leaving big sis to "cook."

Aoife remained silent almost all the way into the terminus. Three years had left a film of sorrow on her skin, but those wrinkles didn't tell the whole story. Kick me if this sounds corny, but there was also an air of serenity about her that endless hours in front of Father Malloy could not have produced. Even with Aunt Moira's threat hanging over our heads, she didn't give in to the pressure. Nor did she ever consider not coming with me and Fiona to Dublin, even if she must have had some brilliant hiding place somewhere. "All for one," she said, as she rang the train station to book our tickets. Something had changed her inner-most, deepest core, and it wasn't the murder. It was something lumi-nous that she kept to herself.

"I have something to show you," she finally said, after most of the train car emptied out in Newbridge just before we reached Dublin.

Fiona and me leaned toward her and saw the object in her hand.

It was a man's wallet.

"I took it out of Jim's pocket," she said, still breathless at the mem-ory. "Don't know why I kept it."

The caramel-colored thing was worn shiny, and I couldn't wait to open it. But I let Aoife do the honors. Inside, I saw what I expected: re-ceipts and a few banknotes. Then my twin thumbed Jim's pink driver's license out of its plastic holster. It was his picture, all right, shiny teeth and lowered sex-eyebrows. But the name belonged to a stranger, which didn't surprise me at all.

"So he's Jim O'Driscoll, is he?" I said.

"Was," corrected Fiona, ever the schoolteacher. "What else ya got?"

Aoife emptied all the scraps out into her hand. But there was noth-ing but an old train ticket and a spent phone card. I noticed that the wallet's bulk was still there, though. I reached a finger behind the li-cense and felt something that had been stuck to the leather from sweat.

A folded-up sheet of paper, yellowed and porous from age, saw the light of day again.

"What's that?" asked Aoife, lowering her voice when she saw the train conductor doing a last check before getting off work.

I carefully unwrapped the inner fantasy life of the one man besides my own father whom I'd ever cared to know anything about. The paper only gave slowly, resisting intrusion, but finally revealed what old Jim had dreamed about between murders.

A hand-drawn old-fashioned treasure map, such as a child might invent, sprawled in all directions. To the north, impassable ice scapes hindered a small stick figure with a cane in his hand. At the bottom, near an ocean crawling with fearsome octopi, a female form lay on a trail near a beach, her neck broken.

"Christ, she looks like Sarah," I said, and the conductor turned his head my way. I covered by laughing and giggling like the girl I never really was, and he walked on, shaking his head.

Near what was supposed to be the east, the map became a forest with gnarled oaks and wizards in pointy hats sending zigzag rays from their fingertips. Fair maidens ran from wolves, which looked like they had plenty of prey to choose from before the sun went down.

But it was one detail, poorly drawn and smudged, that transfixed me.

"That's a castle," I said, holding it up to the light. And it was. Jim had colored the gate black with Magic Marker, and someone sat outside its walls, operating what looked like a radio. A male figure, it looked like. Curly "electrical waves" rose from his head. And you heard me right, he *sat,* because there was a perfectly good reason why he would never again stand up.

His legs were broken. Almost as if someone had run over them on purpose and left him there to die. A prince, I remembered from Jim's fairy tale, who also has magical powers. His horse just fell on him. His brother, Euan, will kill him and steal the crown. The dying prince's name is . . . damn, I couldn't remember.

Outside the train, the first concrete stanchions signaled that me and my sisters would soon be in enemy territory.

"The next station is Dublin Heuston," intoned the announcer's languid voice. "This train is for Dublin Heuston. Thank you for traveling with Iarnród Éireann."

He might as well have told us the train was rushing straight to the walls of Dochas Prison, its black gates slamming shut behind us.

WHEN WE WERE little girls, our mother would always tell us the same kind of bedtime story, especially whenever something had gone bump in the night. It never varied much, but perhaps it grew a bit longer if we were still crying near the end and needed just one more glimmer of hope to chase away the bogeymen under the bed.

Usually, however, we pestered her to tell us the one where we ended up heroes, and the stakes were dire. What's the fun, otherwise? Mother would try with the softer versions first, where unicorns frolicked with elves and such complete crap, until she relented and picked the one where something stared back from the darkness.

"There once lived three brave girls, just like you," she'd begin, tucking our down comforters up to our chins and leaving at least one light on. "Their home was a tree house deep in the enchanted forest. Elves and animals alike loved having them as neighbors. Only the trolls, who preferred the dark and hid underneath rocks during the day, came out at night to stalk the three beauties. That meant the sisters needed to keep their house lit whenever the sun went down."

She'd go on to tell us how the girls leaped into the heavens each night, trying to catch enough stars in their butterfly nets to light up the bedroom until the sun returned. They'd weave comets and starbursts together until they formed a carpet, which they used for a blanket. Finally, the trolls stopped coming around, frightened by the perpetual glare from inside the girls' house.

All was well, until the most jealous of all cave-dwelling trolls decided to steal their starry treasure. She had no name, but even the wolves feared her and would not forage if they sensed her presence.

She waited until the girls were asleep, wrapped herself in a shawl so dense no rays could penetrate, and climbed into the tree house. Her hands burned when she touched the bright quilt, and she nearly cried out. But she managed to stay silent until the thousands of stars were buried in the deepest, darkest hole in the ground.

The three girls woke up because all the other trolls now banged on the front door, trying to get in. "There's only one thing for us to do," said the bravest of the girls. "We must journey below the earth, fighting whatever dangers lie ahead. Because we're the sisters who sleep under the stars."

The bravest. How do you like that? Mother always had a flair for the melodramatic. After a breathless odyssey starring Aoife, Fiona, and me as we battled witches, demons, and dark knights, the sisters finally retrieved the cosmic blanket and lived happily ever after. And mother would leave our night-light on until breakfast, even if it cost her a bundle. I told you she loved us, didn't I?

There was nothing magical awaiting us at Heuston Station.

We took the DART local train up to Malahide, once again falling into a sullen silence as the sleepy waterfront houses rushed past. Once we got there, it was only a short walk through narrow streets where each house looked like it was made of soggy gingerbread.

I was the bravest, I suppose. So I rang the doorbell of number 1 Strand Street, before any of the others could think about it. I remembered the first time my aunt had taken me to buy sweets and felt very old.

There were disciplined staccato steps from inside, followed by a sharp tug on the handle. I had learned to hate that combination of sounds every Friday night, back home in Castletownbere. Then the door opened.

She looked more beautiful than I'd ever seen her. Aunt Moira's hair was long and spilled out across shoulders that were as tan as her face. Her teeth sparkled brighter than Jonno's fake ones, and the dress she wore fit her body as if it had been spray-painted on. There's a flipping time machine in that house, I thought. She has turned back the clock, and Jim never even happened. We're kids again. Our parents will be right along, too.

Yeah, I know, right? Hell of a time to put your head into the sand.

Whatever cancer Moira apparently suffered from had taken a backseat to sunbathing. There were new freckles on her nose. As she regarded us for a moment, she smiled with such genuine happiness I knew that one of us should have brought at least a knife.

"There you are now, my lovelies," she said, making me wonder where she was hiding our starry carpet. "And just in time for some tea."

AND NOW I'M getting that strange feeling again of not wanting to tell you any more.

Because you can guess, can't you? The oddest thing about our time in this house was how civilized, how almost pleasant, it seemed in the beginning. Aunt Moira was hurt, of course, and couldn't hide her anger as she sat us down by the mahogany table we recognized from the old days. She almost apologized for bullying us into coming in the first place. And then, as the sugar lumps dissolved in our cups, she came to the point.

"Bone cancer," said Aunt Moira, nodding at us as if she were introducing herself by that name. "That means I'll fade away like an old napkin. And don't worry. Once I'm gone, you can take back your . . . effects . . . in that chest of drawers, there." She pointed at an oak dresser across the room. The only decoration was the old portrait photograph of Eamon de Valera. The plaster saints hadn't made the journey to Malahide, apparently. The rest of the house smelled like old dust and regret. Nobody really lived here; they were merely staying. Plastic Jesus hung above the doorway, and the wallpaper was the old striped kind you'd expect to find in a dead grandmother's house fifty years ago. There was nothing else but a few chairs that looked like they had been sat on too hard.

"What effects?" asked Fiona, trying hard not to sound like she wanted to wring her neck. "We got yer cigarette lighter, all right, but—"

"What, you don't remember?" teased our healthy-looking aunt, who obliged by bounding over to unlock the dresser drawer and returning with what looked like bags of weed. That's the first time I noticed her necklace. It looked like it was made of iron, or dulled silver. And the pendants hanging from it weren't jewels, but keys. She waved one plastic bag before us that appeared to be filled with dirt and said, "The guards never found this. It had fallen inside a hollow tree, just like in the fairy tales. But I did. Took me a long time, too. I was out there looking as soon as Brianna from SuperValu said my Jim had been by for a bottle of Chablis and was headed up to the beach." She peered at me, and I held her gaze until it became too much to bear. "Trouble of it is, he didn't drink Chablis. Sounded like trouble to me, didn't it? I had that sick feeling even before I knew he was . . ." She paused before having to put her lips around the word *dead*. "Well. Anyway. I had to clear out for a bit when Bronagh and her gang showed up with the dogs. But I returned. I found some real treasures. Even after those stupid women turned it into a shrine, I looked for more. Quite a collection. Don't you agree?"

Inside was the crumpled-up cigarette pack I'd seen Jim throw away, and another bag contained what looked like a button from Aoife's dress. There were more objects in there too, but I wasn't paying attention anymore. Because with that alone, I was sure, we'd get done for murder. Aunt Moira locked her evidence back up and pushed a sheet of paper across the table for us to read.

"And now that you're all here, let's agree on the rules of the house," she said.

It was like being back at school with the nuns again. Get up at six, make her breakfast, and prepare her medication. After that, it was to be housecleaning until noon, followed by lunch for her, more painkillers, and only then some grub for ourselves. Before we were to make her dinner, afternoons would be spent shopping for groceries, with one peculiar stipulation.

"Only one of you can leave the house at any one time," said Aunt Moira, and looked less radiant than before.

"Why's that?" I asked.

"Because I said so." She pointed at a long tan overcoat hanging from a hook by the door. "You are each to wear that coat with a shawl when you go outside. You will only shop at the corner mart down the street, and never buy anything but what's already on the list. Am I understood?"

I looked into her eyes and remembered what Fiona had told me about how she'd looked at Jim when they'd first met. Besotted, I think she'd said. Delirious. We're deader than rabbits in hunting season, I thought, unless we get out of here soon. I looked at the ghost of a smile and was already wondering how best to escape.

FOR A FEW weeks, nothing happened. Fiona shopped, I cleaned, and Aoife cooked, like one of old Dev's fantasies of what proper Irish girls were supposed to do with their time.

And Aunt Moira?

Well, she was only happier than I'd ever imagined she could be, of course. She relished in pointing out mistakes, like when I'd forgotten to clean the toilet all the way around the bowl, or if Aoife had put too much salt in the soup. But I was telling myself it was just for a few more weeks. Please don't think me naïve or stupid to believe that. If you'd seen that woman's inner glow, you too would have been convinced it was nothing but that last-gasp rally of the terminally ill right before curtains.

No guests ever came to the house. In fact, the only other person I've seen in all this time has been the little postman, who used to linger outside as if he wanted to be invited in for tea. I know now I should have yelled at him long ago, but how could I predict what was about to happen to us? He never stayed long on the front steps anyway. I think Moira chased him away.

At night, Aoife would go downstairs and sleep in the basement, where Aunt Moira had made another guest room, while me and Fiona stayed together in a room upstairs. I found a stack of blank notebooks someone had left behind, covered in dust and with the stamp *1941* on the overleaf. You're reading one of them right now, which I'm sure you've already guessed. I even began to make a countdown calendar for our departure, whether or not our dear aunt was belowground by then. Fiona complained of headaches, but I didn't listen to that right away, because I'd seen her sneaking ciggies from the kitchen drawer and knew she couldn't hold her smoke.

No, it was something else that made me realize things weren't as they seemed.

One morning, not so long ago, I awoke at the sound of a key in the lock.

"Hello?" I said, sitting up and rubbing my eyes. I had been dreaming of witches.

"Go back to sleep," Aunt Moira's voice whispered back through the bedroom door, but I knew what I'd heard. I turned the handle but couldn't open the door. She was no longer pretending we weren't prisoners. And as I listened, the iron sound of more locks sliding shut down the hall told me I should have leaped across the mahogany table that first day we got here and wrung her scrawny neck. If my aunt was suffering from cancer, then I was Madame fucking Curie. This was about revenge, pure and simple. And we would never leave this house alive.

FROM THAT DAY, we weren't allowed out of our rooms. Not even when I started to pee blood. I hadn't a clue to begin with why I was feeling busted up inside.

"Can't trust you," said our jailer, who had taken the opportunity while we were sleeping to put cuffs on us, like in a bad movie. "Murderers must be kept under lock and key, now, isn't that right?" She unlocked the door only three times a week, to bring us some slop she called food. We ate it, of course. What else were we going to do, lunge from our beds and kill her? Believe me, I tried. Twice. And she gave me such a beatdown every time I can still feel my front teeth moving back and forth when I chew.

I began to lose weight. Well, of course I did. But this was no normal diet, where yer jeans sag around yer arse. I could see my own breastbone.

"It's something in the food," said Fiona, herself covered in sores she couldn't keep clean.

All I could think of was Aoife.

I hadn't seen her for weeks and wondered if our aunt had killed her out of spite already. Moira had warned us not to signal anyone outside, lest my twin sister suffer the consequences, and I didn't doubt her resolve.

A few nights ago, I heard a faint metallic clanking. Someone was tapping on the pipe that led through our bathroom all the way into the basement. At first, I couldn't make out what it was, because my hearing has gone all sideways, too, but then I got it. It was old Morse code, and I had already missed part of a sentence:

...L...L...R...I...G...H...T...?

Was I all right? My eyes welled up, and I started to shake. God bless Aoife for sitting in our bedroom when we were little, suffering through having me teach her Morse code. "Come in handy, you'll see," I always insisted then, looking at her very serious like. "But why?" she'd asked. "Because what if there's no more electricity left in the world all of a sudden?" I'd replied, perfectly logically, I thought.

I woke up Fiona and picked up the screwdriver she'd found under the bed, so I could signal back.

H...O...W...D...O...W...E...G...E...T...O...U...T...?

There was a second's hesitation before Aoife's answer came back, clear as a telegram from the high court straight to the butcher's block.

K...I...L...L...H...E...R...F...I...R...S...T.

"What's that racket?" screamed Aunt Moira from downstairs. I could hear her heels on the stairs already. "What are you doing?"

"It's the water, Aunt Moira," said Fiona. "It makes the pipes rattle."

"You're plotting something," said our aunt, shuffling back downstairs, sounding as if she were rummaging through all of her secret drawers. "But you won't get away with it. As Jim is my witness, I'll outlive you all."

That was a new one, and I knew old Jim would have smiled. Now even God took a backseat in her fevered mind to West Cork's foremost sex-and-death practitioner.

I waited a few hours, until the yelling from downstairs had ended. Then Aoife and I talked through the pipe about escape, about killing, and about the diaries we had all started to write. We agreed to try escaping that next Wednesday morning, come hell or high water. That's today, by the way, in case yer wondering. And the moon is getting ready to sink into the mass of brick right outside my window. But mostly, we talked about our love for one another, no matter what. She also finally told me why she'd had to go away for as long as she did, and I said I understood. Because how can you not?

There.

The sun is coming up now, and Fiona is sharpening that damn screwdriver one last time. Aunt Moira is preparing something for us, I know it, because she's talking to herself downstairs, dragging something heavy about, and I don't like the sound of it. When crazy people argue with themselves, it's time to end the party, even when you have no strength left to do it. Fiona could tell me something about the three hundred Spartans in front of the Persian army, I reckon, but there's no time for that now. We've agreed to attack Aunt Moira the second she comes in here with the food. Whichever one of us escapes has promised to post the others' diaries. What, you think we're stupid enough to believe we can *all* live through this? Didn't you listen to anything I've said? I can't even stand up, for fuck's sake, much less walk anymore.

But I can still write. And I won't end this diary with something where I make you promise me anything, tell my priest what a good girl I was, blah, blah, blah. Because we don't know each other, and I'm sure you have better things to do. All I wish for is not to be judged too harshly, that's about it. Oh, and for you to try and reach Evvie for me, tell her what happened. Still can't get her out of my mind, ya see. Love that stinker, even if she's with someone else now, and that's the truth. Her family name is Vasilyeva, and they live in Sochi. Okay? Can't be too many like that around, can there?

Here she comes, now, my dear aunt, dragging her miserable self up the stairs. Now? Really?

It has to be, because Aoife is tapping the attack signal, like I'm deaf or something.

N . . . O . . . W . . . !

Part Four

THE
LEGLESS
PRINCE

· 8 ·

Niall hesitated before closing the book. The voices in it seemed so alive, they appeared still to resonate all around him, out here in the world of the living. He held his breath and listened, for it seemed to him that he'd heard someone mumbling. Impossible. The wind howled. He'd imagined it, he knew that, but he still had half his head inside Róisín's last living moments.

Hang on.

Somewhere close by, he again heard a low murmur. It entered through a hole in the ceiling and drifted down onto him like fairy dust.

"This is useless," said a female voice, angry with itself.

At first he thought it was his own imagination. For days, he'd heard voices in his head and begun assigning them to the three women, trapped like rats in the last room they ever saw. He had got to know their quirks, he felt, and not just as the goth radio rat, her elusive twin, and their protective big sister, who took the first swing with that shovel. Those were just thumbnail sketches, surface clichés. No, Niall knew he might be deluding himself, but each girl's personality had become as vivid to him as the image of Jim's wolf, chasing into a forest primeval. Except, perhaps, for Aoife. She still eluded his understanding, having always run faster than the other two.

That's why he nearly answered when he heard the same female voice calling out a second time, somewhere closer. She sounded more afraid than she let on. Niall couldn't imagine why. If the lynch mob from the cemetery was near, she wasn't alone.

"Rain washed his tracks out already." It sounded motherly, concerned. Not a young woman. But where was it coming from? Niall scrunched in the corner where he'd sat down, trying to take up even less space. There was nowhere to hide, unless he wanted to bump into things and give himself away. He could just see his own hand before him in the predawn blue, and noticed what was probably a window on his right. Boots crunched on gravel. Niall nearly jumped. So it ends here, he thought, imagining being hanged from a gibbet and beaten to death by angry townsfolk. He heard someone else, right before he started to ask himself if it was worth dying like this to protect the Walshes' secrets.

"Shh, *Christ*, Vivian," hissed a man, breathing hard. "Ya might as well shoot a flare over our heads!" There was a metallic sound, too. A gun. Or a length of chain. Or anything at all that might hurt.

Niall had heard him speaking before. The voice belonged to the heavyset man he had last seen standing outside Sacred Heart Primary School, looking very much like he'd prefer Bronagh to take a long coffee break and look the other way while he killed the man he was convinced had abused his only daughter. Oh, Aoife, I sure could use that old shotgun now, Niall thought, his eyes adjusting to the changing light that broke through the clouds like a postcard halo. Plastic Jesus, blind them with your wattage and blessed countenance. Mr. Raichoudhury will read my obituary and say, *I told you so, you stupid boy.* But what else could I do, sir? he would have asked his exacting ex-supervisor. Just *forget* about Róisín, Aoife, and Fiona? Excuse me, Mr. Senior Postperson, but are you joking or what?

The woman was getting anxious. There was a quick intake of breath that never made it all the way past the throat and into her lungs. "We aren't supposed to be anywhere near here, Mr. Cremin, this—"

"Don't you think I *know* that?" he almost shouted, forgetting his own admonition. "But the trail ends just down in the field there. Not many places to hide."

"You know the punishment. The *rules.*"

"She turns me into a toad. All that kind of shite, I know. Nobody has seen her since sh—"

"The rules are clear."

"And I'm my daughter's father, okay? He's here. I know he is. Enough with the witchy bollix."

"Then you do it alone, Donald Cremin." She blew her nose, and it seemed to Niall as if she were making up her mind. "Lads?" Several more feet slopped around in the wet grass. Ten? he wondered, perhaps twenty men? Going or coming? Through the broken window, he saw a cluster of black oilskin overcoats, whose owners had already begun to fan out into the field, back the way they'd come. The pink reflection of the sun on their rubber boots would have been beautiful if it wasn't for one thing.

Mary Catherine Cremin's father was still smelling the prey. And he was staying.

Niall held his breath and imagined what Róisín would have done in this situation. Grab a table leg and beat the man in the face with it, most likely. Or maybe just wave about whatever ghostly spell the woman who had just left was so afraid of. He decided to wait until the man entered the house and then hit him low and hard, a rugby tackle. Beyond that, he had no idea.

The boots right outside shuffled indecisively. And then Niall knew why.

Mr. Cremin was afraid, too. He just didn't want to admit it in front of the others. Big strong vigilante, all that. A whining, keening sound rose up from outside, because setting foot inside the house was a risk he couldn't afford, as if the floor were toxic. He finally spat on the threshold and walked away.

"Witches," he mumbled, before the wind wiped the rest of the sentence out across the Slieve Miskish Mountains, and was gone.

Niall let out his breath like a condemned man whose hangman's rope was just cut. He leaned back against the wall, allowing his legs to shake it off before he even looked around the room. And once he did, and the sun smeared bright yellow on the ruined furniture, he knew without a doubt where he was.

He was inside Aoife's abandoned stone cottage.

What Niall had seen on the floor earlier wasn't rat droppings or bat shite. It had been tufts of cotton fabric from inside the couch Jim had disemboweled with a knife, before raping the one sister he wanted to hurt the most. The hole in the ceiling had only grown since then and now cratered downward, leaving just a small half circle of wall that wasn't rotten down to the foundations. Teacups stood primly on the table, and plates, too, probably from the time the girls had left in a hurry to go see their aunt in Dublin. There was still brown liquid left inside what looked like a whiskey bottle.

As Niall buttoned his coat against the sudden cold, he was certain about something else he had been wondering since setting out on this ill-fated odyssey.

Aoife had been the mystery guest in her aunt's basement, suffering in silence with her sisters until she could escape. Not Bronagh or poor Finbar, with some half-arsed rescue operation. Hell, Niall had read the leaked autopsy reports in the *Irish Star*, hadn't he? He didn't even need to guess much to know the geometry of the last stand in that upstairs room. Fiona had duked it out with the jealous troll, who had never got near enough to touch Róisín. But they had all three died, just the same. And Aoife could not save her sisters, Morse code or not.

He closed his eyes and tried to imagine what had gone wrong. Why had Aoife not made it upstairs in time? Was there a locked trapdoor to slow her down? Niall guessed she *had* made it to the second floor, but too late to save Fiona and Róisín, and had only *then* fled with the diaries before the cops could get her, too. "Did you close their eyes, Aoife?" Niall asked the dripping wet curtains. Perhaps she'd even seen the funeral from afar. It was impossible to imagine that she wouldn't have. She draped them in their carpet of stars.

For the first time, Niall felt he had been allowed the faintest glimpse inside the mind of the family's most private sister. She had been so close. The plan to silence their aunt once and for all must have seemed perfect. He was also certain that someone had been back to the cottage recently, because the walls and doorways were festooned with clusters of new crow's feathers and long-dried-up husks of small forest animals. Mumbo-jumbo nonsense to keep the fear of "the lone sister" alive, wasn't it? But then why did he feel so unsettled? What looked like a desiccated fox hung by the tail, swinging like an extinguished lamp in some troll's underground cave. If he'd had pencil and paper, he could have drawn a brilliant forest landscape, where a woman was forever *just* a step ahead of the wolf. Because Aoife had vanished. Again. She was good at it.

"Where would you go now?" he mumbled to himself, suddenly afraid the walls could hear his thoughts. "And why did you leave your sisters to begin with?" Again, he thought of handing it all over to the gardaí—to Bronagh, the tireless crime fighter, and her little helpers. And again, he couldn't. Wherever Mr. Raichoudhury was, he would surely be shaking his wise head and tapping his immaculate fingernails on his grandfather's belt buckle. No, Niall wanted to say, in his own defense, I'm not heeding your advice. And no, sir, I still can't get these images out of my head. Not after reading two diaries written in invisible blood and tears. And so I must pursue this journey to the end, no matter where it leads. It's my job. Perhaps you'll wander through a marketplace years from now, and notice me sitting in front of an image, expending my last breath to make it come alive. We'll just see, won't we, sir?

The wind had got its nails underneath the loose plywood on the roof, and now gave it a playful slapping. Niall looked around and knew he had to leave, but he didn't want to run into Mr. Cremin's gunslingers on the way down. He could still see them, white spots of hair in a sea of green, tooth-combing for him on the sloping hill below. The road back to town was blocked.

That meant he had to go west, back toward Eyeries. But that was just as well.

Because Róisín had buried something sharp underneath a decapitated tree.

DOES HIDDEN TREASURE lose its mystery the moment it's unearthed? Or does the object, once touched by whoever dug a hole for it, retain a kind of magic that never fades?

In Jim's case, you could have buried a caramel wrapper, and it would still have been sanctified immediately upon discovery.

Niall thought of the knife blade that had punctured Jim's lungs and heart and decided its value lay not in the weapon itself but in the myth that had begun to surround it. Once he reached the spot where the *seanchaí* drew his last breath, he knew he was right. Rabid fans had long ago transformed the tree their hero had leaned against as his life trickled into the grass. It was now a shrine to sex-and-death fantasies everywhere.

Elvis and JFK never had it so good. The bark was stripped off halfway up the trunk, and all branches smaller than an arm had been broken off for souvenirs. A bra hung on a surviving twig, next to a laminated card with the words LUV IS FOREVER. NEVER FORGET U, DARLING JIM. KISSES FROM HOLLY, OMAHA, NEBRASKA. Some girls had enclosed pictures of themselves, creating a school yearbook that never ended. The youngest face looked all of ten years old, buck teeth and freckles and dreams of dangerous romance. The grass had become mud. Beer cans and cigarette ends lay strewn about like newly fallen dirty snow. The rain was coming down so hard that Niall figured it was the only reason this place wasn't mobbed.

He looked about, trying to find anything that looked like a tree missing its crown.

The rain cloaked the underbrush in darkness, and all the trunks looked alike. It took over an hour for him to find the place Róisín had described, because the headless oak had in the meantime withered completely, its one remaining branch wizened like an old woman's elbow. Niall's bad ankle pounded, sending jags of white pain up his spine. As he spotted a bent oak halfway up the hill, he couldn't help noticing how much this place resembled the moment in Jim's fairy tale when the old wolf attacked Prince Euan and pronounced his curse. Niall looked around, seeing nothing but wet branches smacking against one another in the wind. He half wondered if the trees had anything to say that he could learn to hear, if only he really listened hard, then decided even asking the question meant he had been in West Cork for far too long. He knelt down between two roots, poking up like bent suntanned knuckles, and began to dig with his hands. The wet, slimy ground made a sucking noise as it yielded. Are you *sure* you want to do this? it seemed to ask. Why not just go back, before someone finds you here, knee-deep in someone else's dirty business?

There was nothing down there, of course. What had he been thinking? This entire place was now sacred ground for all the world's broken hearts, from Frankfurt to Osaka, and had been picked over for years. Niall was covered in mud and felt like giving up. Give all the information he had to the guards and take his chances. He stood, listening to the rain smacking against the leaves. He felt like a total eejit.

Then he stared down one last time and wondered what a napkin was doing down in that hole.

It was nearly rotted through, a square of cotton damask. Just an inch of fabric left, but it was enough to imagine the rest. There was even a floral pattern around the edges that would fit on any dinner table.

Or atop the good china at Aunt Moira's weekly Friday dinners.

Niall bent down and gently tugged at the napkin, which tore with a tired yawn. Róisín wouldn't just have buried the naked blade, Niall realized, feeling his ankle thumping harder now. She'd have taken the time to wrap it, like the properly raised girl she was, despite the demon-child act. He unpeeled the dirty brown cotton and saw what had ended Jim's life.

It was a serrated blade, beginning to rust around the tip. Whatever blood had once been encrusted on the metal was long gone, which would have disappointed any true souvenir hunter of Jim memorabilia.

Niall pocketed it and walked out of the woods as quickly as he could, despite the pain. Because the skies dumped more summer rain now, blurring anything that could be moving toward him between the trees. Padraic and his wolf hunters, crashing through the thicket with the hounds driving the chase, wouldn't have been a big surprise. The trees, even if they knew how to whisper warnings, would stay silent while the dogs made a meal of an ex-postman. Because even trees, Niall imagined, knew when to shut up or risk losing their own hide.

And although he loved a good fairy tale, he knew how *that* story ended.

BRONAGH WAS WAITING for him at the end of the trail, leaning on a fence. All that was missing to complete the image of the Wild West marshal staring down the cattle rustler before gunning him down, Niall thought, was a hand-rolled cigarette in her mouth.

"Wrong day for a picnic," she said, shaking her head.

God, even her *lines* were stolen from a bad movie. Niall had to keep from smiling. "I know," he said, shrugging. "Too wet to make a proper fire. So I left early."

Bronagh looked at the dried mud, which had caked an even milk-chocolate brown all over Niall's clothes. "You never left at all, ever since you got here." She flipped open a notebook, and her eyebrows shot up while she recited, as if to a retarded person. "Illegal entry on school grounds, posing as faculty—"

"I never pretended to be—"

"—exposing yourself to a *child*—"

"Okay, now you're just pissing me off!"

"—ransacking a cemetery, unlawfully occupying private property as late as last night, and now"—she looked at Niall's dirty hands—"defacing public land. As if you didn't have enough problems. I just passed Donald Cremin on my way up here. He's looking for the man who felt up his daughter." A TV cop smile. "And I mean to tell ya, old Donald doesn't wander around the countryside with a baseball bat at half seven in the morning just to feel closer to nature."

"I know what you're doing," Niall said, watching Bronagh's fingers playing with the uniform jacket's zipper.

"Arresting you? Oh—you mean *that?*" She looked back over her shoulder. "Gave you plenty of warning."

"No," answered Niall, remembering how made-up, how *designed* Aoife's cottage had looked. Those brand-new feathers. His pursuers' unnatural fear of the place, which made no sense at the time. "No, I'm talking about your keeping the myth of the cursed Walsh family alive and well, now, isn't that right? Bit of voodoo? Come on, even Mary Catherine's father was shitting his pants to think of going inside that house after me. And he could *smell* me hiding from him! What, did you tell them the curse of the 'stiletto sisters' would put all intruders six feet under?"

Bronagh's eyes blinked faster now, and she wasn't looking Niall in the eye. "You be quiet. You don't know the first thing about how we—"

All the tiny levers and tumblers began clicking into place inside Niall's head. "She came to you, didn't she? Aoife. I'm guessing it happened right after Jim's death. You helped her get gone and stay gone, right? And dressed up her old house with feathers and dead animals to make sure nobody looked for her ever again?"

"That's *it*, you're under arrest for—"

"And then she knocked on your door *again*, around a month ago. Because she'd escaped from that house in Dublin, hadn't she? Just barely, I'm thinking. And you've helped her all this time because you feel guilty about what happened back then. When you sat on your cop hands and let this whole town's darling Jim rape her and did nothing about it. Just as you never investigated him and his creature for the murder of Sarah McDonnell and all the others before it was too late. Remember that? Where is she? In *your* basement now? In someone else's cottage, way the hell out where not even the tourists can find her?" He held out his hands in a gesture of surrender and put on a really bad John Wayne accent. "Put the cuffs on me, Marshal. And take me to that hanging party of yours. I'll tell the *Southern Star* and the *Kerryman* everything I know. Great front pages, I'm thinking. LOST MYSTERY SIS-TER FOUND. Or would MURDER COVER-UP BY GARDA suit better? Great stuff, either way."

Bronagh just stood there, gobsmacked. The wind made her pant legs flap against her ankles, and she didn't stop Niall as he brushed his way past her and began walking down the road toward town.

"Wait!"

Niall heard her voice right after he glimpsed a group of men waiting at a bend in the road, beyond the trees. It was too far to see any of them clearly. But one had something heavy in his hands. He looked like Donald Cremin. The sun covered them in foggy white coronas, like angels of death. No place left to run. Niall turned and saw Bronagh waving him back. She had got into her patrol car already.

"No hanging party, then?" he asked.

"Just get in," Bronagh answered, looking at the men in the field already moving toward the sound of her voice.

When they drove past the crooked turn where the trees met the asphalt, Donald Cremin was close enough that Niall could see how tightly his fingers gripped that bat.

"Why the change of heart?" asked Niall, watching Bronagh feverishly rummaging through the glove box, finally finding a scrap of half-eaten chocolate. "You could have just handed me over to them, returned later, and filed a report. No traces back to you."

"Did you ever have a best friend?" said Bronagh, spitting the chocolate out the window because it had gone bad. "Someone you know so well you can think the same thing the moment before they do?" She rolled the window back up and set her jaw firmly to avoid letting this long-haired mud crawler see into her heart. "Someone who finishes your sentences? And lies for you to her own parents? Ever know anyone like that?"

Niall thought of little Danny Egan back home. That bus. And those wax-dummy child's legs that lived again because he drew them on paper. But he just nodded and let Bronagh continue. The car sped past the old brook at the edge of Castletownbere and continued on past the

Coast Guard station. The only sound inside the car was Bronagh's guilt, which had shape-shifted into a pair of lungs, trying to get enough air for confession.

"When I was seven," she continued, "all I wanted in the world was a pair of black shoes. They were shiny and had a button down the side. Deadly. Most beautiful things I'd ever seen. So I went into the shop right here on Main Street, and waited for the saleslady to take a smoke break. I took a pair, right? Put them into my book bag and walked home as slowly as I could." Bronagh held a whole hand to her lips, as if to help the words find their way out. "They were too big. I had to put newspaper into them to make them fit. But they were only gorgeous. I went to Rosie's house, and we took turns parading them in front of the mirror in the hallway. Then the doorbell rang. The saleslady had brought the gardaí." She sniffled now, and not just at the memory. Because Rosie was dead and didn't have to be. "Róisín didn't even wait for me to blubber some shite excuse. She looked them dead in the eye and copped to stealing the shoes herself. Her father spanked her so she couldn't walk for the rest of the week. And she never asked for anything in return. Not once."

The asphalt wound into serpentine turns with wet pine trees on either side. Niall recognized it as the road he'd wandered like a half-dead pilgrim two days earlier.

"But you *could* do something for Aoife?"

"Look at it this way," said Bronagh, trying to shake off the sorrow. "She was the only one left. What would you have done?"

"Where is she, Bronagh?"

Bronagh pursed her lips in reply and pulled over onto the shoulder. She unlocked the passenger door and reached into the backseat for something that she threw into Niall's lap.

It was a plastic bag, containing the old clothes and drawing paper he'd left at the bed-and-breakfast.

"Mrs. Crimmins said she didn't want the likes of you setting foot in her house ever again," said Bronagh, gesturing for him to get out. "Lots of other people feel the same way, after what you did at Sacred Heart."

"I did nothing. And you know it."

Bronagh sent him a smile as bitter as a walnut. There was no joy in her voice as she set the terms of the deal that would save them both. "Just as you know I haven't a clue where Aoife is or what happened to her. I'm just a dumb garda. Isn't that right?"

"Okay."

"You're a good enough sort, Niall," she said, with a sigh she hadn't meant to let out. "Just came by looking in the wrong places, is all."

Niall opened the door and got out. The trees swooshed in the wind. He had no idea if they were trying to tell him something or if they just talked among themselves. "If you see her again?" Niall said. "Tell her I hope she finds what she's looking for."

But Bronagh had already turned the car around and was headed back to town. Because some answers cost too much.

NIALL HAD WALKED for hours, watching the shadows grow longer. The fog rolled up behind him like it was nosy about where he was going. Then he heard something he thought was another loose spare part from his own imagination. An engine, alternately revving up and downshifting in the curves.

A motorcycle.

Sure, Niall thought with a hysterical laugh, that's just perfect. It's Jim's old Vincent Comet, isn't it, coming to haunt me all the way back to shagging Ballymun? The sound bounced off the cliffs, growing fainter, then stronger again. Niall turned and saw a lone headlight. The cursed rider, he thought, rising from his grave atop the hillside every night, to torment those who refuse to believe in him. He reached into his pocket for the knife blade and held it hidden inside his hand.

When the motorcycle came closer, Niall could see that it was black, not red.

The rider slowed down and came to a stop in front of him. It reached up and flipped open the visor with a jaunty snap. He recognized the face.

"Didja find who you were looking for?" asked the same young

woman who had scared the life out of him once already. Her smile enjoyed that he couldn't find one anywhere on his own face.

"Not everyone," Niall finally answered, pocketing the weapon as discreetly as he could.

"Hop on back," she said. "I'm going east. Your lucky day."

"Don't think so. I want to live to see tomorrow. But thanks all the same."

The rider nodded, flipping the visor back down. Niall was sure her smile was still on, though, because the plastic seemed to glow from the inside. "Don't come back here," she said evenly, and yanked on the gas, propelling the motorcycle up the next hill in five seconds flat. He looked back down the road and saw the fog hovering there, daring him not to follow that advice.

"Rest easy, Aoife," he said as he walked on, away from Castletownbere.

· 9 ·

The train was so empty Niall gave a start each time the announcer came on. He had been dozing, allowing wolves to creep into his dreams and scavenge around. Now he jumped awake and banged his head on the window.

"The next station is Thurles. This train is for Dublin Heuston. Please note that there is no food service until the terminus. Thank you for traveling with Iarnród Éireann."

So this is what total failure looks like, Niall thought, looking out the window. When he'd got to Cork City, he was two euros short of being able to afford the ticket back home on the last train of the night and had to beg in the street near the taxi stand. The cabbies finally grew so disgusted one of them gave him the money, if he promised never to return. The shame had burned in his throat as he said the words. The fella had laughed as he tossed Niall the two-euro piece. It still stung.

The landscape whizzed past outside, blurring all the evening trees into one black drape. Nothing moved out there. Niall began to imagine that Jim's fairy-tale world existed just beyond a horizon that was already too dark for him to see. And why not? Despite mobile phone towers, highways, and petrol stations, something from the past might have survived the march of progress, if only it was hid cleverly enough. Couldn't it? Something like a wolf's lair. Or a golden hall fit for Princess Aisling. Or even a hidden wizard's workshop, from which spells and incantations from an ancient world continued to spill over into ours.

A wizard?

Despite his swollen ankle and aching limbs, Niall bolted fully awake. An image flickered inside his head just behind the eyes and tried to connect with the parts of his brain that didn't want to go to sleep. Because Róisín had described something like that near the end of her diary, hadn't she? She'd sat in a train just like this one (Niall even pretended she and her sisters had huddled in the very spot where he now sat) when Aoife confessed to taking Jim's wallet from his corpse and finding his secret map.

Another thought struck him harder than Donald Cremin's baseball bat would have. What if Jim's map hadn't all been made up? And what if those "electrical charges" emanating from the wizard's head and fingertips weren't meant to be spells but a way to communicate with someone he couldn't see?

It couldn't be. Niall reached back where he kept the diary and yanked it out. His hands shook as he flipped to the pages where he'd read that description. "A male figure," Róisín had written in her jagged script, who was "operating what looked like a radio." And there was something more, if he remembered correctly. The wizard was really a prince, whose legs were destroyed underneath a fallen horse. He was waiting only for his remorseless brother, Euan, to come murder him.

Róisín couldn't remember his name then, but Niall could. Because Jim had told everyone, over and over again, in his fairy tale about Euan's wolf curse.

The legless prince's name was Ned.

Niall was about to close the diary, when a single sheet of rumpled paper fell out of a back pocket of the book that he hadn't noticed before and fluttered to the ground.

"Would you like something from the trolley, sir?" said a voice above him as he bent down to retrieve it.

He looked up into the eyes of a sleepy young woman balancing a top-heavy cart laden with hot coffee and sandwiches. Her uniform had what looked like gobs of old mustard on it.

"Erm, I thought there was no service?" he said, hiding his new treasure inside both palms.

"They never change that tape," said the woman, winking at him. "Some tea?"

"No thanks, love," he said, sucking up the warmth that came with the only smile he'd got in days. She moved on, waving one hand. He waited until she was gone before unfolding the yellowed sheet.

It was Jim's uncensored brain, transformed into ink and poured onto paper.

Here was the dead woman on the trail, and there the massive ice wall that no traveler could penetrate. But Niall traced his finger farther to the east, looking for something specific. The ink had smudged, just as Róisín had said, but he could still make out what it was supposed to be.

It was a castle, with Ned sitting inside, sending his waves out into the ether for anybody to pick up. And there was a detail Róisín either hadn't noticed or didn't have time to write down. A set of double lines ran into Jim's paper forest. It was crude, but it was clear what Jim had intended to portray.

Train tracks.

They ended near a mountain. Jim had drawn flowers all over it, as if the rock itself grew fragile beauty right out of the granite. Magic from the princely wizard's hidden home. Almost a girlish impulse to prettify an otherwise foreboding landscape. Niall closed his eyes and took it all in, trying to remember everything he'd read in both diaries. Jim had said something to Fiona about where he was from, hadn't he? Or had it been someone else who'd mentioned where he lived? Niall rummaged around in his bag for Fiona's tale until he remembered he'd traded diaries with the crafty Mary Catherine. Wait a second. Had it been Róisín's

unknown radio friend, instead, who'd talked about a castle deep in the
forest? He couldn't recall. The train jerked as it slowed. It would be
Thurles in a minute.

He looked up at an Iarnród Éireann intercity map above his head,
following the real tracks as they went toward Thurles, past Templemore
and Ballybrophy. Then he compared the plastic map with the crumpled
one in his hand and saw Jim's clumsy tracks ending exactly where the
train company's helpful cartographer had put the next station.

The wizard, real or imaginary, lived near Portlaoise.

The Slieve Bloom Mountains, covered in purple bluebells in the
spring, lay right nearby. Niall had played on their slopes as a boy. He
and Danny had got lost there once after dark, finding their way home
only because the flower petals reflected the light of the moon long
enough to see the trail.

Shaking in equal parts excitement and apprehension, Niall leaned
back and closed his eyes for a second. The thrill of the chase, extinguished less than two hours ago by a group of heartless cabbies,
throbbed alive again.

If you exist, he said to the wizard he couldn't quite see yet in his
mind, I'll find you. And I've more curses put on me already than you
have up your sleeve, so do your worst.

THE MOON WAS nearly down but would still shine bleakly for at
least another hour, Niall reckoned, as he picked a trail that led deeper
into the forest. From the Portlaoise train station, it had been simple
enough to find the southeasternmost edge of the Slieve Bloom Mountains, which rose out of the ground like a sleeping creature awaiting the
coming of the sun. He found his old boy-reflexes and tried to navigate
his way west as he once had, using the sea of illuminated bluebells for a
guide. But as the last streetlights from Portlaoise vanished behind him,
he realized his first mistake.

The month of May was coming to an end. And the few surviving
bluebells he could glimpse near his boots had withered and died. All
around him, the stalks had turned brown and dry. Ahead of him, there

was the kind of featureless darkness only children know how to conjure up properly in their nightmares.

"Killed off the flowers didja, ya old wizard?" he asked the invisible trail, convincing himself he sensed a presence not far away. "I'll find ya anyway."

Niall had taken a few half-running steps up a hill when his eyes played tricks on him. At first, he thought he had been granted what his imagination had hoped for. Then he accepted that what he saw was real. He knelt down and touched something small and frail, which had opened all five petals to welcome him into its silent world.

The tiniest wood anemone, newly born, stood at attention, drinking in the cold rays of the moon.

Niall barely touched it with his forefinger, feeling the paper-thin texture, rippled like a dragonfly's wing. Then he lifted his head and knew he'd have guidance into even the darkest part of the forest. Because the little flower wasn't alone. As far as Niall could see, the moon was refracted by legions of white anemones lighting up the path before him even more brightly than it had been years ago, when him and Danny tried to get home before their fears got them first.

"A starry carpet, Róisín," he said, feeling something settle inside and give him the only rest he'd felt since picking up that strange package inside the dead-letter cage a million years ago. He steered a path toward the one part of the mountain he'd never visited, feeling the wizard's invisible rays already scouring the treetops, looking for intruders.

NIALL KNEW WELL enough that wizards don't play the piano.

And yet, there it was: expert hands conjuring up what sounded like Cole Porter's "Anything Goes." Whoever it was chose to perform it fast, at almost breakneck speed. He also thought, if only for a second, he could hear humming.

Of all the mythical creatures Niall had ever heard of, it was mostly mermaids who used song to lure travelers into lethal traps. Powerful practitioners of the dark arts, he imagined, would instead enchant the animals of the forest to attack obvious enemies or cast spells to paralyze a stranger like himself. But music, such as he heard seeping through the dense thicket in front of him, belonged inside a smoky saloon back in the 1920s. And as he crept past bunches of ramrod-straight wild arum, their red fruitlike seedheads bursting with spring juices, he could imagine a vaudeville musician entertaining the rabbits and deer in a peaceful grove. He cleared a mess of brambles that tore up the jeans Mrs. Crimmins had given him and cursed.

Just as invisibly as the tinkly piano sounds had emanated, they stopped.

Damn! Niall wanted to kick himself for being so bloody stupid. He should know better than to stumble about in here without a map. If wizards did exist, he thought, they had thousands of years of experience listening to heavy-footed amateur detectives entering their lands. He cleared a copse of birch trees, which had begun to absorb the faint shimmer of dawn. The entire forest, except for a dark spot in a natural valley just past an overhang drop-off less than fifty meters away, was waking up. Niall looked around for his next route and realized something he hadn't paid attention to earlier.

Not once had he heard so much as a mouse clear its throat. No jay scuttled its wings, nor did any badger probe the defenses of its nest. It was as if every creature watched and waited for Niall to find what he so obviously sought. Or for it to find *me*, he thought to himself as he pushed on. The anemones, so plentiful and brave in numbers earlier, grew thinner on the ground and were soon gone. Fear is biological, not intellectual, he guessed. It was, he would later recall, as if they sensed what lay down in the valley below and just out of sight. We've led you this far, they seemed to say, and even we dare not shine the light for you any farther.

He inched out on the promontory until the tips of his soiled boots stuck into thin air. Below, twin wisps of blue smoke competed to see which would reach a low-hanging cloud faster than the other. Niall couldn't see a chimney, or even a roof down there, but it was too heavy a fire to be random campers. There was a house somewhere; he was sure of it. He closed his eyes and smelled what the fire was made of.

There was maple, maybe some ash. Peat, definitely, and lots of it. Someone was getting cozy. Someone who lived there.

Niall was just getting ready to descend when he became aware of a
sound just behind him. It was whiny and mechanical and reminded
him of those remote-controlled cars Danny let him borrow because his
own dad couldn't afford to buy him one.

"Good morning," someone said, sounding pleased to have snuck up
so silently.

"Who is . . . ? Oh, *shit!*"

The old boots Niall had got from Mrs. Crimmins slipped on the
loose dirt, and for a moment he was falling into the abyss. His one hand
had grabbed hold of a branch, purely by reflex. As he dragged himself
back to safety, cheeks aflame with embarrassed rage, he turned and saw
the man.

The figure sitting just behind him wore an old-fashioned red velvet
smoking jacket, accessorized with green commando boots and a black
forage cap. His mustache was sparse and well-trimmed. The eyes above
it gleamed hazel in a way that was neither hostile nor inviting. His legs
were covered with a green woolen blanket. A double-barreled shotgun
lay across his lap like a fossilized pet snake, and he stroked it as if it
would soon awaken with lots of noise.

Why would anybody just *sit* there like that, rather than come up and
challenge me? Niall's brain asked before he saw that the answer was
obvious.

Whoever he was, the young man was in a wheelchair.

Niall's ankles felt cold. He couldn't imagine how to escape fast
enough to outrun two volleys of steel shot. The wizard had found him
the moment he'd stepped foot into his domain.

"I've come to speak with you," Niall said, voice croaking and high.

The legless prince only nodded and waved a hand in the air. Two
silhouettes, each a hundred meters apart on the trail behind them, rose
from the foliage like wolves to the hunt. These men acknowledged the
"Everything's okay down here" greeting by waving their guns in like

fashion and blending back into the trees so seamlessly you'd never know they'd been there.

"Is that so?" asked the wizard, unimpressed. "Then let's see if you know the magic word." He wheeled himself down a trail and bade his uninvited guest follow into a darkened culvert, from which no light at all seemed to escape.

"Do you like ragtime?" he wanted to know. Niall saw his rough hands dance on the all-terrain tires as if he were demanding that they make music, too. "Because if you don't, this is going to be a very long day for the both of us."

NIALL ALLOWED HIMSELF to feel safe when he saw the dogs coming to greet the man in the wheelchair. Springer spaniels, both of them, with that peculiar fixed look of fierce intelligence that makes even their owners feel insecure. A woman in a starched white apron waited near the front door of a classic, early nineteenth-century Georgian mansion with unkempt moss creeping up its walls. It'll be tea and lemon crèmes next, thought Niall, until he felt a hand on his shoulder and looked up into the patient face of one of the underbrush men. His face was as stoic as the trees themselves.

The legless prince spun his off-road contraption around with an impatient jerk. Niall was about to say something when he took another look at the front door, beyond which the servant had wisely retreated with the dogs. It was a gate, really, and painted black as the inside of a pair of miner's lungs. So it's to be a hanging at dawn in front of the Fort of the Wolf, then, he thought, and got ready to duck backward and to the left in order to give the thug an elbow to the nuts.

"Come for the clean country air?" asked the crippled aristocrat, breaking the shotgun open on his lap with a practiced motion and searching all his pockets for fresh shells.

"Now, just wait a minute, please, you've got the wrong—"

"Don't tell me it was the music that drew you here, as if by magic," persisted the gaunt figure, grimacing when he still didn't find the ammo he needed. "Because then I'll get *really* cross with you. So. Declare yourself. Are you simply lost? Or do you have a purpose worth listening to?"

"I've not come to harm you," said Niall, feeling both shoulders pounding as the other helper gave it a generous squeeze.

"I frankly don't see how you could," said the lord of the manor, shaking his emaciated head and triumphantly gripping a single 12-gauge cartridge between thumb and forefinger. "You come all this way, over hill, over dale, into my little hovel, the only other unbidden guest for nine years since some French tourist ambled in here because he'd taken a wrong turn, looking for the train station over in Portlaoise. And you don't even have the manners to apologize?"

"I don't mean to trespass," persisted Niall, eyeing the double-barreled muzzle. "But I need to speak with you. It's important."

Ned no longer pretended to enjoy baiting his quarry. He shook his head, bored already with the entire spectacle. "Important to whom? Little birdwatching Frenchman two years ago, his name was . . ." He glanced at the goon to his left. "Marcel, was it, Theo?"

"Not sure, Mr. O'Driscoll. Think so."

"And when you dragged him away by the scruff of the neck, what was that word he kept repeating, like he was calling for his *maman*?"

"Sounded like 'pity,' sir, I recall correctly."

The wizard favored Niall with a boyish smile, and his eyes widened like camera lenses adjusting focus. "Ah, that's the one. *Pitié*. That'd be *mercy*. Did we show him any, by the way?"

In response, the bodyguard merely smiled at the memory.

"Do you speak any French?" Ned asked, cocking his head at the young intruder whose voice sounded muffled because of the hand clamped tight around his neck.

"No," croaked Niall, as he struggled to breathe.

"Pity," said the wizard, nodding at both his henchmen.

"Want us to take him away now, Mr. O'Driscoll?" asked the lummox crushing Niall's clavicle.

Niall's face had turned blue. "Tell your troll to get his fucking mitts off, or I'll—"

"Or nothing, fuckwank," said Theo, clamping his other hand around Niall's wrist.

Ned lit up in a genuine smile, and now Niall could see how Jim's twin resembled him in every respect but the natural, lethal charm. His brother had no sensuality whatever and had probably never seduced more than his father's porno mag. But neither was far from turning someone's insides out like a summer coat to get what they wanted.

"*Look* at this, Theo. We start the morning off right, rinsing out a wayward traveler's dirty mouth." He bared his beautiful even teeth at Niall and turned down the temperature behind his eyes, like scores of women had seen Jim do right before they drew their last breath. "You couldn't even be bothered to come up with an original excuse for being here. All you can do is swear. Well, that's *verboten* in my forest, don't mind telling you." He turned his wheelchair around and engaged the whirring engine Niall had heard earlier. A hand waved in the vague direction of the other bodyguard. "Break his legs, Otto. And make sure to leave him by the road this time, for the motorists to find. Last time was an awful mess."

"Roger that, Mr. O."

"I know what killed your brother," Niall almost screamed. "And I have it right here in my pocket."

The wheelchair stopped. Ned turned it just slowly enough for Theo to get in another good squeeze. "Surprise me. And then go take your medicine like a good boy."

"Tell this creature to let me go first."

Ned sent his handler an overbearing grimace, and the large man stepped aside.

Niall dug into his bag with the hand the fascist hadn't mangled (Thank *God* it wasn't his drawing hand, he couldn't help thinking, despite everything) and pulled out the picnic napkin Róisín had used to give a murder weapon a proper burial shroud. He held it out to Ned, who steered his wheelchair closer, the tiny motor straining into overdrive.

"He was stabbed with this," said Niall. "And if you want the other thing of his that only I can tell you about, you'll let me go."

Ned had already swiped the dirty object and was unwrapping it like a true relic. When his fingers touched the rusting blade, his eyes lit up as if he held the Spear of Destiny that pierced the side of Christ, not the IKEA veggie knife that punched a raping murderer's ticket. "Astounding," he mumbled to himself, then revealed the smile of a born cynic. "How do I know you didn't just make this yourself, doctoring the linen with your own white hands? Although it *is* quite a good forgery, I must say. Nearly believed it there, for a moment." He threw it to the ground. "Well, toodle-oo. Off you go, then."

Theo and Otto grabbed a leg each and hauled Niall up the trail, back into the woods.

"You're Gatekeeper," shouted Niall at machine-gun speed, clawing at the wet ground and finding no purchase. "You used to get on the ham radio for years, while your darling brother raped and murdered his way through five counties. You said his fatal flaw was women. You even warned Róisín and Fiona Walsh, the two girls who used that knife on him. Do you even know you *spoke* to them? Your brother's killers? I'll bet you don't know they're dead now, either, do ya? I read their shagging *diaries!*" The two men had stopped tugging, and seemed to be reacting to a hand signal Niall couldn't see. "The only reason I found you in the first place is because your brother drew a map. Unless I'm very mistaken, you also have a tattoo of two boys, holding hands. Because you and Jim are twins, now, isn't that right? Answer me, you fucking cripple! You're your brother's keeper, aren't ya, you culchie bastard?"

Theo and Otto helped Niall to his feet and brushed as much dirt and leaves off him as they could. Then they practically carried him toward the house, where the servant had reopened the black gate and the smell of fresh coffee penetrated even his stopped-up nose.

Ned raised his head and regarded Niall with a mixture of curiosity and respect. He had picked up the knife blade again and held it this time with a reverence that couldn't be faked.

"Well, my boy, look at that," he said, shifting his chair into second gear. "You *did* know the magic word, after all."

THE COFFEE WAS strong and made Niall's head swim. Another servant in a white lab coat stood behind him, applying a thermal bandage through the open shirt to the bruised skin beneath.

His host sat at the piano, a scratched-up Bösendorfer concert variety with a raised sail the size of a large dinner table. There came those Cole Porter tunes again, played fortissimo, then furioso, one after the other, until they all sounded the same. It seemed to Niall that the lifeless legs dangling from the stool had lent Ned's arms all their strength and fury. The wizard finished and hesitated, before raising his head and nodding at the servant, who immediately retired and closed the French doors behind her.

"D'you know, it actually feels rather nice with some company," Ned said, sliding into his wheelchair like a soft-shell crab and wheeling himself two rooms away before Niall could answer.

Niall followed, noticing silver-framed family photos of what had to be Ned and Jim as boys: healthy, vibrant, with that arrogant lassitude of those aware of their parents' wealth. Dented cricket bats and hurleys hung above a fireplace. There were oil portraits in the next chamber, which seemed to shun the light. Renaissance glazed vases, too.

But a dusty photo, half hidden behind two golf trophies, made Niall stop.

It showed a young blond woman sandwiched between the twin brothers on a swing set long ago, sweaty summer grins on all three faces. It was impossible to tell whether it was Ned or Jim who had a hand around her waist with just enough possessiveness to notice. Her skin was so white the poor contrast in the old black-and-white picture had turned her eyes into black sockets. Niall could only recall one person that pale and sexy at the same time, and she wasn't even real.

Her name was Princess Aisling. And a wolf first loved her, then killed her.

"In here," called Ned, and Niall followed. The smallest room was also the place where the lone occupant of the house clearly spent most of his time. Stuffed hoot owls were forever caught in mid-blink underneath glass bell jars. There may even have been a few ravens and hawks for good measure, Niall couldn't be sure. Because it was the wolves, sprawling on pictures and posing in clay, that dominated everything. There was even a real wolf's head, mounted right above the doorway, jaws pried open as far as they would go without wrenching the mandible entirely from the skull. It looked like the creature was still in pain, trying to howl its way to safety, the way Prince Euan once had attempted. But someone had caught it first. The only sound in the room was another electronic signal Niall couldn't locate. It was a single beep about every ten seconds, like a slow metronome.

"When did your brother put these up?" asked Niall, choosing the chair farthest away from his host. He wondered if he had the strength to fight back if the intemperate piano player decided to finish him off before the next solo performance.

"*I* did," Ned said, leaning back and staring at the grayback head as if for the first time. He lit a cigarette and waved it about. "I taught Jim everything about animals. Horses, falcons, rabbits, and deer. How to ride them or kill them. And, yes, even wolves. We had to go all the way to Kyrgyzstan to find our old friend up there. We call him Freddie." He waved at the stuffed head. "Say hello to the nice man, Freddie!"

Niall felt like throwing up. The beep sounded again, closer this time.

"Our parents never used this place while my father was alive," explained Ned, adjusting a gilt-edged oil portrait of an elderly man next to a stag he'd obviously just brought down. "But after Father died, Mother felt the Dublin air was too stifling, so we all moved out here." The legless prince sounded nearly wistful, forgetting to guard himself for a moment. "She tried to make it a real home for us—riding lessons and evening prayers by the dinner table. Of course, we all became frightfully bored, I don't mind telling you. And there's no money in the world quite so intemperate as the inherited kind."

"You have a beautiful home," said Niall noncommittally, feeling anxious again. The stag in the picture lay with its bloody snout toward the painter, twisted antlers reaching for the dark sky like antennas.

"You said you had something else to show me," said his host, with the impatience of those born to give dead trophies names better suited for children.

"Here," Niall said, holding Jim's map out as though it might crumple and turn to dust before he could hand it over. "Your brother kept a visual log of the story he told around the country as it unfolded in his head. Look, see there? That's you, I think. With rays coming from your—"

"My fingertips, yes," said the impatient wizard, suddenly sitting thigh to thigh with his guest, poring over the poor rendering like two boys inspecting a rare stamp not belonging to themselves. He gently folded the map and pushed a button on the leather handle of his chair. There was the clacking of heels, and a manservant Niall hadn't seen before discreetly poked his head inside.

"Mr. O?"

"Sam, can we mount this and put it in a lovely frame? Nothing too stark, the drawing's the star here. Good man."

"Right away, sir." The servant took the holy object and retreated in a flash.

Beep!

Niall looked past Ned's withered legs and saw a bulky shape, covered by a green felt cloth. He had thought it was a dresser, or maybe an upright piano. But now he knew what had made the sound. And he didn't need to peek underneath to make sure.

"Clever boy," said the surviving twin, following the direction of Niall's eyes. "Want to see Old Sparky? Afraid I haven't fired her up much recently. Not since . . ." He let the unspoken words fall to the floor and dry up.

"But you used your shortwave radio to warn people before," Niall said, feeling a little braver. Who was this made-up wanker, who spoke like he had his head up the queen's arse? "When Jim was still killing people. Why didn't you just call the gardaí instead, when there was time? Stop him? Or did that become boring, after a while?"

"Why did you come out here at all?" spat Ned, gripping the joystick on the armrest. "To delight in sharing the obvious?"

"I came to finish a job I'd promised to carry out," Niall said, liking the sound of that. It was the first time he'd articulated it out loud, and only wished Fiona, Róisín, and Aoife could be there to hear it, too. "Putting the final pieces together for some friends who couldn't be here themselves."

Ned's eyes grew unfocused and distant. He was in the past, with his brother and someone else his face didn't reveal. "And they didn't listen anyway, did they? All those women? They wanted to love someone dangerous, that's all. I love Jim. You'll notice I don't use the past tense, because the bugger is still my brother. Moment he left here—oh, thirteen, maybe fifteen years ago—I knew what he was going to do eventually. But I couldn't rat him out to the guards, now, could I? Wouldn't have been decent of me."

"And then," Niall said, playing along with the logic of someone with nothing but objects left to occupy his days, "you became aware of a change, didn't you? Something happened. It made the papers. The wolf struck for the first time. And he got used to that blood music in his ears."

Ned looked like he might leap up and throttle Niall, despite his handicap. Then he shrank back, nodding at the memory. "He began by sending me a gift. A keepsake. They just kept coming. Would you like to see?" Without waiting for an answer, the legless prince wheeled over to a cabinet and hauled out a leather pouch the size of a small deflated football. He opened it, and the floor was immediately covered in shimmering women's earrings of every shape and size. Ned picked one up and smiled.

"The first one, the *very* first, was made of cheap simile and brass," he said. "A barmaid or someone on the dole, one thinks. When the fourth one arrived, it had a bit of dried blood still on it. That's when I cranked up Old Sparky to minimize the damage, so to speak. That radio used to belong to Jim, you know. Delightful irony, isn't it? Of course, Mum and Dad went to their graves believing us both to be marvelous gentlemen."

Niall didn't say anything for a while, but just listened to the *beep!* sound and knew how stupid it was of him to have got trapped in here with this piece of work.

"So you're a storyteller, too," Ned said, bemused. "Like my Jimmy? Wizards and dragons and fair maidens for you, is it?"

"I'm no *seanchaí*," Niall admitted. "I'm trying to *draw* the story of my three friends. As a comic book. I'm afraid I haven't got very far yet."

The wizard clapped his magic hands and laughed. "A *comic* book? For children? Oh, how perfectly marvelous! But why not tell Jim's story, instead? Much more dramatic."

Niall looked past the amber gold around Ned's pupils and saw Jim's quicksilver temper inside somewhere, but he didn't waver. "Because all *he* did was tell his own story, over and over. And the women he killed got a notice on page thirty-four of the local paper and a closed-casket funeral."

Ned pushed the red button on his armrest one more time. He looked at his guest with something close enough to regret to pass for genuine. "And I know the story he told, too," he said. "About the prince who kills his crippled brother and is turned into a wolf? Heard it on the radio. Except you've got it backwards. Everybody does." Footfalls outside in the hallway. It could be Theo. It might be Otto. Or both. "I was the one who sent Jim away from home, you understand?" He tapped his dead legs with clenched fists. "I was *born* with these loaves of bread, he didn't leave me under my horse. That's just angry projection. *I* told Jim how to talk to women, what to do with them in bed, that kind of thing. He took things a bit too—"

There was a knock at the door.

"Just a *moment*," he called out, and looked back at Niall. Ned's eyes were wide, and the spell they cast now was Jim in the flesh, limp legs or not. He could have told any story, until the end of time, and Niall would have believed every word of it. "I found him in bed with our big sister, Aisling. It was late summer, as I recall. They weren't playing cards, tell you that. Our father sent her away to school in Switzerland. Old girl was never quite right after that. Did a runner before graduating and moved in with a French punk musician, who taught her what to do with needles. She's buried right out back. Want to see the headstone? It's really quite beautiful. Just like the one I helped put up for Jim in that wretched little town, what is it? Castledown . . . Castlesomething?"

"No, thank you," Niall said. "And if you don't mind, I should be going."

"Should you?" asked Ned, with mock incredulity. "But you know more about my brother than anyone who's come by. So much more to share. Why should I let you leave? Give me just one good reason."

Niall's hands gripped for the knife blade, and he remembered it was no longer there. The wolf's head grinned at him, confident of one last kill even beyond taxidermy. "Because you lie awake at night, wondering if you might not be worse than your brother," he said, rising and opening the door. He stared right into Otto's fish eyes. "And if I walk out of here unmolested, you tip the scales back in your own favor. At least for one night."

There was another faint chirp from the shortwave radio's dying battery, as if it agreed. Ned nodded to Otto and smiled. He seemed relieved. "Otto, would you be so kind as to drive our new friend here anywhere he wishes to go?" He turned to Niall and cocked his head, as if to a worthy adversary. The tattoo with the twin boys holding hands could just be glimpsed on his left forearm, before he buttoned his shirtsleeve again. "You would have made a good man for my security team," he said. "What kind of training do you have?"

"I used to be a postman," Niall said, shrugging. "But I got fired."

"Perfect. A civil servant confidence artist. You bluffed your way in, and guilted your way out. Might have made a decent grifter. I'm sure my brother would have agreed." He leaned forward in the chair, his eternal mobile prison, and gave Niall a smile to remember him by.

"We're not bad people, so park that condescending smile somewhere I can't see it. And have the presence of mind never to come visit me again."

AS NIALL LOOKED out the rear window of the soundless Rolls-Royce taking him home to his shoebox flat in Ballymun, he saw the wizard's black gates closing behind him. Whatever family secrets still lay buried inside would stay forever hidden.

The wood anemones averted their petals from the road and didn't dare look up again until they were quite sure the car was gone.

Postscript

A
KNIGHT'S
REWARD

· 10 ·

It's true what they say about cats, Niall thought, as he picked up Oscar from the biology students next door. You can be gone a moment or a decade, and they'll stare at you as if you've insulted them personally.

His flat looked exactly the way he'd left it, only with a film of gray dust everywhere, and Oscar delighted in stirring it up, because he knew it bothered Niall's sinuses. Mail had piled up in the box downstairs, most of it delinquency notices from his long-suffering bank, a fitness club, and the art school where he still owed a fortune in tuition for learning something he'd never made a dime at. The kicker had been the bright orange NOTICE OF EVICTION—30 DAYS sticker he'd found on his front door. Jennifer, from across the hall, had passed him when he tried to peel it off and pretended not to notice.

Niall made some tea, leaving a few spare bags for Oscar to eviscerate to his heart's content. He'd missed the bugger. Looking around at the humble remnants of his life, there was nothing to suggest he had fought like a medieval knight for fair maidens, two of whom were already dead before he set out on his quest. The answering machine blinked FULL and his mobile had conked out long ago, because he had no money left to pay the bill.

The only proof that any of it had actually happened was the one bent sweat-stained diary he had managed to save. He'd got no treasure for his efforts. No triumphant return to the castle courtyard, with a kiss from the grateful princess. It was back to the salt mines and obscurity.

You should have sent your diary to a *real* knight, Róisín, he thought, as he flipped through it, recounting in his mind the first time he'd set foot in Castletownbere. The three of you deserved a better champion to keep your memory alive. Bronagh was probably dining out on having chased the "dangerous pervert" out of town, Niall guessed, and wondered how good Donald Cremin was at looking up names in the telephone directory. He consoled himself with the fact that he'd soon be history inside the concrete tower he'd come to love like a benign disease. The wizard would keep chasing intruders, Niall guessed, forever denying that his brother had been anything more than an apt pupil at his brother's knee.

O'Driscoll, that's what the no-neck bodyguard in the forest had called Ned, wasn't it? It struck something familiar inside Niall, and he tried to remember something Jim had said about his twin mythological princes. Wasn't O'Driscoll merely a modern form of saying Ua Eitir-sceoil anyway? Wizardry. Smoke and mirrors. He closed the book, which had begun to come apart at the seams, and knew he wouldn't open it again.

He was going to get a good night's sleep. And tomorrow, he'd go up to Malahide and ask Mr. Raichoudhury for his old job back. All right, he'd *beg* for it. Niall pulled a black number-two pencil out of his bag and held it in his hands a moment. Nothing happened, not even a slight tingle to get an image moving from his brain to the lead tip. The story of the man-wolf tearing up the countryside and all the women in it was as dead inside him as an old newspaper. He snapped the pencil in two and tossed it into the trash.

He felt tired, and his eyes hurt. He stared at the black book again.

There was no way he'd keep Róisín's diary, not now. It was dragging him down like a millstone around his neck. The cops? He thought one last time and realized he'd spent the last week running from them all over West Cork. The law would just love a visit from him, once they checked with Bronagh. No, he'd have to throw it away somewhere it would never be found. But first he had to get some Dublin air into his lungs, and go get that bike. With my luck, it's probably stolen, he mused, and pocketed the diary one last time. On impulse, he grabbed a couple of pencils, too, because you just never know. Niall opened the front door and glanced back at the orange tabby, who had jumped onto the kitchen counter to show him how easily an eraser can be shredded into a thousand pieces.

"Feel free to wreck anything you like, ya old bastard," Niall said, pulling the door shut. Behind him, Oscar merely blinked at him, as if to say, And I need *your* permission for that, gyppo?

THE CALENDAR SAID it was summer, all right. But the wind blowing across the river Liffey as Niall pulled his bicycle along the quay felt Siberian.

No one had touched his bike, which he'd forgotten to lock again, of course. One small bounty for staying true to three vanished princesses. And now he just let the arctic breeze carry him from the station down toward the center of town. There was more espresso in the air than lager, and had been for some time in the shiny new city that had embraced New Europe and forgotten it was actually still in Ireland. Niall passed a café, where the slurping sound of someone making cappuccino froth sent him farther on down the footpath. He finally found a dirty pub without a smart name or outside wicker chairs. Perfect, he thought, counting through the fistful of banknotes he'd just got for cashing his severance check. "Yer a god, Mr. Raichoudhury," he mumbled, and went inside.

"Howya," said the barman, adjusting the volume on a TV, where a stern-looking woman was going on about how two lads up in the North had been killed when a helicopter fell on them. "Pint?"

"Guinness, please," said Niall, feeling at home again. He paid for his beer and picked the table farthest away from the door. The foam was thick enough to make a soft ice out of. The chatter of students bragging about last night's accomplishments blended with TV commentary from the British Army about how their helicopter was brought down by "parties unknown, at this stage." A jukebox somewhere played "Brothers in Arms," and Niall hummed along about how every man had to die, while he turned Róisín's diary in his hands like a stone tablet he was itching to plant somewhere far away.

He hadn't seen the figure before it spoke. "Drinking alone is bad luck," it said.

Niall lifted his head and recognized Aoife instantly. The way she stared at him, directly and fearlessly, left no doubt.

"You're . . . What's . . . ?" he said, spilling the glass like an eejit but catching himself.

"Just let me speak for a moment, okay?" she said, sitting down. "Can I do that?" Her cropped blond hair was so short it was barely there. She wore brand-new pink combat boots with her black overcoat and hid something in her lap.

Niall merely nodded and only just remembered to close his mouth.

"You had every chance to go to the guards and tell them everything you know about us," said Aoife, finishing Niall's beer. "And you never did, not even when your own life was at stake. I've come to thank you for that. Been keeping an eye on you ever since you came walking into Castletownbere. And now I need to ask you a question."

"Sure," Niall said, his heart beating into his fingertips. "Anything you like."

Aoife looked out the window at something Niall couldn't see from where he sat. "Why did me and my sisters matter to you that much" she asked, nervously picking at a nail, "that you'd risk everything for our sake?"

"Because they were buried before anybody knew what had happened to them," Niall said. "And because I was the one who found Fiona's diary, not the cops. You mailed both of them yourself. You should know.

I was"—he searched for the right word—"entrusted. After that, what choice did I have?"

"All the choices in the world," she protested, but smiled despite herself. "No one asked you to get chased up the road by Donald Cremin and his gang of mucksavages. Or to get an earful from Bronagh every five minutes."

"She does a good job, doesn't she?" Niall asked. "Keeping your trail cold? And people off ya?"

"Not good enough. *You* found me."

"No, I didn't. Just your tracks."

"Too close anyway." Aoife sighed and eyed the bar. "I made a few new friends along the way, trying to stay hidden. This one girl I met in a shop up north had a motorcycle. Became like a fourth sister, really. She offered to help out wherever Bronagh couldn't." A shake of the head. "A proper desperado, that one. Beat her cheating boyfriend half to death in Tyrone someplace. Reminds me of Rosie." She fell silent and looked at the notebook in Niall's hands. "Is that . . . ?"

"It's for you," he said, pushing Róisín's diary across the marble tabletop. "I don't want it anymore." It was as if the black canvas groaned the moment Aoife's fingertips touched it. She glanced out the window again, smiling at something. "I had to leave them in Aunt Moira's house, once I knew they were dead," she said, gripping the notebook harder. "Do you understand?"

"Anything I tell you about that will be a lie," Niall said, "because before I can answer, I have a question for you, too."

"We're talking about the same thing, then," she said, gripping both his wrists and smiling the way people do if they need to be forgiven.

"The reason you left Castletownbere and your sisters to begin with, after Jim—" Niall began.

"Hang on," she said, wrinkling her brow. "I'm not sure you're getting—"

"And the way you *stayed* gone for nearly three years after that," he persisted, not allowing himself to keep this last secret bottled up. He'd bled for this, got beat up and threatened and fired, and whatever else. The black gates opened one last time and let three princesses out onto the fields before it, alive and well before the wolf or his wizard could reach them. "There could only be one explanation. And it's the same one that made you escape so quickly after you raced upstairs and found both your sisters dead, isn't it? You had something to protect, your sisters wrote. Protect from prying eyes everywhere. From judgment."

Aoife didn't say anything, at first. Then she signaled for Niall to rise and join her by the window.

"Where are . . . ?" he said, but did it anyway.

Outside, people were taking the long way home from work, and a couple of taxi drivers stubbed out their cigarettes before getting on with it. He was about to ask Aoife what he was supposed to be looking for, even if he could guess. Then he saw it: a brown Vauxhall Royale with wobbly tires was parked across the road.

From the backseat, a child's hand waved back at Aoife.

Niall looked closer and saw it was a little girl, most of her face obscured by a waterfall of the blackest curls. He guessed she couldn't be much older than three. An adult in a black leather jacket held her close and grinned at Niall, who stood there, gobsmacked. He recognized her, even without the helmet visor. It was the speed-demon girl on the black motorcycle. A proper desperado.

"My daughter will never know she was fathered by a wolf," said Aoife. "And when I walk out of here, you won't see me again. Poof. Gone. Just like in a fairy tale. Now do you understand?"

"Yes," Niall said, taking a breath and smiling. "Yes, I do."

Aoife put the notebook in her pocket and turned to leave. Two gardaí by the front door leaned in to ask the barman something Niall couldn't hear. The blond pixie looked back at Niall. C'mon, boy, now's yer chance, her eyes beamed. Be a hero. Getcha name in the papers. When she saw he didn't take the bait, she turned around and came back.

"Where did you come from?" she asked him, and smiled wider this time.

"A castle deep in the forest," he answered. "Where all the wolves are long dead."

"Sounds like a wonderful place," Aoife said, and appeared to hesitate. "Don't tell anybody how to find it." Behind her, the law shuffled back outside. She took something out of her pocket and handed it to Niall. It was wrapped in the same kind of laced napkin he'd found around the knife. When she saw he was about to open it, she stopped him.

"Wait until I'm gone." She nodded toward the bulk in her hands. "I nearly threw that in the river many times. But I always thought, If I do, then me and my two sisters will be forgotten for all time. That's why you're the only one I trust with it. I know you will understand. And when you've seen enough, tell our story. I hear that you're a cartoonist. Draw something beautiful."

"We call it 'graphic artist,'" Niall said, feeling his throat getting choked.

"Good luck, Niall Cleary," she said, kissed him on the cheek, and walked out the door. As her left arm swung up to wave at the only family she had left, Niall noticed the handcuff bracelet still there, around her wrist. Must have taken forever to saw through the chain, he guessed. A moment later, the Vauxhall rattled out of its spot and down the quay.

Niall's fingers knew what was inside the package Aoife had left behind. They unwrapped the white fabric and uncovered the last thing, the *only* thing, he would have dreamed of as a reward for his faith and loyalty.

It was a plain black notebook.

He listened for the hidden music that accompanied the pictures inside his brain, right before one particular image manifested itself there. It rose up slowly, blending with the speaker's voice and the rattle from video poker machines nearby.

He opened the book and turned the first page. Aoife had written:

The diary of Aoife Jeanine Walsh, with much love to Niall, a true knight in shining armor. We'll never forget you.

No, there would be no kneeling before Mr. Raichoudhury, thanks all the same, thought Niall, as he closed the book and put it into his bag. His fingers tingled again, and couldn't wait to get around a number-two pencil that would render every detail of what happened when three women defeated a wolf dressed as a man. And the arts academy would just have to keep sending him reminders of how deeply in debt he was. He would give all the money he had left to the landlord, hoping for a reprieve. Because he hadn't completed his quest. The most important part—the telling of it—still lay ahead.

There would be plenty of time to storyboard everything. But the first order of business was a splashy cover. Niall first thought of making several inset panels of all the women Jim had killed, then decided against it. Too morbid. And it wouldn't do the Walsh sisters justice, either. He also decided against a panorama showing all three of them knifing Jim to death down by the beach, with seagulls crying murder overhead.

An image came to him, stronger than the others.

The same one he'd tried and failed to conjure up that night at the post office, when he'd found the first diary.

It was a wolf, fully matured from its frail human existence into a feral predator. He would capture its expression, mid-lunge, at the exact moment when it *nearly* grabbed hold of a woman as she tried desperately to flee into the forest. Because that was the entire story, right there, wasn't it?

Would he love her or kill her?

Niall didn't know yet. But he was too impatient to wait until he got back home. There was a paper napkin on the table next to the empty glass. The wolf coursed through his fingers and made them thrum against the wood in anticipation.

He found a pencil and began to sketch.

A woman appeared on the paper. She resembled Róisín a bit, and was dressed exactly the way he'd imagined Princess Aisling when Euan first saw her.

There was no hiding in the dense foliage growing behind her, because the wolf had already taken shape in the foreground. For the first time, Niall got it exactly right. The fur was thick and rough. Its eye looked like translucent glass. In a moment, either love or death would triumph.

It was forever making up its mind.

Afterword and Thanks

➤❤

L ike Niall, I needed just one spark to begin imagining this tale. It came when I read an Irish newspaper story in the summer of 2000. An eighty-three-year-old woman and her three middle-aged nieces had all been found dead inside a house in County Kildare. According to local press, an inquest determined they had all committed suicide from self-imposed starvation.

I tried to forget about the brief article and found I couldn't. I took it out and read it again. Then I got to thinking: What if it *hadn't* been suicide? What if, instead, a standoff had taken place inside, with only enough time to smuggle two diaries out before the end? Could a grim discovery like that, told from the point of view of each sister, be the portal to a larger fictional drama about a lethal charmer who—in a very real sense—put all four women inside that house? You be the judge, since you've just finished reading. I hope you enjoyed it.

For the last several years, I've walked all over Dublin, Malahide, and counties Offaly and Laois, as well as the windblown hills of West Cork, in researching *Darling Jim*, and received the gracious hospitality of Irish people everywhere I went. That's why certain place-names have been changed, out of respect for institutions or individuals who would otherwise be too immediately recognizable, even in fiction—which isn't the point. Besides, how would I be able to show my face in Castletownbere or Eyeries for a pint ever again? The real Jonnos of this world might never forgive me. If I haven't been discreet enough, be assured that no harm was intended. Any similarity to actual people is entirely coincidental.

Though the Norman invasion of Ireland was all too real, the tragic tale of King Stiofán and his twin sons is entirely my invention, as is the foreboding Fort of the Wolf.

Seanchaí may still be found all over Ireland, but not easily, since true storytelling is a wandering profession of great skill. And none of them, to my knowledge, has ever harmed so much as a hair on anybody's head. Should you be lucky enough to find one, take a seat and listen. Tip well. It's worth it.

A round of thanks are in order: To Máire Moriarty, Kieran Finnerty, Eileen Moriarty, Miriam McDonnell, Louise Cody, Sue Booth-Forbes, and Kathryn Brolly for their help and advice. Any mistakes in the text are mine alone, not theirs. I must also thank Neil Jordan for making sure I found my way to the Beara Peninsula in the first place.

Last, I'm indebted to Howard Chaykin for graciously agreeing to lend Niall his talent and his quiver of pencils. The poor kid would've never got it right, otherwise. Thanks, pal.

Christian Moerk
Inches
Eyeries, County Cork
September 2007

About the Author

✦

Born and raised in Copenhagen, Denmark, CHRISTIAN MOERK moved to Vermont in his early twenties. After getting his BA in sociology and history from Marlboro College and an MS in journalism from Columbia University, he wrote for *Variety*, was a movie executive for Warner Bros. Pictures, and later wrote about film for *The New York Times*. *Darling Jim* is his first novel published in America. He lives in Brooklyn.